Also written by Leif Mills

Frank Wild—a biography, published 1999 and reprinted 2007

Men of Ice—biographies of Alister Forbes Mackay and Cecil Henry Mearcs, published 2008

Contents

Chapter One

The Hotel

"Mrs Smith?"

Leila looked at the receptionist: small, young, greased hair and a rather sallow complexion. She smiled at him.

"Yes, I'm in for this night and am just checking in. I am meeting Mr Carmichael in the bar later."

"Yes," said the sallow youth. "I believe he checked in yesterday."

Leila finished completing the hotel form. She took the proffered key.

"Mrs Smith?"

Leila turned and saw a rather smooth looking middle aged man standing behind her—with strands of his hair swept over his rapidly balding pate. She thought to herself, why did balding men do that with the thin pieces of hair? It was so obvious and looked ridiculous. But then, so was much else and why bother anyway?

"Yes."

"I'm John Carr from Group HR. We're meeting later on and I just wanted to say hello and make my number with you". No offer to shake hands.

Leila thought he sounded a bit like a telephone salesman. What was this about a meeting later on?

Carr smiled. "You do know about the meeting don't you?"

Leila smiled in return. "I'm meeting John Carmichael this evening. He may well have fixed up an informal meeting but if so, it would be with David Stannard."

"Ah, no, alas. He's no longer with the company. Had to leave in somewhat of a hurry. Good chap and all that but needs must."

Leila thought he now sounded like a telephone salesman with a bit of a drink problem.

"I'll see you later then" she said and turned away. As she walked up the stairs by the reception desk Carr made one last effort at ingratiation.

"I'm sure we can work all this out."

Leila went to her room on the first floor. It was a reasonable hotel and it had been a long journey from London to Liverpool; in fact, one hour late because of a derailment up ahead on the line. It was also a hot day and the air conditioning on the train had worked only fitfully.

She put her bag on the bed and sat in the one chair in the room.

Leila Smith was the number two in the union—the Deputy General Secretary of the 260,000 strong Clerical and General Union. She had come to Liverpool, where the UK Head Office of Industry 3M was, to meet the Union's General Secretary, John Carmichael. He had come the previous day to meet the Union's leading representatives in the evening and then hopefully meet the company's personnel director that morning for an informal talk on how to process the union's claim. The personnel director was David Stannard and now he was gone and the oily Carr was down from group. What was going on?

Leila undressed, took a shower and then dressed again. It was just past six o'clock and, with a bit of luck, she might still be able to contact her secretary at the union's head office. She phoned the direct line to Muriel, her secretary. Fortunately she was still in the office.

"Muriel, it's me. What's going on with Industry 3M?"

"Thank goodness you phoned. I left a message for you at the hotel. There's been developments. John's meeting last night was successful but the company's just had some sort of blood bath. Stannard was dismissed this morning and they've brought in some creep from Group. I don't know what else has happened."

"Yes," said Leila. "I think I've just met him. The hotel didn't tell me about a message and I've phoned to see what the score is. I'm meeting John shortly but wanted to talk to you first."

"John phoned earlier today. He met the company this morning and apparently things went from bad to worse. That new man from Group was dreadful and it looks as if there's going to be trouble over the pay deal. That's all John said so I don't know any more."

"Right Muriel, thanks."

Leila put the phone down and decided to go down to the bar.

When she got there she saw Carr with two other men, heavily built, sharp suited, whom she knew were the chief and his number two from the UK arm of Industry 3M.

Carr saw her arrive and smiled greasily. She smiled somewhat reluctantly in return and ordered a glass of red wine from the barman, sat down by herself and got out the papers she had on the company. Carr and the other two resumed their conversation. They were too far away for Leila to hear what was being said but at various times she noticed the three of them casting glances in her direction.

John Carmichael, the union's General Secretary, entered the bar and joined Leila. He was in his late fifties and looked hot and tired.

"Hello there, Leila. Drink?"

"No thanks John. I've just got one. What's going on?"

Carmichael ordered a pint of bitter and sat down by Leila.

"It's not too good. I met the reps yesterday evening and that went well. There were eight of them. They agreed the line to take on the claim and I saw the company this morning. I thought it should have been quite straightforward and then intended to get hold of you this afternoon to fill you in before we met this evening. One thing and another it all went pear shaped. I couldn't contact you on the mobile so phoned Muriel instead. The blasted meeting with the company went on all morning."

"What about Stannard—and who else was there?"

"There were those two over there"—indicating the two men talking with Carr—"and Stannard. I set out the position on the claim, the views of the reps last night and said I just wanted an informal chat on how the actual negotiations would go. Instead they insisted on giving me a lecture of the company, its profit and loss and how they didn't know whether the negotiations could start tomorrow at all. Then Carr joined the meeting and things went straight downhill."

"But," said Leila, "the negotiating meeting tomorrow was fixed a couple of weeks ago—"

Carmichael cut in. "I know, but the atmosphere was terrible. Stannard didn't say much at all and in fact looked bloody miserable. We argued for a bit and then Jones"—the taller of the two men with Carr who was the company's chief executive—"rehearsed the lecture he had given earlier and said they would be prepared to have an informal meeting this evening with me—and I told them you would be coming as you'd be directly involved in the negotiations tomorrow. Again they said that the issue of a negotiating meeting tomorrow was still undecided but they would meet the two of us this evening."

Leila was taken aback. The union had written to the company two weeks earlier and outlined their pay claim and the claim for the introduction of a new job evaluation scheme. They had agreed that the formal negotiations would take place the following day when the union's team would be Leila and the two leading representatives from the company. David Stannard had agreed that on the telephone with Carmichael and Leila thought she was just going to get an update from Carmichael so she could meet the two reps in the morning and then go into the formal negotiating meeting.

Leila rehearsed the position to Carmichael.

"I know, Leila but now it's changed. Just after I left the company about lunch time I got a message from Jones—read to me by his secretary—that Stannard was leaving the company and that Group had decided that their man Carr would be attending the informal meeting this evening."

"I don't like the look of him."

"I don't like his looks or his attitudes" said Carmichael. "I tried to speak to Davis and Bristow"—the two representatives who were going to join Leila in the formal meeting the next morning—"but when I phoned Head Office I was told they were unavailable."

Leila sipped her wine while Carmichael quickly finished his beer and got another pint. Leila hadn't seen him like this for a long time. It was clear that something had made him angry.

David Stannard had been a reasonable man to deal with. He was the company's personnel director and had been with the company for over ten years. Previous negotiations with him had generally been cordial and though Stannard was no push over, negotiations had generally been positive and settlements reached. This time the union had decided on a major pay claim with a claim for a fundamental look at the company's payment structure and job evaluation system and had proposed their own scheme which, Leila knew, was radical and could be far reaching. Previously Stannard had conceded that the system needed re-examination and Carmichael—and Leila—had thought there would be no problem on that part of the claim, or at least she fervently hoped there would not be. Crucially it was the most important element of the claim.

Leila told Carmichael that she had imagined the negotiating meeting would be the usual claim presentation and then, after a few opening attitudes struck, there would then be arrangements for a further meeting. The usual practice.

"I know Leila" said Carmichael. "But for some reason the whole thing's changed. What was going to be another claim and another set of negations has now become a problem. Stannard's gone; Group has come in and we don't know whether there will be a meeting tomorrow and I couldn't get hold of our reps."

"What about the Group man this morning—what did he say."

"Not too much but what he did say made things look bleak. The UK arm of the company is not doing well; Head Office in Atlanta is not happy and—whatever he means—things will have to change. It was evident that Stannard was not happy and he wasn't able to say much at all. When he did contribute, Carr chipped in and repeated that Head Office was very concerned."

The bar was filling up with people. Several youngish men were ordering drinks at the bar while two women—of indeterminate age, thought Leila—were looking at them expectantly. Next to them a florid man wearing cavalry twill trousers and a tweed jacket was talking animatedly to a much younger and smartly dressed woman. Leila looked briefly at them. Boss and secretary she thought. The man was talking away; the woman was listening and, Leila imagined, trying to look interested. They wouldn't be talking so much if they were husband and wife and certainly a wife would not bother to even look interested. More people came into the bar. It was getting quite crowded. Carr then came over to Leila and Carmichael and smiled greasily again. Leila wished he wouldn't smile. If he scowled it might be better.

"Sorry for butting in" Carr looked at Carmichael—"but we can have an informal chat now if you like. We've booked a private room here on the first floor in the hotel where we will not be disturbed. My two colleagues "—indicating Norman Jones, the chief executive and Tom Chance his deputy—"are ready and are anxious to explain the position to you."

"Explain?" said Carmichael. "I thought—"

Carr cut in again. "If we went to the room now then you will get a chance to say your piece."

Leila smiled thinly. If Carr could, she thought, then she could, though not as greasily.

"Our piece?" she queried. "By all means, let's have a chat but—"

Carr cut in again but dropped the smile. "Let's go to the room now and we'll explain how things are."

Carmichael finished his second pint. "Let's go to the room and we'll explain our position."

"Of course we will listen to what you say but I think it's best discussed in private, don't you? And people here are looking at us."

That was true. Their voices had been raised and some in the bar were looking at them curiously. Leila noticed that even the tweed jacket man had momentarily stopped talking and was looking at them: they must have been talking rather loudly.

Carmichael and Leila stood up. Jones and Chance came over and nodded to Leila. Leila was about to offer her hand to the two men when Carr broke in. "We will save the introductions till later."

"That's all right" smiled Leila. "I know Mr Jones and Mr Chance already. How are you?"

Both men ignored her question. Jones said to Carr "come on John, let's get going."

The company men and Leila and Carmichael left the bar.

I was feeling fed up. I didn't like the man Carr. I had quite liked Stannard and had always had a good relationship with him from the days when he was first appointed and I was then a national officer with the union. Had he been pushed out because he was reasonable and did Carr come in because there was going to be a confrontation?

We entered the private room. Jones, Chance and Carr sat down behind a big table. Leila and I took the seats on the other side. I thought I would let them start and try and assess which way the company wind was blowing.

Jones started first. "We thought we would explain the company position to you so you can get a better understanding of where we are."

I sighed, audibly. Jones looked at me: "There have been some changes and you will have to appreciate what the actual position is."

I sighed again and said "look, I realise that you kick off first but let's get this straight. I came up to have a meeting with David Stannard to sort out the procedure for dealing with our claim and then Mrs Smith here would attend the first formal meeting tomorrow morning and things would go on from there. Instead we had that confused meeting this morning and now I see that David has disappeared."

Jones went a bit red. He was clearly uncomfortable but that wasn't my fault and I didn't want to listen to some management lecture.

Jones, though, ploughed on. "We want to explain why the situation is different now. We're not in the position of just receiving a claim from you and then negotiating it. Things have changed. Mr Stannard is no longer with us and Group have asked John Carr to sit in." He turned to Carr. "John?"

I groaned, but inwardly. I could feel Leila getting uncomfortable beside me.

Carr smiled again—like Leila, I began to hate his smile—and said "Group have asked me to handle the HR side here but it has to be in the context of where the company now is."

Carr then went on at length. I knew the background but what I didn't know was what had changed to cause the current kerfuffle.

Industry3M was a multinational supply company with it head office in Atlanta in the US. Its European Group Head Office was in London and that was responsible for the eight subsidiary companies on the Continent. The UK head office was in Liverpool with some 2,000 staff. Originally Industry 3M had started life as a small oil consultancy—Oil 21—in America with marine engineers, geologists, surveyors, petroleum analysts mineralogists and a host of other 'ologists' and a lot of other specialists all hired for particular jobs that oil companies asked Oil 21 to undertake. Basically oil companies had decided to contract out for tasks that had previously been done in-house. Oil 21 found the right people for the tasks. That had been nearly twenty years ago.

Their business had boomed, particularly with the oil exploration expansion in Alaska, the Gulf and more recently the far east. They then had widened out to supply other industries—timber, coal exploration, transport—and then into the service companies. Within twenty years they had become one of the US biggest service supply companies and while they hired the specialists for particular tasks, it meant that they needed increasing numbers of clerical people. Especially as they went down market—as Time magazine had described it—and began to get into the office, and even domestic, market: cleaners, electricians, plumbers, secretarial staff, IT programmers.

Ten years ago Oil 21 had then decided to change their name and some bright fellow had suggested Industry 3M. Apparently they liked to be 'Industry' as, although they supplied the service sector as well, the word Industry had some sort of masculine, worthwhile ring about it. The 3M was that they were designed for the third millennium.

There was no doubt about it, I thought. Whatever their marketing and hype, they were a very big company and I knew they were expanding well into the UK market, pushing some of the small supply companies to the wall and taking over others.

"So," continued Carr "although globally we are doing reasonably well—". I broke in, "Global profits of nearly six billion in the last financial year."

Carr decided to give up smiling.

"If you had been listening, Mr Carmichael, you would have heard me mentioning the trends which in the UK are not so healthy as they are on the continent nor as good as they could be in the far east."

I realised the force of his last point. Much of the secretarial, administrative and IT work could be transferred to a India, Sri Lanka, Singapore and possibly, later, to China even. But it hadn't happened yet.

Jones decided to step in.

"On your claim, we have had a look at it. The pay element is of course far too high and, quite frankly, we don't understand the new payment structure you're proposing. I don't see how we can start negotiations when there's such a difference between us."

Jones, I thought, had got his spiel half baked. Of course the pay claim was a bit higher than we would eventually accept but the new payment structure—? "The new structure was something I wanted to chat with David Stannard about this morning. That was the whole point of the meeting—and discuss with you, naturally. But, as you know, for various reasons—" I left the implication in the air—"we didn't get round to discussing that at all. All that happened this morning—though I must say it took a hell of a time - was that I had a lecture of the sort that Mr Carr is giving now."

Tom Chance, always the quicker and more antagonistic of the two, said "Clearly you didn't understand the lecture then. That's why Mr Carr is saying it again."

I decided to shut up for the while.

Carr paused and then went on. He went over the trading position in Europe, their hopes of expansion and returned again with a gloomy set of forecasts for the UK part of the company. It didn't make much sense. The UK profits were good; they had gone up each year, turnover was increasing, new contracts being agreed in the public and well as the private sector. There had to be a reason why Carr was painting such a bad picture. I started to get a foreboding about the whole thing.

After what seemed like ages but, to be fair, was probably fifteen minutes, Carr began to slow down.

"It's against that background that we have had to look at your claim."

There was silence. I looked at Leila and raised an eyebrow. She smiled and opened her mouth to speak when Carr began again. "There's one other thing. I understand that negotiations with the union have usually been at national officer level so we don't quite get why have the two most senior officials in the Union—though we're flattered of course." The greasy smile appeared again.

Leila looked at me and I nodded. It was time for her to have a go.

Both Leila and Carmichael had deliberated long and hard about the claim and it had been discussed many times with the union's committee in Liverpool, the union's company and national executive committees and its policy sub-committee. Industry 3M was the first company in which they were proposing the new payment structure and both Leila and Carmichael had wanted it to be a success. Because

Carmichael knew, and had got on well with, David Stannard they reasoned that getting a positive response from Industry 3M was worth a good try, and, if they were successful in pursuing it, then the ramifications for a host of other companies were considerable.

Leila knew she had to be careful about all the background.

"Normally a straightforward pay claim would indeed be handled by one of our national officers," she agreed, "but in this case he's away sick and will be for another three months." She noticed no interest in this explanation. "Cancer," she added. Still not much interest.

"So, because of the relationship with the company and the union in the past which"—she smiled obliquely—"has always been positive we thought we'd do it this way. As you may know, I have a particular interest in payment systems and structures and I suggested to the General Secretary that I would actually lead the negotiations. With—" she added—"our two leading representatives in the company."

"Ah," said Carr, "that's going to be difficult."

"Why."

"Because of the new context which I have just been explaining" responded Carr.

"I heard what you said about the company and we would like to discuss that in depth with you but we have the procedure with you and naturally I must have the two leading lay officials with me. That's what the procedure allows."

There was silence. Jones and Chance looked at each other and both looked at Carr. It was clear to Leila that they both looked to Carr to take the lead. In fact, she thought, it was clear too that Carr was the most important of the three.

"The bottom line," said Carr, "is the current trading position in the UK. We have the UK head office here and eight other offices in the UK. Your claim covers five thousand people and the job evaluation part could be a huge cost. That is, if it makes sense at all. What is this self assessment all about?"

Leila waited. Carr looked at her expectantly. "Well?" The greasy smile had gone again.

"It's a new scheme, designed to get people more involved and deliberately done to demonstrate fairness and proper reward for effort. A far cry," she added, "from some of the performance bonuses that were so fashionable a few years ago. For senior management usually, as you know." She smiled sweetly at the three men. She knew they were all on performance bonus schemes and all had benefited well in the last few years.

Leila then outlined the basis of the scheme and how it tied in with the pay claim. After ten minutes she paused. "That's an outline and I want to go into detail tomorrow at the meeting.

Carr said "I'm afraid the meeting tomorrow will have to be cancelled—it's too soon and we're not ready."

"Ready for what?"

Carr ignored her. Chance chipped in, "You must understand that a new scheme will cause us considerable time and effort to digest and then respond to."

"Of course," replied Leila, "that's why I want to outline the scheme tomorrow and then we could fix up a series of meetings to negotiate the whole thing."

Jones looked up. He was clearly embarrassed. "Look," he said, face going red, "let's not beat about the bush. We want you to understand that we will not be meeting tomorrow, the position has changed, our outlook is not too good and our relationship has to change."

Leila knew this was the heart of the problem: "in what way change?"

Carr responded. "We have five thousand employees here in the UK part of the company. There's Liverpool and eight other offices, not counting Group in London. I understand—" he looked directly at Leila—"that you have just over two thousand members. The question Group, and may I add, Head Office in Atlanta is asking is what about the other three thousand? You're a minority union. You don't represent the majority of staff."

Carmichael could see that this was behind the whole events of the day: the company was going to try and push the union out. He looked at Leila and winked.

Leila smiled back. "I think Mr Carmichael and I would like to recess for a while. But, so as I get the position quite clearly, you are actually proposing de-recognition of the union. That's what this is all about isn't it? You are using the excuse of the complications of a job evaluation scheme and the size of the pay claim instead of sitting down with us on a procedural basis."

She went on, "and for the record our membership is over two thousand six hundred: you've forgotten the cash payers and the four hundred we recruited in the last two months—particularly because they were attracted by the new JE scheme."

"Ah," said Carr, "so the new scheme is a recruiting gimmick is it? What about this fairness stuff?"

Carmichael got to his feet. "We'll be back shortly". He and Leila left.

We stood outside in the corridor. I didn't want to go to the bar downstairs in case they came to look for us. It was a favourite trick of some employers to imply that the union officials they dealt with were "fond of a drink", implying that they were disposed to drink too much. From there it was a short step to spreading the news to junior management in a company and then to other companies.

One of my colleagues in the steel union had indeed liked a drink but, as far as I knew, had always managed to control it and had never let the union side down in any negotiation. The one mistake he had made was to call for a recess in a negotiating meeting and then suggest he and his union team discuss the issue in the bar. One of the employers negotiating side had come looking for them after a while. The rest was history. "We were sitting there, prepared to negotiate and the union side was in the bar"; "how many did they have?"; "they had had a drink before we started"—all the phrases and statements were spread. It wasn't just the active members who heard the rumours then portrayed as facts. It was the trots who had spread the stories all over the place. From there it was a short to step to portraying the official as an alcoholic. In that particular case the man concerned had then taken to drinking too much and the whole thing had become a sort of self fulfilling prophecy.

I knew the trots were gunning for me. They always had been. One or two were trying to spread the story that if anyone wanted to see me they could always find me in the bar. That was why the successful prosecution of the claim and negotiations with Industry 3M were so important.

Leila knew that and I knew that she knew that.

"Well, Leila" I said. "What do you think?"

"I see their tactics and I think I see their strategy. They are using the claim as an excuse to start derecognition moves. What I don't see is why they want to start the derecognition process."

I said I agreed. Leila was smart and we had both worked together for a long time. She was one of the few officials I could absolutely trust and I respected her judgement.

"Perhaps someone in Atlanta is pushing it—or perhaps someone in Europe HQ is anxious to ingratiate themselves with Atlanta. The one thing I am confident about is that Stannard would have not been involved. That's why he was looking so glum this morning."

Leila said, "why don't we rehearse the position—for the record—and then adjourn. If they refuse an adjournment and just say the meeting is ended—and they still refuse to meet us formally tomorrow morning—then we should say we're going to ACAS."

"The only thing," I cautioned, "is how we are going to explain this to the troops. As I told you I couldn't get hold of the leading two about this morning's meeting."

Leila smiled. "I've got their home numbers—let's ring them now."

I should have realised that Leila would have come prepared with the details and contact points. The trots called her pedantic. To my mind she was thorough.

"Look," I said, "let's go back in shortly, ask for a date for a meeting in a few days time—that'll make their point about more time less relevant. Then, what about a meeting of the reps tomorrow evening? You could call Davis and Bristow tonight and see if it can be done. Or"—I was having second thoughts—"what about an open meeting for the members tomorrow? This could all get serious and if we have a good turnout tomorrow the company might realise that it's not going to be too easy for them."

Leila didn't respond immediately. I could see she was trying to remember something.

"I know," she said. "I've got it. I remember now where I had heard about Carr before. I didn't know his name but when I happened to meet the Group chief at that CBI reception, he mentioned the personnel man from Group who was clearly ambitious and who was going then to Atlanta for a senior course."

She went on: "I think I can see it now. Carr was the man. He goes to Atlanta. There had been some changes in the head office and the main board in America. He's very ambitious. He puts it to the new management that they could make much more progress, particularly with things like outsourcing, if they could get rid of the union."

I repeated, "let's go back in, suggest another negotiating date and perhaps call an open meeting for tomorrow evening. Timing's tight but if Davis and Bristow can get the word round—and fortunately the office is all one big building—then take it from there. One thing, though," I added, "I have to get back to London tomorrow morning. There's the TUC executive committee at ten. I must go. So you'll have to handle the meeting yourself."

Leila smiled. She said she would be pleased to do the meeting herself and I realised that I had made it sound that she might not be able to handle it herself. I knew she would able to.

We went back in to the room.

<hr/>

The three Industry3M men were sitting down when they entered the room. Chance looked ill at ease, Leila noted and wondered perhaps if he and Jones were fully up to speed with what she surmised Carr was planning.

Carmichael said they had briefly discussed the situation and took on board the statement they had made about the complexity of the JE part of the claim. They therefore suggested the meeting scheduled for the morning be postponed for a couple of days to give more time for consideration. In the meantime they would need to discuss the matter further with their members.

Leila could see that Carr realised the tactics.

Carr said, "we obviously can't stop you having a meeting outside office hours but that's your problem. But we can't have a meeting in a couple of days. I repeat that the UK situation is serious. I don't accept"—looking at Leila with a half smile—" the membership position of your union. The company is seriously concerned at dealing with a union that doesn't represent the majority of staff and then imposing any settlement on the majority. I think we now need to consider the whole issue. The claim's far too big. The job evaluation thing is, to be blunt, pie in the sky."

Leila tried to count the number of non-sequiturs in Carr's statement but gave up.

Carmichael said, "so where does that leave the matter? We're willing to meet you any time but our members have got to be told about the delays caused by the company."

Jones leaned over. "What you tell your members is up to you. I shall tell the staff the real position. I think this meeting has now finished."

Carr was openly smiling. Leila thought he must be pleased at the backbone that he seemed to have implanted in him.

Carmichael tried once more.

"We submitted our claim under procedure. I had the meeting with you this morning but that proved to be abortive. I see that David Stannard is no longer with you. Mr Carr here seems to be calling the shots. We're willing to negotiate and when Mr Carr gets on to Atlanta he better be prepared to tell them why the UK part of the company is having so much trouble."

Carr did not rise to the bait that Carmichael had dangled before him. He turned to Jones and Chance. "I think we must go".

The three got up and left the room.

"Don't forget to write" said Leila. None of the three smiled.

"Well," said Carmichael, "now we better make some calls."

***

We went down to the bar. It was now about nine o'clock. Leila had telephoned the two union reps and briefly told them the seriousness of the position. Both were reasonable people and they appreciated what Leila told them. Leila had suggested a meeting of members the following evening and said she would try and book a room in the local Friends Meeting House. Bristow had said he would phone round a number of the key people then and there and would spread the word the following day. Leila urged him to be careful. Any hint that Bristow was using office time on union business might put him in jeopardy—and give Carr an excuse for further intimidation. Davis said he would telephone the leadings reps in the branch offices: he had the home numbers for some of them and hoped they would have the numbers of the others. It was unrealistic to expect them to come to the meeting tomorrow evening—although some from the nearer offices might try and make it—but principally he wanted to update them before the management sent round a bulletin to all the UK branch offices.

I had made some notes about what we could do in the wider context. Perhaps I would be able to have a quick word with the TUC General Secretary tomorrow just before the Executive Committee started. I was catching the breakfast train in the morning and should get to Congress House, the TUC headquarters, about half past nine.

I brought Leila a glass of red wine and another pint of bitter for myself. The bar was quite full but we managed to find a quiet corner where we could sit and talk.

Leila said "in one sense it could be a temporary hiccup: Carr trying to impress but then moving on to something bigger when he realises the problems he's created. In another sense it's pretty serious. A complete rejection of even discussing the claim with us and a clear threat of de-recognition. And there's the wider position—" Leila looked at me.

I knew exactly what she meant. Altogether we had over eighty procedural agreements with different companies, some big, some small with the majority about middle sized with five hundred plus staff. Industry 3M was one of the bigger companies but by no means the biggest. However, as I knew from other unions, a de-recognition by one company could affect both our attempts at getting new agreements and cause some of the other employers with whom we dealt to think they might like to follow the example. Most of the companies we dealt with were reasonable in their attitude to the union, but there was no getting away from the fact that a number of them would be delighted if they didn't have to deal with us at all.

"I might try and see if I can have a word with Stannard: I have his home number. And I'll try and have a word with the TUC tomorrow morning. I know they are always hellishly busy but a quick word might be appropriate."

Leila nodded. "I will try and get our membership position checked tomorrow and have a word with Dan at head office."

Dan was the man in charge of the union's membership department. The records were of course all computerised. Most of the recording was straightforward as we had simple check-off arrangements with most of the companies. The difficulty was with the cash payers. Those members who paid in cash—a declining number but still an administrative problem—had the money collected monthly by one of the representatives in each office. They were then banked locally and a cheque sent to head office. I knew it was a cumbersome—even absurd—way of collecting union subscriptions in the twenty first century but many people did just not realise the practical problems in organising a union. The cash payers didn't want their employer to know they were members of the union and we had to respect that.

"There's another point", said Leila. She paused and looked at me again. "The trots."

I groaned. "Yes, there's a problem there. There's only a few in the company but they do have credibility."

I was referring to about ten of the two and a half thousand members in the company. They were bright—but not too bright—and mostly employed in the computer department of the Liverpool office.

"They will certainly be at the meeting tomorrow evening. Anyway, you'll have to be careful how you handle them."

Leila said "I know that John. They're not part of my fan club."

"Well, Leila, tell me how you think it ought to be played."

Leila outlined how she saw the position. She would try and check the membership position in the morning. She would also try and contact one of the accountant's department staff at the UK Group in London—some one she had known for some years. I had often wondered whether there was more than just a friendly relationship with the chap but it was none of my business. She would book the meeting room and meet Davis and Bristow at lunch time when they could get out of the office. She would also check with the international trade secretariat to see if there were any problems that unions had encountered similar problems in the other countries where Industry 3M was based. She said she would be interested in hearing what David Stannard said, if anything.

I looked for Stannard's number in my diary and lifted up my mobile. "No time like the present," I said.

There was an engaged tone from Stannard's home number. I said that if I couldn't get him tonight I would try in the morning on the London train.

Just then my mobile rang. It was Stannard phoning me.

"John? It's David Stannard."

"I was just trying to get hold of you. What's going on—and sorry to hear that you've left the company" I said.

"Pushed out, more like" said Stannard bitterly. "Look, John this is between us—" I nodded instinctively though I knew Stannard couldn't see that. "Yes, of course" I replied.

Stannard then said "you must have seen I was looking unhappy this morning" I nodded again, and then grunted assent. "Well it all happened very quickly. We were told that Carr was coming over—"

I interjected "told when and by whom?"

Stannard replied, "about a week ago. The Group chief telephoned Jones to tell him. Jones only told me yesterday. He must have known I would query the thing but he's always been frightened of Group. Anyway I was formally told that Carr was going to sit in at the morning meeting. That was all." I could tell that Stannard was relieved to be able to tell someone what had happened but I equally knew that Stannard would not try and deliberately talk down the company. He was a company man but a good one. It was just that he and I had known each other for ten years and I think we had a mutual respect. Several times in the past I had had some informal meetings with him when I was the national officer dealing with them and we had tentatively come to an understanding about how to process a claim.

It had never been the two of us stitching up a private deal. I had never done that with any of the employers I dealt with, though I believed some union officials had tried that with other companies. It wasn't my style and it wasn't right. But we had discussed procedures and timings and generally those informal chats had been helpful.

"Then this morning," Stannard continued, "just as we were going into the meeting, Jones told me that Carr would be leading for the company. I didn't have time to protest before the meeting started and you must have realised from my expression that I was not happy."

I grunted again.

"But what happened afterwards," I asked, "did you get the heave-ho?"

"And some," replied Stannard. "I was called into Jones' office immediately after we broke up this morning. Chance and Carr were there. There was ice in the air. Jones asked Carr to speak.

Reorganisation; change of attitude; difficult trading and all that. To cap it all, Carr accused me of being too friendly with you and the other union officials. I was asked to resign and they would be generous to me: if not, they would sack me and find some excuse. In the end it was money or take a risk with an employment tribunal for unfair dismissal."

I grunted for the third time. I had heard the story many times. Employment protection legislation was, of course, good but there were many who had been seeking ways to circumvent it even before it was on the statute book.

"I don't blame you David," I said, "but what's the real agenda?"

"Just that. To de-recognise the union and then after that to outsource a lot of the work. There'll be no union to cause any problem. Everyone happy—except the staff, of course."

I spoke for a few more moments with Stannard and suggested he and I should meet when he was down in London next. He said he would be there the following week and undertook to phone me.

I turned to Leila and briefly told her what Stannard had said. "You got that?" Leila nodded.

I paused. Originally I had thought when the claim was submitted that we were on a good wicket: a brand new concept of job evaluation, get it introduced into Industry3M, then follow up with similar claims in other companies and also hope its success would make recruitment in the non-unionised companies that much easier. Pay claims were one thing—but memories were short and a good deal one year could always be forgotten if the following years pay deal was not equally as good. A different pay structure, however, was something else. A fair—and seen to be fair—system which involved the individual and made career progression so much more open was another thing: and one that would last for some years. One of my executive had described it as a win-win situation. At the time I had smiled. Now I could have laughed.

Industry3M was going down the road of de-recognising the union and the job evaluation claim had given them a spurious justification for it. If that happened then it wouldn't take long for others to follow suit. The union's executive would huff and puff, the trots would shout and accuse but—all in all—if Industry3M got away with it, then the consequences were dire.

Leila was looking at me. I saw her glass was empty.

"One for the road?"

"Please," she replied. "And I think we ought to go over the options again."

I agreed, got the drinks and then invited her to spell it out.

"You're going back to London tomorrow morning and will try and have a word with the TUC. I'm going to check up with membership department our figures. I'll also have a word with van Megeren in Geneva "—he was the General Secretary of the international trade secretariat to which we were affiliated—"and shall meet Davis and Bristow at lunch time. Now—" she leaned towards me—"the key is what do we advise the troops?"

I sat back and looked at her again. She was good looking and bright. She must be about late forties and had worked for the union for twelve years. Prior to that she had been a leading lay union official in the civil service. Then her department had been hived off into becoming an executive agency, and then it had been privatised. I remembered that there had been a dispute with the former civil service union about which union could organise the employees but the TUC had sorted it out with a disputes committee and we had won. Leila had led the move to us then.

I swallowed another mouthful of beer.

"Well, Leila," I said "it's your call. What do you advise."

I knew she would have thought about this already. In contrast to many of the officials—however good they might be—Leila was always willing to take the lead and put forward her views.

"I will outline the issue tomorrow evening and suggest we have another go at a negotiating meeting with the company. But the resolution I'll get Ted Davis to put will say that if there is any difficulty then we should immediately approach ACAS and also seek approval from our executive for a one day strike ballot."

"OK" I said—"and you'll give me a buzz in the afternoon?—or better still at home in the evening after the meeting?"

Leila agreed.

It was now just gone ten and the bar was as crowded as ever. Voices were getting louder as the drink seemed to flow faster. I had to up early to get the breakfast train so I thought it was time to go to bed.

"I think I'm off" I told Leila. "You know, this could all be resolved in a few days but I get a feeling that it will run and run."

"So do I" replied Leila, "and we'll be—in one way—fighting the early nineteenth century battles of unionism in the new twenty first century."

As it turned out, it was a prophetic remark.

⟡⟡⟡

Carmichael left the bar. Leila stood up and thought it was about time she went to bed as well. The bar was still full. Tweed jacket was still there and it seemed that he and his lady friend were getting on very well, sitting together with her laughing uproariously at whatever he was saying. Perhaps the drink had made him sound interesting.

"Mrs Smith?"

She turned. A young man, tall and athletic looking. He smiled at her.

"Joe Turner, *Liverpool Daily Post*," he said. "Can I get you a drink?"

Leila smiled. He seemed nice enough and she thought she could have one more drink. It was a good job she had had a meal on the London train. Once she had had too much drink with no food inside her. The result was embarrassing but, fortunately for her, the occasion had been a small group of members—in her previous union—after a celebratory dinner. She couldn't remember what the celebration was about but she could remember that she was not the only one the worse for wear.

"Thanks, a glass of red wine will do nicely."

Turner got the drinks and came back to her. She motioned to the two chairs she and Carmichael had been sitting in and they sat down.

"I've just finished with the chap from the Council that's leading the opposition to the new planning regime" Turner explained. "Then I saw you in the corner here. Was that John Carmichael, the General Secretary, you were with?"

"Yes, he's just gone up. Has to catch the breakfast train tomorrow."

"I was at your conference in Manchester last year," explained Turner. "So what brings you to Liverpool? It's not Industry3M is it?"

Leila remembered him from the union's annual conference last year. He was bright and pleasant and he had given a fair account of the conference in the paper. Did he know something about Industry3M? It was always a difficult question of judgement of how much to tell any journalist at any time when talking about relations with employers or even particular claims. In a sense one couldn't win. If you said a lot then you could be accused of seeking publicity for yourself and even damaging the negotiations. If you said nothing then you could be accused of losing an opportunity to publicise the union and perhaps attract adverse criticism from the papers concerned. Even worse when journalists started reporting difficulties inside a union.

Leila thought a piece in the *Daily Post* might be helpful and, anyway, she had to make an instant decision (and, as she often reminded herself, that was one of things she was paid for) and decided to be as open as possible with him.

"A good guess."

Turner smiled deprecatingly. "Well, not difficult. Industry3M is one of the big employers in Liverpool now. The docks are a fraction of what they were. Several of the big banks and insurance companies have merged, downsized, re-located—whatever jargon you like: the net effect being that many of the head offices and regional offices have gone. So, anyway, what would the number two in one of the big unions be doing up here with the General Secretary?"

"We have a claim submitted to the company. The GS was up this morning at an informal meeting and he and I met the management—again informally—this evening."

"Yes," said Turner, "but, if you don't mind me mentioning it, what's so important for the two top officials of the union to be both involved?"

"One of our national officials would normally deal with the company but he's off on prolonged sick leave. And—" she decided she might as well give him the total background—"it's the first time we've submitted the new job evaluation scheme."

Turner asked her about the scheme and Leila explained in some detail its basis and the key of self assessment that could make the scheme both transparent and popular. She stressed that the central point of the scheme was fairness but also there had to be safeguards to ensure the scheme was not abused and there had to be rigorous checks on the accuracy—and perceived accuracy—of self assessment. One of her executive members had jokingly referred to it as a scheme where you could write your job description, assess your own worth, grade yourself how you liked and then attach what pay scale you wanted. But it wasn't like that and had to be seen to be not like that. Leila explained to Turner the checks and balances in it.

Turner said it sounded interesting and made some jottings in his notebook.

"And, what's the company reaction?"

"Well, we have submitted the scheme and there have been two preliminary—and informal—meetings on it. This morning John Carmichael and the company, and then this evening John and I with the company. We were going to have the first formal negotiating meeting tomorrow morning but the company wanted more time to consider the claim—and the pay claim too."

Turner made a few more notes and asked some more about the implications of the job evaluation scheme and whether it could be introduced into manufacturing industry, its application to other service sectors and how it fitted in with civil service grading—if it was ever to be introduced into the civil service.

Leila was actually quite proud of the scheme. She and the head of the union's research department had worked on it for some months. She was pleased that Turner seemed so interested in it and seemed to be asking all the right questions. She looked at her watch. Just gone half past ten.

Turner looked at her. "Thanks for the background. Now what's all this about David Stannard?"

Leila kept a straight face. He had been tipped off. He must have heard—and could the company, particularly Carr, have told him? And for what reason? Could she trust Turner?

It was a stupid question she then thought. She could not expect any journalists not to try and get as much information as they could and use it to get the best possible story. At least Turner was accurate in his reporting and seemed to be as impartial as any reporter could be. But someone from the company must have spoken to him: or would Stannard himself have done it?

Leila thought there was no point in trying to deny she knew about Stannard. But then, what else did Turner know? Had Carr—if it was Carr who had spoken to him—indicated the difficulty the company had posed to the union. If so, when? Then Leila realised—and mentally kicked herself for not realising earlier—that when she and Carmichael had been talking, Carr could easily have buttonholed Turner elsewhere in the bar. She quickly looked around the bar. She couldn't see Carr, or Jones or Chance come to that. She could see tweed jacket and his girl: what a long evening they have had, she thought.

Leila looked again at Turner. "He's gone, apparently."

"Why?"

"I don't quite know" responded Leila. "I haven't actually spoken to him "—a true statement but not the whole truth—"so you had better contact him. Or, if you want the official version, then get hold of the Group HR man."

"Who's he?" Turner said, keeping his face straight in turn.

"Joe, you know quite well, I think." Leila stood up. "Anything else you require?—oh, by the way, is there much of a story in this or are you keeping it just for background?"

Turner smiled. "I'm not sure." He motioned to Leila's glass "One more for the road?"

Leila shook her head. "Let me know if I can help any more."

It was a good tactic. Always try to be helpful to the reporter, and, in some cases, actually do be helpful. If Turner wrote a factual piece based on their conversation this evening then all would be well. If he speculated on Stannard's departure then it might cause waves. She couldn't see, though, how anything Turner would write could be harmful to the union's position—and it might indeed be helpful. If she had not spoken to him much at all, then it could be bad—stories that the union was "tight lipped" or, worse, "too anxious to make any comment" could be distinctly unhelpful.

Turner smiled. "Thanks again for your help. If I find anything out about Stannard, perhaps I could give you a ring." He consulted his notebook. "Yes, I've got your number and your home number." They shook hands and Leila watched him make his way through the bar to the door.

It was then that she noticed Carr sitting down at the far end of the bar with a youngish woman who seemed to be making notes of what he was saying.

Leila didn't recognise the woman—another journalist perhaps? If so, it seemed that Carr was working fast on his plan, if there was a plan. Yes, there must be. De-recognition of the union, brief some of the local and regional press first, then some of the nationals later. Then some deep background notes for the heavyweight magazines. Of course it all depended on how the company's strategy was working out but the local press was stage one.

Leila walked over to where Carr was sitting. He looked up, somewhat startled to see her standing by his chair.

Leila said, "just to say goodnight and we'll meet soon then." She smiled and turned round to face the door. But not before she had seen Carr look a bit embarrassed and clearly searching for the right words in response and the woman reporter—if that was what she was—look startled.

Leila went out of the bar and climbed the stairs to her room. If Carr had been telling the reporter dark tales about the union as a precursor to further stories, then it didn't hurt to appear to be on good relations with him. In one sense it would make Carr's attitude appear misguided, and, in another sense, make him appear hypocritical.

In her room Leila made some notes on what she needed to do the next morning. First was to check with Davis and Bristow—preferably by telephoning them at their homes before they left for work—to confirm arrangements for lunch time and update them on the conversation with the *Liverpool Daily Post.*

She would also speak to Dan at the union's membership department, try and get hold of van Megeren in Geneva and also book the room for the meeting. She had told Carmichael that she would try and get hold of her friend in Group HR. It was Chris Rodd, the number two in the chief accountant's office in London. She had met him at a financial management seminar and thereafter at various ACAS, TUC and CBI one day conferences and discussions. Although she knew that a number of her union colleagues had wondered whether Rodd had been her lover—some had immediately assumed it was so—he had been nothing more than someone she chatted to and who had seemed a pleasant man.

It was getting on for eleven o'clock and she decided she would try and get hold of Chris on the telephone in spite of the lateness of the hour. She dialled the number on her mobile. No answer. The answering machine came on. She left a message. She would phone him in the morning—but, as with some of the others, early in the morning at home and not at the company.

It was time to go to bed.

Chapter Two

The Meeting

"Mrs Smith?"

Leila was already awake when her early morning call came. She looked at the clock by her bed. Six thirty. She lifted up the telephone.

"This is your wake up call."

"Thank you" said Leila and put the telephone down. At least it was a human being on the phone and not an automatic recording. Time to get up.

She would make some calls before she went down to breakfast. First, she thought she would try Chris Rodd and dialled his home number on her mobile. She could hear the ringing.

"Yes". A rather angry response from a woman whom Leila imagined was Chris' wife.

"Sorry to ring so early. This is Leila Smith. I wonder if it's possible to speak to Chris."

"Do you know what time it is? It's only six thirty. And who are you?" The woman sounded more angry.

"It's Leila Smith from the union. I left a message last night on your answer phone. I am sorry to call so early but I know Chris gets to the office early and I wanted to speak to him before he left."

"How do you know he gets to the office early?" Angry and suspicious. Leila began to worry that she had caused a problem.

She had never met Chris' wife and wondered whether there was a difficulty.

"Look, I am sorry but it is quite important, Mrs Rodd."

"Just a minute." The woman put the phone down and Leila could hear her call for her husband. "Chris, some woman for you." It sounded as if it wasn't the first time. Then Chris Rodd came on the phone.

"Hello?"

"Chris, sorry to call so early and I think I may have upset you wife. It's Leila Smith."

"Oh, Leila. Yes, my wife doesn't like early calls. Still, what can I do for you?"

Leila briefly explained what had happened with the company the previous day and how she was anxious to get some feel for what the company really wanted and whether Chris could help. When she had met him he had always been friendly and forthcoming about the company.

"I see," said Chris. "But what can I do? I'm an accountant, remember?"

"Is there anything behind all this? You see we have a meeting—which I hope will be a mass meeting—this evening and I didn't want to speak to you at the office as it might have been a bit difficult. I don't want to presume on our acquaintance but is there any guidance you can give me?"

Leila realised as soon as she said the words that perhaps she had gone too far. She didn't really know how Chris really felt about the union in the company and from upsetting his wife she had probably upset him.

"I can't tell you anything, Leila. Look, it's a bit hectic here first thing in the morning. Children off to school and that sort of thing. My wife's not feeling too good anyway."

"OK," replied Leila. "Look, once again apologies for disturbing you—" she started to put the phone down.

"Just a moment Leila." Chris' tone became more friendly. "There's not much I can say. All I know is that there have been a series of meetings between the company and Group and there's a man called Carr who's been brought in to devise a new strategy."

"Strategy for what?"

"I'm afraid that's all I can tell you Leila."

It was clear to Leila that the phone call was a mistake. She had presumed too much on her previous meetings with Chris, couldn't really expect him to tell her any inside information and—to cap it all—had seemed to have upset his wife. Or, Leila thought to herself, given grounds for suspicion? Perhaps there was some background to this. But how could she know?

"Look, Leila," Chris went on. "I'm here in London. We don't always know what's happening in the UK offices and I've told you all I know. Perhaps we could meet for a drink sometime."

"Thanks. Sorry again."

Leila put the phone down. Not the best start for the day.

She got up, showered and dressed. She thought she would try Ted Davis again and dialled his home number.

"Hello Ted, it's Leila Smith."

"Ah, Leila" came the booming voice of Davis. A big man in his fifties who was the senior union lay representative in the Liverpool head office of Industry3M in the UK. He was one of the best representatives that Leila knew. Solid and reasonable. Leila knew he wasn't particularly well thought of by the company and had been passed over several times for promotion. Some of his colleagues would have put this down to his being prominent in the union; the company, Leila thought, may have thought he was too pedantic and slow. But the union members seemed to respect him and always voted for him as their leading representative.

"How did it go yesterday after we spoke?"

Davis responded that he had made contact with the main union representatives and spoken to leading reps at some of the other UK offices. He and Clive Bristow would meet Leila at lunch time.

"We could meet at the Kings Arms off Water Street. But we'll be drinking orange juice." He chuckled.

"Fine" said Leila. She knew the pub he had mentioned. "I think I shall be joining you in the orange juice. See you at one then, and I'll have a draft resolution that you might put to the meeting, if all goes well." She rang off.

Leila decided it was time for breakfast. She left her room, went down the stairs, picked up a copy of the day's *Liverpool Daily Post* at reception and went into the dining room. A few people were already there. She saw the tweed jacket again, but by himself this time. He looked a bit hung over. Leila smiled to herself.

As she ate her scrambled eggs she opened the newspaper. At first she couldn't see any piece by Joe Turner and then at the foot of one of the inside pages she saw a news report captioned "Union meeting of Industry3M members". It read "There will be a meeting this evening of union members at Inudstry3M to discuss developments in the union's pay claim. Industry3M is one of Liverpool's biggest employers and the Clerical and General Union represents the staff there." So far, thought Leila, so good, and continued: "Included in the claim is a new job evaluation scheme which the Union has drawn up. Mrs Leila Smith, the Deputy General Secretary of the Union, and one of architects of the scheme, is to address members on how to pursue this and the pay claim. It is understood that the company may be prepared to take an aggressive line as changes have taken place in some of the company's senior management and the company's head office in Atlanta, in the USA, is said to be taking a keen interest in the matter." The piece then gave some more details about the company and the actual amounts in the pay claim. He got that bit about being more aggressive from John Carr, Leila decided, but it was accurate. She wished Tuner had included a bit more about the job evaluation scheme, but she couldn't really complain.

I finished my breakfast as the train neared Watford. It was going to be on time. A quick tube train to Tottenham Court Road and I should be in well before the TUC executive meeting at ten. I phoned the TUC number, managed to get through in spite of all the overhead cables and tunnels and asked to be put through to John Miller, the General Secretary. Miller's secretary came on the phone.

"Oh, hello" said the secretary when I said who I was. I asked it if was possible to have a quick word with the GS about nine thirty. "I'm afraid John's tied up at the moment but I'll tell him when he's finished that you want to see him before the meeting and that should be all right."

Sheila Meadows, the secretary, was always pleasant, I thought, as I switched off the phone. So far, so good.

I got to Congress House just before nine thirty. Although it was a fine June day the TUC building—Congress House in Great Russell Street—still managed to look its grey concrete and dull windows worst. I went up to see John Miller. He had been the General Secretary of the TUC for about eight years now and was highly respected by the affiliated unions and—by all accounts—by many of the country's leading employers. He was in his late fifties and could retire at any age between sixty and sixty five. He got on well with the senior figures in the Government whom he had known since the days when the Labour Party seemed perpetually to be in opposition. His number two, the Deputy General Secretary, Len Arkwright, was expected to be selected to take over but I knew there were mixed views on him. He was able but known to be a bit weak. Had he the strength to be the top man? And who would the left wing unions support? Arkwright had been a bit close to them recently. Anyway, that was not my immediate concern.

Miller greeted me warmly in his office and I sat down.

"What's all this about John?" Miller asked. "Not the trots again" as he smiled. He knew, as did a lot of my fellow general secretaries on the TUC General Council, that the trots had become quite active in my union. Although there were several extreme left wing organisations involved in various unions. I usually referred to them all as trots—erstwhile Trotskyists—as did Miller and the majority of those on the General Council of the TUC. In fact, in many ways, my union—private sector and service orientated—was an ideal breeding ground for them.

"It's Industry3M. It may be nothing John," I said "but I wanted to update you in case things turned nasty."

I spelt out to Miller the pay claim and the job evaluation scheme we had lodged and gave him some background on the company and how, if all went well, the job evaluation proposals could be very popular among a whole range of companies and could be adapted to fit several different industries.

"Well then" said Miller, "what's the problem? If all goes well you could be on a winner with the JE scheme—and think how you could use it as a recruiting weapon."

I smiled. "We had indeed thought of that John. But the whole thing could go pear shaped."

I briefly told him what had happened the previous day, about the man, John Carr, from Group HR and how derecognition seemed to be the company's objective.

John Miller was no fool and he realised that if a major company could get away with derecognising the union then a whole range of other companies might be tempted to try the same. Of course Miller knew the employment laws and regulations backwards but he was also well aware of the mobility of membership figures, particularly among the white collar unions. It was one thing to have a clear position of fifty percent plus one membership to get recognition—and employment legislation did help there—but it was another thing to maintain or increase that figure given staff turnovers, the use of temporary labour, outsourcing many functions, early retirements and the fact that in many companies—and Industry3M was one of them—the membership could be spread over a number of locations. The days of large locations employing hundreds, if not thousands, of people almost from cradle to the grave were now long gone. Union recruitment was difficult, expensive and took a lot of resources and money.

"Who's this chap Carr? The name rings a bell but that's all."

I told Miller that John Carr was a bit of an unknown quantity in terms of experience and that all we really knew was that he was currently based in London at the company's European headquarters. I also told him about Stannard being eased out and how Carr had kept on about the wishes of Group head office in Atlanta.

Miller mentioned to me the importance of keeping recognition in American companies. Even now there weren't many American companies that dealt with British trade unions and to lose one of them—particularly an expanding service one like Industry3M—could be bad news for a lot of unions. He knew full well that I was aware of this but he said it to reinforce the point with me that he was fully alive to the wider context of what I had described to him.

Sheila Meadows came into the room.

"John, it's five to ten."

Miller thanked her and got up from his chair.

"Look John," he said to me, "keep me posted. In the meantime I'll try and get some gen on this man Carr. And I'll have a word with Bob Wilson at DTI to see if he knows anything about Industry3M that could be helpful"

Bob Wilson was one of the ministers of state at the Department for Trade and Industry and he had been a union official before being parachuted into a relatively safe seat at the general election before the last one. He and John Miller were old friends.

I told Miller that I didn't intend to raise the position at the executive now but would have a word with some of the other unions afterwards.

"Oh, by the way," I said, "I've no doubt the trots will stir the whole thing up in their incoherent way but I think Leila Smith can cope with that."

Miller knew Leila Smith and smiled.

It was time for the TUC executive meeting.

⁂

After breakfast Leila had telephoned the Friends Meeting House from her room and, fortunately, they were able to let her book the large meeting room which could hold about a hundred and fifty people. It was always difficult when booking a room when there was no reliable pointer as to how many people would actually turn up, but she hoped that the word would spread now following the calls from both Davis and Bristow. If they got a hundred people to the meeting, then that would be good. One of the problems always was to get a good cross section of the members. There was nothing more she could do now; it was up to the lay members to spread the word.

She then telephoned Dan Michael, the official in charge of the union's membership department. She briefly explained the situation with Industry3M and the need for the latest details of the union's membership there. The union's computer programme listed just over 2,100 members recorded through the check off arrangement whereby their subscriptions were deducted from payroll by the company and the money transferred monthly into the union's account. It was similar to the position in the other companies with whom the union negotiated. The problem was the cash payers. A number of the members did not want the company to know they were members and preferred to pay by cash. These had to be collected by the union representatives in the various offices. The system relied on someone voluntarily making sure the subscriptions were collected—usually monthly, but sometimes quarterly or, sometimes, annually. It was cumbersome and the system often fell down as the collectors changed due to relocation or leaving the company.

Of course many of the cash payers in different companies paid their subscriptions direct to the union by direct debit through their bank. The problem was that all employees of Industry3M had to have their salary paid into the company's nominated bank and the company had stressed that they preferred their employees to use that bank account for their domestic affairs. The result was that several hundred of Industry3M employees would not use their own bank account for direct debits to be made to the union. Leila had often thought it was almost the ultimate paradox that while Industry3M was at the forefront of new computer practices and systems, some of their staff paid their union subscriptions in the nineteenth century way—by cash. But many American companies were anxious to know all about their employees—the company's chairman had done a video sent round to all branches called "Our happy family". All staff had had to see it. Cringe making, Leila reminded herself. And, given the attitude of the American owners of the company, it was remarkable that they had the membership in the company that they did have. That was why, she knew, it was so important to retain union recognition.

Leila well knew the subscription system was not fool proof and if industrial action were contemplated and a strike ballot was actually taken and a strike was subsequently authorised, then the union had to supply the company with a list of the members concerned. This posed a particular problem in that the company would then discover who the cash paying members of the union were. Inevitably, thought Leila, a number of cash payers would then resign from the union rather than have the company know that they were members. It was a result of one of the many pieces of union legislation that had been passed in the 1980's. It was all very well, thought Leila, for some unions to shout about repealing all the legislation governing unions amid calls for secondary action and no need for secret strike ballots. For her, the difficulty of giving lists of members to the company was significant and, in trying, as the TUC had, to get the Government to repeal that particular aspect of employment legislation they had had no success. Any move by Government, or so the Government decided, to repeal any of the union legislation could lead to newspaper headlines about industrial relations going back to the 'bad old days' of alleged union power and militancy.

She asked Dan "I thought we had recruited a number of members in the last moth when the details of the pay claim—and the new JE scheme—had been circulated in the company".

Dan replied that this had been the case and was why the figure of check off members had risen from 1970 to now just over 2,100 and there should be some more to add when the next check off payment was made. He added that the number of cash payers, at the last count, had been four hundred. That still made it marginally over half the total staff. He told her that it was not uncommon in foreign owned companies for the number of cash payers to be so large. It wasn't only the American companies that were difficult to organise. The same was true for some of the Japanese companies and even a couple of French companies where the union was established.

Leila knew that one of the reasons for the increase in the previous fifteen years of foreign investment in British companies, and the establishment of direct foreign owned companies, had been the relative peaceful nature of industrial relations. Some commentators had called it the result of the decline of union power and influence. Some politicians had called the current position one of 'labour flexibility'. Whatever it was called, Leila knew, the result had been considerable difficulties in actually recruiting and organising the staff of those companies. The flexibility had been one sided in the main. But that was how it was and all the unions had to deal with it.

She asked Dan to fax her the membership details to the hotel's fax machine. She wanted the precise figures in case the issue arose at the evening's open meeting.

She then tried to speak to Hans van Megeren, the General Secretary of Staff International—the international trade secretariat to which the union was affiliated which was based in Geneva. There were about sixteen of these secretariats, known as ITSs, covering all trades in both public and private sectors. Van Megeren spent a great deal of his time travelling from his headquarters in Geneva to meetings of affiliated unions and officials of the various international bodies in different countries. When Leila had last looked at van Megeren's list of activities in his annual report to affiliated unions, it had seemed like a massive travel compendium. More like the itinerary of a travel agent, John Carmichael had once described it to her but he knew, as did Leila, that such travel was inevitable.

Luckily van Megeren was in his office when Leila phoned and got through to him.

"Leila" he said "how goes it? And what can I do for you?"

The Clerical & General Union was one of his largest affiliates and while there some bigger American, German and Swedish affiliates, he knew the importance of retaining the affiliation of the biggest white collar private sector union in Britain. In fact, little of his activity was expended on the big unions; much more was spent on liaising with the many and small unions in east and west Africa and in south east Asia but he could not afford to neglect union affiliates like the CGU.

Leila briefly outlined the position with Industry3M.

"I'm sorry to hear this Leila. But you know that our German and Swedish affiliates also negotiate with that company. The Americans of course, do not negotiate with Atlanta but that's the same in a number of other companies." Many American companies in the European countries had had to deal with unions there while at the same time steadfastly refusing to deal with either of the two American private sector white collar unions back in the US. Although, as in the UK, there was employment legislation providing for union recognition—dating from the legislation passed under Roosevelt's New Deal programme of the late 1930's—it was a long and tortuous process. At any time the company could call for a ballot of how many members in the companies wanted a union to represent them. There were many firms of lawyers who specialised in employment and industrial legislation in the USA who advised companies on how to get round union campaigns for recognition, most of them successful. The problem was exacerbated by staff retiring or leaving the companies earlier: at any time the company could demand a ballot of staff on how many were actually in the union at a particular time and, especially with the difficulties of recruitment, this meant the unions had to run fast just to stay in the one place of majority membership—and if the number of union members dropped below a majority of staff at any time and the company demanded a staff ballot, then the whole process of claiming recognition and going through the long tortuous process would have to start again.

"By the way Leila," van Megeren continued, "thanks for sending me the booklet on the new job evaluation scheme. I've sent copies of both to Germany and Sweden. Both unions might well contact you about it."

"That's just what I want" replied Leila, "and I would like their telephone numbers from you." She explained she was in Liverpool and didn't have the numbers with her. Van Megeren gave her the numbers for the large Swedish affiliate which was the equivalent to Leila's union (the Svenska Arbeiter Forbundet) but—although the total Swedish workforce in the economy was not quite one quarter the size of that of the UK—the SAF had over three hundred thousand members—significantly more than Leila's CGU. He then gave her the number for the German affiliate, the white collar section of the large Deutsche Gewerkshaft Bund, the equivalent to the British Trades Union Congress.

Leila then asked if he would send a note out to all affiliates, particularly stressing the new job evaluation scheme and how any union affiliate would be welcome to get more details from the CGU.

"For you Leila, anything" joked van Megeren.

Next Leila telephoned the Swedish union. The telephone receptionist answered in Swedish and then switched to perfect English as soon as Leila announced who she was. Lars Tolmark, the General Secretary, was not in but his assistant, Per Ulric, was. Leila knew him from many of the ITS meetings: young, articulate but very serious. Leila knew that even some of his colleagues thought he was too serious—and that was something for the Swedes. She remembered the time when he had attended the CGU conference in Blackpool. In the evening some of Leila's colleagues had got him drunk but instead of making him smile, it only succeeded in making him go to bed early. The next morning he said he had no recollection of the drink the evening before.

Leila explained briefly the situation with the UK head office of Industry3M.

"Yes," said Ulric, "I have read your booklet about the new job evaluation scheme and I am most impressed. I think the self assessment point is good."

Leila said she was pleased and wondered briefly if anyone she knew could read and understand a job evaluation scheme written in Swedish.

"What's the position in Industry3M in Sweden?"

"Well, it's not a very big company. As you know they only started here five years ago—but they are growing fast. We have about eighty per cent membership there but that only adds up to one hundred and fifty members."

They spoke some more about the new scheme and how negotiations went in England and in Sweden. For all his good points, Ulric could be very boring in his monotone of an English voice. Then she sat up.

"Yes, I have had copies of the booklet made and the company committee is going to discuss it next week."

"You mean you might lodge a claim for its introduction?"

"Yes, that is exactly what I mean. I would be grateful if you would keep me informed on your progress; and I will tell Lars of your call. I am sure he would send you his best regards."

Always polite, the Swedes, thought Leila. She thanked him again and promised to keep in touch.

She then tried the German affiliate of the ITS. This time she was not so lucky. She had got through to the head of that union's research department. Yes, he had received the booklet but had not had time to study it yet. Yes, they did negotiate with the German part of Industry3M but as part of the last two year pay agreement they would not be pursuing any further major negotiations until the end of the following year.

"is there anything to stop you putting in a claim for a new job evaluated structure outside of a pay claim?"

"Not necessarily," replied the German, "but it could be argued that we were going against the spirit of the two year agreement."

"But it's possible—if you wished to do it?"

"Anything is possible" was the reply. Leila imagined the German smiling as he said it.

"However, I shall speak to the General Secretary and I shall read your booklet."

Leila thanked him. She realised she ought to sketch out what she intended to say at the meeting that evening and took out some paper from her briefcase. She knew basically what she was going to say but wanted to cover all points that might arise.

***

The TUC executive committee meeting finished just after twelve o'clock. As we all got up from our seats I moved over to Dick Whetter of the main civil service union and suggested we went for a drink. I had known him for years and though we had had the run in with them when Leila's department had been privatised and then joined us, Dick was sensible enough not to let that rankle with him. I knew he would have done the same if the positions of the two unions had been reversed—and he undoubtedly knew that I knew.

We went to the pub at the back of Congress House and I got pints of bitter for him and myself.

"How are things, John? Got the trots under control?" Almost the same words as John Miller had used with me earlier. I told him about Industry3M and our claim.

"Yes, I have read your job evaluation booklet. It's a corker of a scheme. In fact I wish we had thought of it earlier. It must be good for recruitment."

We discussed how the scheme could be used in both private and public sectors and why I thought it so important. After a while Dick smiled.

"Are you selling me the scheme so that we can claim it in our negotiations?"

"Well," I said, "you said it's a good scheme. You might consider it."

I then asked him about how he was getting on with the trots in his union. There were several groups of them particularly in some of the large Government benefit offices. A few years back they had published their own newsletter and were vitriolic about the union leadership. One edition had referred to Dick as 'Bed Whetter' and I knew that Dick did not think that was very funny.

"I think we are slowly winning," said Dick. "It now depends on the next executive elections."

After a couple more pints each Dick said he had to go back to his office. He promised to consider the scheme and asked me to keep him posted on how things went in Industry3M. It was the best I could have wanted him to say. Just before he left he turned to me and said "by the way, how's the lovely Leila doing?"

"As good as ever" I replied, "in fact the JE scheme is really all her doing. I'll tell her you were asking after her."

Dick grinned and then left the pub.

I was about to leave when a voice called out my name. I turned. It was Oliver Listle from the *Financial Times*. I noticed he had been with the two general secretaries of the big manual unions. It was fairly well known that they were discussing a possible merger. Both unions were big—one with three quarters of a million members and the other over a million. But ten years ago they had both had over one and a half million members each. The reduction in the number of manual workers and, particularly, in manufacturing had caused a significant loss of members for them. They had both tried to expand into the growth area—private sector white collar service—but neither had been successful. Both had also approached me in the last couple of years about a merger but I had politely declined.

Listle came over to me.

"Pint?" he enquired.

I had had three pints and decided that was enough.

"Sorry, Oliver" I said. "I've got to go but perhaps we could meet tomorrow. There's some news you might be interested in. Perhaps lunchtime?"

Listle said he could meet me about one o'clock and we agreed to meet at the pub near my union's headquarters. I told him it was about Industry3M and he said he would be pleased to learn of any news about that company. It was one the companies that the *Financial Times* had reported on many times in its coverage of American companies and their expansion into Europe.

"You negotiate with them, don't you" said Listle as I put my coat on and prepared to leave.

"Yes," I replied "and there might be a story there—but it will be a lot clearer tomorrow—and I hope Leila Smith will be available to come along as well."

"Ah," said Listle. "The redoubtable Mrs Smith."

It was how a number of the labour and industrial correspondents of the press referred to her after she had appeared on a memorable interview on the BBC's *Newsnight* programme. John Dryden, the number two in the CBI had also appeared and the general consensus was that Leila had wiped the floor with him.

"Yes."

I thought I had said enough and left the bar.

It was half past one and it was time I was getting back to the union's headquarters in Clapham. I knew I must speak to the union's two senior lay officials—the President and Vice-President. In many ways I had always considered the title of President to be absurd in any union and that the word 'chairman' was the appropriate one. But tradition lingered and, anyway, the two current office holders were not too bad. As I went to Tottenham Court Road tube station I wondered how Leila was getting on.

Leila had gone down to the hotel's reception and got the fax from Dan Michael on the unions' membership figures in Industry3M. At the last count it was 2560. Still over fifty per cent, but only just.

She had drafted an outline of what she intended to say at the meeting and had also done a resolution that Ted Davis might put to the meeting. Clive Bristow was the chairman of the union's branch in the Liverpool head office and, at the appropriate moment he would ask Davis to move the resolution.

She left the hotel and went to the King's Arms to meet Davis and Bristow. It was just before one o'clock when she got there. The main bar was half empty and she bought a large orange juice and sat down at one of the empty tables. After ten minutes there was still no sign of the two representatives. Leila began to get worried. She knew that the staff were allowed one hour for lunch and someone like John Carr would undoubtedly have urged the company management to make sure that this was not abused. Five more minutes elapsed and there was still no sign of them.

The bar was filling up. Leila looked a bit conspicuous by herself at the table and she noticed some of the bar's customers looking at her. A single woman drinking orange juice by herself—it could indeed look a bit odd. Two men in business suits were now openly looking at her and one of them started to move towards her table when the door opened and Davis and Bristow came in.

"Sorry to be late Leila," said Davis. He seemed a little out of breath. "Collins buttonholed me just as I was about to leave." Leila knew Collins was Stannard's number two in the personnel department and presumably John Carr had spoken to him.

"Bloody cheek," said Davis, "he started asking me about the branch and the meeting. He was waving a copy of the *Daily Post* about."

The two men sat down at the table. Leila went to the bar and got them both orange juice and another for herself.

She knew them both and knew that they liked her. She asked what progress had been made about circulating the news about the meeting that evening.

They had both telephoned some of the representatives in the various departments and Bristow had spoken to two in the Manchester and Leeds branches of the company. Then at work they had spread the word to their colleagues and from the feedback they received it seemed that there would be a reasonable attendance at the meeting.

"Are we going to get a hundred?" asked Leila.

Bristow nodded his head. "We hope so."

Davis added "and at least ten from the IT department."

Leila said "well there's a surprise."

The three of them knew full well that the Information Technology department contained most of the left wing members—particularly the Socialist Workers Party members who formed the main group known as 'the trots'. They would be certain to attend.

On the surface it seemed incongruous that an American owned company should employ people who were Socialist Workers Party and Militant Tendency members and even more incongruous that such members would want to work for an American company. Leila had discussed this several times with John Carmichael and knew that he had discussed it with David Stannard. Of course the company could not openly refuse them employment if they met the requirements of knowledge and experience even if they knew about their political activities, which in many cases they did not at the time of recruitment. But Carmichael and Leila also realised that in many ways—providing things were kept under control—it was useful for the company to employ such people. Paradoxically they were usually a thorn in the union's side rather than the company's and in, some cases, their union membership actually deterred other members of staff from joining the union. The key for the company was to keep things under control and not let them get too numerous and certainly not put them in senior positions.

Leila remembered that one of them had been appointed deputy manager of the department some three years previously and almost overnight his political fervour had been transformed into an ardent advocacy of company policy and attitudes, but—to be fair—that was exceptional.

Leila asked for any feedback on the meeting the previous day and also whether the news about David Stannard was known.

"Oh yes" said Davis. "Everyone seems to know about Stannard. Pity about him because most people had a high opinion of him—unlike Collins. But there's a lot of talk about the Group HR man Carr and Collins mentioned him to me just as I was leaving. He referred to him in glowing terms"

"Well, there's another surprise" said Leila. "But what about the company's attitude to the claim?" She didn't mention the implied threat of derecognition but she didn't need to. Both Davis and Bristow commented that it could be a serious issue and both clearly understood the implications. The response, though, from what they had heard seemed to be that the claim was popular—particularly the job evaluation scheme—and the members wanted it strongly pursued.

They talked about the draft resolution Leila handed to them. Leila said she would amend the resolution in the light of their conversation. She would speak to the meeting, Bristow as chairman would then call for comment and questions. Then the resolution would be put.

Leila stated that there would have to be a meeting of the Industry3M national committee if the resolution was carried. This was the union's policy body for Industry3M matters. It comprised two members from each of the company's eight UK branches and four from the Liverpool head office. Any recommendations on industrial action ballots would go from there to the national executive committee which under the union's constitution was the only body that could authorise such ballots and any subsequent action that the members voted for.

Davis said, "I don't think there's much chance of getting time off for a national committee meeting."

"I know" responded Leila. "Although the procedural agreement provides for time off there's that clause about subject to the company's requirements and, with John Carr about, there will undoubtedly be a lot of company requirements. If we try and meet with only half the committee able to be present then the company will shout loudly that the meeting was unrepresentative. So we'll probably have to hold the meeting on a Saturday, possibly this coming Saturday. In the light of what happens I'll have a word with the GS about a special national executive meeting afterwards."

The three agreed that was the best course of action.

Davis then mentioned the news item in the *Liverpool Daily Post*. Both he and Bristow had thought it fair and apparently a number in the office had read it before getting to work.

"This chap Turner's not coming to the meeting is he?" asked Bristow. "That wouldn't go down too well."

"Of course not," said Leila, "but I did say I would keep him informed. If we have a good turnout and the resolution is carried with a big majority then I'll follow it up with Joe Turner. I'll ask John Carmichael to fax through a letter to the company tomorrow morning with the text of the resolution and we'll do a newsletter to go round. We can still use the notice boards can't we?"

"So far," replied Bristow "but we can't use the e-mail route—even Stannard didn't want that." Some time ago Davis had used e-mail to pass on news to the members but as it was on company time and using company computers, the company had issued a notice prohibiting it.

Leila mentioned the calls to van Megeren and the Swedish and German unions she had made. She didn't mention the abortive call to Chris Rodd.

Leila asked if they would like another drink. Both declined. Clearly, thought Leila, one orange juice was more than enough for them.

"We'll be able to have a decent drink after the meeting," said Bristow, "that pub near the Friends Meeting House is not bad."

The two men then left after arranging to get to the meeting room about half an hour before the meeting to have a further talk with Leila.

Leila returned to the hotel, telephoned her secretary at the union headquarters to see if anything urgent had arisen in the morning, asked her to book a hotel room in London for a possible national committee meeting on the forthcoming Saturday and then sat down to go over her draft speech. Hopefully, all would go well. She could handle the trots providing they did not get much support from the others but things partly depended on whether the company had done anything during the day.

⬦

I had spoken to Les Martin, the union's President, and also Jane Toff, the Vice-President. Les worked for a large oil company as a marketing manager. In a way he was an unusual man to be a union President. There weren't many members among the white collar staff of his company and there was certainly no negotiating procedure. Les had worked there for thirty years and was well respected by the company. Over the years a number of staff had joined the union largely at Les' bidding but I would be surprised if more than ten percent of those eligible were actually members. The last time I had asked Dan Michael for the figures the number was just under eight per cent.

Les, though, was a stalwart in his union membership and belief. He was also good at his job—a combination that was a huge advantage for any union. I knew that in many companies a number of the leading union members were all too often those who had failed to progress in their job, lacked any drive or enthusiasm and not been given any appointed position in their management structures. Leila once had referred to them—somewhat unkindly but also accurately—as the unappointed and the disappointed.

One of the union members in Les' department had some years back been hauled up before the company's personnel director on a charge of sexual harassment. Les had been the link with the union's headquarters and while the union did not negotiate with the company, the union could represent individual members in a disciplinary situation: a right that was now enshrined in employment legislation. One of the union's national officers had represented the member and eventually the charge was found to be clearly unsubstantiated—the result of a malicious and untrue accusation—and the member was completely exonerated. Since then the union's membership had never been under threat but equally it had not grown much at all. Still, I thought, Les was able to participate fully in union activities and a year ago the company had agreed to let Les have the appropriate time off for union duties after he was elected union President.

I had told Les about Industry3M and mentioned that Leila was drafting a resolution to put to the meeting which would probably include a reference to asking the national committee and the national executive of the union for a ballot on industrial action. He had agreed with me on the importance of the situation and how a special meeting of the union's executive committee might be necessary if the national committee were to ask for one.

Jane had been equally supportive. She was an administrator in a fairly large travel agency with which we did negotiate. Again, she was good at her job and, though she had several children and a husband who seemed, as far as I had gathered, to drift in and out of work, managed to find time for her union duties. She had been the surprise victor in the election of the union's vice-president. The executive's choice—much against my own wishes—had been one of the most strident feminist activists that we had. The ballot at the Manchester conference of the union had been close but Jane had emerged the winner.

There was one other call that I thought I ought to make. Jim Bradwell of the local government union had been absent from the TUC's executive meeting that morning and I had wanted to speak to him. He had given his apologies for absence; he was involved in negotiating with the local authority employers. Hopefully his meeting would have finished.

I was lucky and got through to his office to speak to him on the telephone. I had never really got on with him but he seemed pleasant enough. He never stayed behind meetings for a drink and at the annual TUC Congress he could never be seen at any of the various union receptions that were held. Still he headed an important union and was always polite when I had spoken to him in the past.

I asked him how his meeting had gone and he stated that it was but the first of what would be a fairly long series of meetings. It was coming up to the annual pay round. Then he mentioned something that woke my interest.

"Also, John, there's quite a lot of feeling that the grading system needs a complete overhaul."

I asked him what the issues were.

He described the national grading framework that had been negotiated at national level some years ago and was now being interpreted and applied in many different ways by different local authorities. I was then surprised a bit more.

"I saw you union's booklet on job evaluation the other day, John. How's that going?"

I explained that the scheme had been drawn up by Leila and the head of our research department. The union had agreed that we should pilot the scheme in Industry3M first but we had encountered early problems. We spoke for a few more minutes. I felt I had achieved my objective—Dick Whetter had expressed interest in the JE scheme and now Jim Bradwell had seemed very keen.

"Perhaps," said Bradwell, "we could get Leila to come and talk to our executive about the scheme."

It was more than I could have hoped for. I agreed to get Leila to contact him and then wished him success in his negotiations and rang off.

There was nothing further I could do about the Industry3M position until I heard from Leila after the meeting. I thought I ought to now spend some time on the problems of the other nearly 260,000 members we had in the union.

By half past four Leila was nearly ready for the meeting. She had ordered some sandwiches and coffee from the hotel room service as she knew there wouldn't be an opportunity to eat anything after the meeting. Time to eat and for one last reading of her speech. She normally managed to memorise the salient points in a speech and that way could look directly at the audience when she was speaking. It was useful to see how it was going down though on more than occasion she had noticed one or two members nearly drifting off to sleep. Even when John Miller of the TUC had spoken at a big indoor rally of the union in Birmingham Leila had noticed a couple of older members nodding off. It could happen to the best, she thought. But, hopefully, not tonight as it was so important for the meeting to go well and her speech was the key.

At a quarter past five Leila gathered up her papers into her briefcase and left her room. The Friends Meeting House was only a short walk from the hotel and, fortunately it was a clear warm evening.

She was the first to arrive. The meeting room was well laid out, with chairs for a hundred people. The platform for the chairman and speaker was at the end of the room facing the door. There was space round the side of the room for a number to stand.

Davis and Bristow arrived next. Davis waved a piece of paper at Leila.

"The company's view" he announced.

Leila read the paper. It was headed 'The company and the union's claim' with the name of Norman Jones, the chief executive, at the bottom.

"Yesterday the senior management of the company met officials from the Clerical & General Union for informal talks about the large claim the union has submitted. The company made it clear that the claim for a minimum pay increase of eight per cent was far too high and the claim for a whole new job evaluation scheme—to replace the existing scheme which has worked so well for many years—is totally unrealistic. The union's scheme is too complicated and although the union pressed us for a negotiating meeting very quickly, we made it clear that we would need considerable time to consider the scheme in detail and we see no prospect of an early meeting." So far, Leila thought as she read it, it was expected. Then came the sting in the tail. "The company has also been giving thought to the current negotiating procedure with the union and is considering ways in which the views of the thousands of staff who are not union members can be taken into account in the future."

Leila looked at Davis and Bristow.

"Not much comfort there, is there. And to talk of thousands of non members is giving a deliberately false impression. There's just over two thousand."

"Still, said Bristow, "we might step up recruitment with the claim but I heard a number of anxious voices in talking to people this afternoon."

Leila nodded. It was a normal reaction and the company circular seemed designed to increase that anxiety. She outlined what she was intending to say and then gave them the resolution which she had refined in the afternoon.

"I've got about thirty copies here. Sod's law. The hotel's printer broke down after thirty. Still, it should be enough."

Davis and Bristow voiced their approval of the resolution. People then started to come into the meeting room. Leila smiled at a number of faces she recognised and then went with Bristow to the platform. Davis would sit in the body of the hall and at the right moment would get up and move the resolution. He moved off to give copies to several of the members he knew he could rely on.

By six o'clock nearly every chair was taken. Bristow and Leila were sitting on the platform and Bristow said he would wait another five minutes as people were still coming in. He leaned over to Leila.

"Look, there's Mark Fuller from Manchester. He must have driven like the wind to get here on time and I know Jean Asah from Leeds is coming. She already had booked the day off as holiday. She was going to see an aunt in hospital but, good for her, she's come here."

"I hope her aunt agrees." Bristow smiled at Leila's words.

"I understand that her aunt goes into hospital every few months and they can never find anything seriously wrong with her. By the way, I see the trots are scattered about the room—clever tactics. Never congregate in a heap but spread all over the bloody place."

Leila said, "as usual." Bristow nodded.

The sides of the room were now filling up with people standing against the walls. Bristow looked at his watch. Eight minutes past six. Time to get started. He rose to his feet.

"Colleagues." he said, "can we get started please."

The noise in the room quietened. Leila thought there must be about one hundred and fifty people present.

"We have called this meeting," said Bristow, "to hear from Leila Smith on the union's current claim and the informal meetings with the company. There was a factual piece in the *Liverpool Daily Post* this morning and most of you will have seen the company's newsletter which was circulated today. I'm going to ask Leila to speak and then there'll be an opportunity for members to put questions and express their own views on what they think we should do. I've already been given notice of a resolution—(which, Leila thought, was a nice way of putting it)—which we'll take a bit later. First, over to you Leila."

"Good evening colleagues" she started. She never addressed members as comrades though some in the union did. "I want to give an account of what's happened since the national committee approved the claim for an eight per cent increase in pay and the introduction of the new job evaluation scheme. I also want to be factual and then put to you what we ought to do. It's your decision, of course, but the views of this meeting will be passed on to the national committee which we hope will be able to meet this Saturday. I hope too that the other branches will be able to pass on their views as well. Also John Carmichael is standing by to write to the company with views expressed here if our position is determined this evening."

She noticed a hand go up. She didn't know the name of the person but recalled him from previous meetings. One of the IT trots. Bristow waved the hand down. The hand stayed up and the man got to his feet. Leila paused.

"Why isn't the General Secretary here?" he demanded. A few voices uttered 'hear, hear'. It's started early, thought Leila.

"The General Secretary met the leading reps on Monday evening and then had an informal meting with the company yesterday morning. As you know, Tim Burke—the union's national officer who's responsible for negotiations with the company—is seriously ill and is unable to be present and because of the importance of the claim we decided that the GS would start the ball rolling and then I would carry on. John and I both met the company yesterday evening and then John went back to London this morning for the TUC executive committee meeting." She smiled at the questioner. "Satisfied?"

The man grunted and sat down.

She continued with a outline of Carmichael's meeting on Monday evening, the apparent dismissal of the personnel director, David Stannard, and then the meeting she and the General Secretary had had. She mentioned John Carr from Group head office.

"We've called this meeting because it seems that the company is going to be very difficult and we want your views and support to demonstrate that they must negotiate properly with us."

Another hand went up. This time from an elderly man whom she recognised as one of the long standing union members who had been at the union's annual conference in Manchester. The man looked anxious.

"What's the rush? Why all the hurry?"

Bristow turned to Leila. "You might deal with that now, Leila."

She explained the importance of the company, the importance of the job evaluation scheme and the need to be clear on pursuance of the claim.

"I know how quickly things can move and with the disappearance of David Stannard, the involvement of this new man from Group—and the company's circular—I think it's right to be clear on what we ought to do. Above all, we have to make it clear at the outset that we will negotiate on our claim and the company must not break our procedural agreement with them."

The old man seemed satisfied.

Leila then wound up with brief details of the reason for the eight per cent and the basics of the proposed job evaluation scheme, why it was fairer than the existing scheme and how it could be introduced. Altogether she had spoken for thirty five minutes. Bristow nodded at her as she sat down. It had, he thought, been a good competent performance, but then Leila was like that.

"Now," said Bristow. "Comment, questions."

Several hands went up. Bristow pointed at a large red haired woman. He knew she also worked in the company's IT department was and was close to the trots there.

"I think this is a very serious situation, comrade chair". 'Comrade chair'—that was a giveaway to her politics, thought Leila. "It's clear the company are using the claim as a trial of strength. We must get all the reps here and in the other branches involved and I want to propose that we set up a committee of the reps to lead the campaign."

"No," said Bristow. "This is a meeting of the union branch and we have the leadings reps from Manchester and Leeds here. There are branches in each of the company's eight branches apart from here. The governing body of the union in the company is the national committee. There's no need for another committee to clog things up."

Another hand went up. Bristow saw it was Tony Hammond from the IT department, tall, thin and angry looking.

"I support what June has just said" pointing to the red haired woman.

"So do I" said another voice from the back of the hall.

"And I" said another voice from the side.

Leila saw it was almost a classic manoeuvre. Put people in different parts of the room and then give the impression of widespread support throughout the meeting. She got up.

"Can I reinforce what Clive Bristow has said. We have a democratic structure. The other branches should be able to brief their delegates in the next couple of days. A fax is going out from HQ to the branches tomorrow morning. We hope the national committee will be able to meet on Saturday and we've deliberately picked Saturday as the company may be a little difficult about leave for a weekday meeting. The national committee will pass on their views to the national executive and I know John will have been in touch this afternoon with the President and Vice-President about a possible special meeting. Another committee would cause confusion and be outside the union's structure."

Leila knew that the trots would always try and diffuse the union structure. If they could get a lay representatives body set up then they would find it easier to influence as most of the positions on the branch and national committee were filled with members whom she knew were, on the whole, sensible whereas some of the union reps were recently elected and had not the experience of knowing the real agenda of the trots. Also, the creation of another layer in the union structure—in a sense, a dual structure—would be confusing.

Leila knew that was what the trots wanted so that they could exploit the confusion and uncertainty that such a dual structure would create but a number in the meeting were picking up the point. And if ever a committee of lay representatives were set up, she knew that the trots would have their own caucus meetings before the committee met and in many ways it would be far easier to control than a union branch or the national committee.

Voices boomed out: "What's wrong with the reps?" "Why not trust the reps?" "Who does the work?" And then, in Leila's mind, came the ultimate paradox of accusation with the shout of "bureaucracy!"

Davis began to think it was time he got up to move his resolution when more hands went up round the room. Bristow pointed to a young woman standing against the wall who was shouting "brother chair! Brother chair!"

"Yes, you,"

"I demand to know," said the young woman, "what action Mrs Smith thinks we ought to take."

"You can certainly ask that question," said Bristow, "but I object to your use of the word 'demand'". A cry of '*ooohhh*!' went up. He turned to Leila and whispered that he didn't recognise the questioner.

Leila got to her feet again and the meeting quietened again.

"I think that we demand—" another cry of '*ooohhh*!' went up and Leila smiled—"Yes, we can demand of the employer a negotiating meeting and if, the company refuse, then we must use the services of ACAS, the Government appointed arbitration and conciliation service, keep the TUC informed and seek authority from the national executive for an industrial action ballot. Above all, as I said earlier, we must make it abundantly clear that we are not going to stand idly by and let the company ignore our procedural and negotiating agreement with them."

There was applause from many in the room.

It was a risk strategy, Leila knew. Things had moved very fast in the last two days and to talk about industrial action at this stage could well deter some of the members. On the other hand, Leila realised full well, the issue had to be raised and it was better for Leila to raise it herself.

More hands went up. Bristow pointed to a young man at the back of the room.

"Yes, you."

He recognised Larry Brent, a young fair haired man, one of the newer members of the branch committee.

"Mr. Chairman," began Brent, "aren't we being a bit premature with talk of industrial action. I've only been a member for twelve months—". A cry of 'shame!' came from Tony Hammond. Brent turned to him. "I only joined the company twelve months ago and I joined the union the day after." Several of the audience laughed and some clapped.

Bristow called for order.

"Carry on, Larry."

"I joined the union twelve months ago," repeated Brent, "and so I don't know all the procedures the union has with the company but I understand that there's an actual procedural agreement with the company which lays down how negotiations will take place. Surely we can take legal action if the company don't conform to it."

A groan went up from some of the audience, led by Hammond and June Trevor, the red haired woman.

"It's a fair point," said Leila as she got up again. "But the agreement is specifically not legally binding and—if someone asks why not—it was at the company's insistence, not ours, that that should be the case."

Leila recognised that it was odd that an American owned company specifically had asked for the agreement not to be legally binding. In the USA most union agreements with companies were legally binding and that was one of the reasons why lawyers and the law played such an important part in collective bargaining there.

Bristow allowed a few more questions which Leila answered. She referred again to ACAS and what they could and couldn't do. Some in the room were now clearly getting restive. It was also getting hot. Bristow looked at his watch. It was gone half past seven.

He motioned to Ted Davis to get up and move the resolution.

"As I have said," announced Bristow. "I have been given notice of a resolution and Ted Davis is going to read it out."

Davis rose and in a slow and loud voice read: 'This meeting of members of the Industry3M head office branch in Liverpool fully supports the union's claim for an eight percent pay rise and the introduction of the new job evaluation scheme and calls upon the company to enter into immediate negotiations. Further, this branch calls on the union to involve ACAS in the event of any difficulty and urges the national Industry3M committee to ask the national executive committee to consider an industrial action ballot if the company refuses to negotiate and thus break the procedural agreement. The form of industrial action to be determined at a later date'. Mr Chairman, I move."

There were cries of support as he sat down. Bristow called for a seconder and several hands went up. He then asked Davis if he wanted to say anything more. Before Davis could speak, Hammond rose and asked why his colleague June Trevor had not been able to move her motion calling for a committee of lay representatives to lead the campaign. There were several groans as he said this. Bristow pointed out that the point had already been dealt with and was unconstitutional. Several of Hammond's supporters shouted dissent and a few were shouting 'strike!' The atmosphere was becoming very heated. Leila got up to speak and looked round at the audience. She then noticed a thin man, who looked to be in his late twenties, and was standing near to June Trevor, reach into his pocket and take something out. She hadn't seen him before and she continued to look at him. He looked a little furtive.

Bristow was calling for order but the shouts continued. Someone threw a piece of paper made into an aeroplane. Someone else threw a screwed up piece of paper. Both pieces of paper didn't get to the platform. Bristow's call for order was being ignored and the noise of people in the meeting increased with talking, shouting and several people starting to argue amongst themselves. The noise was getting louder. A few people—Leila noticed Tony Hammond among them—started to give a slow handclap.

"Colleagues," Leila shouted, "let's be clear—".

She didn't finish her sentence. She suddenly saw the thin man near June Trevor pull his arm back and throw something straight at her. It was an egg and quickly she threw up a hand to catch it.

She realised later that the whole proceedings could well have gone downhill fast if she had not been lucky and managed to catch the egg without it breaking. Immediately she threw the egg back at the man and, again fortunately, she managed to land a direct hit on the man's chest. The egg broke and splashed over his jacket and some went on his face.

Most people had seen the incident and the meeting had gone suddenly quiet when Leila had thrown the egg back. When Leila's throw hit her target the meeting erupted into a storm of applause, with cries of 'good shot' echoing round the room. Leila smiled. The heat of the room seemed to have cooled.

Bristow called for order and the meeting again quietened down.

Bristow said, "I don't know who you are," looking at the thin man, "but you deserved that."

Again, a round of applause came from most of the members.

Bristow turned to Leila and said loudly "I think you've made your point Leila." Further applause came. The thin man looked aghast and tried to move towards the door. The crowd of people standing meant he could not move.

Leila, who was still standing, said "I don't think the egg was constitutional Mr Chairman."

Laughter came from several of the members. The tumult had dissipated and the atmosphere became noticeably more friendly. Leila could see Tony Hammond glaring at the thin man who had thrown the egg: he realised that the man had played into Leila's hands—as, he ruefully admitted to his friends afterwards, he had the egg. Bristow asked if Davis wanted to say anything more about his motion. Hammond's repeated question was ignored. Davis declined saying that he hoped it was clear and would deal with any points in his right of reply. None of those who had offered to second the motion took the opportunity to speak.

"Anyone?" called Bristow.

Hammond made to get up but was loudly booed and sat down again. Bristow then called for a vote in favour of the motion. Most hands went up. When he called for a show of hands of those opposed to the motion no one did so.

"I declare the motion to be carried *nem con* and Leila will take that back to the union and the General Secretary will communicate it to the management and get a circular out to the branches. I'd like to thank all for coming this evening. We've had a full and frank exchange of views "—more laughter greeted this remark—"and we're now clear on what we want." He turned to Leila again. "I also want to thank Leila for her speech and the way she has dealt with the questions—and the egg."

There was more laughter and applause. The meeting then broke up and people started to leave. Davis came up to Leila on the platform.

"That was great, Leila. What a good shot you are."

"Who was that thin chap?" asked Leila.

"I don't know" said Davis. "He looks a bit familiar but I've never seen him at a branch meeting before." He asked Bristow if he knew him. Bristow said he couldn't remember where he had seen him before but he had noticed Hammond glaring at him, so presumably he was not one of the IT trot members. As the people were leaving the meeting room Larry Brent went up to Leila. He congratulated her on her speech.

"Thanks," said Leila. She hadn't met Brent before, but he seemed an articulate and pleasant person. She guessed he was one of the company's graduate trainees. "Do you know who the egg thrower was?"

Brent said, "I think his name is Carter. If I'm right I think he works in the personnel office. When I joined the company last year I remember seeing him when I went up for my interview with Collins."

The penny dropped. Leila exclaimed "I reckon he's not a member but sent here by Collins"

"Well," said Bristow, "it was an open meeting of members but we have never refused entry to non-members in the past. In fact I know we have sometimes recruited one or two."

"Yes, of course," said Leila, "but I think, whether he's actually a member or not, he was sent here by Collins to try and disrupt the meeting. Presumably Collins was acting on instruction from John Carr." She looked at the others. "Just imagine if that egg had broken in my face." She grinned, "how's that for a conspiracy theory?"

Davis said, "yes, but it could also be true. A pity in a way that the press weren't here tonight."

Leila said she had promised to contact Joe Turner of the *Liverpool Daily Post*. She wondered if he would be in the nearby pub; that would be even better than trying to telephone him. He would get a good impression of the meeting now that things had gone well.

The others agreed with Leila that if the egg had broken in Leila's face the whole meeting could have erupted. Some in the audience would have laughed, some would have shouted and some would have been angry. Some would have tried to get at the thin man who had thrown the egg Whatever the different reactions, Bristow as chairman would have found it very difficult to restore order and the meeting could well have descended into disorder. That would have been just what the company wanted.

Davis smiled as he said to Leila "Your good catch and throw saved the day. Time for a drink I think."

Mark Fuller from Manchester and Jean Asah from Leeds came over to them. They both congratulated Leila on her speech and on her egg throwing skill. They would contact their members in the morning and arrange committee meetings for the Friday evening so their delegates to the national committee could be briefed.

They all joined the others leaving the meeting and headed towards the pub.

I had just got home after nine o'clock from one of the union's London branch meetings. The telephone rang as I entered the house. It was Leila Smith. She was talking from the pub and I could hear quite a bit of noise in the background. There seemed to be a lot of laughter and one or two cheers.

"It sounds quite a party, Leila" I said.

Leila gave me an account of the meeting and read out the resolution. It sounded fine. She mentioned that the journalist from the *Liverpool Daily News* was in the pub and she would be having a word with him. She would get the same breakfast train in the morning that I had caught this morning and be in the office about a quarter to ten. I asked how the trots had performed.

"As expected," said Leila, "particularly Tony Hammond but they didn't get very far. It's going to be difficult, though, as there is fair amount of anxiety about and the company's circular is quite threatening. I'll phone the other branch officers when I'm in the office and arrange the national committee meeting on Saturday." She paused as if there was something else she wanted to tell me.

"There was an incident at the meeting which, fortunately, turned out in our favour."

She then told me about the man throwing an egg at her and what happened. She intended to tell the *Liverpool Daily Post* man about it and how it seemed that the man concerned might have been sent by the company to cause trouble at the meeting.

"You can check tomorrow whether he's a member or not," I said. "If he turns out he's not and that he was sent by the company, then that would be great. The company gets egg on its face."

I could almost see Leila smiling at the other end of the phone.

"That," said Leila, "was what I'm going to tell Joe Turner of the *Daily Post*."

I told Leila she had done a good job and we ended the conversation. I was glad she was dealing with the claim. The situation could get very serious.

My wife looked at me as I went into the sitting room.

"For once," she said, "you look quite happy."

Chapter Three

The Office

"Mrs Smith?"

It was the early morning call.

Six o'clock this time, but Leila had been awake for some time. It had been quite a busy evening and yet she hadn't slept very well. After she had spoken to John Carmichael at his home, she had gone over to Joe Turner who was standing with a group of members at the far corner of the bar. There was a bit of banter from the members when she approached them: "mind out Leila, he's got some eggs in his pocket!", "don't let her hit you Joe"—but it was all good natured. Leila smiled at them.

"I must have a quick word with Joe" she said and had motioned him to the back of the bar where they could talk quietly. It was clear that some of the members had told him about what had gone on at the meeting. One of them had given him a copy of the resolution. They had spoken for about a quarter of an hour then he had had to go and write his piece for the morning's paper.

Leila had a couple of drinks with the members who had been talking to Turner and then gone over to Bristow and Davis. She had thanked them for their support and then decided it was time to go back to the hotel and to bed. She had left amidst protestations of goodwill from many in the pub. Tony Hammond and several of his

IT colleagues had just looked at her as she had passed in the bar and made for the door.

She got up, showered and dressed. As she put on her lipstick she looked closely at herself in the mirror. Forty nine years old, her hair still brown although she could see some strands of grey, a few crows feet under her eyes, perhaps half a stone over what her ideal weight should be and her chin didn't seem quite so firm as it used to be. Still, she thought, not too bad considering the life she led. She thought how much her daughter—now in her mid twenties and married with one small daughter—looked like her. The grand daughter didn't look like Leila at all but was more like her father; which could be a pity, if she continued to look like him Leila thought, as he was a big heavy set man with what looked like an ever expanding beer belly.

She never talked about her private life to her colleagues in the union, especially the fact that she been married for fifteen years and then divorced. It really wasn't any of their business and she knew unions were notorious places to spread both gossip and rumour. She didn't think many knew she was a grandmother; but, then again, she didn't really care. She put those thoughts to one side. It was time to get moving.

She quite liked the breakfast train. She could do some work during the journey and arrive at the union's office in reasonable time. She had made a mental note to phone Muriel, her secretary, from the train and get her started on booking a hotel for the projected national committee meeting on Saturday and contacting all the twenty members to confirm the date, venue and time of the meeting.

As Leila arrived at Liverpool Lime Street station she bought a copy of the *Liverpool Daily Post* as well as the *Financial Times*.

The train left on time and, while eating her breakfast, Leila read the piece in the *Liverpool Daily Post* that Joe Turner had written. The headline on it was 'Industry3M gets egg on its face.' She smiled and read on. It was largely a factual report of the meeting and quoted the resolution and the company circular. Turner had mentioned some of the interventions of the trots and had mentioned Tony Hammond by name. Then the piece concluded with: 'the meeting had been going well although discussion had been heated at times. The deciding factor was when one man threw an egg at Leila Smith, the union's Deputy General Secretary. She managed to catch the egg without breaking it and then threw it straight back. She hit her target and the man who had thrown it—believed to be a non-union member who works in the company's personnel department—was left with egg on his face, as indeed was the company.'

The piece concluded with a note that Tuner had attempted to contact the company for comment but had been unsuccessful.

She sketched out what she would put in the circular that would go out to the union's Industry3M branches that day and drafted a letter for John Carmichael to consider faxing through to the company. As the train passed Watford she telephoned Muriel Blythman, her secretary, and told her to start making the arrangements for the national committee meeting. She had a quick look at the *Financial Times* as the train neared London. She noticed an item in the company news 'Industry3M buys Indian IT company'. She would read it when in the office.

The train arrived on time. She got a taxi from Euston station and arrived at the union's headquarters at just before ten o'clock. It was a large, grey, concrete office building: a relic of 1960's architecture and planning consent, originally deemed 'functional'. She to admit to herself, though, that while it was ugly it was useful to be located just off Clapham High Street—and the union had bought the freehold of it some twenty years ago. It would be worth considerably more now and the figures looked good in the union's balance sheet.

I was just about to ask Frank Hallard, the head of our research department, to come to my office when there was a knock on the door. I shouted "come in" and Hallard's number two, Sam Askari, small and well dressed as ever, entered.

Askari had joined us two years ago. Previously he had worked as a civil servant in the Treasury, as a junior economist. I could never understand why he had left there and joined us. He always said it was because he was committed to trades unionism and wanted to work for a union full time rather than just be a branch official in a large Government office. His father came from Egypt and his mother from England. He had been educated in England, a Cambridge graduate and was certainly very bright. At his interview he had impressed the panel, though I was not wholly sure about him. In the two years he had been with us my original reservations seemed to be right. He was certainly bright and his research work was good but he had a very prickly attitude and seemed to be to be always looking out for insults, actual or perceived.

The staff of the union—all one hundred and fifty of them in our headquarters and our seven provincial offices (though I kept reminding myself not to call our Cardiff and Glasgow offices 'provincial')—who were below the level of national officer had their own bargaining unit to talk to the executive committee about their own pay and conditions. It was an arrangement that most unions had. After all we could hardly not practise what we preached.

In fact it was a sub-committee of the executive that was responsible for dealing with the staff bargaining unit and Leila, as Deputy General Secretary, was the full time official responsible for negotiating with them. The system had worked reasonably well for some years but things had become more difficult when Askari had become the chairman of the unit. Although it was a bit unusual for him to become chairman after only two years service in the union he had been quite keen to take it on, and, also, no one else had wanted the job. Life inside the union often reflected life outside the union.

"Hello Sam," I said, "I was just about to ask Frank to come and see me. What can I do for you?"

"It's about a very serious matter, Mr Carmichael."

"Well, what is it?"

"One of our members has complained to me about a case of sexual harassment" said Askari looking directly at me.

I looked back.

"An *allegation* of sexual harassment, you mean," I responded.

Askari looked aggressive.

"It's a very serious matter, Mr Carmichael."

"You've already said that—and you know that Mrs Smith is the official who deals with staff matters."

Askari swallowed hard.

"I thought you would like to know immediately. Sexual harassment is a serious issue," repeated Askari and then added, "I thought you would be concerned."

I had many problems to deal with this day and I knew Leila was on her way shortly and I wanted to discuss the Industry3M situation with her. I knew, on the other hand, that a wrong remark about what Askari had said or, even worse, apparent indifference could well cause further problems.

I asked Askari who the complainant was. He told me that one of the women in Dan Michael's membership department had complained to him first thing this morning that Dan had made sexual overtures to her just as she was leaving yesterday afternoon. As chairman of the bargaining unit he thought it his duty to inform me immediately.

"All right, Sam. Thanks for telling me. Mrs Smith will be in shortly and I will advise her to have a word with you later. OK?"

Askari nodded and realised he was not going to get any further at this stage. He repeated for the fourth time that it was a serious issue and then left my office.

I made a mental note to mention it to Leila when she arrived and then lifted the internal telephone to ask Frank to come and see me. Our national committee in Hokkaido, one of the major Japanese motor car companies in the UK, which represented the white collar staff there, was meeting the following week to consider its annual pay claim and I wanted Frank to give me some advice on what would be a realistic claim for them to pursue. I asked him to contact Brian

Hall, the national officer responsible for Hokkaido, and ask him to join us.

Frank, Brian and I spent half an hour discussing the possible claim. The pay of the staff in Hokkaido was not too bad but the company was very profitable and the members there considered their jobs to be insecure—in many cases with good reason—and wanted the claim to be as high as was thought to be achievable. There were also a lot of other issues: weekend working, shift arrangements, overtime qualification, holiday rosters and, in the case of the more senior staff, deputisation payments.

Brian said he would do me a draft of a claim, said he had to rush to a meeting of one of the other companies he dealt with and then left. He was always in a hurry, but was one of the better officers we had.

Frank was getting up to go when there was a knock and Leila Smith popped up head round the door. She asked if it was convenient to have a talk.

Frank said, "We've just finished, Leila". He turned to me, "by the way, what's all this about a sexual harassment case in Dan's department?"

Leila was surprised and looked at me. I groaned and lifted my eyes to the ceiling.

"How news travels" I said. I explained how Askari had just come to me and mentioned the alleged incident yesterday afternoon. He must also have told other people in the building.

"Well," said Leila, "who's the complainant?"

I replied that I had not asked this of Askari but had said I would mention it to her who would deal with it. I knew that several of the full time officers would joke about sexual harassment cases and not treat them too seriously, a practice I deplored, but Leila was a different matter. She would be objective—but also ruthless in establishing the facts.

Frank said "I can't believe Dan would be involved in anything like that."

"OK Frank" commented Leila. "I'll be dealing with it."

Frank then left and Leila sat down. She told me about the meeting, the item in the *Liverpool Daily Post* and then pointed out the news item in the *Financial Times*. She had finished reading in it the taxi from Euston.

Well, it was clear that what Industry3M was doing was the same as a number of other companies in the UK, whether they were British or foreign owned companies. We were all in favour of a national minimum wage and decent pay levels, in fact that was one of the major reasons for our existence, but we no control over a company if it decided to outsource some its work overseas. And there was no doubt about it: there were thousands of bright information technology staff in India who would normally be paid about a third—if that—of what IT staff in the UK would get. If a company could get some of its back office work done well but cheaper in India or elsewhere in the far east then it would try and do so.

I knew that several of my colleagues in other unions had managed to get agreements with a number of the employers they dealt with which limited the amount of work that could be done abroad; but I reckoned it was only buying time. The trend could become irreversible—unless pay in the other countries matched that in Britain—and there was fat chance of that happening. We had to learn special skills and do what we were best at—the problem was that no one quite knew what that was. We hadn't really got to grips with globalisation.

Leila said "It's becoming clear, John, that Industry 3M are anxious to get out of the procedural agreement they have with us so they can switch their staff costs around, both here but more particularly in other countries. They see us as a drag on their expansion."

"I know, and looking at it objectively, there is some truth in that. But," I added "unions have sometimes had to be a brake on what I would call irresponsible expansion."

Leila then handed me a draft letter to the company and a draft union newsletter. I looked at them both: short, succinct and to the point.

"OK, I'll fax the letter to Norman Jones and you get the newsletter moving. All in hand for the national committee meeting on Saturday?"

"Yes, Muriel's working on that now"

Just as Leila said that, there was a knock on the door. I shouted. Muriel Blythman came in looking a bit flustered.

"Sorry to interrupt John," Muriel said as she entered.

I smiled at her. Muriel was the ideal secretary: competent, bright and usually calm. This time, though, she was agitated. I asked what the matter was. She told us that, when telephoning the members of the national committee, all had been going well until she spoke to Tony Hammond at the Liverpool head office of Industry3M. Apparently he had not only been cold and unhelpful but had then started calling Leila all sorts of names and in the end Muriel had put the phone down on him.

"I am sorry, Leila" said Muriel, "but this time I think he's gone over the top. I shouldn't have to put up with that sort of talk—and neither should you."

Leila said she understood, and I knew she did. But there was more than one way to deal with him. Leila said she would leave the matter until she saw him on the Saturday.

"That's the other thing," said Muriel, "I've really come into to say to you Leila, don't forget you're due at the Nottingham weekend school on Saturday."

Leila made a face. She had forgotten. It was one of a series of weekend courses for leading lay representatives in different companies which our education officer had arranged in different parts of the country over the next three months. Leila had been due to speak on the Saturday afternoon.

Leila looked at Muriel.

"You're quite right. I had forgotten. Look, Muriel, get on to the Nottingham office and ask if I can speak to the course on the Sunday morning instead. I'll catch the Nottingham train on Saturday after the national committee meeting, stay overnight and take the morning session—if it's OK with them."

I knew Leila had been working over the two previous weekends and this would be the third.

"Look, Leila" I said, "we must be able to find someone else."

Leila said she would be fine. She liked speaking at the courses and I knew she went down well. I also knew that I would probably be retiring from my job as general secretary in three years time and Leila was held to be the strong candidate to get the position. She had never mentioned it to me neither had she made any public declaration about running for my job. It was just assumed she would.

Under the current employment legislation there would have to be an election for the GS position as there was for Leila's job. There were bound to be several candidates in the election for General Secretary and the trots were certain to put up one of their own. It was natural that Leila would want to consolidate her position by attending as many meetings and courses in the union as possible but it did make life rather busy for her.

Leila asked Muriel to get on to the Nottingham organiser and said she would speak to Chris Tuckell our education officer.

Muriel left and Leila and I then discussed what else needed to be done for the national committee meeting.

"What about you, John," asked Leila "do you want to be there?"

I had the so-called away day of the TUC General Council on Saturday. I could get out of it but explained to Leila that it would look a bit bad. I had been on the General Council for ten years now and—with a bit of luck—I should become the TUC President in two years time, my last year of office. It was one of those positions that was filled purely by what the older members called 'Buggins turn': in other words it was purely by seniority. It was the best way rather than let the position be subject to elections and then lobbying by the different groupings of the TUC. Not everyone agreed with me and I had been one of those a few months ago that had successfully led the

defence of the procedure against some of those who wanted to move
to a contested election system.

Leila said she quite understood. I then told her about my chats
with the union's president and vice-president and calling a special
national executive committee meeting. We agreed to schedule that
for two weeks after the national committee meeting. That would give
time for the company to respond—hopefully—to my fax and also for
ACAS involvement if there was trouble.

We finished our discussion with me telling her that I had arranged
for Leila and I to meet with Oliver Listle of the *Financial Times* at
lunch time. I had also mentioned it to our press officer, Julia Cardon.

"In the George and Dragon?"

I nodded. The pub most of the staff used was The Partridge just
near our building. The George and Dragon was a bit further away.

"How much can we tell him?"

I said that we should be quite open with him but emphasise that
we hoped for the company to agree to a series of negotiating meetings
and we were not rushing into industrial action ballots.

Leila said she expected Oliver had his own sources in Industrty3M
and it would be up to him how to play it.

"We'll leave here about twelve thirty. OK"

Leila agreed. She had a lot to do, but then so did we all. And
the last thing she wanted from me was words of sympathy about her
work load.

Just then I remembered.

"Oh, don't forget."

I reminded her about Askari and the case of sexual harassment
that he had mentioned to me that morning.

"I'll get on to it this afternoon," said Leila as she left my office.

Leila asked Muriel to get the newsletter over to Julia who dealt
with publicity and the press and ask her to get it out through the fax

to all the offices and—if possible—the different departments and sections within each office—by the afternoon. She reflected that it was a far cry from sending out newsletters by post. Although the company insisted that staff should not use the fax facility to communicate with the outside on any non-company matter, that did not stop the union from faxing newsletters to inside the company. They did this in a number of companies. In some others there was an arrangement for the company to distribute union newsletters themselves. That was the best method as it went to all the different parts of the company. Industry3M had never agreed to that but in the past had turned a blind eye to the union faxing material: not, Leila knew, that they could have done much about it.

Leila sat down in her office. She hadn't been in since Monday and there was a considerable amount of post to deal with. She did not have direct responsibility for any of the companies with whom the union dealt but in a sense had a watching brief over all of the ones that the national officers dealt with. Altogether the union employed eleven national officers—for research, press and publicity, membership department, organisation and education with the remaining six dealing with negotiations in the different companies with whom the union had a procedural agreement and companies in the various sectors where the union was seeking to get established.

All the national officers reported directly to Leila and—as in the case of Industry3M with the illness of Tim Burke—she would step in and deal with negotiations where one of the national officers was on sick leave. She held regular meetings with all the negotiating national officers so that all concerned were abreast of how things were moving. Carmichael held regular meetings with Leila and all of the eleven national officers to cover all activities within the union. In special cases—as again with Industry3M—he could get involved if the need arose. The system had worked fairly well but it meant that Leila often seemed swamped by paperwork.

She looked at her watch. It was nearly eleven o'clock. She phoned Askari on the internal phone and asked him to come to her office at three in the afternoon. He started to talk about the matter but she cut him off abruptly.

"Save it Sam. And bring the person who makes the complaint—by the way, who is it?"

"Sarah MacKenzie in membership department and—"

"Save it, Sam, I said. I'll see you both at three and we'll take it from there."

She spent the next hour looking through the large amount of paper on her desk. There were daily summaries of press reports on the union, the TUC and the companies with whom the union negotiated which were circulated to the national officers, Leila and Carmichael. The reports of negotiating meetings and the minutes of the different national committees were also circulated. Then there were letters addressed to her personally from members, branch and regional officials. She noticed the programme for the weekend representatives course at Nottingham and Muriel had also placed on her desk the programme for the one day TUC conference on employment law which had agreed to attend on the Friday. She would only attend the morning session and then come back to the office in the afternoon.

She was a third of the way through the papers when she looked at her watch. It was nearly half past twelve. She must find time that afternoon to sketch out her remarks to the Industry3M national committee on Saturday. She must also look again at the draft talk she had prepared for the Nottingham course. And she had to see Askari and Sarah Mackenzie at three. It would be some time before she left the office in the evening.

Leila and Julia, our press officer, both came to my office on time and the three of us left and walked down to the George and Dragon. It was a sunny day, the pub was not crowded and I was looking forward to a drink. Oliver Listle was waiting for us in the main bar.

Oliver greeted us with a smile and "it's my shout". Leila and Julia had a glass of red wine each and I had a pint of bitter. We sat down round a small table.

"Cheers." We all seemed to say it together.

Oliver knew both Leila and Julia. He looked at me.

"Well, what's new?"

I motioned to Leila to start. She quickly rehearsed the events that week with Industry3M and finished with the news item in the FT that morning.

Oliver said he understood the company was looking for partner companies—as they called them—in India and in China. They weren't the only British company to do so. Several British companies had merged with, or taken over, Indian companies for some years. Now that China was opening up to foreign investment any number of American, French, British or German companies were anxious to get in there. Of course it would have an effect on the home base.

I explained how we had been involved with Industry3M for over ten years now. They had been an early player in the UK, right from they days when they were Oil2. It had been a major coup for the union to get an agreement with them as there weren't many American owned companies that dealt with British unions then and, as the company grew into Industry3M and expanded, so our membership had grown and it was now one of the largest single employers we dealt with. We had been lucky with the previous chief executive of the UK subsidiary and with David Stannard as personnel director. Now it had changed. The previous chief had retired and Stannard was now out the door.

Oliver had heard that Stannard had been fired. He had also heard of John Carr.

"What's the form on him?" asked Leila.

"Fancies himself as a bit of a hatchet man. Clever in a way but you could not call him straightforward. Even to call him devious would be an understatement. But I believe there have been some changes in senior management in Atlanta and Carr has seen his chance to make his name with them."

I thought I might as well be open with Oliver.

"I reckon he's thought that derecognition of the union would be a feather in his cap—not for quoting by the way—and come at the right time with the outsourcing abroad."

We then discussed what Oliver could quote from us. He was well clued up on the company. Julia, who knew Oliver and all the leading industrial and labour reporters and who herself had worked on a couple of specialist economic magazines as a reporter, was making a few notes as we talked. Then she interrupted.

"Sorry to barge in, but just before we go any further, has Stannard spoken to you?"

It was a good question. Perhaps the way Oliver had mentioned his name earlier had given Julia the idea. Anyway, it worked. Oliver blushed a little.

"Very good, Julia. Yes, I did speak to him yesterday evening. He's one bitter man and he more or less confirmed what John has just said. But, more to the point, what happened at the meeting? I saw the note in the *Liverpool Daily Post.*"

Leila went over the events of the meeting.

I said, "don't forget the egg." Leila told him about that. Oliver said it would be amusing to ask John Carr about that.

In fact we gave Oliver the complete story and told him what the national executive committee might do in a couple of weeks. I emphasised that I had faxed the company this morning and was expecting a reply soonest. If the company agreed an early date for a negotiating meeting, then all would be well. Oliver said he understood that and would put the stuff about outsourcing and the company's longer term plans as background.

I got some more drinks but both Leila and Julia declined. They did ask for a sandwich though. Oliver and I stuck to beer.

I had known Oliver Listle for some years. He was one of the most astute industrial correspondents with many contacts among the unions and the employers organisations. He was currently the chairman of the labour and industrial correspondents group—a group that covered all the national newspapers as well as radio and television stations. I asked him to stress that we were hoping for a peaceful set of negotiations and he agreed that he would put that very point to Carr if he could get hold of him.

When we left the pub Oliver agreed that Julia could contact him for any news from the company. I said that we would probably hold a press conference after the national executive committee meeting in two weeks time and, in the meantime, would not court undue publicity.

A useful meeting, I thought. But at the end of the day all the publicity in the world—while most times very helpful—was but ancillary to the key: if the company did try and derecognise the union, what were the members prepared to do?

Leila had one hour before the meeting with Askari and the sexual harassment case. She went over her diary with Muriel. She would go to the one day TUC conference on employment legislation in the morning but come back to HQ for the afternoon. Muriel had checked with the union's education officer and the Nottingham organiser. They had changed the programme at the weekend round and Leila would now be expected on the Saturday evening and would speak to the course on Sunday morning. There would be about thirty of the leading lay representatives from the companies with offices in the East Midlands. She would speak on the role of the union in the wider trade union movement, TUC structure, relations with other union and the union's participation in Staff International. She had talked on this at several union education courses.

Muriel commented that the following week did not look too bad. Leila hoped for an ACAS meeting that week—depending, of course, on any reaction from Industry3M to Carmichael's fax. She also had one of her regular meetings with the union's national negotiators. Muriel mentioned that Jim Bradwell of the local government union had telephoned while she was in the pub to ask if she could talk to a sub group of his executive committee on the new job evaluation scheme. She asked Muriel to fix a date and make sure that Frank Hallard could join here. She also mentioned the possibility of a national executive committee meeting in two weeks time: but that had yet to be decided and, anyway, Carmichael's secretary would be making all the arrangements.

Muriel asked if Leila required her at the national committee meeting on Saturday. Leila thought that Tim Burke's secretary could handle it. She normally took the minutes and, although Burke was off with his bowel cancer, she was still the appropriate person to attend.

She started to read some of the paper in her in-tray but soon there came a knock on the door. She shouted for the person to enter and Askari put his head round the door.

"Mrs Smith?"

"All right Sam, come in."

Askari entered her office, followed by Sarah Mackenzie. She was a large woman in her mid-thirties with dark hair curled into a pig tail at the back. Leila knew she had worked in Dan Michael's department for five years. Apparently she was efficient at her job but was known as a gossip and Dan didn't think very highly of her.

Leila asked them to sit down and then explained the complaints procedure as laid down in the agreement between the union and the bargaining unit. She emphasised how she regarded any accusation of sexual harassment as extremely serious and then invited Askari to speak.

Askari said he had been told by Mackenzie of an incident on Wednesday at five o'clock when the clerical staff were going home. She had come to see him first thing in the morning and he had thought it right to tell the General Secretary and he, in turn, had said he would ask Leila Smith to deal with it.

"OK, Sam. I think we all know that. But, now, what's the actual complaint?"

Mackenzie then spoke up. She had a rough voice and—at times Leila had heard her loud and rather grating laugh. But she wasn't laughing now and seemed a little nervous.

"It happened on Wednesday. Dan Michael did it, and that's why I complained."

"But, Sarah, what do you say he actually did?"

Mackenzie swallowed hard and then coughed.

Askari said, "can I tell you, Mrs Smith, what Sarah told me this morning?"

"I would rather here it from Sarah herself."

Mackenzie coughed again.

"Well?"

Mackenzie then said, "Mr Michael touched me and said some nasty things to me."

"You'll have to be a bit more precise than that. Where did he touch you and what did he say."

Leila sighed inwardly. This could take some time and she had a lot of things to do before she left the office that evening. But she knew full well that the allegation had to be thoroughly investigated and she could not be seen to be treating it lightly. Not, anyway, that she intended to treat it lightly.

Gradually she elicited from Mackenzie that as she and one of the other members of the female clerical staff were leaving the membership department Dan Michael had pushed his body against her breasts and then said to her—Mackenzie was blushing by now—that he would like to go to bed with her. After some questioning by Leila she stated that well, what he had actually said was that he would fuck her.

Leila then asked who the other member of staff was and stated that she would have a word with her. Did Askari now want to say anything? Askari repeated what he had said right at the beginning and then said for about the sixth time that it was a very serious matter. Leila noticed that while Mackenzie had been speaking he had been unnaturally quiet and seemed a little embarrassed. Leila then said she would be speaking to Dan Michael and would ask him if he wanted to bring a 'prisoner's friend' to accompany him. She would then get back to Askari.

"I would ask you to keep fairly quiet about this. It won't be doing anyone any good for the whole thing to be openly discussed; the details might get outside of HQ here and comment might well be prejudicial to dealing with the allegation."

Mackenzie then said, "You keep calling it an allegation but it's what happened and I don't think it's right—" Askari put his hand on her arm and motioned her to stop.

"We will wait to hear from you Mrs Smith and I will inform the other person who witnessed the incident that you will want to speak to her."

The two left the office. Leila lifted up the internal telephone and called Dan Michael. She asked him to come to her office in ten minutes time. She wanted to sort out her report to the national committee meeting on Saturday and she also wanted to phone Ian MacCallister, the chairman of the national committee, to have a word about the meeting. Then there was the TUC conference tomorrow. She would probably want to speak at that. Luckily she could probably use some of her speech to the weekend course at Nottingham: but she wanted to make sure it was up to date. She's have to look at that on the train on Saturday evening.

She knew though that she had to deal with the sexual harassment case quickly and fairly—and she wanted to do that. It was all very well for some officials to pay lip service to sexual harassment codes and procedures—and for it to be the subject of banter down the pub—but it was a serious issue and one she felt strongly about.

She also knew that if an allegation was made against one of the union's officials and found to be true, it could be very damaging. There would be only too many people—among the employers, in the press, in some other unions and even within her own union—to make fun of the issue and then contrast the union's principle of urging action against al forms of sexual harassment and with having one of its officials being found guilty of it.

She wondered whether Sarah Mackenzie had been telling the truth or had she—accidentally or deliberately—invented the whole thing? Difficult if there was a witnesses, but then what would she say? Anyway she decided to speak to Dan Michael first.

Just then the telephone rang. It was the switchboard operator.

"It's a Mr Chris Rodd asking for you. Shall I put him through?"

Leila remembered their brief conversation the previous morning.

"Yes please. Oh, hello Chris."

"Hello Leila. Sorry I couldn't speak much yesterday morning when you phoned. Things are a bit difficult at the moment."

Leila wondered why he had phoned. She had phoned at an awkward time but his wife had sounded abrupt and more than a little annoyed. Perhaps there was some tension there. Chris was a good looking man in his early forties: was there something else to it ? But it was none of her business. She waited for Chris to say something.

"There's been a lot of gossip and rumour flying around here, and I thought you might like to hear it."

"Go ahead then, Chris."

"Well, apparently the meeting you had last night didn't turn out how the company wanted. I've seen the company circular but the effect of that has been nullified by what happened at the meeting—particularly the egg incident."

"Oh, you've heard about that?"

"I should say so and it appears that the chap who threw the egg has not only had his card marked but has actually got his cards."

"You mean he's been dismissed?"

"Yes. He worked in personnel department in Liverpool, his name's Leslie Curtis. The story being put about is that his last annual report was not very satisfactory and he hasn't improved since then so—fortuitously they claim—he's been given his notice. In fact more than that, he's been told to leave now with three months money in lieu of notice."

Leila was surprised. It sounded like a rather poor television drama.

"How did you hear all this?"

"You know what a large company is like, Leila. News travels quickly and it would appear that there's a man called Collins in personnel department, the number two to the departed David Stannard, who's been telling people all about it. Of course, there's the counter theory that Collins dreamt up the idea of the egg to ingratiate himself with this chap Carr from group. But it would seem that Carr's distanced himself from it all. There's even one rumour that it was Carr's idea in the first place and Norman Jones, the chief, was furious at Carr. So someone had to take some action and this chap Curtis caught it."

Leila made the obvious point that if he had caught the egg things would have been different. Equally if the egg had splashed all over her face then the meeting could have ended in turmoil.

"Just imagine," she said, "if the egg had broken on me there would have been uproar and it would have been difficult to settle things down." She knew the trots would have taken advantage of the uproar. The company would have been delighted. The impression would have been of an unruly meeting rather than a complete show of support for the union's position.

"It's a good job you caught the egg," said Rodd. "Anyway, I thought you would like to know."

She thanked him and said she had to go.

"Oh, and don't forget, we must have that drink sometime."

Leila said she would remember. She thought, as she put the phone down, she might remember. If there was any domestic trouble in Chris' house, then the last thing she wanted was to get involved. She regretted even more now that she had phoned him in the first place. She had thought he was in a more senior position than possibly he was. He was just repeating rumour and didn't seem to have any inside knowledge of the incident. Still, water under the bridge—and it was nice to know that the company was in a spot over the egg throwing incident.

She looked at her watch. It was nearly four o'clock. She must see Dan Michael now and then sort out some of her paper work. She decided she would take her papers about Industry3M home and draft out her notes there. She must though speak to MacCallister about the meeting. Best to do that before she spoke to Michael.

She could have done without the sexual harassment case; but, she reminded herself for the third time, it was an important issue.

She got through to MacCallister. He was a good solid union member, and seemed to be progressing well in the company. There had been some talk that his union involvement, particularly his chairmanship of the national committee for the last three years, had militated against his career but there was no way of proving it. And MacCallister himself had not raised the matter. He was still only in his mid—thirties and time enough. There were some cases though that Leila had raised with different companies where time off for union duties and union activity had seemingly counted against some members in their promotion opportunities.

She spoke for some ten minutes with MacCallister. He was ready for the meeting. He and Bruce Cannon, the other delegate from the Glasgow office, would be flying down to London first thing on Saturday morning. The meeting had been timed to start at eleven o'clock and they would get to the hotel in Bloomsbury about ten. He would see Leila then. She went over the resolution the meeting had passed and said she would have another resolution ready for him to look at on Saturday. She mentioned the trots at the meeting and the need to be aware of their likely tactics. Tony Hammond, the apparent leader of the trots, was one of the four delegates from the Liverpool head office on the national committee and he was bound to be present at the meeting.

Thank goodness she could rely on someone like Ian MacCallister. And she was also fortunate she had people like Ted Davis and Clive

Bristow in Liverpool. There were, she knew, many such members throughout the company. She was determined not to let them down.

There was a knock on the door and Dan Michael came into her office. As he entered Leila thought he looked a bit flustered. He was tall and fairly well built. She knew he used to play a lot of squash and generally keep himself fit. In recent months though he seemed to have been putting on weight. Probably eating too much and not taking enough exercise: but then hadn't she heard something about his marriage being a bit rocky? If so, Leila thought to herself, it would be a shame. She had met his wife once and she appeared very pleasant and they had three children. Still, she had to sort out the allegation.

Michael sat down on the chair opposite Leila.

"I can't believe all this" he muttered and wiped his brow with his handkerchief.

"Take it easy, Dan" said Leila. "You know that all such incidents or alleged incidents like this come under my wing and I have to investigate them—and, I stress, I want to investigate them properly."

Michael looked at her and opened his mouth to say something, thought better of it and nodded.

Leila rehearsed the allegation made by Sarah Mackenzie, how she had contacted Sam Askari as chairman of the bargaining unit and Askari had formally raised the matter through the union's internal disciplinary procedure. She reminded Michael that he could have someone with him as a sort of 'prisoner's friend' if he wanted to. Michael declined. Leila asked for his comments on the allegation.

He seemed a it reluctant to speak at first, then took a deep breath and spoke quickly. He had known Leila for ever since he came to work for the union and respected her. He decided to tell her everything.

Things had been a bit difficult at home. Relations with his wife had been a bit strained and he had suspected her of having an affair with another man. He had had too much to drink on several occasions in recent weeks—sometimes at lunch time. Yesterday had been one of those times. On the previous evening as work finished he had been rushing to get out of the office to get to the station. Sarah Mackenzie and another woman—he thought it was Eliza Astobe, the bright young graduate from Ghana—had been moving towards the door at the same time. He thought that they would move out of the way when they saw him try and rush through, but Mackenzie had stood right by the door and made a point of not moving out of the way. Instead of waiting for her he had squeezed through the doorway and inevitably had brushed against her. She had cried out that he should stop pushing against her breasts—tits she called them—and he had muttered 'fuck you'. That was it, Michael said.

"I'm very sorry it all happened. I was short tempered and I was in a rush. I wasn't paying proper attention and I should not have squeezed through the door as I did nor should have I had said what I did say." He took a deep breath. "However, to suggest that I was sexually harassing her is ludicrous and I certainly did not mean what she alleges I meant when I said 'fuck you'."

Leila asked him about the people in his department—there were six women working there—and how he got on with them. How long had Sarah Mackenzie been there? Had he any particular problem with her? What about the other women?

"Everything's always been fine, Leila," responded Michael. "Though—and I'm not just saying this now because this incident has happened—Sarah has often struck me as a bit tarty—" he paused and looked at Leila. "I'm sorry but—"

"Look Dan, you can say what you like to me. I want to get your side of the story and then the next thing will be a meeting with Sam, Sarah Mackenzie, you and I—and the apparent witness Eliza."

Michael decided not to say anymore. He thanked Leila for your understanding, said he would await her call for a meeting and left the room.

Leila called Muriel to come into the office again. She asked her to arrange the joint meeting with Askari and Michael and the others for early the following week. She then picked up a pile of her papers and stuffed them into her briefcase.

"I think I'll get more done at home now," she said. "So, Muriel I'll see you tomorrow afternoon."

Leila lived in Wimbledon, in a small house in a road just off Wimbledon hill. It was about fifteen minutes walk from the station and that was probably just as well. As often as not, the walk to and from the station was about the only exercise she got in most weeks. It would be nice to get home and she could sort things out for the next three days. And, she suddenly thought, she must telephone her daughter. She would be unable now to go and see her and her grand daughter on Sunday. Little Helen, the grand daughter, would be disappointed but Deborah, her daughter, would understand. She had lived with her mother's style of life for years.

❦

The TUC one day conference on the Friday morning had, Leila decided, been quite good. There had been the usual rhetoric and declamatory statements but some useful points had been made by several of the union delegates there. During the coffee break several had asked Leila about Industry3M. The article in that morning's *Financial Times* by Oliver Listle had been quite comprehensive and generated considerable interest. Even John Miller, the TUC General Secretary, had smiled as he passed her to go on the platform in the conference hall and asked her not to throw any eggs.

She was particularly pleased that Joe Cobb from the local government union had mentioned that his General Secretary was hoping that Leila would come to their executive committee sub-group to talk about the job evaluation scheme. Leila explained that her secretary was in touch with Jim Bradwell's office to fix a date. The sooner the better, she added.

Leila had been one those speaking at the conference. She had listened enough, she thought, to some of the calls for a repeal of all the employment legislation introduced in the 1980's; that was never going to happen and it just meant that reasonable points about the existing legislation were forgotten in the general call for all out repeal. She had mentioned her concern at the effect of the legislation on the conduct and timing of industrial action ballots and how—if any further such legislation was implemented as some of the country's major employers were seeking—they could all end up with an industrial relations system similar to that of the USA whereby lots of bargaining and disputes were decided in courts of law rather than round the bargaining table. Her remarks had been well received.

She decided to head straight back to the office after the morning session. It would have been too easy to go to the pub with several of the delegates from other unions but she still had lots to do and she wanted to see if John Carmichael had received any reply from Industry3M.

<hr />

I got the fax from Industry3M just after I came back from the pub at about two o'clock. Sheila, my secretary, handed it to me as I went through to my office.

It was signed by Norman Jones the chief executive. I quickly read it and then read it again more slowly. It was not good at all. I knew Leila would be with me shortly as she was intending to leave the TUC conference as they broke up for lunch. Then Julia, our press officer, telephoned.

"Oliver from the FT has just phoned me" she said. "Apparently Industry3M have sent him a copy of the fax that they have sent you and he wants to know if you have any comment."

I explained that I was waiting for Leila to join me and then I wanted Julia to come to my office as well and we would agree a response. I said I would give Julia a ring as soon as Leila came into the office.

The phone rang. The switchboard operator said it was John Miller from the TUC. I asked her to put him through.

"John? John Miller here. You mentioned to me yesterday about your tussle with Industry3M and I said I would try and have a word with Bob Wilson at DTI. I nearly mentioned this to Leila this morning but thought I would speak to you direct."

I knew that was typical of the TUC General Secretary. He was always very conscious of the need not to go outside the formal lines of authority in any of the affiliated unions. If he did, then it could all go very wrong particularly if there were internal problems in any of them. He was the leading man in the TUC and he would never interfere—or be seen to interfere—in any union unless that union specifically and formally asked him.

"Any joy?" I asked.

"Well Bob has met the Group people in London and once he met the deputy chief from Atlanta. Anyway, the long and short of it is that Industry3M is an expanding company, as you well know, and like a lot of companies is seeking to shift a lot of the basic clerical work to overseas. I know, I know—" he quickly interjected as I started to break in with my view on outsourcing to other countries—"apparently the company is seeking further mergers here in the UK and the Government doesn't want to upset them."

I told him that my worry was that the company was trying to go down the road of derecognising the union so as to give them a free hand in outsourcing.

"I understand that John. I'm just telling you what Bob Wilson told me. Of course he realises the union anxieties but he's concerned that if Industry3M were to cut their increasing investment here in the British economy it could frighten some of the other foreign companies that the Government is anxious to help get involved here."

"So," I told Miller, "the long and short of it is that there's nothing formal or informal that the Government will, or can, do."

There was a lot more I could say but I knew that John Miller would know what I was going to say and he knew that I knew. I thanked him and put the phone down.

There was a knock on the door and Leila entered my office.

"Just the person," I smiled. "There's been a reply from Jones at Industry3M. Just a moment while I get Julia to join us."

Leila briefly told me about the TUC conference that morning and how quite a few of the people there had commented on the piece in the *Financial Times* that morning. There was another knock on my door and Julia came in. The three of us sat down at the small meeting table in my office.

I showed Leila the fax from Norman Jones.

"Read it aloud," I suggested, "so Julia can get the gist of it. Sheila's photocopying one for you now."

Leila read the fax. Jones had said he had received my fax—he didn't thank me for it and then came the response.

"I have noted what you have said about the union meeting on Wednesday evening. I assume you have also read the company circular that was sent round the offices on Wednesday afternoon. That circular stated our position and your fax does not affect that at all." Leila's voice was rising slightly as she continue to read out the fax. "We are giving serious consideration to the position between the union and the company and in particular the cost to us of all the time off and other arrangements that up till now we have allowed for union members. You will appreciate that the cost is significant and as there is some doubt as to whether your union actually represents the majority of our staff you will understand our concern."

Leila looked at us. "It then concludes with saying he will be in touch with you at a later date."

Julia mentioned that she was getting a number of calls from different newspapers, and from the BBC and ITN. They had seen either the piece in the *Liverpool Daily Post* on Wednesday or the piece in the *Financial Times* this morning or both. Julia said she had replied factually to each of the queries but suggested that a press conference might now be appropriate.

Leila looked at me. She suggested she get in touch with ACAS this afternoon and we hold a press conference after an ACAS meeting rather than delay one until after the national executive committee meeting. In the meantime Julia should continue saying that the union was considering various options, the national committee was meeting on Saturday and once an ACAS meeting was arranged she could mention that. I emphasised to her that the one point she should stress to each of the callers was that we did represent a majority of the staff.

"That is right, isn't it Leila?"

"Absolutely, John. I checked the figures with Dan Michael on Wednesday morning from Liverpool."

I told Julia that I would phone Oliver Listle now and she could wait in my office while I did so and then she could know exactly what I said. Leila said she would get back to her office. She said she wanted to sort out her papers before the national committee meeting and the Nottingham course. She would either phone me with the result of the committee or ask Julia to do so. It would depend on when the meeting finished. I nodded and wished her luck.

Chapter Four

Further Meetings

"Mrs Smith?"

Leila lifted up the phone, grunted and glanced at her watch. Seven o'clock. She had been fast asleep but it was time to get up anyway.

"Leo Patullo from the Press Association. I understand your Industry3M committee is meeting today. Any chance of a word afterwards?"

"Not really," replied Leila. "I don't think there will be much to report as any recommendations will have to go before our national executive and that's not meeting for another couple of weeks."

"Why so long?"

"We are having a number of meetings of our branches and we hope to meet ACAS next week. But, if you like, I'll give you a ring after the meeting. Oh, and we shall be holding a press conference possibly after the ACAS meeting but definitely after the national executive: there'll definitely be some hard news then."

The PA man persisted.

"No chance of a quick meeting this afternoon?"

"Afraid not, I've got to go to Nottingham after the meeting—nothing to do with Industry3M; but I'll ring you when I can."

"Thanks. And sorry to call you so early" he said as he finished the call.

He didn't have to say that, Leila knew, but at least he had been polite. And it was early for him too. Leila would try and phone him, or at least ask Julia to phone him; and she would have to phone the GS as well as Julia who were both probably going to get press queries that day.

She showered, dressed, made some breakfast and left the house at a quarter past nine o'clock.

She wanted to get to the meeting early. She wanted to speak again to Ian Macallister. She had arranged for Tim Burke's secretary, Samantha Riley, to bring copies of the articles in the *Liverpool Daily Post* and the *Financial Times*, as well as the company's circular, John Carmichael's faxed letter to Norman Jones and his reply.

As she got the train from Wimbledon to Waterloo she remembered her telephone conversation with her daughter Deborah the previous evening. She had arranged to go over to her house in Basildon on Sunday but now couldn't and was very sorry not to have let her know earlier. She was full of remorse that she had to disappoint little Helen, her grand daughter, but she had no alternative. Deborah had said she quite understood but her voice had been a little weary: this had happened so often in the past. Leila knew it was difficult for her, particularly as only a year ago Richard, her husband, had walked out on her and not come back. At the time Leila had been almost relieved as she had not liked him much—or, she smiled wryly, his beer belly.

But, what was it, she wondered, that made both mother and daughter should have unsuccessful marriages? In her own case, of course, it did have something to with the nature of her job, the late evenings, the many nights away, the working weekends, the interrupted holidays. However, she knew that some of her colleagues in the union—and in other unions—had stable marriages: so was it an excuse or not? And, in Deborah's case, had Leila's experience with her husband made her very wary of her own marriage?

Leila had finished the conversation by asking Deborah and Helen to come over to her house the following Sunday and they would all go out for lunch at a recently opened, and apparently very good, Indian restaurant. Deborah had said they would be pleased to.

The national committee meeting was in a conference room in a hotel just close to Euston station. It was handy for the delegates from different parts of the country and the union had often used it for meetings. Leila went by bus from Waterloo station and got there just before half past ten.

Macallister and the other branch delegate from Glasgow had not come down by airplane but had caught the overnight sleeper train and were there when Leila arrived. She waved to Clive Bristow, Jean Asah from Leeds and several of the other delegates who had also arrived. Then while Samantha was distributing the papers round the committee table she told Macallister how she hoped the meeting would go. She explained she had contacted ACAS the previous afternoon and they had provisionally fixed up a meeting for the following Thursday at its London headquarters. She gave him a copy of a resolution she had drafted the previous day.

By eleven o'clock the delegates had all arrived and sat round the committee table. She noticed Tony Hammond sitting next to Jean Asah and frowned. Was Hammond, the leading trot in Liverpool, and indeed in the whole company, getting too friendly with Asah? She hoped not and made a mental note to speak to her when they broke for lunch.

Macallister called the meeting to order at just gone eleven. Leila reported that there were three apologies for absence. Each branch was entitled to send two delegates to the national committee but one delegate each from Leicester, Manchester and Bristol had sent apologies. He then asked Leila to report to the national committee on the events of the last week but before Leila could get to her feet, Tony Hammond raised his hand. "Point of order" he exclaimed.

"What is it Tony?" asked Macallister.

"Why isn't the General Secretary here? He wasn't at the meeting on Wednesday evening? Is he interested at all? Is he—"

"That's quite enough Tony," broke in Macallister. "That, as you well know is not strictly speaking a point of order."

Leila leant over to him and whispered about the TUC General Council's away day meeting.

"The TUC General Council have a special meeting today and John, as a senior member of the Council, and also because he chairs the Europe task force, really has to attend. And as Tim Burke, our national officer, is away getting treatment for his bone cancer, we have Leila, DGS, here instead. Now, Leila—off you go."

Hammond groaned as if he didn't find Macallister's response convincing at all and muttered something to Jean Asah. She didn't smile but looked a bit shocked.

Leila noticed and said across the table to Hammond, "by the way Tony, what was that you called me when speaking to my secretary on Thursday?"

Hammond went red and was silent.

"Next time, Tony, tell me to my face, will you?"

The room was quiet as the delegates realised there was a sub-text to the questioning. They all looked at Hammond. He shrugged his shoulders and remained silent.

Leila then got to her feet and gave her report. She went over the whole sequence of events since John Carmichael's meeting with the leading union representatives in Liverpool on Monday, referred to the papers handed out before the meeting started and finished with the provisional ACAS meeting the following Thursday and the interest shown by other unions. Macallister thanked her and said he now intended to go round the table and ask each of the delegates for their comments.

Five of the eight union branches had held special branch meetings and three had passed resolutions supporting that carried at the Liverpool meeting on Wednesday. One had not passed any resolution but had given its delegates an open mandate to support whatever seemed to be reasonable and the consensus of the national committee. The fifth branch, Bristol, had passed a motion simply urging negotiations between the company and the union. The other three branches had not been able to hold meetings in the short time available.

Leila offered to go and speak to each of the three—Brighton, Norwich and Newcastle—in the next two weeks and try and get them on board. She knew Bristol could well be a problem as evidenced by their motion avoiding any mention of any sort of action except negotiations, which the company gave every sign of ignoring. Membership in the Bristol branch office of the company was the lowest of any of the company's eight UK branches. There had been difficulty in finding union branch officers at the last annual general meeting. Brighton, Norwich and Newcastle could also be difficult.

Macallister asked Clive Bristow to speak on the UK head office branch feeling. Bristow explained that there was considerable feeling among the members—and some of the non-union members he had spoken to in the previous two days—that the company was deliberately seeking confrontation with the union and the general mood was more determined than at the Wednesday meeting. Macallister then called on Tony Hammond who also chaired the IT branch.

Hammond always looked intense, Leila thought, and appeared angry and humourless. To be fair, it had to be admitted that union membership there was high, particularly among the programmers and the operators, though not so high among the analysts and other senior IT staff. Altogether, membership of the union among the IT staff was some seventy percent. Although the majority of them were not what Leila referred to as 'trots' they were happy—or seemed to be happy—to let Hammond take the lead in union matters. Leila had wondered often how much the other members knew of Hammond's views and what the agenda of him and his few close supporters actually was.

Hammond said his members in the IT branch—why did he always refer to the members there as *his* members Leila asked herself—were determined to take action and then posed a series of questions. What plans for industrial action had the union officials prepared? What were going to be the arrangements for strike pay if a strike was called? Was there going to be a national demonstration? Had other trade unions been solicited for support? And he finished with: "and what about our sister unions on the continent who organise the company's staff? What was the ITS, Staff International, doing? I know that there are a lot of international junketings—sorry, I mean meetings—but what practical steps were being taken there?"

Leila knew he was planting the idea—not a new one she had to admit—that the union's involvement in Staff International was an excuse for a lot of travel abroad, dinners and a bit of sight seeing rather than anything positive for concerted union action. It was part of the feeling generated that involvement in the ITS was merely subscribing to a travel agency, and all at union members expense, though Leila found little difference between a meeting in a hotel in London and meetings in hotels in Madrid, or Rome or Brussels or Berlin. The latter might sound better or more exotic but union meetings were union meetings wherever they were held and often the need for simultaneous translation made them very tiresome. But some people would never be convinced; perhaps Leila thought, it was a continuation of the old English theory that as soon as you left the UK for some foreign place then you were somehow 'living it up'. That, and a bit of the 'little Englander' nostalgia.

Leila got up again.

"I have been in touch with Van Megeren at Staff International and also with the Swedish and German unions who negotiate with Industry3M in their own countries. Both those unions are interested in the job evaluation claim and possibly one or both of them might submit a claim for a similar scheme there. I'll be in touch with them again in the next two weeks. In the meantime Van Mergeren is circulating all affiliated unions about our position with Industry3M."

She went on. "The GS has been in touch with the TUC General Secretary and some of the other unions. Again there seems to be considerable interest in the job evaluation scheme of ours and I hope to be meeting one of them soon. I did mention the interest of other unions earlier. As far as strike pay is concerned, if there is a strike, then it will be for the national executive to decide. On any form of industrial action I'll say something later on in the meeting but first I want to hear what the committee thinks about it."

Leila turned to Macallister. She said she wanted to widen the issue a bit. He told her to carry on.

"You've all read the company's circular and the fax reply to the GS letter. What with those and the remarks of John Carr that I mentioned were made at the meeting with them on Tuesday evening, I am in little doubt that the company is looking at a possible derecognition of the union." She went on to tell them about the latest membership figures, the importance of the procedural agreement and the strength of feeling shown at the Liverpool meeting.

Hammond started to get to his feet but Macallister waved him down.

"You've had your shout, Tony. I want any other delegates who haven't spoken yet to make their comments."

The delegate from Brighton raised her hand. Leila looked at her. She was Lilian Fairweather, mid-fifties, brown hair almost white, thin faced and one of those members who never volunteered an opinion but had seemed content to sit on the committee ever since the national committee had been formed when the union first signed the procedural agreement with the company.

Macallister asked her to speak.

"Why is there all this talk of action, Mr Chairman? Everything seems to have been happening very fast in this week. What's the rush?" She always referred to the 'chairman' of a meeting and never 'chair'. Leila thought that if anyone could be called old fashioned, it was her. But, she knew, there was no harm in that and she made a great contrast to the Tony Hammonds or, Leila remembered, the Sarah Mackenzies in the union's membership department, and was undoubtedly representative of a good many of the union's members in the company. And, her question was a fair one.

Leila got up again. She admitted the relevance of the question. She explained the significance of the company's apparent attitude and how she very much hoped that there could be a negotiating meeting with the company on the union's pay and job evaluation claims. But it didn't look hopeful and the committee had to look at what might happen next. She saw the dismissal of David Stannard, the previous personnel director, as a bad sign and the involvement of John Carr from European Group head office as particularly bad. She very much hoped she was wrong and that negotiations would take place in the normal and proper manner but the union had to be prepared for the worst.

Lilian Fairweather nodded. It would be wrong to say she was happy with the answer but she did see the logic of it.

Macallister looked round the table. Hammond raised his hand again.

"OK Tony, one more question and then we'll go round the table again for suggestions for the future."

Hammond rose and in his rather thin and nasal voice asked what steps were being taken to involve the lay representatives in any union action. Leila saw this at once: it was another way of getting some sort of lay representative committee as an alternative to the existing structure and one which the trots would be more easily able to influence.

Before Leila could get to her feet to respond, Clive Bristow jumped up.

"Mr Chairman" he said loudly. "Mr Hammond—" *not* Tony, Leila noted—"raised a similar point on Wednesday at our meeting and got the answer he knew he would get then. We have a proper union structure of branch and then national committee for the company. Of course the lay representatives are important: after all, I'm one of them and I would say that, wouldn't I?" A number round the table laughed. "I wish Mr Hammond and his followers would try and put forward practical suggestions and support the union and their colleagues and not continually push their own separate agenda. The union belongs to all of us—not, thank God, Mr Hammond and his cronies."

Most of those present were taken aback at what was said and some clapped. It was strong stuff thought Leila. Hammond jumped to

his feet and started shouting 'point of order' and then demanded that
Bristow apologise for his remarks. Bristow laughed at him. A number
round the table looked askance; others looked pleased that Bristow
had actually taken Hammond on, and—it seemed—won. Two other
delegates started to rise to their feet to speak.

Macallister banged the table and the two delegates sat down.
Gradually the noise stopped. He reiterated that he was going to
ask each delegate for suggestions for future action and any form
of possible action. He reminded them that there was a provisional
Thursday date for an ACAS meeting but what he wanted to know was
the strength of feeling in the branches and what sort of action, if any,
would have support.

<hr />

The TUC's General Council 'away day' wasn't going too badly.
It was being held at the St Ermine's hotel close to Victoria Street.
Previously similar meetings had been held n the TUC's education
centre in north London but that was closed at the moment for repair
and redecoration and—if some of us had our way—for putting up
for sale. It was too far from the centre of London and the take up
by unions for education courses had been declining. It was difficult
to let out the space to outside organisations because of its awkward
location. Anyway, I thought, the St Ermine's was fine and there were
some good pubs in the locality.

The day had been organised by Len Arkwright the Deputy
General Secretary and, to be fair to him, was well structured. We
had an academic from Warwick University first talking about the
shifts in employment patterns, the growth of part time employment,
the continuing drop in manufacturing and the big move towards
outsourcing jobs, particularly to Asia. It didn't make for complacency
and in fact would cause considerable alarm if the trends continued.
Then we had two case studies of union recruitment, one in the public
sector and one in the private sector.

The public sector unions seemed to be doing reasonably well. There wasn't much outsourcing there yet and the growth in new employment in the last few years had been mainly in the public sector. I had often thought that recruitment was much easier there, particularly before Government had started hiving off a number of public bodies to be executive agencies determining their own pay and conditions. In the old days with a common pay and grading system for most of the civil service for example, recruitment to the union had been almost automatic, though some of my colleagues would have denied this. Now it was different, not only with the creation of the agencies but also the move towards each Government department being able to set its own pay and conditions and a uniform system for the whole of Government departments being dismantled. Still it was far easier than in the private sector.

My colleagues often accused me of being biased but I knew well that recruitment in the white collar private sector had always been difficult. There the tradition of unionism was not pervasive and, in some cases, was non existent. There weren't many—if any—large employment sites as there used to be with car manufacture or steel production where the traditional manual unions used to organise. There were far more different types of employers too than in the public sector and increasingly now we had to deal with foreign owned companies. I realised that this was becoming similar to unions in the manufacturing sector who now had to deal with American or Japanese owned companies but even there the tradition of belonging to a union was still about.

I realised I was almost becoming a bit self pitying but I also realised that the new picture of employment and unionisation that was spreading across the whole UK economy made companies such as Industry3M so important to us.

During the discussion that followed the academic, John Miller the General Secretary, who was acting as the chair of the session, asked me if I would like to say a few words and I leapt at the chance.

I told the rest of my colleagues on the General Council—about thirty five of the forty one members were present—how some twenty of the eighty odd procedural agreements we had with different employers were now with companies that were either partly or fully owned by foreign based companies. I then moved on to Industry3M as a prime example and how it seemed that changes in management at their Atlanta head office could have direct effects on the staff over here. And the American white collar unions had made no impact on trying to organise the staff in the USA so we could not call on them to assist.

Miller then referred to the Government's attitude to foreign investment, while careful not to mention Bob Wilson, the DTI minister, by name. A number who spoke referred, quite rightly, to the important role the international trade secretariats could play not just with the European affiliated unions but now with the Indian, Japanese and south east Asian affiliates. In spite of the indifference—and sometimes direct hostility—in my union over our ITS, Staff International, I was more than ever sure our affiliation to it was vital.

The private sector union case study by the Commercial and Technology Union had mirrored much of what my own union was dealing with and I resolved to have a word with the General Secretary, Peter Moorhouse, in the pub when the day was finished.

Before we broke for lunch we had a presentation from John Miller on the changes in General Council composition in the last ten years and some suggestions on further changes that should be made to take account of the new economic and employment scene. In the afternoon we would see if we could get agreement on amendments to the TUC's rules to put to Congress in September which would allow for changes in General Council composition to be introduced in the following year. Some of the media who reported on TUC's activities found such matters as profoundly boring but they had to be considered. There were too many people complaining (as had always been the case) that the TUC was out of date: and we had to try and reflect the developing nature of unionism, the changes in employment and recruitment and unions' own internal structures.

Several times during the talk and the subsequent discussion I wondered how Leila was getting on at the Industry3M national committee. The dispute with that company could well be a catalyst in whether a union could deal successfully with modern management in the twenty first century—even though that management might revert to almost nineteenth century practices.

The national committee reassembled after lunch at just gone two o'clock and the remaining branch delegates who hadn't yet spoken gave their opinions on their branch members' feelings.

From all the responses to Macallister's questioning of the delegates on the committee it seemed that most of the eight branches—and the members in the Liverpool UK head office—were considering that some form of industrial action might have to be taken and would be supported. Leila would speak to the three branches which had not yet had a meeting.

Although in the previous ten years the procedural agreement with the had worked reasonably well, and agreements on pay and conditions had been successfully negotiated, there was a feeling now that things would get harder. There had been a few straws in the wind over the last six months: time off for union activity had been curtailed; merit increments on the anniversary of appointment to a particular grade had been reduced; promotion opportunities had been limited and there had also been an increase in the number of middle to senior positions filled by people coming in from outside the company. Now the company circular and the fax letter that the General Secretary had received from Norman Jones, the chief executive, had crystallised concern. Things had been getting a bit more difficult since Jones took over two years previously and Stannard's dismissal had been greeted with alarm among many of the staff.

Although Tony Hammond had tried several times to seek support for various immediate forms of action—which Leila reminded the committee would mean the union breaking the terms of the procedural agreement if 'immediate' meant not observing the time limits set out in the agreement and if anyone intended to break the procedural agreement it should not be the union—he had little support. There were only two others on the committee who had any sympathy for any of his points. It would be different, Leila thought, on the national executive of the union. Hammond was a member of that as well, and at least two of the other fifteen national executive members were more or less open supporters of the Socialist Workers Party or Militant whom she designated as 'trots'.

Macallister then read out the terms of the resolution that Leila had handed to him. It urged support for effective and immediate negotiations with the company, called on ACAS to assist if those negotiations did not take place and asked the national executive to consider authorising a ballot of members on industrial action if all else failed.

There had been some debate on what form of industrial action should take place. It was a classic problem. If the action was limited to a ban on overtime working or even a one day stoppage, then it could be that it would have little effect on the company though it might be well supported by the members. After all, Leila reasoned, if work stopped for a day, then the next day and all the following days it would continue as before: though, it could be different if new supply contracts that Industry3M was hoping to sign with some UK companies were seen to be jeopardised. On the other hand, if the action envisaged was to be an indefinite strike it was highly likely that, even if a majority vote for such action was achieved in the secret ballot that would have to take place, it would not be supported by all the members. In that case, the union's ultimate weapon would have been used and if it failed, the position of the union in the future would have been irreparably weakened—and not only in Industry3M. Other employers would quickly have surmised that perhaps the union was a toothless tiger after all. A far cry from when the union had called a strike in a small insurance company some years previously and within days—largely because of the company's need to avoid any hint of staff problems when it was engaged in a fairly big and expensive advertising campaign—agreement had been reached between the union and company. Later the company had realised they had been foolhardy to agree to what they deemed a large pay settlement but it was then too late. The union had made a big impact through what was seen as an effective and well run industrial dispute, and a number of other companies had signed agreements with the union as a result. But it would be very difficult for the union to repeat that success. Now it was always better to give the impression that the union could take indefinite and damaging action rather than put it to the test.

In the end Leila had suggested a form of words that would allow the national executive to determine the type of industrial action that would be balloted upon.

When Macallister put the resolution to the vote two of the delegates abstained (how could they do that? Leila asked herself) and only Lilian Fairweather voted against. Tony Hammond voted for; but then he would have to as otherwise he knew some of his enemies would quickly spread the word that he had voted against industrial action and that would never do. He thought though that the resolution had been too weak and indecisive about action. Still, it was a step and his supporters would try and build on it at the national executive meeting.

As the delegate members of the national committee left the room Leila phoned Julia Cardon on her mobile. She knew it was Saturday afternoon and she knew that Julia had a small child and that she valued her weekends when she could be at home, but she also knew Julia would be getting calls from various of the media about the national committee meeting and anyway she would want to know what had happened. She gave her a brief rundown on the meeting and quoted the resolution. Julia told her she had had some press calls already. She would get back to them and Leo Patullo of the Press Association in particular; she would also give John Carmichael a ring later in the early evening while Leila was on the train to Nottingham.

On the Sunday morning I saw a piece about the national committee meeting in *The Observer* while I was eating my breakfast. It wasn't bad and contained the essence of the resolution that Julia had told me about the previous evening. I assumed that the other Sunday 'heavies' would also carry a report. I decided to wait for them until I got to the office on Monday. Julia would have a press digest ready for me.

My wife Claire said she was going shopping after breakfast. The new shopping centre near Croydon was now open on Sundays. Claire had made it clear to me, in her gentle but firm way, that she would prefer to go by herself as she was intending to purchase a new outfit for our daughter's wedding which was coming up in the middle of next month. She also said she would be meeting two of the wives of our friends who were coming to the wedding and they would all have lunch together.

Our daughter was already living with her fiancee in a flat near Dorking; our son had his own flat near Manchester and so I was going to be alone most of the day. That suited me fine and I told Claire I would probably go down to the pub for lunch. There were lots of things to do at home but I decided I would read the newspaper and then possibly some of the union papers I had stuffed in my briefcase when I left the office on Friday. The garden would have to wait.

I had once again almost—but not quite—finished *The Observer* crossword and was starting on the news pages when the phone rang. To my surprise it was David Stannard: then I remembered that I had given him my home number some time ago. After we had exchanged the usual pleasantries he mentioned our brief chat earlier in the week. Would I be available later this day for another chat?

I jumped at the offer and suggested that, if he could, he should come round to our house and we could then go down to my local pub, The Crown, for a drink. I knew of course that Stannard lived in Liverpool but when he came down to London he stayed at his son's house in Ewell and that was only a bus ride away from our house in Epsom. He asked for directions and then said he would be around my house about half past eleven.

I thought I had better get my union papers out and see if there was anything I should note before Stannard came. They were mostly reports from the various officials on their negotiating meetings, minutes of the various union committees—why did there have to be so many committees?—and some correspondence which I had not had an opportunity to read before.

I noticed a letter from the Industrial Foundation. This was an independent body set up by a number of employers and unions many years ago. It organised lectures and, more recently, employed people to advise companies, and unions, on implementation of the various pieces of employment legislation, the latest interpretations of that legislation and the impact of employment tribunal judgements. I had spoken at some of their meetings in recent years and I knew that Leila had as well.

The letter was from the Foundation's director. He referred to the work they had done on job evaluation and how they had seconded some of their staff to companies in the past to introduce different job evaluation schemes. Particularly he mentioned the press reports in the last few days about our troubles with Industry3M and asked whether I could arrange for Leila to talk about the JE scheme we had presented to the company.

I would mention this to Leila in the morning. Monday morning she would be in the office and there were a number of things we needed to talk about first thing. I thought she had a meeting with the negotiating officials later in the week and I presumed she would be raising the JE matter with them. Also, I wondered, were there any other companies with whom we dealt in which we could claim the introduction of the scheme? And, had she fixed a date with the local government union? I almost thought of phoning her at the Nottingham hotel where her talk to the lay reps was taking place but decided to leave it until tomorrow.

I was halfway through the pile of papers when the doorbell rang. It was Stannard. I thought he looked a bit worn out when he came in. He was a tall man, usually smartly dressed and looking relaxed. At the meeting with the company on last Tuesday morning he had been distinctly gloomy. Now he was rather scruffy: baggy grey trousers, a crumpled shirt and a tie that was askew, even his jacket looked as if it had seen better days. I made some coffee and we sat in the lounge to drink it.

I jokingly said to him that he looked as if he had been on the booze the night before.

"I almost wish I had," he said. "It's been a rough week."

He seemed reluctant to speak at first but after several promptings from me he poured it all out.

For some months apparently the company had been toughening its attitude to the union as a deliberate policy. I said it had been reported to me that things had been tightened up; leave for some of our members had been curtailed, some of the recruitment visits by our organisers had been delayed, a meeting to discuss a possible type of European works council for the company had been postponed indefinitely, there had been problems over merit payments and a lot of promotions had been going to outsiders. Stannard put it down to the arrival of Norman Jones as the chief executive and the instructions that must have been given to him by the new management in Atlanta. He had raised concerns about the way things were going with Tom Chance, the deputy chief, and once with Norman Jones, but had been fobbed off. The arrival of John Carr from European group head office had hastened the process along and the meeting I had had with them on Tuesday was the culmination.

Stannard said he had been told just before that meeting had started that his services were no longer needed by the company and—as he had told me on the phone on the Tuesday evening when I was in the hotel with Leila—he had no realistic choice other than to go.

I commiserated with him and we then talked about some of the events in the earlier days of the union's relationship with the company. He seemed to relax a bit as we talked but stopped every now and then. There was clearly something else he wanted to say. He had always been a good man to deal with and, though we had never been friends, I thought he respected me as I respected him.

"And, John," he continued, "that's not all. I don't think you've ever met my wife Jane." I shook my head. "Well things have never been plain sailing between us; in a way she's always been more ambitious than me and she took my dismissal—for that's what it was—very badly. In fact we had a blazing row about it. I told her there was nothing I could do about it and she accused me of being weak and a wimp and—". He paused.

There wasn't much I could say. I was always a bit uncomfortable listening to any of my colleagues talking about problems with their wives or children. In a way I was very lucky. Claire and I had been married for thirty five years and, in spite of inevitable ups and downs, we had what would be described as a successful marriage. Our two children were also doing all right. I felt sorry for Stannard. As he said, I had never met his wife, but I could imagine the difficulties there would be with an ambitious wife and, I suddenly remembered, someone had once told me that they only had the one child, although they had been trying for another one for several years. Was that a contributory factor? Well, there was absolutely nothing I could do about it. Still, that didn't help Stannard as he then continued to tell me about his problems with his wife over several years.

On the Thursday morning his wife had said she was going to stay with her sister, had packed her bag and left. Apparently she had made a point of saying that she didn't know when she would be back. Stannard had been taken very much aback. They had often argued—and they had often gone several days with hardly speaking to each other at all—but never had she walked out on him. Yesterday he had come down from Liverpool to spend a few days with his son.

But it seemed that wasn't all he wanted to say. He looked embarrassed. I suddenly looked at my watch and asked if he had time for a drink at the pub. I had never known him to be a drinker but he accepted my offer with alacrity. I said we could carry on our chat there; there would be a quiet place in the pub where we could talk.

Stannard explained to me as we walked down the road to The Crown, my favourite pub, that his son would pick him up so he would give him a ring on his mobile to say when. The Crown was a fairly tatty looking place and in all honesty you couldn't say it had much charm. It was a far cry from some of the trendy and upmarket pubs and wine bars that seemed to be mushrooming all over the place but it had three distinctive advantages as far as I was concerned: there was no music played inside, the furniture was old fashioned but comfortable and, above all, the beer was usually excellent—a fine selection of real ales.

While I was getting the beer Stannard phoned his son. He looked at me. "One thirty be about right?"

I nodded. That would be good as I could afterwards then have something to eat. I brought the pints of beer over to the small table at which we sat.

"Cheers."

Stannard swallowed some of his beer, took a deep breath and then said: "look, John, I didn't really want to unload my domestic problems on to you. But there's something you ought to know about the company and what they might do."

"Derecognition?" I queried.

"It's not just that, though undoubtedly that's what the company want. They are going hell for leather in outsourcing a lot of their basic admin work and, as far as possible, outsourcing it offshore. But there's more."

Stannard swallowed another mouthful of beer. I felt sympathy for him. He looked rough and was clearly unhappy. In all the meetings I had held with him he had always played the game. He also had never criticised the company in any of our private conversations. It must be difficult for him.

"David," I said. "I'm sorry you got the chop from the company. They've treated you appallingly. I'm sorry too about your wife. But there's more isn't there—though I don't know what could be more than derecognition."

Stannard gave a wry smile.

"I assume," he said, "you will be having some sort of industrial action ballot. I assume also that any meeting with ACAS won't be productive—the company will see to that. And, yes, I reckon the company will give you notice about terminating the procedural agreement, but there's a particular point you ought to be aware of."

He then told me what he had really come to see me about. It was what the company had done in order to prepare for a confrontation with us and their desire to ensure they would win. He talked about the procedural agreement; he accepted that the agreement allowed for the union to take industrial action if all the procedural steps had been taken and no agreement in negotiations achieved. The key was the union membership in the company. I interrupted him to say that our latest check showed we had 2,600 members and that was a majority of the staff. If we had to, then we would ask ACAS or the Central Arbitration Committee to hold a ballot of the staff and, if the result was a majority in favour of the union, then under the law the company had to recognise us.

Stannard shook his head.

"I know the law, John," he said. "But the problem could be the cash payers in the union."

I explained that there were cash payers in almost all the companies with whom we negotiated, although the number was disproportionately higher in Industry3M.

"That's the point" said Stannard.

I looked at him.

"What's the point then?"

Stannard then told me that he knew there were a large number of union cash payers in the secretary's department and in the payroll administration of the company, both in the Liverpool head office of Industry3M in Britain. I said I knew that but didn't ask him how he knew. But he then told me.

The union member who collected the cash for subscriptions in payroll administration had left the company last year. His replacement as the union collector, a woman called Sophie Elwin, had told Stannard about the numbers of cash payers and—much worse—had given him a copy of their names. He had done nothing about it but she had also told Collins, his number two in the personnel department. Stannard reckoned that Collins had told Tom Chance, the deputy chief executive and presumed he had also told John Carr.

The implication was clear to me. If the company had a list of names of those who paid their union subscription by cash then they could start to put a lot of pressure on them. They only paid by cash so their union membership would not be revealed to the company unless they were going out on strike and, if the company did know, some of them—perhaps many of them—might well think twice about continuing their membership. If enough of them were to buckle under company pressure, something we would have great difficulty in proving, and resign their membership then our membership could well fall below the magic fifty per cent plus one that legislation demanded in the event of compulsory recognition.

Stannard looked distinctly unhappy as he told me this. I was appalled but appreciated how it must have been very difficult for him to tell me. He went to the bar and got two more pints of bitter.

"I have thought long and hard about this, John," he said as he sat down again, "but in the end I thought I ought to let you know. Collins is a creep and has seen his opportunity to ingratiate himself with the company and as for Sophie Elwin—well, she is one of yours."

I didn't know her and would speak to Leila in the morning about her. But if she had given a list of the cash payers to the company then there was not much we could do about it. Theoretically we could bring a charge against her for bringing the union into disrepute and eventually expel her from the union. The prospect of doing that now was not appealing. It would take time, probably receive a lot of bad publicity—the company would see to that—and could well frighten off many members from supporting the union. I didn't know why she had chosen to give Stannard a list or Collins, come to that. Perhaps she was trying to get in the company's good books: or, perish the thought, the company had persuaded her to join the union in the first place so she could be the collector for the cash payers.

I thanked Stannard for his information and for coming to share it with me. Of course I promised him I would not reveal anything he said, except in confidence to Leila and I knew she would respect that confidence. We had one more pint each and then Stannard's son came and they both left. I thought he looked a bit unsteady as he went through the door. He had only had three pints but, then, he was not a drinker. It made me realise that perhaps I should not drink as much as I did, but Claire had often said that to me and I had not taken much notice. I kidded myself that life was too short to worry about things like that.

On Monday morning Leila and Carmichael had a long talk. Carmichael told her about the Industrial Foundation letter asking her to speak on job evaluation and Leila said she would contact the director about it. She then said she would have a talk with Dan Michael about the membership figures in Industry3M. She was appalled to learn what Stannard had said on the list of cash paying members in the company. She didn't know Sophie Elwin but would speak to Clive Bristow about her, She agreed that there was not much they could do about the membership lists.

Then Julia Cardon joined them and they went over the weekend press reports. They agreed to hold a press conference after the

ACAS meeting which Leila said she would now fix definitely for the Thursday afternoon, assuming the ACAS officials could manage that. Her regular meeting with the union's negotiating officials was being held on Wednesday morning and she would both raise the job evaluation proposal with them and also stress to Alan Whitchurch, the national officer responsible for union organisation, that the union's organisers should make every effort to recruit members in the company's branches and do that even at the expense of any other recruitment campaign in other companies that he had going at the moment. It wouldn't be easy if the company proved obstructive about access to the branches but it had to be tried. Leila understood the importance, especially in the light of what Carmichael had told her about Stannard's information. If the union could go to ACAS and the CAC and win a ballot on recognition then that would be fine and perhaps industrial action would not be necessary.

As soon as they finished Leila went back to her office. She called in her secretary and again went over her diary for the next two weeks. Muriel told her that Sam Askari had been on the internal phone twice that morning to see if a date had been fixed to process the sexual harassment case. Leila almost groaned but didn't. The case had to be dealt with in spite of all the other pressures on her time; and she wanted to deal with it fairly.

She asked Muriel to arrange with the branch secretaries at Industry3M's offices in Brighton, Norwich and Newcastle, that special branch meetings should be held in the next two weeks and that she would be pleased to speak to them. She emphasised to Muriel that the three meetings had to be held before the national executive meeting on the Saturday week.

Usually the national executive committee of the union met on a weekday but she and Carmichael had decided that as the attendance of the Industry3M members was so important—even though, thought Leila, one of them was Tony Hammond—that they couldn't afford to go ahead without them; and the company could well refuse leave of absence for them by referring to the clause in the procedural agreement that leave could be withheld due to special company pressures of work. So it had to be held on a Saturday.

Leila looked at Muriel.

"I've got the negotiators meeting on Wednesday morning, the ACAS meeting on Thursday and—hopefully we could fix one of the branch meetings for Friday evening, either Norwich or Newcastle, and then the other the following week. What about having the sexual harassment hearing tomorrow, Tuesday? And see if the Brighton meeting could be held on the Wednesday evening."

Muriel said she would contact Askari and Michael and also make sure that Eliza Abbotke was there together with Sarah Mackenzie. She knew that Leila wanted to deal the issue as soon as possible.

At ten o'clock on the Tuesday morning there was a knock on the door of Leila's office. It was Sam Askari. Leila asked him to come in together with Mackenzie and Abbotke. Leila didn't really know Abbotke; she had seen her around the office and remembered talking to her at the staff Christmas party ; she had heard she was very bright and a graduate but that was about all. She looked at Askari and Mackenzie. Askari looked quiet and a little nervous. Mackenzie looked aggressive. Then Dan Michael knocked on her door and joined them.

They all sat round the table in Leila's office. Leila rehearsed what she had been told about the incident and said Michael had told her it was all a misunderstanding and he had certainly not made any improper advances towards Mackenzie.

Mackenzie interrupted, "well he would say that, wouldn't he? But I know what happened."

"Please, Sarah," said Leila. "You'll get your chance in a minute. I'm just relating what I have been told. Now I am going to ask Sam to speak first, then you Sarah, and then Eliza as the witness and finally Dan. You'll each have an opportunity to question each other. If you each have no objection I shall ask my secretary Muriel to come in and take notes during this hearing. Any objections?"

No one objected and Leila called in Muriel. She sat at one end of the table with Leila at the other. Askari, Mackenzie and Abbotke sat on one side and faced Michael on the other. He had told Muriel that he did not want anyone with him. Leila thought that could be harmful to him but he was adamant.

The meeting went on for over an hour. Askari gave a brief summary of what he had been told and then stressed again how important the matter was and how there should not be any incidents of sexual harassment, particularly in a trade union. Mackenzie embellished the account she had given to Leila the previous week and said she had been most upset and hadn't been able to sleep properly since then. Leila then asked Abbotke to speak.

"I was going out of the door with Sarah," she said, "when Mr Michael came rushing down. He was in a hurry and pushed past us." She paused and looked at Mackenzie. "I moved back to let him through but I saw him push against Sarah."

"You mean that you got out of the way?" asked Leila. Abbotke nodded. "Did Sarah get out of the way?"

Mackenzie broke in. "No, why should I? He just tried to barge through and made a point of squeezing against my breasts. He did it deliberately—and then he said he would like to fuck me."

Leila asked Abbotke whether she had heard Michael say that. She paused against and looked uncomfortable. Leila asked her again. She then said she had heard Michael say something but wasn't quite sure what. Mackenzie got annoyed at this and turned to Abbotke and said she had clearly heard, why had she changed her story? Abbotke looked more uncomfortable and claimed she hadn't changed her story at all.

The argument went on. Dan Michael then said he had been rushing through the door. He should not have barged through but he was in a hurry and Mckenzie had made no attempt to move out of the way.

"Why should I?" demanded Mackenzie.

Michael ignored her. Yes, he had pushed against Mackenzie but that was only because he could not get through the door without touching her. He hadn't meant to; he should have waited and there was certainly no attempt at any sexual harassment.

Leila asked him what he had said. Michael looked embarrassed but admitted that because Mackenzie had not got out of the way he had said something—he thought it was under his breath—and it was something like 'sod you' or even 'fuck you'. It was an instinctive reaction and was all due to him being in a hurry. He repeated that he should not have said that and was sorry if he gave any offence, but it was clearly not sexual harassment.

The argument continued. Michael was clearly upset, Mackenzie insistent and Askari looked worried. Finally Abbotke spoke again.

"I didn't hear what Mr Michael said. I could see he was in a rush and not thinking." She looked straight at Mackenzie. "I don't think there was any sexual harassment. It was a spur of the moment thing and—" she looked then straight at Leila—"I was certainly not a witness to any sexual harassment."

Askari and Mackenzie looked shocked. Mackenzie tried to speak but Leila asked her to be quiet. She turned to Askari.

"Sam, sexual harassment is a very serious charge. If it is proved it could mean that Mr Michael here would be disciplined, and that would be quite right if the charge is proved. But we've just heard what Eliza said—what do you say?"

Askari was even more worried. He had not really asked Abbotke what she had seen but relied on Mackenzie telling him that she had witnessed the harassment. He said that any accusation of sexual harassment was extremely serious.

Leila said she was well aware of that. It was serious both for the alleged victim and the alleged perpetrator, but what were the facts? She asked each of them if they had any more to say. Mackenzie repeated her story and was clearly getting excited. Michael repeated that he had been in a hurry and again he was sorry if any offence had been taken but certainly none had been intended. Askari repeated for the umpteenth time that it was a serious matter. Leila looked at Abbotke.

"I am sorry about this," she said. "Sarah asked me to be a witness here and I agreed. I have been thinking about this and gone over the incident in my mind. But I did not see any sexual harassment."

Mackenzie started to interrupt and shouted "but he said he wanted to fuck me."

"No, Sarah," replied Abbotke, "that's not how it happened at all. I'm sorry to go against you but I must tell exactly what I witnessed. There was no sexual harassment."

Mackenzie looked savagely at her and muttered under her breath. Leila said she would now consider the matter, look at the notes that her secretary had taken, and let them have her judgement later. She would do a report to the General Secretary and let each of them have a copy. She asked again if anyone wanted to say anything more but no one did. She stressed that they were not to give a copy of her report to anyone else and that there should be no outside publicity about the matter. She knew that what she said there could almost be inviting Mackenzie to create some publicity, but she reckoned she had to say it and take the risk.

The meeting then finished and the four of them left her room.

As Michael was leaving Leila called out to him that she wanted to discuss the membership figures in Industry3M and would he do a complete printout for her.

❦

Thursday afternoon was a bright day and I had managed to get rid of a lot of the paper work that had been building up. I had also spoken to our solicitors about the procedural agreement with Industry3M. The agreement was specifically not legally binding and there didn't seem much we could do if the company decided to break it and refuse negotiations. I had also decided that I would go with Leila to the ACAS meeting. She could do most of the talking but I wanted to be present. Julia would be with us and we would hold the press conference afterwards. ACAS would let us use one of their rooms for this purpose.

I had had several chats with Leila over the previous two days. She had told me about the sexual harassment case with Dan Michael and how she would be doing me a formal report. She had decided there was no case to answer; she thought Sarah Mackenzie had tried it on and how Eliza Abbotke had been impressive. She hoped that would be the end of the matter and I told her I hoped she would make it clear to all of them that the matter was now resolved. Rumours of any sexual harassment could be unsettling, and even damaging, in the union.

She also had told me about her meeting with the negotiators yesterday. There were several companies where they thought we could pursue the job evaluation scheme: the white collar staff of one of Britain's largest chemical companies, several computer companies, administrative staff in some of the new leisure companies that were combining video and digital manufacturing as well as sports complexes, the staff of a major hotel complex and the payroll and clerical staff of one of Britain's biggest road transport firms. Leila had arranged another meeting with them all the following week.

The previous evening Leila had spoken at the union's Brighton branch of Industry3M and had had about thirty members there. Apparently, she told me, there had been considerable anxiety about doing anything at this stage. She mentioned that several of the members had been advising others that they should wait for the ACAS meeting and not rush into anything. She reminded me of what Lilian Fairweather from Bristol had said at the national committee meeting. I remembered Lilian, she had been a union member for many years and had joined Industry3M from another company at the time we had first signed the procedural agreement with them. I was not surprised to hear Leila tell me; there were probably quite few like her but they didn't concern me as much as the cash payers on the list that Stannard had mentioned. In the end, Leila said, the Brighton branch had passed a resolution calling for negotiations to take place but then asking the national executive to consider forms of action if negotiations did not take place.

Leila and I had discussed what to say to the people on the cash payers list in Liverpool She had telephoned Clive Bristow and Ted Davis on Monday evening at their homes. They thought it best to have a quiet word with some of them, not spread any alarm amongst them but to leave dealing with Sophie Elwin at the moment. I agreed with their idea. It wouldn't do us any good if we made a big fuss about Sophie Elwin, and I wouldn't put it past the company to try and portray her as some kind of union martyr. Leila had also gone over the list of cash payers with Dan Michael. There were about three hundred and twenty and as Stannard had told me were mainly in secretary's department and payroll.

I had also mentioned to Leila that I had had a chat with Peter Moorhouse of the Commercial and Technology Union and he had asked if Leila could have a word with his officials about our proposed new job evaluation scheme.

The three of us entered the London regional office of ACAS at three o'clock on the Thursday afternoon. I had been there—and to ACAS headquarters in south London—many times. This time we were seeing Tino Malik, the regional conciliation officer who would probably have a couple of colleagues with him. Malik had told Leila on the telephone that he had contacted John Carr about the meeting and, after a lot of dithering, Carr had said the company would attend; but he had insisted they meet in the London office and not in Liverpool. I wasn't sure why but it would suit us. If there were further meetings possibly involving the European group head office of Industry3M it would also be easier for us to meet them. Leila had tried to get our national committee chairman, Ian Macallister to attend as well. He had been willing but yesterday evening he had telephoned Leila to say his leave had suddenly been stopped and it was now too late to get anyone else from the company. I knew Leila would tell the ACAS officials that but there was nothing else we could do about it now.

Malik was tall, quite good looking and certainly looked younger than his forty eight years. His father was an Indian immigrant and mother was Scottish. He had been to Cambridge University and, if he had one fault, it was that while he was clever, he knew he was clever and couldn't help wanting other people to know. He had previously been a civil servant in the Department of Trade & Industry but had sought—and been successful in getting—a position within ACAS. He had two officials with him.

Malik explained it was a bit unusual to meet in the London regional office. Normally the meeting would have been held in Liverpool as that was the head office of the UK part of the company but John Carr had insisted. Leila had already told me that he had said all that but Malik was a bit pedantic and wanted everything down on the record. I asked him who would be representing the company. He said it would be John Carr and an assistant called Collins.

"That's ridiculous" I exclaimed when Malik told us this. "Carr's from Group and not the UK company and Collins is only the number two in personnel. Either the chief or his deputy should be here and preferably both."

Malik shrugged his shoulders and said that they had no power to enforce any particular representation from the company. Did we want to continue? I said we did of course, wanted my point noted and also that Ian Macallister was unable to be present. I told Malik that Leila would be leading for the union and she then explained the events of the previous eleven days.

"Isn't this meeting and talk of industrial action
 a bit premature?" asked Malik.

"Not really," replied Leila. "The procedural agreement allows for either side to request a negotiating meeting and it also says that after such a request, then arrangements for such a meeting should be notified to the other side within seven working days. The reality is that the company have so far refused to meet us or talk about a date."

Having got that out of the way Malik then asked a number of questions about the company. What was all this about querying our membership, what had happened to the UK personnel director and why were we concerned about outsourcing, given the nature of the jobs that the company provided for a whole range of firms?

Leila dealt with it all well and Malik seemed satisfied he understood the position. He and his two colleagues left us while they went to talk to the two company men who were sitting in another room.

Half an hour later they came back and again Malik shrugged his shoulders. He didn't look too concerned and, if anything, looked a bit bored by the whole thing. He explained that Carr had read out a company statement that the job evaluation scheme was confusing and could not be taken seriously; the pay claim was far too high and, as they had already mentioned to us, they were querying our membership figures.

For the next hour we spoke to Mailk and answered his questions which he had put on behalf of the company and he then went back to the other room to ask the company the questions we had posed. Although we asked him several times to get Carr to agree to a face to face meeting he was unsuccessful.

Mailk then summarised the position as he saw it. He could not force the company to agree to a joint meeting or even, whatever the procedural agreement said, fix a date for a negotiating meeting with us. He explained—rather pompously I thought—to us that conciliation could only work if both sides were clearly ready to compromise and wanted a resolution of a dispute. He didn't say that he thought the company's position was justifiable; indeed that was not his function. But he made it clear that there was nothing more he could do. He would write up a brief summary of what had happened and send us and the company a copy.

Malik then smiled and concluded our meeting by what he obviously thought was a clever remark: "In many ways this is a case of *de minimis*".

Leila smiled: "you could say rather *de maximis*."

Malik went a little red. He had presumed his remark had gone over our heads. One up to Leila, I thought; though I must confess I didn't really understand either remark.

We thanked him for his efforts and he mentioned the room he had set aside for our press conference. He would leave it to us.

As Leila, Julia and I entered the room allocated for the press conference I was surprised to see twelve people present. I had thought there would only be a handful. It must be either what the press called a slow news day or there was a genuine interest in what could be a battle between a trade union and an expanding American owned new type of company.

, We sat down at a table facing the correspondents. I noticed one from BBC radio with his tape recorder and looked at the others. I think I recognised them all except one—a large red faced man wearing a loud check suit.

Julia opened up by thanking them all for being present and introducing me and Leila. We had decided amongst us that I would make a brief introduction and then had over to Leila. And we had agreed that we might as well tell them of our concerns at possible derecognition and how we would stop that. Or, I thought to myself, how we hoped to stop it. But there was no point in beating about the bush and we were going to be as open as we could be. Ideally such publicity would cause the company to back down a bit but, having met Carr, I doubted that.

I thanked them for coming and explained how important the position was with Industry3M, how we had secured recognition in the first place and the many agreements we hade with them in the ten years since the procedural agreement was first signed. I then handed over to Leila.

Leila explained the number of procedural agreements we had altogether and how many of those were with foreign owned, or partly owned, companies here in the UK. She stressed our majority membership in Industry3M and, as I had done, the ten year old procedural agreement. She said a bit about the proposed job evaluation scheme and its importance, then mentioned the resolution passed by the national committee the previous Saturday and how the meeting they had just held with ACAS had not resolved anything, the company had refused to meet us face-to-face and then asked for questions.

The man in the check suit spoke first.

"*Wall Street Journal*" he said by way of introduction and that explained his presence to me. "Bearing in mind the nature of Industry3M and the number of people it employs, what's your concern about outsourcing?"

It was a fair question.

"There are about five thousand staff employed here in the UK," said Leila, "and, of course many of their jobs can't be outsourced overseas because other companies use Industry3M for people to work on specific tasks and projects and that means their physical presence here. But there are also many employed on backroom work, processing, administration and the like which could be done overseas without jeopardising the company's main selling point to other companies."

"Well," said check suit, "how many jobs do you think could be outsourced to other countries?"

That was a slightly unfair question and Leila knew that if she were to give a fairly definite figure then that could be interpreted as the union accepting that these jobs could, and probably would, go overseas. She decided to play safe.

"It could be hundreds or even more."

I recognised Oliver Listle's number two from the *Financial Times.*

"What are the chances of Industry3M trying to derecognise you?"

Leila smiled: "I think the chances are high but the prospects of success are very low."

It was a good answer, I thought, and hoped it was right.

There were several questions on the form of industrial action that might be taken. Leila kept emphasising that we wanted a proper series of negotiating meetings to resolve the union's claim. It was inevitable, though, that the labour correspondents of the newspapers would concentrate on the likelihood of industrial trouble and the possibility of strikes. There hadn't been many days lost through industrial disputes in the whole economy in the last few years. The prospect of a dispute, and subsequently a strike, in a white collar area, particularly in a company that was American owned, made a heady mix that was bound to get publicity.

I admitted to myself that we had been a trifle disingenuous in calling a press conference now, realising that a lot of the publicity would be about industrial action. It could frighten off some of our members and potential members in the company, but it should bring us a lot of coverage and expose the company's tactics. It should also get us a lot of support from other unions and, hopefully, from members of Parliament and Government ministers. It was all a bit of a gamble but then, as some commentators persistently said, industrial relations was all a bit of a gamble.

The *Times* and the *Guardian* both asked questions about our number of procedural agreements and how many of those were with British companies as compared to those that were foreign owned or else had a substantial foreign shareholding.

Several more questions were asked on the likely effect of any action and the possible response of the company. Were we planning an overtime ban and, if so, what effect would that have? What would the company do? Who did we think was responsible for the dispute that the union seemed to be having with the company?

Leila was careful not to talk disparagingly about Norman Jones or John Carr. When asked by the *Daily Telegraph* about David Stannard she merely said she regretted his going but they would have to speak to him about any of the personal circumstances.

The *Wall Street Journal* had another go.

"Do you really think you can win against a major player in the US economy like Industry3M?" It was asked in a quizzical rather than hostile manner.

Leila replied that we wouldn't be going down the road of a ballot and possible industrial action if we thought we had no chance of winning—but she hoped that there could be sensible negotiations on our pay claim and the new job evaluation scheme. And, if derecognition was pursued by the company, then we could always ask the CAC for a vote of the entire staff under the recognition law.

The check suit grunted and mumbled what I thought I heard as 'good luck'.

After a few more questions Julia called the conference to a close. The BBC man asked if he could do an interview for the late night Radio Four comment programme. He asked me but I suggested Leila would be more appropriate. It would be daft, I knew, to try and steal unnecessary publicity for myself when Leila was effectively running the campaign.

The correspondents then left. The check suit man winked at me as he went out the door. I mentioned to Julia that she must get hold of a copy of the next edition of the *Wall Street Journal*. It could be a useful contact.

We waited while Leila recorded her interview with the BBC and then went over to the pub across the road from the ACAS building.

It was mid-morning on the following day that John Carmichael's secretary Sheila received a fax from Industry3M. It was signed by Norman Jones and contained two pages. She took it into Carmichael's office. He was on the telephone to Les Martin, the union's President. He glanced at the fax, said he would phone Martin back and put the phone down.

He looked at the two page fax and having quickly read it, asked Muriel to make some copies and to get Leila Smith and Julia Cardon into his office. The fax letter was not surprising but he always hoped that things might not be quite as bad as he expected. This time they were.

Muriel brought the original fax back to him. Jones' covering letter had been brief. In it he gave formal notice that the company was withdrawing from the procedural agreement they had with the union. The company no longer believed that negotiations with the union were in the interests of either the company or the staff and that furthermore the company thought the union was increasingly unrepresentative of the staff's views. Jones had attached a copy of a company circular that that being sent round to staff that afternoon.

The circular was a bit longer than the letter.

"Yesterday the company went to the offices of the Government's Advisory, Conciliation and Arbitration Service at the request of ACAS officials. Apparently the Clerical & General Union had asked ACAS to arrange the meeting—" that's rich, thought Carmichael—"but there was no agreement on any of the issues that the union raised. We reiterated that the pay claim was far too high and that the claim for a new job evaluation scheme was cumbersome and, in our view, entirely inappropriate for a company like Industry3M."

Carmichael was getting increasingly annoyed. They hadn't even met us face to face, he thought, and then they give this impression. And the job evaluation scheme was drawn up specifically with companies like Industry3M in mind. He hadn't lost all his youthful idealism; he could still get irritated by some employer arguments and stances and wasn't completely cynical, he thought ruefully.

He read on: "Furthermore the company has been increasingly concerned that the union does not seem to represent the views of all of our staff and that the procedural agreement seems bureaucratic and unwieldy. We have therefore informed the union that the company intends to withdraw from the procedural agreement."

Just as he finished reading both Leila Smith and Julia Cardon had come into his office. Sheila had given them both copies of the fax. Carmichael looked up as they entered.

Leila smiled: "It's a long time since I saw you genuinely angry John," she said. Carmichael smiled back and motioned to them both to sit down.

They discussed the implications of the company's letter. It was cleverly written. It didn't say that the company was derecognising the union or indeed withdrawing any union facilities but the implication was clear. They hadn't either given the requisite three months notice of withdrawal. But, as they all knew, the withdrawal from the procedural agreement meant that there were no ground rules by which the union could operate in the company nor could the union claim for matters such as time off for meetings, access to offices or, fundamentally, the right to negotiating meetings.

Leila knew that when they had originally signed the agreement ten years previously there had been some surprise that the company had not wanted to make it legally binding, particularly in view of the general American preference for recourse to law. Now, there was nothing legally they could do about it. Not, as Leila well knew, that many British unions favoured using the law for industrial relations issues in any event. And even not giving three months notice would be difficult to raise in a legal context. It would probably take well over three months to pursue the matter in any legal manner.

Carmichael asked Leila what she thought they ought to do.

"Well," said Leila, "this isn't really a surprise is it? I think we must get a circular out soonest, issue a press statement—I assume the company will have released this to the press—" she turned to Julia—"you better check that Julia—and obviously do a note to the national executive. I can take care of that if you like, John. But the real thing is what practically can we do about it before the executive meeting?"

Carmichael nodded. "My concern, exactly."

Julia then handed round copies of the press reports that had appeared after the press conference the previous afternoon. The heavy tabloids and the berliners (what Julia explained used to be known as the broadsheets) had covered it well but the reference in the 'ordinary' tabloids was sketchy. The *Wall Street Journal* had printed quite a large piece and included a lot of background material on the growth of Industry3M in the US and more recently in Europe.

Carmichael particularly noted that the paper had a quote from the managing director of the parent company in Atlanta. Harold Stuckman junior had told the *Wall Street Journal* "It's a competitive world and Industry3M must always be looking to be dynamic and modernise to face growing global competition. It's in that context that we look at how all our European companies are doing."

He read it out to Leila and Julia and asked "what the hell does that mean?"

Julia smiled, "perhaps we could try and contact Harold Stuckman senior to find out what junior means."

Leila said: "it's clear that the head office in Atlanta is aware of what's going on over here. I wonder how much John Carr is driving this or if he's just a front man."

Carmichael snorted derisively, "I wonder how long Carr will last if this dispute really gets off the ground. Now, more important in the immediate is what steps are we going to take?"

Leila said she had proposals in mind for the national executive but first wanted to clear her mind on what was happening in the following week. She started by listing what she was going to do: meetings of the Industry3M branches in Norwich and Newcastle; meeting the sub-committee of the local government union with Frank Hallard of research and attending a meeting of the union's finance and administration committee on the Thursday at which she would raise the issue of strike pay. This was a sub-committee of the union's national executive and was responsible for overseeing all the myriad of matters affecting both the day-to-day function of the union and making longer term recommendations on the financial state of the union and its headquarters and regional offices. It also dealt with items raised by the staff bargaining unit in dealing with a sub—committee of the main committee. Sam Askari as the chairman and principal spokesman for the bargaining unit normally led for the staff and Leila spoke for the finance and administrative committee.

Carmaichael interrupted her: "yes Leila, but what steps are we going to take in the current dispute?"

Leila swallowed. She had so many balls in the air that she wanted to get them in some sort of order but realised she had made a mistake. She had momentarily been thinking of the sexual harassment case and the report she still had to do on it.

"Sorry, John, I was just trying to clear my own mind on the next week."

Carmichael nodded and invited her to continue.

"OK," said Leila. "There's a meeting with the negotiators on Wednesday and this is to follow up the meeting this week on where we could submit claims on the job evaluation scheme in other companies. I'll be having another word with van Mergeren and the Swedish and German affiliates to see if anything is happening there. I suggest you have another word with Miller at the TUC. I'll be raising the issue of strike pay at the finance and admin committee on Thursday. As far as the national executive is concerned I suggest we go for an industrial action ballot for a ban on overtime and a one day strike. We could also include the option of a three day stoppage if the one day doesn't spark any movement by the company. I think we should leave open the question of an indefinite strike. I hope it doesn't come to that and I don't know if the membership would support it but we shall have to consider it if all else fails. Sorry John," she added, "to be a bit cautious but I think we have to be realistic."

Carmichael nodded again: "I agree and as well as informing John Miller at the TUC I shall ask him to have another word with Bob Wilson at DTI." He turned to Julia—"please don't mention that to anyone Julia."

Julia Cardon said she hadn't heard what he said. It was her way of saying she wouldn't tell anyone.

They discussed what to say to any press queries. Julia said she was sure the company would have released their statement but she would check first. Assuming they had sent out the statement then the union also ought to send out the company's fax and include a comment from Leila so they had the two pieces in one go.

Leila said her comment would be that the union was disturbed by the company's attitude, would be reporting the matter to ACAS and seeking their involvement, would be notifying the TUC and would be using the hard line taken by the company to intensify its recruitment campaign in the company.

Leila's latter point was, she knew, more in hope than expectation. True, she did hope for some non-members to realise that the company was not perhaps the benevolent employer that it pretended to be and that union membership was even more needed now, but also she thought that some existing members—and Lilian Fairweather's name sprang to her mind—would think twice about continued support for the union. It was a classic dilemma but she thought they had to go all out in their dispute and try and face down the company at every step.

Carmichael agreed with Leila's suggested comments and added that he would be writing to the company's head office in Atlanta about the position. He knew that John Carr would be most annoyed at the union communicating direct with Atlanta but, then again, it depended on whether the company's head office was totally supportive of what its European—and particularly its UK—head office was doing. If it was fully supportive then a letter to Atlanta would achieve nothing. But it was worth a shot.

Leila said she wondered whether the finance and admin committee would take a fresh look at the question of payment if there was a strike. It was the practice of the union not to pay strike pay as such. Although the union's annual turnover was nearly £30 million a year its financial position could not be considered too healthy. It was no different from most unions. The union had property assets and some investments but in recent years had only barely managed to cover its annual expenditure from its income. Payment of strike pay on a regular basis—especially if such pay was to be significant—could well mean utilising a fair bit of their investments. She knew that some would say that that was what the investments were for—and she could imagine Tony Hammond making this point strongly. Again, though, it was a question of balance. She knew of two unions that had almost become bankrupt in the past because of prolonged payment of a high level of strike pay.

Normally the Clerical & General Union agreed to pay what they called hardship money to members who lost pay through taking industrial action and this was when individual members spelt out their own particular circumstances that would justify such payment. The practice also meant that the majority of members who did not claim any hardship money had to face losing significant amounts of money as their employer deducted pay for strike days from them.

Carmichael made the obvious point to both Julia and Leila that if they had to contemplate an indefinite strike ballot and then action, they would have to rethink their policy on strike pay. They could hardly expect members to take indefinite action and lose all their pay by doing so. It was something that they all knew the company would be well aware of. The key was how effective would limited action be?

Carmichael then said that they should meet again on Friday morning in the following week, with Alan Whitchurch the national organiser and Dan Michael of membership department, to go over the options for the national executive meeting on the Saturday. In the meantime he said he would liaise with Leila and Julia should contact her for any further statements.

"What are you going to be doing John?" asked Julia.

Carmichael smiled: "There are other matters Julia. I have to meet the chaps at Hokkaido and the senior management over a possible European Works Council. There's the north-east regional council meeting I'm going to on Thursday. I've got two TUC committees and there's the General Council meeting on Wednesday. Oh, and I've got to speak at the pensions conference of the CBI Tuesday afternoon."

Julia blushed: "Sorry John."

Carmichael said "I know this is a trying time for all of us and there's a hell of a lot to do but we must make this a success. I know it's particularly difficult for you Leila as Tim Burke is off with his cancer and this is really his patch. But, needs must. And you can always get a message through to me at the TUC when I'm there."

Leila thought his remarks sounded as if he wasn't sure whether she could cope and wished he didn't have to say that, especially in front of Julia but she knew that Julia was sensible enough not to attach any particular significance to it.

As they left Carmichael's office Leila turned and told him that she would have her report on the sexual harassment case on his desk later that afternoon. She would show him she could cope with all that was happening but then she knew he would expect her to.

When she got back to her office she asked Muriel to chase up the branch secretaries of Norwich and Newcastle about meetings. Ideally she could do the Norwich one on Tuesday evening but would have to do the Newcastle one on Friday evening. It would mean coming back to London on the overnight sleeper train in time for the national executive committee on the Saturday morning but, as she again reminded herself, she could cope.

She took out the notes Muriel had done on the sexual harassment case hearing she had held earlier in the week and read them one more time. She then got Muriel in and started to dictate her report.

First Leila summarised the complaint by Sarah Mackenzie, the statement of Dan Michael and then the meeting she had held earlier in the week. She emphasised the seriousness of any complaint of sexual harassment and how any such harassment was not to be tolerated within the union. She referred to the union's internal disciplinary procedure for dealing with staff. She paused and for a moment wondered whether she should be quite as forthright as she intended to be. Well, why not, she asked herself.

She dictated: "I have thought long and hard about this case and want to stress that the matter has been dealt with properly and in strict accordance with the procedure. If any of those involved dispute my conclusions which I set out below, then they can appeal to the union's national executive." She almost added "but I hope they would not" but realised that would be almost an incentive for Sarah

Mackenzie to do exactly that. She had decided that the complaint was in fact spurious and that it was clear from what Eliza Astobe had said that there was really no case to answer. Dan Michael had been daft to rush through the doorway when he could have seen that Sarah deliberately did not move out of the way for him; and he should not have muttered what he did mutter. But that was all. She would speak to him about this.

She carried on: "However, after due consideration, I conclude that there was no sexual harassment in the circumstances described by those involved and therefore no disciplinary action is to be taken against anyone involved. The incident is to be regretted but that is all."

Leila wondered whether she should add anymore and decided that she might as well.

She went on: "Sexual harassment is a serious matter but it can be the case that actions can be misinterpreted by individuals. However, I do hope that all staff will think seriously before invoking the procedure unless they are clear in their own minds that there is a case to answer and that, if there is any doubt, shall try and discuss the matter with those involved first."

This would be taken by Sarah Mackenzie as a slap down, and by Sam Askari as being most unfair. But, Leila thought, so be it. Sexual harassment was indeed a serious matter and she was not going to see it trivialised as there was no doubt in mind Sarah Mackenzie had done. She hoped the point would not be lost on all the staff.

She asked Muriel to give a copy of the report to John Carmichael, Sarah Mackenzie, Eliza Astobe, Sam Askari and Dan Michael. For good measure she also told Muriel that a copy should be circulated to the finance and admin committee. She would also recommend to John Carmichael that a copy of the report be pinned up on the union notice boards in headquarters and the regional offices. She guessed that not only some of the finance and admin committee would have heard about the matter but the majority of union staff would also have done. It would be best to try and kill the matter now but if Sarah Mackenzie intended to appeal then she would have to face that.

***

After Leila and Julia had left my office I asked Sheila to get me Les Martin, the President and Jane Toff, the Vice-President on the phone. I wanted to update them on the latest development. It took me twenty minutes to do so. They were both alive to the situation and concurred with the line which Leila had suggested for the national executive. I realised again how fortunate I was to have two such reliable people as the two most senior lay officials in the union.

I had often wondered how some of my colleagues in other unions managed when their senior lay people were often from the extreme left, or, in one case some years ago, a senior lay official who had been an office holder in the National Front. It was almost what the Germans called *schadenfreude*—delight in other people's misfortune—on my part. I knew we had our fair share of trotskyists—the trots as we called them—and there were at least three on the national executive committee but we didn't have any in the individual senior union positions; at least, not yet.

I recalled that thirty years ago the main problem in the union had been the influence of the Communist Party. There had been groupings of the CP in a number of unions both manual and white collar. At least, though, we had known who the people involved were—or, at least, I thought we had known. But there was a structure to the CP and its members were disciplined. The problem with the trots was the lack of any coherent plan or aim other than to cause as much trouble as they could with the union organisation and policies: always ask for more, always challenge the official line, always press for changes whether they were needed or not.

Perhaps I was being naïve in thinking there was no proper structure for the trots. There didn't seem to be but on reflection I knew that there was a hard core of trots who co-ordinated their activities in the union and who also discussed a common line with similar groupings in other unions.

I asked Sheila to get me John Miller at the TUC and, fortunately, he was in his office. I rehearsed what had happened with Industry3M and the company fax in particular.

"It could well be a green light for a lot of foreign owned companies John," I said and then suggested he had another word with Bob Wilson.

There was a pause and then he agreed and to let me know.

It was something and I thought I would go and tell Leila about it to cheer her up. As I entered Muriel's office, next to Leila's, Muriel said she was on the phone. Apparently our West Midlands organiser was asking her if she could speak to the seminar on Sunday that he was holding in Coventry for a number of the leading lay representatives. It was a similar thing to the Nottingham course at which Leila had spoken the previous Sunday. I entered Leila's office.

"I would love to come Jack" Leila was saying to Jack Treeman the organiser, "but Sunday's a bit difficult and—"

Before she could continue I motioned to her to give me the phone. She looked at me in some surprise but then handed it over to me.

"Hello, Jack" I boomed. "John Carmichael here. How goes it?"

Treeman was startled at first but then started to tell me about the seminar and the interest there was in the Industry3M dispute and why he thought it would go down well if Leila came to speak.

""I know Leila's got something on next Sunday but, if you like, I'd be happy to come and speak: again I stress, if you want me."

I heard Treeman chuckle and then he thanked me profusely. I knew he meant well. He had been an organiser with us for twenty years and was a solid and loyal official. He wasn't, though, the brightest pebble on the beach.

"That's fine Jack," I said, "I'll get my secretary Sheila to phone you in a few minutes to get all the details and look forward to seeing you on Sunday morning."

I hadn't intended to give up another Sunday but I could sense that Leila was getting a bit swamped by all the extra work that the

Industry3M issue had caused; the fact that the national official responsible for dealing with the company, Tim Burke, was away with cancer had aggravated the whole thing. I'd have to square it with Claire but I didn't think we had anything planned for the weekend.

I smiled at Leila: "don't take offence Leila but it's a long time since I spoke at one of these weekend seminars and I'd quite enjoy the experience again."

Leila had started to protest but quickly stopped. It was good of Carmichael and she appreciated his action. Though, ordinarily, she would have been happy to go to Coventry on a Sunday she did not want to cancel the arrangements for her daughter and grand daughter to come over that day; and she was looking forward to seeing them then.

"Thanks, John," she said. "Much appreciated."

I told her about my call to Miller at the TUC and how he was going to have another word with Bob Wilson at DTI. It could be something or nothing; but it was worth trying. I also handed her a copy of my faxed reply to Norman Jones at Industry3M. I had pointed out that three months notice of abrogating the procedural agreement was needed and asked again for an early negotiating meeting. I had also stated that if the company doubted our membership figures then we would be happy for ACAS to conduct a membership or audit or, alternatively, we would go to the CAC for a ballot on recognition. I remembered all that David Stannard had told me about the cash-paying members but I thought I might as well be upfront with the company.

Leila told me she had done the report on the sexual harassment case and briefly told me her conclusions. I knew Sarah Mackenzie and remembered her getting drunk at the office Christmas party. I didn't really know Eliza Astobe but made a mental note to have a word with her in the near future.

I asked Leila what she thought Sam Askari would say about her conclusions.

"He won't be happy but then he's been a bit daft. He made no attempt to enquire into the allegations but simply swallowed all

Mackenzie had told him. He's bright in some ways but he lacks a lot of common sense."

I agreed that Leila's report could be put up on the notice boards and then wished her a good weekend and left.

I t was the Saturday of the national executive committee meeting. Leila had got the overnight sleeper train down from Newcastle and was now having breakfast in the restaurant at Euston station. She looked back on the week: it had been a busy time—another busy time she thought—but quite productive.

She had spoken at the union's Norwich branch of Industry3M on the Tuesday and Newcastle the previous evening. Both meetings had been well attended—thirty five at Norwich and nearly fifty at Newcastle—and both had gone well. It seemed that the members were getting quite determined to support the union in its struggle and some new members had been recruited. The company's circular had not gone down well and there were a lot of rumours about who was to fill David Stannard's job as UK personnel director. The union circular—which had gone out partly by fax and partly through the post—had on the other hand been well received. Leila had been firm and positive but had resisted the idea of slagging off the company.

At the negotiating officials meeting Leila had been pleased that four of them had consulted their various company committees and were now going to submit claims for the introduction of the same job evaluation scheme that had been submitted to Industry3M. She had arranged a follow up negotiators' meeting for the end of the next week.

The finance and administration committee meeting on Thursday had also gone reasonably well even if it was just as boring as usual. Sometimes Leila got exasperated by the minutiae of administration— particularly as some of the committee members loved to get their teeth into very minor and even petty issues. Perhaps, she had thought, it was an easy alternative to thinking about the broader strategic issues facing the union.

As she had expected, the committee had decided to recommend that hardship pay only be paid if there was a strike of Industry3M members but also were telling the national executive that they would wish to reconsider the matter if there were to be any prolonged industrial action.

What had particularly pleased Leila was the news from the Swedish and German unions that dealt with Industry3M. She had telephoned Van Mergeren and he had circulated a summary of the job evaluation scheme as well as a brief account of the dispute with Industry3M to all the eighty four affiliated unions of Staff International. He had made a particular point of stressing to Leila that the Malayasian affiliated union had contacted him and asked for more details of the JE scheme. Leila had told him she would write direct to the union. He had then mentioned that both Lars Tolmark of the Swedish union SAF and the German white collar section of the DGB had contacted him to say they were actively considering whether to submit claims for the job evaluation scheme and that he had told them that Leila would now be contacting them again direct.

Leila and Frank Hallard had also met a small sub-committee of the local government union's executive to outline the JE scheme and that had gone well. She had telephoned the director of the Industrial Foundation and made a date to speak at one of their seminars on job evaluation. She still had to fix a date for talking to the Commercial & Technology Union about job evaluation but Muriel was chasing them for a date.

All in all, she thought, it had been useful week and the meeting she and Carmichael had had with Alan Whitchurch and Dan Michael on the Friday morning had also been encouraging. Whitchurch had reported that thirty new members had been recruited in the company, some by existing members and others as a direct result of organisers visiting some of Industry3M's branch offices.

The most enjoyable part of the last seven days, though, for Leila had been the lunch she had had with her daughter and grand daughter on the Sunday. Helen had been delightful and enjoyed the Indian meal. Deborah, her daughter, had been more relaxed than previously and had seemed to be getting over her husband having walked out on her. She had mentioned a man she had met at one of her visits to the local gym and how she was going out for a meal with him later in the week.

Just as she was finishing her coffee she heard a voice call her name. She looked up. It was Chris Rodd.

"Chris, what are you doing here?"

Rodd was looking fit, she thought, and was carrying his set of golf clubs.

"Off to St Andrew's: I've been invited by the committee there to take part in a sponsored match with the Scottish CBI."

The CBI—the Confederation of British Industry—had a Scottish arm and most of the leading Scottish employers were members of it. She remembered that Rodd had always been a keen golfer.

"Why didn't you fly? The train will take hours," she asked.

Rodd said he enjoyed a long train journey and anyway the golf tournament was not starting until the Sunday. Just then he looked round the restaurant and smiled. Leila turned and saw he was smiling at a woman eating breakfast by herself at a table by the window. She had waved a hand.

"Can't stay, unfortunately," he said hurriedly, "but we must have that drink sometime and I'll see what I can do about the current troubles with the company." He moved over to the table by the window before Leila could respond.

Leila realised she had been daft ever to get friendly with him in the first place. He was going away for the weekend with a woman who was obviously not his wife. No wonder, Leila thought, his wife was a bit irritated on the telephone that time. And clearly he wouldn't be much help in the dispute with Industry3M. No doubt he kidded himself that he was in touch with everything but in reality he was in touch with nothing, at least nothing of any significance in the company. When she had met him before at various courses and receptions he had talked as if he was well up in what was going on in the company: in hindsight now she realised that it was all a bit of a show. She resolved to avoid having a drink with him in the future.

Leila got to the hotel at half past nine. John Carmichael was already there and talking to Les Martin and Jane Toff. Altogether there were fifteen members on the union's national executive committee and that included the President, the Vice-President and the Honorary General Treasurer. Five years ago the committee had consisted of thirty one members, partly because of guaranteeing seats for other unions and staff organisations that had transferred engagements to the Clerical & General Union.

A committee of that size was widely recognised as being too unwieldy and at a rules revision conference two years ago it had been decided to cut back the number to fifteen. The union had eight regions throughout the UK and each region had one seat on the committee. There were the three top honorary officials and then four seats for what were called 'specific areas': these were for members employed in information technology in the different companies in which the union was organised, members in legal departments (including a few qualified solicitors but mainly more junior staff) and members who worked in finance departments. Some of the latter were qualified accountants but—as with those in legal departments—the majority were junior staff. The fourth special area was for those lumped under the heading of 'specialists'. These were members who worked for firms and companies that were not part of major employing institutions and who had some specialist qualification. They included staff from firms of architects, quantity surveyors, charities and voluntary organisations.

The eight regional members were elected by postal ballot of all the members in each region. Normally only about thirty per cent of the members voted but then, as John Carmichael kept telling everyone, that was usually above the norm for local government elections. Those in the press and different employers who derided the low level of voting were always challenged by Carmichael who consistently wrote to the newspapers—and used the point in speeches—arguing that those who claimed that trade unions were therefore unrepresentative of their own members should likewise believe that local authority members throughout the land were even more unrepresentative. He also used to refer to the number of shareholders voting at company annual general meetings. He usually finished such letters and speeches by stating that one of the joys of democracy was that people had the choice of whether to vote or not, and that was something to be prized.

The four members in the special areas were elected by the members in each such area. Tony Hammond could have chosen to stand for election as the member for the Merseyside region but instead stood for election by all the IT members in the union. He had been elected for the last three years.

Leila thought the fifteen strong committee was a distinct improvement on the old much larger one. But it did mean that they had to be very careful to try and ensure that a particular faction or clique in the union did not get an undue influence and she knew that the particular area of concern now was the growth in the extreme left representation. There were three trots on the national executive committee, including Tony Hammond and a number of others' in certain key regional positions.

She went over to speak to Carmichael.

All in all the national executive meeting wasn't bad. By three o'clock all the necessary decisions had been taken and the meeting finished.

I had agreed that Leila would do most of the reporting. I would start off by mentioning the broader context of the dispute, my discussions with John Miller of the TUC, the ACAS meeting and my letters to Norman Jones at the UK head office of Industry3M and my letter to the managing director of the company in Atlanta. I was still awaiting responses to both letters.

There had been a full attendance for the meeting and in the end the motion authorising a ballot of all members in Industry3M on three options—an overtime ban, a one day stoppage and a three day stoppage—had been approved without dissent. Tony Hammond had been a pain as usual and at one point he had moved a motion calling for an indefinite strike and also a mass demonstration outside the company's head office in Liverpool. One of the other two trots on the committee had seconded it but such was the hostility of the rest of the committee that Hammond had decided to withdraw it.

The clincher had been Leila's argument that an indefinite strike might be an option if all else failed and if the company made no move at all towards a settlement, but to suggest it now would be both risky and foolhardy—and, more important, it would give a weapon to the company to demonstrate to its staff that the union was becoming more extreme and out of touch with its members. We had to ensure that the company was seen as being unreasonable and that the union had no alternative but to take the action we were going to take.

Tony Hammond's way would blow that all to pieces. Leila then cleverly made an oblique reference to that perhaps being the agenda for those who were against the union. Hammond didn't rise to the bait but the point was not lost on the other executive members.

Leila had made a good report at the beginning of the debate and given a full account of the last three weeks. She also made it clear that the union had a god weapon in the new job evaluation scheme. It would be a good scheme in Industry3M and could also prove attractive to other companies. She stressed that if other unions—both here and abroad—were to pursue it, then it could be a winner. She had mentioned the branch meetings in Brighton, Norwich and Newcastle since the national committee meeting and the recent increase in membership.

There had been a long debate about strike pay and in the end the recommendation of the finance and administration committee had been carried. The union's Honorary General Treasurer had spoken at some length on the union's financial position and emphasised the need to balance the conflicting demands of supporting those who suffered financial hardship while on strike and the need to keep a careful eye on the union's expenditure. The executive had—it seemed to me—to appreciate this and agreed to reconsider the matter if there was to be a further ballot for a longer strike.

After the meeting Leila and I had given another press conference. Julia had arranged it for four o'clock so the timing was quite good. Both Les Martin and Jane Toff stayed behind for the press conference but the other executive members went straight home. Again, the reaction of the press—all fifteen of them this time, including I was pleased to see, Joe Turner of the *Liverpool Daily Post*—had been positive and the *Wall Street Journal* had been particularly helpful. Afterwards I had a brief chat with him and arranged to meet him for a drink the following Tuesday evening. He asked for Leila to be there as well and I said I would be glad to ask Leila along.

On this occasion it was Oliver Listle of the *Financial Times* who attended the conference. As he was leaving after the conference he came up to me and said that he thought Leila had been impressive in her handling of the press. I told him that she was impressive in all the union work that she did and that I couldn't think of a better official to run the dispute than her. Listle said he would like to do a profile of her for his paper and I suggested he fix that up with Leila now.

I saw him go over to Leila and, while he was talking to her, saw her write something in her diary. Then she approached me and asked if I was available on Monday morning to deal with all the matters that we now had to deal with as a result of the national executive decision. I said we ought to have a meeting with all the relevant national officials so we could co-ordinate exactly who was dealing with what. Leila said she would telephone those concerned when she got home that evening to make sure they would be available.

Not for the first time I realised I was very fortunate to have Leila as the number two official of the union. I said to her as she left: "not time for a drink?" She declined saying that no doubt there would be many drinks in the next few weeks and smiled as she said it. I wondered whether she had anyone to go home to; it was what—ten, fifteen years?—since she had got divorced and she must now be in her late forties but she was still an attractive woman. However, it wasn't really my business.

I smiled back and wished her a happy weekend. I knew that there was some time before Les Martin and Jane Toff had to get their trains so I suggested to them that we went to the pub. My suggestion was carried without dissent and, indeed, with some enthusiasm.

Chapter Five

The Ballot

"Mrs Smith?"

Leila had got into the office early. She had two telephones on her desk: one was connected to the switchboard, the other was a direct line. It was the direct line that had rung.

"Yes."

"Good morning, Tino Malik here."

It was the regional conciliation officer from ACAS. The one she had exchanged Latin summary descriptions with, or at least that was what she imagined they were.

"You're nice and early," said Leila. "I was thinking of calling you later today."

Malik chuckled: "beat you to it."

Leila thought he did sound friendly. Perhaps he knew he wouldn't impress her as easily as he tried to other people.

"You gave me your direct line number at our meeting," explained Malik. "I was reading yesterday in the Sunday papers about your national executive committee deliberations—" he may be sounding more friendly, but he was still very pompous, thought Leila—"and I wondered if ACAS could be any help now. Would you like us to try and arrange another meeting with the company? Or would you just like to come into the office and explain your union's current position?"

Leila replied that a meeting with the company would be helpful but emphasised that he should stress to the company that they should be prepared to meet with the union on a face to face basis. She mentioned that neither Norman Jones, the chief executive in the UK nor Stuckman the CEO of the company in Atlanta, had replied to John Carmichael's letters. Carmichael would be writing again to Norman Jones telling him of the national executive committee's decision on an industrial action ballot: but to be able to talk about it with the company direct would be a distinct help.

Malik said he took the point and would do his best. He asked if Leila had any preference for a meeting date. Leila said that any date would do but preferably the Wednesday afternoon would be best. She knew Carmichael was free then and she also knew he would like to come to the meeting. If that was not possible then she and Carmichael would have to juggle their diaries if they could: a meeting with the company at ACAS would have to take priority. The only exception Leila told Malik was the forthcoming Friday morning. Then she had agreed to speak at the seminar of the Industrial Foundation on the job evaluation scheme of the union.

Malik said he would try and contact the company now and would get back to Leila as soon as he could.

At ten o'clock that morning Leila went to the small conference room that the union had in its headquarters building. It was useful for small meetings of up to ten—or twelve at a pinch—people. It was no good for the national executive committee as a number of officials attended that as well as the fifteen members. The union's finance and administration committee met in the conference room and Leila used it for her regular meetings with the union's negotiating officials.

On the Saturday evening and Sunday morning she had contacted the various officials about the meeting that morning. Surprisingly, but fortunately as well, they could all make it: Alan Whitchurch, the national organiser, Frank Hallard, head of research, Dan Michael of membership department, Julia Cardon and the four national negotiating officials who had previously told Leila that they would be submitting the job evaluation scheme to some of the companies they dealt with. She had also asked Muriel to come along to the meeting and make a note of who was going to do what.

Carmichael opened the meeting by briefly summarising the national executive committee's discussions and decisions on the situation with Industry3M. Leila then referred to the call from Malik of ACAS that morning. She reported that she had also contacted the Electoral Reform Society before the meeting and agreed a timetable for the proposed ballot of the Industry3M members. A lot of trade unions used the ERS for ballots. They were independent of the unions and employers organisations and the Clerical & General Union had always used them.

Leila said that ballot papers would hopefully go out in the next couple of days to members' home addresses and members would be asked to return them not later than the Friday of the following week. She knew it meant that members who were away on holiday wouldn't be able to participate in the ballot, and that the timetable was tight, but then she reflected, you couldn't win. They needed to have the ballot quickly now the national executive decision had been taken.

Leila asked Dan Michael to get working on producing the list of members' home addresses for the Electoral Reform Society and invited him to tell the others about the latest union membership position in the company. As he spoke she thought he still looked a bit rough and—if anything—slightly more dishevelled than when she had had the meeting in her office over the sexual harassment allegation.

Michael said the latest membership figure was 2,650: an all time high but reminded those present that the total staff in the UK part of the company was 5,000. If they got a fifty per cent ballot return then that would be just over 1,300 voters. If they got a majority of three to one—which would be very good by normal trade union standards—that would mean something over nine hundred in favour. He left the point in the air.

Leila carried the point further. A fifty percent ballot return would be good by any standards and a three to one majority would be significant but that meant that only just over nine hundred people out of a total staff of 5,000 would had voted to take industrial action. They all took the point. She stressed though that naturally they would all hope that all the union's members would support the action once the ballot result was known.

Carmichael then asked Alan Whitchurch about the organisers stepping up their recruitment in the company. As ever, the organisers were engaged on a number of campaigns but Whitchurch said he would make rearrangements so that Industry3M would be the priority. He reminded his colleagues that all new members that they recruited in the next two weeks would not necessarily be able to vote in the ballot. Under the union's constitution and rules members had to have been members of the union for at least ten days before being able to participate in any union ballots. This was designed to stop people from joining and voting almost on the same day or, as had happened on some occasions in the past, join the union one day for one particular issue, vote in a ballot, and then let their membership lapse or, worse, resign almost immediately afterwards. It did mean, though, that new members would be able to participate in any industrial action.

Frank Hallard reported that there were an increasing number of enquiries about the new job evaluation scheme. He mentioned the Swedish and German unions' interest and the sub committee of the local government union's executive which he and Leila had addressed. Leila mentioned the Commercial and Technology Union and that Muriel was fixing a date for her to speak to them.

Alan Whitchurch interrupted: "communications would be a lot better if they merged with us." He smiled as he said but there was a real issue there.

All the officials knew that there had been tentative merger talks with the Commercial & Technology Union two years previously. At least John Carmichael and Peter Moorhouse, the C & T Union General Secretary, together with the Presidents of both unions, had met a couple of times and discussed if there was any desire for the two unions to get together. The discussions had been friendly enough but had not led to any formal talks: both the General Secretaries had said to each other that there would have to be a groundswell in favour of a merger before any meaningful talks could take place. And that groundswell had not been there then.

The Commercial & Technology Union had about 150,000 members—significantly smaller than the Clerical & General Union. Many of the C & T Union's members had been in the public sector. Privatisation and the growing number of information technology companies had prompted the expansion of a relatively small electricity managers union, originally in the public sector before electricity had been privatised, into what was now the Commercial & Technology Union. Logically Leila and the others knew that a merger of the two unions would make sense—and would be significantly beneficial in financial terms—and it was good that the abortive discussions of two years ago had ended amicably. She had no doubt the issue would arise again.

Carmichael then asked the national negotiating officials how claims were progressing in their companies for the new job evaluation scheme.

Brian Hall referred to the comprehensive claim that he and Carmichael had discussed for the white collar staff of Hokkaido, one of the major Japanese owned car manufacturing companies. The Hokkaido national committee had agreed to include a claim for the JE scheme and he had written to the company with the claim. Hazel Bellini, the youngest national official in the union and—Carmichael had often said to Leila—one of the brightest they had, said she had a meeting of the national committee for Leisure & Sport and they would be deciding on whether to submit a claim at their meeting the following Monday. Leisure & Sport was a big company in both television and radio manufacturing and also in sports complexes. They had settled their pay in a two year deal the previous November so the job evaluation claim would be dealt with separately from other conditions.

Carmichael asked Adam Turnbull about Transport International, one of the UK's biggest transport companies. Turnbull said his national committee was meeting the following day to discuss including the JE scheme with their annual pay claim. He had discussed it with some of the leading lay officials and they were sympathetic to the claim.

Mathew Singh, the fourth national negotiating official at the meeting, said his national committee for the white collar staff of Teening & Sykes, a major British chemical company, had met the previous Friday and they had agreed to submit a claim for the job evaluation scheme.

Leila suggested that Frank Hallard as head of research should go with the negotiators to meetings with the companies concerned. If, she acknowledged, Frank could not be in two places at once then he should get one of his colleagues in the department to go. She queried whether Sam Askari could go and Hallard said he would discuss it with him.

Carmichael asked Leila to summarise the timetable for the Industry3M ballot and any subsequent action. Leila referred again to the ballot papers hopefully going out on Wednesday and for just over a week to let the members return their completed papers. As agreed the ballot paper would ask three questions: whether the members were willing to ban overtime, to have a one day strike and to have a three day strike.

The national executive committee would then have to meet again to authorise the action—provided there was a majority in favour of the action, at least one of the three possible actions but hopefully all three actions. On a few occasions in the past Carmichael had circulated the national executive for a decision on a strike by post but he knew this was most unsatisfactory. This time he insisted that there would be a meeting to determine action. Apart from anything else, he could imagine what some of the newspapers—to say nothing of the company—would say, if word got out, that the national executive had not deemed the issue important enough for a meeting to be held. They would have to hold the national executive meeting on a

Sunday—two days after the ballot closed—and that would allow the national committee for the company to meet on the Saturday.

Leila then looked at Carmichael as she said there should be another meeting of all the officials concerned when the ballot result was known. They could then discuss arrangements for the industrial action if there was a ballot majority for it. Assuming they got the ballot result from the Electoral Reform Society on that Friday morning then the meeting would have to be on that Friday afternoon. Then Leila could go to the national committee on the Saturday and the national executive committee on the Sunday with a detailed proposal. Hopefully, she reiterated, the ballot result would be good majorities for all three possible actions. Carmichael nodded as she was speaking and said his secretary would be in touch with them all as soon as the ballot result was declared.

<hr />

I thought the meeting had gone well and all seemed enthusiastic about the future of the dispute. I thought, though, that Dan Michael had looked rough. Leila had told me in confidence about his own domestic troubles and, if appearances were any guide, they must be continuing.

As soon as I got back to the office I had a call from John Miller at the TUC. He had spoken again to Bob Wilson at the DTI and reported that this time Wilson had seemed more sympathetic to the Clerical & General's view. Wilson had hinted at something he knew about Industry3M but didn't go into any details and he, Miller, had decided it would be unwise to push him. I remembered as we were speaking that Leila and I were due to meet the man from the *Wall Street Journal* the next evening. I told Miller this and said I would try and get some news on the company from him. In the meantime, Miller emphasised, there was nothing the Government was prepared to do publicly nor—at least in the immediate future—in private.

I thanked him for his call and repeated that I would keep him informed of developments. I started to plough through the pile of papers that had appeared on my desk that morning. After about half an hour there was a knock on my door and Leila entered the office. She looked a bit irritated and I asked her what was up.

"I've just had Tino Malik on the phone again" she said.

"I could see you didn't think much of him before," I commented, "you shouldn't let him get to you." I meant it as a sort of joke but apparently I was wrong.

"No, no, it's not him. It's the company again."

She explained that following his call first thing that morning Malik had telephoned John Carr of Industry3M and suggested a meeting, and, at the same time, had stressed that in his view it would be best if the company and the union were to meet together under his—Malik's—chairmanship. Carr had apparently prevaricated and then said he might be able to persuade his colleagues to have a meeting with the union but he would object to Leila being present. Leila had exploded on the phone and Malik has hastened to assure her that he had told Carr that his proposal was totally unacceptable. Carr had then said he would have to think about the matter.

I told Leila that in a sense she should take Carr's attitude as a bit of a compliment. It could be that the company was apprehensive of her and realised she could make Carr look a bit of an amateur at industrial relations. I told Leila, somewhat ruefully, that the company clearly couldn't have much of an opinion of myself.

We agreed that there was nothing more we could do about an ACAS meeting and that we would just to wait for news from Tino Malik.

Sheila, my secretary, then came in carrying two letters which she had not opened. I looked at them. They had both come from Federal Express and that was why they hadn't come with the main post. One was from Atlanta in America and the other from London. Both were from Industrty3M and marked 'strictly private and confidential'.

I opened the letters. One was from Harold Stuckman, the managing director, or chief executive officer as American companies usually called their top man; the other was from John Carr of the European Group head office in London. I read them both quickly and passed them over to Leila. As she read them her early irritation increased.

The letter from Stuckman had been brief. It said that his company—and I noted that phrase *his* company—had a policy of good staff relations and, where appropriate, would deal with various types of staff organisation. However he understood that the Clerical & General Union no longer represented the majority of staff and therefore the company did not wish to continue with their previous arrangements with us.

The letter from Carr was longer and a little more devious. He had reiterated that our pay claim was 'ridiculously' high and the job evaluation scheme 'inappropriate for a company like Industry3M'. He had then rehearsed the point about union membership, stressed that they no longer wished to meet with us 'under the procedural agreement' and how they would be examining other forms of staff representation.

"It's quite clever," said Leila. "He's not actually saying that they are derecognising us and he says too that they are not against staff representation *per se*. And he doesn't do what I believe some US companies do and call the company one big family."

"Nor," I commented, "suggest all the staff should sing the company song every morning."

I remembered years ago that in the London branch of the Bank of China the staff there had to listen to extracts from what was described as 'Chairman Mao's little red book' every morning. It just happened that the management of the Bank's London branch were pro-communist at the time of the Chinese revolution in 1949 while the other branches—New York, Sydney and Singapore—were pro Kuomintang, the previous governing party of Chiang Kai Shek which had subsequently fled to Taiwan. So when Mao launched the cultural revolution in the 1960's his little red book was distributed everywhere and staff of Chinese companies made to listen to it being read out and also encouraged to read it themselves.

I remembered, too, how many of us had laughed at the idea at the time and proudly proclaimed that we would not do such things in western countries or companies. Then in more recent years some of the US based companies in Britain and elsewhere in Europe—particularly in the retail trade—had started the appalling concept of the 'company song'.

I told Leila of my memory. She smiled.

"These things can be circular," she said. "Remember what Bernard Shaw said about the Communists and the Nazis in the thirties—the only difference between them is the colour of their shirts?"

"Or was it George Orwell?" I asked.

"Touche." Leila smiled again.

We arranged that I would circulate the letters to the national committee for Industry3M and the national executive committee of the union. I would get Julia to send the stuff to the press and Leila said she would put a suitable comment on the press release. I would telephone the President and Vice-President and Leila would phone Ian Macallister of the national committee and also update him on the ballot timetable. There was nothing we could do about ACAS at the moment. Leila would pursue with the Electoral Reform Society the ballot arrangements and particularly try and ensure we got the result by the midday of the following Friday.

She then mentioned that she thought Dan Michael had looked a bit rough that morning. So we had both noticed. I made a mental note to have a word with him. Surely he would have been relieved at the outcome of the sexual harassment charge?

Leila suggested she went up to the union branch committee at the UK head office of the company in Liverpool and I thought that would be a good idea—and reminded her to watch out for some more eggs. She also said that if action was authorised following a successful ballot then she would arrange for Alan Whitchurch to see that the union's organisers attended each of the eight union branch committees we had in the company. We then discussed about the European Group head office staff in London. It was a bit of a nonsense having the two head offices in the same country and undoubtedly they would be merged at some time. That, however, was not my concern. I was always interested in company structures and organisation and knew that a great many of them could not be described as logical. But then, neither could a lot of trade union structures.

There were only about forty staff in the London Group head office and they oversaw Industry3M's separate companies in Sweden and Germany, where the unions did negotiate with the local management, and also in France, Italy, Spain and the Netherlands, where the local unions had failed to make any inroads. We had tried in the past to get the London staff into membership and had held meetings for them but the response had always been negative and our procedural agreement with the company had only covered the UK company. Leila suggested that we have one more go at the Group head office staff and I agreed. She would have a chat with Alan Whitchurch about it.

I said I would write back to both Howard Stuckman and John Carr and Julia could include those letters in her press release. I reminded Leila that we were due to have a drink with the *Wall Street Journal* the following evening and I would get Sheila to phone him and fix a convenient pub.

❦

Tuesday, the next day, saw Leila arrange for the address labels for all the union members in Industry3M to be delivered by courier to the offices of the Electoral Reform Society together with the ballot papers which the union printed in house. Ballot papers were to go out the next day by first class post and, because the papers were going out first class, that would give another day or two for the papers to be returned. It would cost the union more by going first class but it would be worth it. She knew, though, that time was not so important as might be imagined and experience showed that the big majority of union members usually voted in a strike ballot by return of post. However, this time there could be no excuse for late return of the papers or people complaining they did not have sufficient time to complete them, at least those who were not away on holiday—but there shouldn't be too many of them at this time.

She telephoned Ian Macallister in Glasgow. She told him about all the arrangements that were now in hand, read out the text of the two letters from the company and asked what the strength of feeling among the members now was. He assured her that feelings in favour of the union's position were still strong but a number had queried with him why the union didn't go for a straight recognition ballot through the Central Arbitration Committee rather than a strike ballot. There still was a feeling that things were moving perhaps a bit too quickly.

Leila explained the time a recognition ballot would take as the CAC would have to consult the company over it and undoubtedly they would prevaricate: anything to delay matters would, she said, suit them and from their point of view hopefully diminish strong feelings and, anyway, the company had not actually said they were derecognising the union but withdrawing from the procedural agreement. It was, she admitted, a distinction without much of a difference but legally it was not actual derecognition. She deliberately didn't mention the cash payers to whom David Stannard had referred though she got the impression he knew something about it. Perhaps Clive Bristow had been in touch with him. Well, she reckoned, no harm done provided the news did not get out widely.

Leila outlined the ballot timetable and said she would of course phone him as soon as the news was available on the Friday. He agreed that it would be necessary to have a meeting of the national committee to recommend implementation of the strike ballot provided that the figures were clear—a good turn out and a big majority in favour of the proposed actions. If there was no clear cut decision from the ballot then there would still have to be a meeting of the national committee and both Leila and Macallister agreed: it would have to be on the Saturday. In the meantime Leila would send out some more newsletters and would particularly mention the attempts by ACAS to arrange a meeting and how the company was stalling on that. She would also circulate the national committee with arrangements for their meeting on that Saturday.

The whole timetable was tight and Leila knew it would seem unnecessarily cumbersome and bureaucratic to have a national committee on one day and the national executive committee the next day. But that was the price of a democratic structure and they had to be seen to be following the correct—and union constitutional—procedure. She would not put it past John Carr to try and get a union member to raise an objection with the Government union watch dog, the Commissioner for Trade Union Affairs, that the procedure had not been followed properly and that could be disastrous.

After the telephone conversation Leila went to get a cup of coffee from the machine just outside the staff rest room at the end of the corridor. She saw Eliza Abbotke there and smiled at her. Abbotke looked worried and just looked at Leila in a sort of distressed way.

"Hello Eliza," said Leila, "you don't look too cheerful. What's the matter?"

Abbotke cast her eyes down and murmured something that Leila could not quite hear.

"Sorry, didn't catch that. What's the problem?"

Leila looked at her and it seemed as if tears were welling up in her eyes. She felt a premonition that there was some bad news.

"Eliza, come along to my office for a little chat." Abbotke seemed reluctant but Leila almost insisted and she then agreed.

In her office Leila asked Eliza Abbotke again what the matter was and then Abbotke started to cry. After a while she recovered sufficiently to tell Leila what had happened.

It appeared that the previous afternoon Dan Michael had called her into his office, asked her to sit down and had thanked her for speaking up for him at the sexual harassment hearing. She had said she had just spoken the truth and she was glad to do that. Unfortunately Michael had not left the matter there. He had come round to her and put his hands on her shoulders. Then, before she realised what was happening he had started whispering in her ear and then puts his hands on her breasts. She had got up and then he had tried to turn her round to face him and made to kiss her. She had been shocked and pushed him away. He had continued and her protests seemed only to excite him further. After a short struggle she had managed to break free and rushed out of his office.

Leila was taken aback and asked her if she was sure about her recollection of what had happened. Abbotke started crying again and then angrily through her tears demanded why Leila didn't believe her. Leila said she did not doubt her story but wanted to be absolutely sure. This would be bad for Michael and she would have to take the matter further. What a bloody fool he was. No, worse than that. She wondered whether there might, after all, be something in what Sarah Mackenzie had alleged but then dismissed the idea. That matter had been properly dealt with. This was something else.

Abbotke quietened down and again told Leila what Michael had tried to do to her. She emphasised that what she had said at the previous sexual harassment hearing had been true and that she thought Mackenzie had deliberately distorted what had happened when Michael had brushed against her when trying to get through the doorway. This time, though, there was no doubt: she had been sexually harassed by Dan Michael.

Leila realised that this had happened not too long after the meeting with the officials that she and Carmichael had had and how both she and Carmichael had commented afterwards that Michael was looking stressed. She said that Abbotke should go and tell Sam Askari as the main staff representative and chair of the bargaining unit and she would see them both the next day. She would also see Dan Michael. She assured Abbotke that she took the matter very seriously. Abbotke then thanked her and, drying her eyes, left the room. Leila waited for her to go and then called Dan Michael to come to her office right away.

It was just after five o'clock and I was putting my papers back into my pending tray when Leila came to my office. We had arranged to see the *Wall Street Journal* at six thirty that evening. Sheila had told him we would be in the fairly quiet bar of the Hole in the Wall, a pub just near Waterloo station. Yes, it was fairly quiet but it also was a bit rough but I knew the beer was good and it was handy for us going up from Clapham. The *Wall Street Journal* might well prefer some rather trendy wine bar but, I reasoned to myself, this was England after all and I had said that I would fix the venue.

I was a little surprised to see Leila as we still had about half an hour before we had to leave but then she told me about the allegations of Eliza Abbotke. It was appalling and I said so. It went without either of us saying so, that we all had enough to do without having an incident like this. I started to curse Dan Michael and Leila waited while I then calmed down.

Leila told me that she had called Michael to her office and confronted him with what Eliza Abbotke had said. He had started to deny the incident but then swallowed hard and admitted it was true. He was looking even more dishevelled and had almost broken down when saying this. Then he had poured out all his domestic problems again, had said he had originally just wanted to thank Abbotke but had then lost control. He was desperately sorry, referred again to his wife's affair and how their marriage had seemed almost over and said he couldn't understand why he had behaved the way he had. Leila said she had said she would have a formal meeting under the internal procedure with him, Abbotke and Sam Askari the next morning. He could bring someone with him to the meeting but—as he had done on the previous occasion—he declined this.

Leila told me that if the allegations were true—and Dan Michael had admitted them—then he would be guilty of gross misconduct and could be suspended from his job. Suspension though would not solve the issue and it could well be that he would have to go. She would consider the matter again after the meeting the following morning.

I nearly said that this was the worst possible time for such an incident to occur but quickly realised that there was no such thing as a good time for such an incident and knew that Leila would take the right decision.

We then left the office and made our way to the station to catch the train to Waterloo. We didn't want to miss the *Wall Street Journal*.

We got to the pub at just past half past six. The small bar in the front was nice and quiet, but I could hear the noise growing in the large bar at the back. The *Wall Street Journal* was already there in the small bar and, to my surprise, was drinking a pint of beer.

"I'm glad you fixed this pub," he said, "there aren't too many where you can get some decent beer. My name's Charles Pitney, by the way. Most people call me Chuck. It's John and Leila, isn't it?" He finished his pint and added "it's my shout."

I liked him already and after we had got some drinks—Leila nursing a small gin and tonic and Pitney and I with pints of bitter—we sat down at a small table. Pitney got his notebook out and asked if we minded him making some notes as we conversed. Neither of us objected and off we went. I referred to the importance of Industry3M as an American company dealing with us as a British trade union and Leila then updated him on the ballot timetable and our current membership figures and gave him copies of the letters from the company.

I was looking at Pitney as Leila spoke. He was a big man and, as I had noticed before, seemed to have quite a red face. His hair was a bit ginger and his moustache quite luxuriant. In many ways he looked like a typical English beer drinker, but, I reasoned, that was no bad thing and I knew that the *Wall Street Journal* was an influential paper both in the US and here. He made a number of notes and then when Leila had finished he closed his notebook.

"How much do you two know about the company's position in the US?" he asked and then without waiting for a reply launched into a potted history of Industry3M.

Harold Stuckman had originally started Oil21 as an oil consultancy and as a private company. It had gone well and when it had progressed he had changed it to Industry3M and after a couple of years had turned it into a public company with a flotation on the New York stock exchange. Then Stuckman had retired—he was over seventy years old—and his son, Harold Stukman junior had been appointed as CEO. Junior had worked for the company since his father had started it but Pitney thought he was not the man his father was and he had made some strategic mistakes in trying to diversify the company too quickly. All had gone well for a while but in the last three years a number of the stock holders in the US had been making noises about the direction the company was taking.

This was useful information to us and we both admitted that we had had no detailed knowledge but had accepted that the company's annual reports, glossily and exaggeratedly presented, had been accurate. Pitney said that at the company's last annual general meeting some critical questions had been raised about the costs of the expansions into other countries. Unlike most British companies which were largely financed by share issues, Industry3M—in common with many other US companies—relied heavily on bank finance. In the economists' jargon, the debt to equity ratio was very different. That was fine as long as profits were sufficient to finance the bank lending but it appeared to some commentators in the US that Stuckman junior had had to borrow more and more to finance the bank lending and the profits were not apparently enough to finance that in the medium to longer term.

I interjected, "but then clearly the company doesn't want any adverse publicity. On the other hand, I always thought its UK part was quite profitable."

"Yes," said Pitney, "but the key question is whether the actual level of profitability is sufficient to underwrite the increasing lending—and it might be now that it isn't."

I was going to ask him another question but he thought we ought to have another round of drinks first before he answered any more.

Leila looked at me as Pitney was at the bar and raised her eyebrows. "That might be why they're so keen to get rid of their relationship with us?" I nodded.

When he came back to the table with the drinks Leila asked him about the profitability of the company's subsidiaries in continental Europe.

"Well," answered Pitney, "I believe that in Sweden and Spain they're doing OK. The other subsidiaries are just about breaking even but Stuckman has been telling the stock holders that the move into the Far East is the solution: low overheads, less running costs because of low wages and not the competition there is in Europe and the US."

He asked us about our contacts with the other parts of the company and Leila explained the union contacts we had through our membership of Staff International. He seemed quite impressed by this.

I asked him whether he knew anything about John Carr and had he heard about David Stannard. Pitney said he knew nothing about Stannard but he had heard about Carr, and what he had heard had not been very complimentary. Apparently Carr had been appointed the human resource man in the European head office over the head of an American called Tiller. Tiller had been with the Atlanta office of the parent company and when the vacancy had occurred had been hoping for the job. Stuckman, though, had thought it would look better over in the UK for a European—even an Englishman he said smilingly—to get the position.

After I got another round of drinks I was beginning to like Pitney more and more. He was not the rather smooth and superficial American journalist that I had wrongly visualised.

"This is all very helpful, Chuck," I said. "By the way what's your background?"

"Journalism all my working life," he responded. "That's why I like a proper drink". He gestured to the fresh pint of bitter he had.

"There must be more to it than that" I said.

Pitney smiled. "OK, you've got it. There's a lot of Irish in me. My family came over to the US from Ireland in the nineteen thirties. I like the Americans and I am an American, but I've been to Ireland many times and now I've been the *Wall Street Journal* man in the UK here for the past eighteen months."

Leila asked him about his trade union contacts. He replied that he knew some of the British trade unionists, including at the TUC, but not too many because there was little interest in the industrial relations scene in the UK for readers of the *Wall Street Journal*. Industry3M was an exception because of its American ownership. He mentioned that he did know the leading people in the US equivalent to the British Trades Union Congress—the American Federation of Labour-Congress of Industrial Organizations. Years ago the AFL and the CIO had been separate bodies and sometimes very antagonistic towards each other. Then they had merged and, although American trade union membership was only fifteen per cent of the total American workforce—"if that" Pitney emphasised—it was still influential in a few industries like steel and motor car production. It also had influence with some of the leading lights in the US Democratic Party.

"But," Pitney admitted, "there's not much unionisation in the white collar sector. Some in retail and in the public sector like state and local government, and teaching of course. But the unions have never made much headway in the private white collar sector. That's one of the reasons why your dispute is interesting. And there's one more thing you ought to know."

He paused, took another long swallow of beer and continued: "although Industry3M has this basic dilemma over short and medium to long term profits and profitability to bank lending, it still is very much an attractive company. Stuckman senior had the idea of branching out from oil and, with the privatisation of state assets in so many countries, the idea of supplying so much labour under a contract basis is very attractive. That's why a number of the large US institutions—including some of our major banks—have been eyeing the company with a view to a possible takeover."

Leila asked him outright if he thought the union's proposed action would cause the company to think again. Pitney looked at her and then shook his head.

"I hope I'm wrong," he said, "and they certainly don't like bad publicity and their US stockholders will get even more jumpy if the bad publicity gets worse for them. But the strike here in itself is unlikely to cause them to change their attitude. But I understand why you are doing this. However—" he looked at Leila and then me—"the big unknown is, in my opinion, what's going to happen to their expansion in the far east."

It was all interesting stuff and I thanked him for giving us all this information and his opinion. He said he would be doing quite a big background piece for the paper anyway and he thought we ought to know. I asked him if he wanted one more pint and he accepted. Leila declined another drink and said she would be getting off back home. After she left and I had got another two pints of bitter Pitney asked me about Leila. He had heard about her from his TUC contacts as one of the brightest union leaders around and he was impressed by what he had seen in the last few weeks.

We chatted a bit more and exchanged home telephone numbers. Then I decided it was indeed time to go. I was not too surprised by what he had said about our chances of getting the company to change its mind about the union, but I knew he would accept that we had to be seen to be doing something. And his remark about the Far East was worth pursuing.

On the Wednesday morning Leila checked with the Electoral Reform Society and they were all geared up to dispatch the ballot papers that day. She was pleased too that Tino Malik from ACAS had telephoned to say that John Carr had agreed to a meeting at the ACAS offices and would be prepared to meet the union on a face to face basis under his, Malik's, chairmanship. The meeting was fixed for the Thursday afternoon and Leila knew she would have to get another newsletter out to the company's offices to tell them this. Malik emphasised that Carr had said he would attend a meeting to listen to what the union had to say. Surprisingly he had also said that he would probably bring Norman Jones, the UK chief executive, with him. Leila noted the way that Malik had put that: clearly Carr was the senior man.

She looked at her watch and saw it was half past nine. She had got Muriel to arrange a meeting with Sam Askari, Eliza Abbotke and Dan Michael for ten o'clock that morning. She had provisionally allocated about an hour for the meeting. After that she had agreed that Oliver Listle from the *Financial Times* would be coming to her office to interview for the profile he was doing for the paper. He asked her to have lunch with him but Leila had declined. She was not one for smart lunches in smart restaurants and, anyway, time was precious. Listle hadn't minded in the least and said he would be with her about half past eleven.

The telephone rang and Muriel said it was Dan Michael for her. Leila asked her to put him through.

"Hello Dan. We're meeting this morning so where are you?"

"I'm sorry Leila. I'm in bed. I feel bloody awful and can't make it this morning."

Leila was not too surprised but asked if he was going to see his doctor. He said his doctor was coming round later that morning and he would telephone Leila afterwards. There was a pause with each waiting for the other to mention the sexual harassment case. Finally Leila thought she had no alternative but to spell it out for him.

"Look Dan, there's never a good time for this. If you can come in—say tomorrow—we could have the hearing then. But if you're going to be off for some time then I have to do something."

Michael broke In: "can't we leave all this until the doctor says I'm fit?" He was almost pleading with her.

Leila thought for a moment and then said: "I think what is best is that I suspend you—on full pay—until we can hold the hearing and then we'll take it from there."

Michael started to protest that that would make it appear he was guilty. Leila reminded him that he had admitted his actions with Eliza Abbotke. He started to protest again but then lapsed into silence. There was another awkward pause.

Leila said, "so, Dan, I'll drop you a line suspending you on full pay until such time as the charges are determined. You let me know what your doctor says. If you're back in a few days then we can go ahead with the hearing—" she could almost hear him wince as she was speaking—"but if you're going to be off for any length of time then I'll have to come back to you."

There was a further pause and then in a very low voice Michael said he understood and rang off.

Leila sighed but the issue had to be dealt with and in suspending him on full pay she reckoned she was being reasonable. Why on earth had he done it in the first place?

Leila then sorted out her diary with Muriel. She would go up to Liverpool to speak to the branch committee there and would ring Clive Bristow about it. She would check with Ian Macallister whether she ought to go to the Glasgow branch, speak to Alan Whitchurch again about the organisers visiting the union branch committees as well as recruiting in the company offices—if they could get access—and then spoke to Julia Cardon about the press release and the company's two letters.

On Thursday afternoon Leila and I got to the ACAS offices in good time for the meeting. Julia came with us and she had again lined up a press conference for immediately afterwards. Both Julia and I had read Oliver Listle's profile of Leila in the *Financial Times* that morning. Oliver Listle had headed the piece 'the redoubtable Mrs Smith'. It was pretty good and I could see that Leila was pleased with it.

That morning Leila had told me that she had got a medical certificate for Dan Michael from his doctor. The doctor had written a note with it saying he didn't know when Michael would be fit to return to work. He had diagnosed him as suffering from 'nervous exhaustion' and it could be some time before he recovered. Leila had got Muriel to acknowledge the note. She had already written to Michael that morning confirming his suspension on full pay. She would have to consider the position further in two weeks time. In the meantime she had spoken to both Sam Askari and Eliza Abbotke and told them the position. Apparently Askari had asked her to hold the disciplinary hearing any way but Leila had told him that was not on.

After we had checked in at reception Malik came out of his office to meet us. He smiled and asked us how everything was going. We went into the small conference room as he explained that he had just had a phone call from John Carr to say that he and Norman Jones would be a bit late. We sat down and Leila updated him on developments, particularly the industrial action ballot and the likely timetable for a one day strike if the ballot showed a decent majority in favour. This time Malik seemed genuinely interested whereas previously he had not seemed to give the matter much attention. He must have read the various bits in the press and realised that this was becoming quite a high profile dispute.

He asked a number of pertinent questions and then left us to see if there was any message from Carr. He came back and said that Carr had telephoned to say they would be another twenty minutes. It didn't augur well, but there was absolutely nothing we could do about it except sit and wait.

In fact it was half an hour before Malik came in again and this time he was followed by Carr and Jones. It was the first time I had seen Norman Jones since the meeting in the Liverpool hotel. He seemed tired and raised a half smile when he saw us. He waved but made no attempt to shake hands. Carr just nodded at us. They sat down opposite us and Malik took the chair at the head of the table. One of his colleagues sat further down the other end to make a note of the meeting.

Malik summarised the position as he saw it. I then referred to the letters from both Stuckman junior and Carr and the replies I had sent. I said I hoped for a positive response from Stuckman.

Carr broke in: "why should he write to you again. He's already explained the position to you and there's really nothing more to say."

It was deliberately provocative but I declined to rise to the bait and merely said that if the UK part of the company was facing a strike I thought he would have something to say. Carr shrugged his shoulders. Norman Jones looked uneasy but said nothing.

I then suggested Leila should outline the position and she made a fairly long statement about negotiations in the past with the company, the pay claim, the new job evaluation scheme and the strength of feeling in the company. She mentioned her meeting with the branch committee the previous day in Liverpool. The meeting had gone well and there was support for the ballot and—though she didn't mention it—even Tony Holland had been supportive without causing any trouble. She mentioned too that Carr's letter had seemed to exacerbate the situation and asked what Carr had meant by the company looking at other forms of staff representation.

Carr said "it means exactly what it says. And these things take time. It seems to me that the union is hell bent on a strike and that must be because of a fundamental weakness in the union's position."

Another provocative remark and Leila stated that it was not helpful. Norman Jones was looking more uneasy by now and asked what the union hoped to achieve.

"It's quite simple," said Leila. "We would like a negotiating meeting to pursue our claims but if the company refuses then we have to pursue them by other means."

Malik looked at Carr. The strands of hair covering his largely bald pate seemed to have gone awry and he went red.

"We agreed to come here because ACAS asked us to," said Carr. "We came to listen to what you have said, but there's nothing in what you have said to encourage us to think that you are not deliberately stoking up the situation and we have no intention of negotiating with you on the claims." Carr then sat back in his chair.

Leila stated that we had majority membership in the company and that it made no sense for the company to say they were looking at other forms of staff representation.

Carr smiled grimly and said that if that was the case then why didn't we take them to the Central Arbitration Committee with a claim for recognition. He knew of course that that would take considerable time and that the company would claim they had not derecognised us as such, only withdrawn from the procedural agreement. It would be rather spurious and really a distinction without a difference but, I supposed, technically correct. Also it was clear to me that he knew all about the cash payers and thought the company might put pressure on some of them—or most of them—if there was a ballot of the entire staff of the company. If that happened and we didn't get the magical fifty per cent plus one in a recognition ballot, then things would be grim indeed for us.

I responded that we didn't want to wait for the CAC to be able to negotiate on our claims.

Leila then outlined the ballot timetable, looking at Jones as she spoke. She mentioned that their membership was increasing as a result of the situation and particularly the publicity the dispute was getting. She finished by asking Jones direct why couldn't they fix a date for a negotiating meeting now and then the union could suspend any action as a result of the ballot. Jones opened his mouth to speak but before he could do so Carr said that Leila had already had the answer to that.

It was clear who was running the company's policy. I looked at Malik and he looked at Jones but he said nothing.

I asked if I was going to get a response to my letters to Stuckman and to Carr. Carr said he would be writing to me in due course but there was nothing really to add to what he had already said. I pressed the Stuckman point but Carr repeated that he didn't think Stuckman had anything to reply to.

"It's all been said" he concluded.

I made one last effort.

"This dispute could get very serious" I said. "There's a lot of interest in it and I know the Government is watching it closely". That was an exaggeration on my part but there was no doubt in my mind that Bob Wilson at DTI would be interested in what happened. It could affect foreign investment and particularly investment from the US. I remembered some years ago when Japanese companies had come to the UK in a big way and the concern then expressed by Government at any suggestion of unions taking industrial action in those companies.

After I had finished there was no response from Carr or Jones. Malik asked them if either wanted to say anything but both declined. He then looked at Leila and me and asked if we wanted to add anything.

Leila said she would like it recorded that the union had tried to get a negotiating meeting so the claims could be pursued peacefully and that I had emphasised how the dispute could get very serious for all concerned. Malik nodded and said that would be recorded and then said the meeting was closed. Carr and Jones left without saying goodbye or even looking at us. I thanked Malik for his efforts and said Leila would be keeping him informed as to what happened next. Then Leila, Julia and I left to go to the room Malik had set aside for our press conference.

On the Friday morning Leila went to the offices of the Industrial Foundation which were situated in a close just off the Mall. Frank Hallard went with her and took a parcel of pamphlets outlining the job evaluation scheme with him. They had discussed the likely attendance at the seminar and both had pitched it at under thirty. Much to their surprise when they got to the offices the director met them with the news that there were nearly one hundred people attending. There were quite a few people from public companies—personnel and human resource professionals—from some Government agencies, a few Government departments and somewhat surprisingly a number from different local authorities. There were also some from management magazines and consultancies. The conference room was only intended for a maximum of seventy and the others were crammed in and standing round the walls. The director seemed delighted and said he was sure all the recent publicity must have sparked the interest.

The press publicity following the abortive meeting at ACAS had again been quite considerable. Charles Pitney had brought along copies of the previous day's *Wall Street Journal* to give to Leila and Carmichael in case Julia Cardon hadn't managed to get hold of a copy. He had done a half page on the dispute. He had referred to stockholders' concern in Industry3M and sketched out the background of the company. It was mainly what he had told Leila and Carmichael in the pub though he had toned down some of the concern about the company's borrowing and profitability. He had, though, mentioned the proposed expansion in the far east. The other newspapers had concentrated on the ballot timetable and the likely sequence of events if there was a ballot majority for action. *The Times* had asked about Government involvement and Carmichael had merely said he was keeping the TUC informed and that he had no doubt they would be keeping the Government informed.

The director of the Industrial Foundation was chairing the seminar session for Leila. He introduced her with a few words and then Leila spoke for nearly one hour. She referred—almost in passing—to the dispute with Industry3M but spent the large part of her speech on the principles of the job evaluation scheme and how it should be implemented. After she had ended the director called for questions and there were many. Some were hostile to the scheme but most were genuinely inquisitive.

Leila explained how the essence of the scheme was to combine the elements of self assessment and objective assessment into a scheme that was workable and could improve efficiency. One of the questioners claimed the combination was impossible, another that it was excessively bureaucratic. Leila dealt with both and then—with the director's agreement—invited Frank Hallard to deal with some of the technicalities of the scheme. All in all, the session was a big success for Leila and she and Frank Hallard got a good round of applause when the director called the session closed.

Hallard left the pamphlets with the director and said he would be happy to meet with the Foundation's staff to go into the scheme in more detail if the director wanted. As he was speaking one of the participants came up to Leila. It was John Dryden, the deputy director of the CBI—the Confederation of British Industry, the main employers organization in the country.

"Leila," he said, holding out his hand. "We've met before. John Dryden of CBI."

Leila remembered him and shook his hand. He was a small and rather fat man but Leila had been impressed when she had previously heard him speak at a management seminar and had also met him when he had attended part of the previous year's annual Congress of the TUC. He had worked in the motor industry many years previously and then set up his own management consultancy before getting the number two job in the CBI.

Dryden asked Leila whether she had time for a chat and suggested they go to his club, the Oxford & Cambridge in Pall Mall which was not far away. She looked at her watch. It was just coming up to midday and she was going back to the office.

"I was going back to the office but I would be happy for a chat." She turned to Hallard who had just finished talking to the director.

"Frank, I'm just going for a drink and a chat with John here. I'll see you back at the office."

Hallard grinned and said he quite understood. He knew Leila well and often pulled her leg with suggested innuendos that she was starting illicit relationships. Leila grinned too and replied that she thought he would say that and then left with Dryden.

As they entered the Oxford & Cambridge Club and went up the stairs Leila asked Dryden if it was all right for a woman now to enter the club's bar. Dryden smiled and said it was now open to women as well as men. Like several of the Pall Mall clubs women had not been allowed in the members' bar but, again like most of the other clubs, the rules had been changed and women could join as full members with full access to all the facilities. "We had a vote to admit women but didn't get the right percentage of those entitled to vote even though we had a majority of those voting" explained Dryden. "So we had to have another ballot to change the rules to allow for a majority of those voting but before that we had to have a ballot to reconsider the matter then before the original period of years designated for reconsideration was up. Almost Jesuitical" he smiled. "The TUC would have been proud of us. And women can now have the privilege of paying the full subscription."

Leila smiled and they both entered the bar. Dryden got two gin and tonics and handed one to Leila. They sat down and Dryden said how much he had enjoyed Leila's talk.

"Job evaluation" he said "is not the most exciting subject but I thought you explained it well and certainly your union's scheme is ingenious but has it been tried anywhere?"

Leila explained that really the scheme was an amalgam of many of the current schemes currently in operation but had the added refinement of being capable of adaptation to changes in the structure of the workforce and the nature of the jobs carried out. She emphasised that the trouble with a lot of the current schemes was that they were not transparent in their implementation and didn't take account of the increasing pattern of part time working or job sharing. Above all, she said, the self assessment process would make the scheme easily understood and be seen to be fair.

She started to say more but stopped. "But you know this John, because I saw you taking notes as I was speaking."

Dryden nodded and swallowed his gin and tonic in one go.

"Yes, you're quite right. But what I wanted is to see how far your union is going in getting it accepted. Am I right in saying that no company has yet accepted it?"

"Yes, you're right but someone has to be first and it just happens that we tried it our first with our national committee for Industry3M. The pay claim was up for submission and we thought we would combine it with the JE scheme. But there are quite a few other companies where the claim has now been submitted."

"I suppose you can't tell me which those companies are?"

Leila saw no problem with that and mentioned Transport International, Hokkaido and Teening & Sykes. She didn't mention Leisure Sport because she knew Hazel Bellini was raising it with her national committee on the Monday.

Dryden grunted. "They're all members of ours but—as you probably know—Industry3M is not a CBI member. How do you normally get on with them?"

Leila told him about her involvement, particularly since the absence of Tim Burke, the national official, on prolonged sick leave with cancer. She mentioned the attitude of the company and especially that of John Carr from the company's European Group head office.

"Yes, I've heard about him."

Leila noted that Carr seemed to be well known in some quarters but also noted that Dryden seemed a bit dismissive in his mention of his name.

They chatted for a bit more about the existing job evaluation schemes in other companies and Dryden accepted that since the original introduction of job evaluation schemes in the late 1960's and early 1970's it was clearly time for schemes to be looked at again and employers could not stand still in ignoring the changes of employment structures on the existing schemes.

Dryden got another two gin and tonics while politely refusing Leila's offer to buy them. "You're not a member here so you can't buy anything" he said. "Anyway it was me that asked you over here." He said it pleasantly and Leila smiled.

"Your union could be on a winner with this JE scheme, then" he said. "A number of my people have read about your dispute with Industry3M—and I particularly noted that piece in the *Wall Street Journal*. There's a meeting of our employment committee in a couple of weeks and I'm due to attend that so I thought a chat between us would help me clarify the position with the committee."

Leila mentioned that there was interest in the scheme with some of the foreign affiliated unions in Staff International but didn't go into any detail. She respected Dryden's point and wanted to be forthcoming but, as she reminded herself, he was a major employers representative so she did not want to give him too much information. He was bright and experienced but his viewpoint would inevitably be different from hers even if at times they would appear to coincide.

On the Monday morning Leila gave me a report on her talk with John Dryden of the CBI. I had met Dryden on several occasions and always found him realistic and easy to get on with. It was one of the reasons, I supposed, why he had got the CBI job in the first place. It was perfectly reasonable for him to chat with Leila and it was far better for him—and the CBI employment committee to which he would be reporting—to have our side of the story rather than rely oh what version they might or might not have heard from Industry3M. It was interesting, though, that Industry3M was not a CBI member but the other companies where we had lodged the JE claim were.

The rest of that week was, as usual, pretty busy. Leila had gone to a meeting of the Glasgow union branch committee of our Industry3M members and that had apparently gone well. I knew Macallister was a good man and not likely to be alarmist about some of the circulars the company was issuing.

They had issued two more circulars that week. The first was about our ACAS meeting where we had met face to face. It was signed by Norman Jones the chief executive but clearly was written by John Carr. It said we had proposed nothing new and were obviously hell bent on provoking a serious industrial relations problem. The company reiterated that there was no point in a negotiating meeting with the union when there was such a gulf between the union claims and the company's attitude. Again they did not say that they were derecognising the union but were looking at the whole issue of staff representation.

The second circular was a direct appeal to union members to take account of the effect of any strike on the company's competitive position and finished with the rather ominous statement that the company would have to respond to any industrial action and warned staff that no one owed them a living and that they could not stand idly by if the union was jeopardising the company's trading position.

Leila had issued three circulars in the week and had given our view as to the somewhat abortive ACAS meeting, the growing membership in the company—our membership department had reported it now stood at 2,700—that claims on the new job evaluation scheme had been lodged with a number of other companies and given the latest industry wide figures on average pay settlements, price inflation and average earnings.

Our organisers had met the committees of all our Industry3M branches or—where the committees had not met—the leading lay officials of them. Even the more doubtful committees, including the Bristol branch committee, had reported strong support for the union's position—but I wasn't sure how deep those feelings would prove to be—and that the company circulars had not made any significant change in members' perception of the dispute.

So far it was looking reasonable so when Leila and I met with the officials on the Friday afternoon to discuss the ballot figures the mood was optimistic.

On the Friday morning the Electoral Reform Society had faxed Leila the ballot result. A total of 1600 members had voted in the ballot. There were just under 1200 who had voted for action. Almost all of those had ticked the boxes for the overtime ban, a one day strike and then a three day strike. About sixty of those had voted just for the overtime ban and against the strikes. 410 had voted against any form of industrial action.

We all met in our small conference room and I asked Leila to report on the figures.

Leila said the participation in the ballot was high by any trade union ballot standards—over sixty per cent had voted. Frank Hallard commented that that was higher than the percentage vote in the last parliamentary general election, twice as high as the usual turnout at local elections and significantly higher than in most shareholders annual general meetings. The majority of basically three to one in favour of action—some 1200 to 400—was again high and as good as we could expect. Leila made the valid point thought that the company would be bound to point out that the figures only showed 1200 out of a total staff of 5000 were in favour of action and they would trumpet the fact that 1200 out of 5000 was less than a quarter. This meant for us that if industrial action was authorised then every effort should be made to maximise support for it, whether individual members had voted for or against it or had not voted at all.

Alan Whitchurch reported on the accounts from the organisers on their branch visits and Val Holloway—Dan Michael's number two in the membership department—referred to the recent membership recruitment figures. No one asked specifically about Dan Michael. Leila had reported that he was on sick leave but I think a number of those present had heard rumours about the new sexual harassment allegations.

Julia Cardon had done a good job in providing everyone with a file of all the press cuttings on our dispute since the original Liverpool open meeting. Then the three officials concerned reported on the submission of the job evaluation claims in Teening & Sykes, Transport International and Hokkaido. Hazel Bellini was the last to report. The national committee for Leisure & Sport had met on the previous Monday but had wanted to defer any submission of the JE scheme. However they would be reconsidering the matter at their next scheduled meeting in three weeks time.

We all agreed that we would recommend that the Industry3M national committee should propose implementation of the action to the national executive committee at its meeting on the Sunday. But there was one worrying point when Hazel Bellinin stated that the main opposition in the Leisure & Sport national committee to submitting the JE scheme to their company came from the two extreme left members. I knew that there was an unofficial grouping of the trots who sat on the various union national committees and I suspected they were in touch with similar groupings in other unions. If the trots were not all in favour of submitting the JE scheme wherever we could then there must be some ulterior purpose. I couldn't for the moment understand what that might be.

Leila had picked up the point when Bellini had spoken and said she would like a chat with her after had we had finished.

All in all, though, things were as positive as they could be. I asked Leila to set out a timetable for the proposed action if the national executive committee gave the go ahead. She reminded everyone about the period of notice that we would have to give Industry3M under the current employment legislation and said she wanted to meet Alan Whitchurch, the national organiser, on the Monday morning to go over the organisation for the action. Whitchurch and the others would all be at the national executive committee on Sunday so they could hear the debate on the ballot result and feel the atmosphere at the committee. Once the decision was taken, however, there would be a great deal of work to be done on organising the action.

In a way I thought I was almost glad that Tim Burke, the national official for Industry3M, was away on sick leave but then instantly regretted the thought. He did have cancer. It was just that I couldn't think of a better official than Leila to deal with the whole dispute. If Burke had been at work I could always have asked Leila to take charge but no national official worth his or her salt would take too kindly to having the union's Deputy General Secretary drafted in over their heads.

The industry3M national committee meeting was in the same central London hotel as before and again Leila got there on the Saturday morning in plenty of time. She wanted another word with Ian Macallister. Apart from the meeting with the Glasgow branch committee she had spoken to him several times on the telephone in the week and he had always sounded very calm and supportive. This time there was only the one item on the agenda: the ballot results.

Again there was a full attendance of the committee. Julia Cardon also attended and—as with the officials on the previous day—handed round the sheaf of press cuttings to the members of the committee. Alan Whitchurch had also asked Leila if he could attend in case there was any question of the allocation of organisers if there was industrial action in the company and Leila had readily agreed.

Macallister opened the meeting by stressing the serious nature of the business they had to discuss and then asked Leila for a report.

Leila spelt out the ballot results and Muriel, her secretary, handed round the copy of the fax from the Electoral Reform Society. She referred to the meetings held by the organisers of the committees and leading lay officials and spent some time in detailing the ACAS meeting held with the company. She wanted to make it absolutely clear that there had not been the slightest intention of the company to reach any sort of accommodation with the union and how it was now evident that John Carr was the man in charge. She specifically mentioned the recommendations of the union's finance and administration committee on paying hardship money rather than strike pay and concluded by stating that both the General Secretary and herself recommended that the national committee should ask the national executive committee to authorise the overtime ban and the one day strike in the light of the ballot result. The national committee should also recommend that the national committee should authorise the General Secretary to implement the vote for a three day strike if there was no move towards a peaceful resolution of the dispute after the one day strike.

Macallister then called for questions and comment.

Leila looked at Tony Hammond, thin faced and angry looking as ever. He didn't speak at first but waited for several of the others to ask about the timing of the strike, the monitoring of an overtime ban and arrangements for picketing offices for the one day strike. Both she and Alan Whitchurch dealt with the questions and all seemed satisfied.

Hammond then put his hand up to speak and Macallister pointed to him.

"Yes, Tony, your point?"

Hammond started slowly but then spoke faster and faster until in the end he sounded almost breathless. He asked about publicity and newsletters. He said there had not been much press publicity and there was a total lack of sufficient union newsletters. The company was winning what he called the battle of publicity and it was almost too late for the union now to do anything about it.

It was so blatant that even some of the committee members who rarely spoke at all seemed to gasp in disbelief. Leila smiled as Hammond was speaking and that had only made him the more angry. Leila knew that his statements were carefully designed to lay the ground for blame if at the end of the day the company still refused any sort of agreement or compromise. And it was always easier to blame the union rather than accept the fact that industrial action had not succeeded. It was also so simple, she thought, to blame an alleged lack of publicity because there was no magic amount of publicity that everyone would accept as sufficient. It would also be a marker for criticising the union's officials if the dispute was not won. It also gave the impression that it was only members like Hammond who were alive to the realities of the position.

Leila then calmly went over the total number of newsletters since the Liverpool open meeting had been held—twelve in total—and the amount of press publicity as evidenced by the reports that Julia Cardon had circulated. The rest of the committee seemed more than satisfied and Hammond said no more.

Leila had had a chat with Hazel Bellini after the officials meeting the previous afternoon. It appeared that the two trots on the Leisure & Sport national committee had advocated waiting before submission of the JE scheme because they said it might not be appropriate to their company. The number of part time staff was disproportionately higher than in most other companies and the company might be more easily resist such a scheme because of this. Leila knew the argument was fallacious: the number of part-timers in Leisure & Sport was high but the scheme was deliberately drawn up to allow for different mixes of full and part-time staff. Hazel Bellini said she had mentioned this but the way the two trots had put the point had seemed to be reasonable and the majority of the national committee had gone along with them. She assured Leila that at their next meeting she would push hard for the scheme to be claimed at the earliest opportunity.

After further discussion the Industry3M national committee had voted unanimously for the motion calling upon the national executive committee to authorise the overtime ban to start in two weeks time, the fifteenth of July, and the one day strike to take place on the same day. The timing of the three day strike would be left to the General Secretary to determine in the light of what happened. Leila noted that even Lillian Fairweather from the Brighton branch had voted for the motion.

John Carmichael had agreed with Leila that he would not attend the national committee meeting; he had every confidence that Leila could handle it and he had a one day TUC conference on health and safety at which he would be one of the speakers. Leila noted too that when she had given Carmichael's reason for non attendance at the national committee, Hammond had not said anything. Undoubtedly though he would have noted the fact.

The TUC's one day conference had gone well and about eighty union members and officials from the TUC's affiliated unions had attended. My own speech had been reasonably well received. I had taken the opportunity to have a word with John Miller at the conference about the Industry3M position and also mentioned to him what Charles Pitney of the *Wall Street Journal* had told us about the company's financial position. Miller told me that he would be keeping Bob Wilson at DTI informed and suggested that, assuming the one day strike would go ahead, Leila and I should seek a private meeting with Wilson.

The national executive committee on the Sunday was successful. Les Martin, the union's President, had conducted it well and the national committee's recommendations had been carried without dissent. Leila had again spoken succinctly on the dispute, the ACAS meeting and the ballot results. I noticed that Tony Hammond didn't mention anything about publicity even though Leila had told me of the tirade he had made about it at the previous day's national committee.

The recommendation from the union's finance and administration committee on hardship pay—as distinct from regular strike pay—had been agreed with a specific proviso that if a three day strike was necessary and was implemented then before any further ballots or action there would have to be a fundamental re-think on the whole issue of strike pay.

After the meeting finished we had yet another press conference. This time nearly twenty journalists had turned up at the hotel. I chaired the conference and left all the talking to Leila. She told them the ballot figures and then the agreement of the national executive committee for the overtime ban to start on 15 July and the one day strike to take place then. She emphasised that we all hoped the company would negotiate with us before then and try and reach a sensible settlement but made it clear that if the company did not move at all from its current stance then the action would definitely go ahead. She also mentioned the distinct possibility of a three day strike following that if there was still no movement from the company.

We had discussed before the national executive meeting what to tell the press. It would have been daft to try and keep the information secret as inevitably some of the journalists would contact some of the national executive members and, with the best will in the world, they were bound to find out. We wanted a clear and factual report in the press and the only way to secure that would be to tell them straight.

It also meant that the company would learn of the strike date from Monday morning's papers rather than from us but again there was no way round that. I would fax a letter to Norman Jones the chief executive first thing on the Monday morning but there was no way I could contact him on this Sunday.

A number of the questions from the press were obviously on the likely effect of the overtime ban and the one day strike and Leila answered them realistically.

Overtime was patchy in the company. There was quite a bit of overtime worked in the Liverpool head office but not much in the branches. The one day strike would affect the company in that new contracts would be delayed and some of the client companies would be inconvenienced. It could also make some companies think twice about using the contract labour services from Industry3M. Leila also said that the Atlanta head office of the company would not like the publicity the action would generate and—hopefully—would tell the UK head office to settle the dispute.

Charles Pitney from the *Wall Street Journal* asked when a three day strike was likely and Leila said that if such action was necessary it would probably take place fairly soon after 15 July. If that failed to move the company then both the union's national committee in the company and the national executive committee would hold further meetings to consider further action.

The reporter from the *Daily Telegraph* asked what members thought of damaging their company by going on strike and thereby jeopardising their own future. Leila replied that that was the classic dilemma in any industrial dispute and that was why they hoped the company would agree to a negotiating meeting. What else could the union do?

I thought Leila had handled the press well and told her so as we collected our papers and left the room. Les Martin and Jane Toff had both attended the press conference but had not said anything. They clearly were pleased at the way the day had gone and suggested we went over to the pub across the road.

The suggestion was agreed by all concerned without dissent.

On Monday morning Leila dictated a note to Muriel, her secretary, on all the things that would have to be done between then and the fifteenth of July. The union's organisers should again visit the branch committees in the company; Leila herself would go up to Liverpool and meet the committee there. She would also go up to Liverpool on the evening of Sunday the fourteenth of July and stay until the Tuesday. Muriel would book her into the hotel for the two nights. She would suggest to Clive Bristow that they should consider a march through Liverpool on the fifteenth which could start by the company's offices and end at the river Mersey just by the old Royal Liver building. The local police would have to be informed as would the police in all the places where the company's branches were. Each of the branches would be picketed from seven in the morning until seven in the evening.

Leila knew she would have to speak to Alan Whitchurch as soon as possible as he would be responsible for arranging the members to be on picket duty, draw up the rosters, arrange for placards and arm bands and also get Julia Cardon to print out leaflets which the pickets could hand out to the public. The organisers would need to discuss with the local officials whether to hold open meetings on the Sunday evening—doubtful in that probably not many would turn up—or the Monday lunchtime. She thought the latter would be the best and she would need to suggest speakers at each of the meetings. In some cases the organisers would speak but perhaps some of the union's national officials could step in.

She would suggest that the General Secretary should be in the union's head office and that she would be the focal point in the Liverpool hotel on the actual day of the strike. All the organisers could report direct to her there. Alan Whitchurch could also be with her at the Liverpool hotel. Julia Cardon would stay in Clapham and handle press queries there.

Muriel went to print out the note and said she would call Alan Whitchurch to come to her office when it was done. Leila decided she would then have a chat with John Carmichael and outline the arrangements. She would suggest to Carmichael that they have a meeting of all the union's national officials at the end of the following week, the Friday, so that all could be briefed on the position. In the meantime she would contact ACAS again and see if another meeting with the company was a possibility.

Leila knew there were lots of other things to do as there always were in any industrial dispute and the next two weeks would be very busy. She also knew that the rest of the union's activities did not stand still and there were all the union members—other than those in Industry3M—whose needs should be met, and for whom claims be pursued, meetings held and individual problems taken up. The union had some 260,000 members grouped in 420 union branches in eight regions throughout England, Scotland and Wales. There were altogether eighty national committees corresponding to the eighty different procedural agreements the union had with companies.

Take away the Industry3M members she thought, and there were still over a quarter of a million union members who wanted their interests pursued and protected.

Chapter Six

The Strike

"Mrs Smith?"

Leila was awake before the telephone rang and it was ten minutes before her alarm call was due. It was Monday the fifteenth of July: strike day. And she had been awake for the last hour.

"Leo Patullo here again. Press Association. I'm sorry to make these early calls a bit of a habit."

Leila grunted and managed a "good morning".

"Sorry to call so early," said Patullo again. Leila looked again at her watch. Half past five in the morning. Did the Press Association never sleep? Then she realised that was a daft question. They acted as a service for all the main newspapers and media outlets and usually had someone on duty all the time.

"I just wondered what your movements would be today. And Julia gave us your number at the hotel as the contact point."

Leila sat up in bed and collected her thoughts.

"The pickets will be there from seven this morning. There should be about five or six there at the front door with a similar number at the other entrance at the back. And then they'll be relieved at about two hour intervals. We finish the picketing at seven this evening. I'll be there when they start and when they knock off. But Leo—"she thought she knew him well enough to call him by his first name and she knew he was only doing his job so she didn't have to be crotchety—"you might like to come along to the march and meeting. We start from the company's offices at half past twelve and finish with a rally by the Royal Liver building on the waterfront."

"I'll be there," said Patullo but perhaps I might catch you at the picket line to get a comment."

"Fine," said Leila. "If you don't catch me there then I'll be here in the hotel. As you say, we're using this as the focal point and there will either be me or one of my colleagues here all the time."

Patullo again apologised for calling so early but said he was being pushed for some copy for the papers. Leila said she quite understood and was getting up soon anyway.

As she showered and dressed she reflected that the amount of press interest was quite considerable. Admittedly there were not nearly so many industrial disputes these days and nowhere near the number of strikes that there had been twenty years ago, but, even so, Leila thought it was still surprising that so many papers were interested in the dispute. She was certainly glad though as she knew that publicity was really their most powerful weapon.

She hoped the strike would be a success today but then, what was success? Even if all the union members came out on strike for the day there would still be nearly half the workforce working and the company would undoubtedly trumpet that it was business as usual. In many ways she reflected, it was the press publicity leading up to a strike that was the most powerful weapon in their armoury, particularly with the inevitable speculation about how well supported the strike would be and what would be the impact on the company's business.

Anyway, the die was cast for today. She had arranged everything for the day, the pickets had been organised, the leaflets printed and distributed to all the relevant union officials and members, the police had been informed and the programme of marches and speakers had been sorted out for Liverpool and the other eight places where the company's branches were. Her attempts to get another meeting at ACAS had come to naught. Art Malik had done his best, she believed, but apparently the company had simply said they would not meet the union unless the union withdrew its claims. What was the point of that Leila had asked and Malik had told her that in his view it was clear the company had no intention of seeking a compromise in the dispute: but he had insisted to Leila that she could not quote him as saying that.

It must be the American angle, she thought. That was why the media was so interested. There was no doubt that Industry3M was one of the new type of companies—supplying labour to a whole range of different companies—but it must be the fact that it was American owned that made it newsworthy.

Muriel had booked a suite at the hotel and as Leila left her bedroom she saw that Alan Whitchurch was already sitting the lounge room of her suite. He had been booked in at a bedroom further along the corridor.

"Nice and early, Alan" she said.

"Of course. I've been here for hours."

It was not true as they both knew but Whitchurch had been there for half an hour. He had arranged with Leila that he would be in the room for the first couple of hours while Leila went to join the first picket at seven o'clock. He had asked the union's organisers in each of the eight cities where the company had branch offices to contact him at regular intervals throughout the day and that way he could get a picture of what was happening. Leila would then telephone Julia Cardon at the union headquarters in Clapham with appropriate items for the press and she would also keep Carmichael posted.

Leila liked Whitchurch and was glad he was with her in Liverpool. She could rely on him to keep a level head as the inevitable conflicting reports came in from the picket lines. She also thought wryly that it was just as well that he was gay so there would be no jokes about sharing a hotel room with him.

"I'm off to have a cup of coffee in the dining room and then to the pickets. I'll be back just after nine and see you then." Leila smiled as she left the room.

Leila walked from the hotel to the company's UK head office. It was a nice morning; warm and a clear blue sky. She felt relieved now that the actual strike day had arrived but she just hoped all would go well.

Leila got to the company's head office at about ten minutes to seven. She wanted to be there when the large office doors of the company's UK head office opened at seven o'clock. As she approached the company's office she saw Clive Bristow and Ted Davis outside with four others. They had armbands on saying 'official picket' and some placards saying 'official strike—Clerical & General Union'. She recognised three of the four but didn't know the young woman talking to Davis. She seemed to be wearing what looked like an army greatcoat and wore big black boots and didn't have an armband on.

Leila smiled at the pickets: "good morning for it, isn't it?" They smiled back, all except Davis and the woman he was speaking to. He seemed to be getting increasingly irate. Leila went over to him.

"What's up Ted?"

Davis looked at Leila, exasperated and angry.

"I don't know who this is," he said gesturing to the woman, "but she's not one of ours and I'm trying gently to suggest that she should not be here."

Leila had another look at the woman. Probably in her twenties and apart from the greatcoat and the boots she was wearing a pair of jeans and a T-shirt which bore the legend 'justice now!'. She must be hot in that coat, thought Leila, even though she didn't have it done up.

"What do you want?" Leila asked her.

"I'm here to help you on the picket line." She said it defiantly.

"No, I'm afraid you're not" said Leila. "This is an official union picket and you're not a union member, so please leave."

"That's just what I've been telling her" said Davis. "But apparently she wants to show her solidarity."

Leila waited for the woman to respond. Thin, tight lipped and angular. Why she had on an army greatcoat on a warm July morning was, Leila thought, a question she had no intention of asking. But she could guess what she was doing. Just then two young men approached. They were both wearing jeans and similar T-shirts to the woman. None of the union members on the picket line showed any hint of recognition at them. One of them nodded at the army greatcoat woman. They looked at Leila.

"We're here to help" one of them said.

"We don't want your help" replied Leila. "Now please move on."

Clive Bristow and the other three on picket duty had gathered round.

One of the jeans and T-shirt men said "we want to help. This is a strike isn't it? And we're socialists who support the strike, so what's the problem?"

Leila guessed they were from the Socialist Workers Party or a similar group. Invariably they would turn up on picket lines whenever a strike was going on. In former days before employment legislation had curtailed unions' ability to launch and run strikes, the trots—Leila lumped them all under that title—would fasten on to picket lines, marches and rallies. She remembered on a TUC protest march in Manchester once, the trots had marched alongside carrying buckets into which they urged members of the public to put cash. Several people did put some cash into the buckets, thinking it was towards the TUC's official campaign. It was part of what some critics had called 'side entryism': get involved, or even join—on the fringe at first but then gradually in the middle—a campaign, a march or a rally and distribute their own banners, placards and leaflets.

"The problem," said Leila slowly, "is that you are not union members and we don't want you here. You are not helping. And there are limits on the number of pickets the law allows."

The woman shouted out "but Tony said we could join you."

Leila was certain she must be referring to Tony Hammond and she had no doubt that Hammond would have said that.

Bristow said "Leila, there are some people coming in." He pointed across the street where several people were heading towards the company's front doors. They were obviously members of the company's staff and were going to work. It was seven o'clock and the doors were being opened.

Leila grasped the woman's arms and pushed her out of the way, with the two men starting to pull her back. This was just what she didn't want to happen but then she saw a policeman coming down the road towards them. It flashed through her mind that things were going very wrong so quickly. The picket line was there but the three trots were causing trouble and it would be ironic if a policeman had to intervene to sort it out. One of the men was clutching at Leila's arm. She turned and put her face close to his and muttered savagely at him. He appeared surprised and let go of her am and motioned to the other two to move away.

Thank goodness, thought Leila. But the greatcoat woman had to say something: "your strike's going to fail. You know that don't you." The woman and the two men then moved off.

People were crossing the picket line and entering the company's building. The pickets handed over leaflets which most of the people entering took. One or two threw them on the ground. Some smiled at the pickets. After all they were staff of the company and clearly Bristow, Davis and the others knew who they were.

The policeman stood a little way off and then went over to Leila and asked whether there was any problem.

"No, all OK, thank you" said Leila.

The policeman looked young to her but then, she reflected, most of them did now. The union's north west organiser had telephoned the police in both Manchester and Liverpool to give them details of the location and timing of the pickets.

The policeman hesitated. He was tall and broad shouldered and looked friendly. He raised his eyebrows at Leila.

"Do you mind, madam, if I ask you what you said to that man to get those three to move away?"

Leila replied "no, I don't mind but I don't want you to think I speak like that all the time." She paused and then carried on. "What

I said to him was that he should fuck off right away or else I would accuse him of making a sexual assault on me. I don't think he had expected me to say that."

The policeman looked surprised and then grinned.

"Well, it seems to have done the trick, doesn't it? Anyway if you have any trouble then let me know or ring the station." He went over to chat with Davis, Bristow and the others.

By a quarter past seven Leila estimated that about fifty staff would have crossed their picket line and gone into work. The company operated a form of flexitime with core time being ten until three. The hours outside that were left to the individual but the majority preferred to come in early, between seven and eight o'clock. So fifty staff coming in then wasn't too bad at all, thought Leila. It depended how many had entered by the back entrance and, of course, how many would arrive later: but it was a good start. She told Bristow that she was going round to see the pickets by the back entrance to the building.

On the other picket line she recognised Larry Brent from the meeting at the start of the dispute. He told her that about thirty staff had entered the building and one had turned back after listening to what he had said. Altogether, including the IT staff in a separate building, there were some twelve hundred staff working in the Liverpool offices. So, eighty staff going in so far was certainly not too bad at all.

"Good stuff," said Leila. "Any problems?"

"Not so far but it's a pity we don't have the regional organiser here."

It was an understandable point. Leila knew full well that the union's resources were always stretched when it came to industrial action. Each of the unions eight regions had a full time organiser based in a small office. The north west regional organiser was based in Manchester. Liverpool was part of his region but he was in charge of the picketing of the company's office in Manchester.

Leila briefly explained the position to Brent. She knew they should employ more staff but finances were tight. The absence of Tim Burke through cancer was an added blow but, she told him, she was there and Alan Whitchurch was in the hotel. The regional organiser was the only official in Manchester. Whitchurch would be coming down to the pickets as soon as Leila went back. She spoke to the other pickets there and then moved off to the separate building housing the company's information technology department.

The building was on the right hand side of the main office and reached by a small side road. It had one entrance and Leila saw five people on the picket line there. She saw Tony Hammond and June Trevor, red hair shining in the morning sunshine. She had heard there about ten trots in the IT department and she presumed the pickets were five of these: she knew that Tony Hammond seemed to have the union committee packed with them. Then she noticed the young woman in the army greatcoat and black boots was there as well but she moved away as soon as she saw Leila.

"Good morning Tony. How's it going?"

Hammond smiled thinly at her. "All OK so far. No one has come in yet."

Membership among the IT staff was the union's highest in the company but there was over twenty percent of the staff who were not members, so if no one had crossed the picket line then that was indeed good news.

Leila asked about the IT managers because she reckoned they would try and run the centre on a limited basis. Hammond explained that they didn't normally come in until eight o'clock and they would not be able to do much when they did. She wondered whether this was just a hope or a reality.

"We're fairly solid here," he said proudly. "By the way what was wrong having Sylvia—" he gestured to the retreating figure of the army greatcoat—"to help out."

"You know the answer to that as well as I do, Tony."

Leila turned to the others and asked them how the IT staff were feeling. At first they reluctant to speak to her—goodness knows what Hammond would have told them about her, Leila thought—but after a while they seemed to thaw and the conversation got quite animated. The IT membership had been particularly keen on the job evaluation scheme and several of the pickets asked Leila about how the claim was going in other companies. Leila briefly brought them up to date and made a point of mentioning that the union's national committee at Leisure & Sport had decided to defer submitting a claim for the scheme. She noted that Hammond didn't say anything at this and presumably, she thought, the others had no knowledge of it.

After a few more minutes Leila said she was going back to the other pickets and then would be available in her hotel room if there was any problem. She wanted to see how things were going with the other pickets at the company's eight branches throughout the country. Before going she reminded them of the march planned for twelve thirty. Hammond assured her they were geared up for that and would ensure that the picket line was fully staffed as well.

I had got to the office at eight that morning. I knew that Leila would not be phoning in until after nine but I wanted to be available in the office in case there was an emergency. I remembered one occasion some years ago when we had had a strike in an electronics factory in Leicester and the organiser had failed to notify the police of the pickets. There had been a big kerfuffle but it was eventually sorted out by me telephoning the police superintendent and eating humble pie. Every time since—and there had been a few—I had wanted to be sure personally that everything was going all right.

I reflected on the events of the previous two weeks since the meeting of the national executive committee meeting. There had been some good publicity. I had written to the company's Atlanta head office telling them about the action and asking them to get the

UK part of the company to agree to proper negotiations but received no reply. I had written to Norman Jones as chief executive of the UK company but received a short reply from John Carr saying that the company had no intention of negotiating under what he called 'threats' and urging me to call off the proposed action.

I had written to Bob Wilson, the minister of state at the DTI, asking if Leila and I could have a meeting with him. Wilson had been a senior official of one of the manufacturing unions before getting parachuted into a safe Labour seat two general elections ago. He had made rapid progress since then and was tipped for a future Cabinet post. To be fair to him, he had kept in regular touch with John Miller at the TUC and had spoken at some TUC one day conferences. I had heard nothing from him for ten days and had last Friday decided to telephone him. To my surprise I was able to get through straight away to his diary secretary and fix up a date for the end of this week.

My diary was already looking a bit crowded for the next few weeks and I asked Stella to come in and we went through the various engagements. She reminded me that I was due to go on the TUC delegation—about six of us—to meet the employment committee of the CBI. Leila had told me all about her chat with John Dryden after her talk at the Industrial Foundation and I thought there might well be a chance to have a chat with him myself.

She also reminded me that van Megeren of Staff International was pushing me to go to a special conference he was arranging on globalisation in Prague and be one of the speakers there. I had not wanted to go as I was tied up with a number of meetings in Scotland that week where I was due to go round several of the union branches there and also speak to the national committees of two fairly major Scottish companies and have some informal meetings with the senior management of the companies concerned and a trip to Prague and back would take at least a couple of days.

I asked Stella to check with Muriel whether Leila could go in my place and then I would speak to van Megeren and, assuming Leila was available, hopefully fix it with him.

About half past nine Leila phoned in. She had gone back to the hotel and checked with Alan Whitchurch what the reports from all the pickets were. I t seemed that everything was peaceful, though she did mention about the woman in the army greatcoat. From the reports it appeared that about five hundred staff had gone into work. I knew that this was bound to be a moveable figure as flexitime meant that starting times could be anywhere between seven and ten o'clock in the morning. But our of a total workforce of five thousand that a good result, so far.

Julia Cardon was in my office when Leila phoned and I relayed the information to her. She then left to get out a press statement and to telephone some of the leading papers direct.

⌘

At a quarter to ten Leila was in the lounge area of her hotel suite. Alan Whitchurch had just come back from his visit to the pickets. Then for the next fifteen minutes it seemed that their mobile phones and the phone in the room were ringing continuously. They dealt with the calls as quickly as they could but each time they answered a call the news seemed to get worse.

The organisers at each of the eight pickets at the company's branches were each phoning in with a similar story. A large number of the company's workforce were coming in together—almost marching—to the offices as if they were all coordinated. Leila added up the figures as the organisers reported them to her and Whitchurch.

Clive Bristow reported that a large number of staff—several hundred he reckoned—had entered the head office in one go. He had seen several of the senior management leading them in. He mentioned that Ted Davis thought the figure was approaching five hundred and with the eighty that had gone in just after seven o'clock that meant about half the total staff of the UK head office were going to work. Leila asked what the normal pattern of starting was between seven and ten in the morning and Bristow had explained that the usual starting time varied but it was now obvious that a concerted effort had been made for the majority to come in just before the core time of ten o'clock.

The organisers had reported similar situations with anything from one to three hundred coming in together at the other offices. Leila's summary of all the figures was that by ten o'clock something like 2,800 staff had gone into work. That was well over half the total 5,000 staff of the company and that meant too that it could be that nearly three hundred of the union members had also gone into work.

Whitchurch looked grim as he finished his conversation with the last of the organisers to phone in.

"Don't look too glum, Alan" said Leila. "The other way of looking at the figures is that nearly ninety per cent of our membership has come out—which is a remarkably good figure."

"Point noted," replied Whitchurch, "but it's clear that it's all been carefully orchestrated by the company and I bet they will have taken photographs of the people marching in: and what will that look like in the press? And I've had a call from Hammond outside the IT building. After a bit of waffle—and a few slogans—he admitted that he estimated about thirty per cent of the staff had gone in; and that means some of their members have gone in there too. I assume that the IT department will therefore be functioning."

Leila was dialling the union headquarters as he was speaking. She was not surprised at the news from Hammond but it did mean that in that case some seventy per cent of the IT staff had come out. She asked the headquarters telephone operator to be put through to Julia Cardon. She explained the latest figures to her and said she must telephone the leading newspapers again with the news that ninety percent of the membership had come out on strike and that was a good result. She asked her to tell Carmichael was what was happening and also to ring round the regional television companies to see if any of them were going to cover the lunch time rallies that they were holding at each of the locations.

"I'm going back to the pickets, Alan. You stay here but for goodness sake put a positive spin on the figures when you're speaking to the organisers or indeed anyone else."

Whitchurch nodded and Leila left the room.

When Leila got to the first picket she saw that Clive Bristow and Ted Davis were still there. The arrangement had been for the pickets to change every two hours and it was now after ten o'clock. They greeted her as she went up to them. Davis explained he and Bristow had left the picket at nine o'clock and had some coffee in a nearby café and then decided to return. They had got back just as the hundreds of staff were crossing through the pickets and going into the offices. They both said to Leila that the situation looked a bit grim.

"I've got the figures," said Leila, "and they are not too bad. It means that almost all our membership has stayed out—many more than voted for action in the ballot."

Both Bristow and Davis were realistic and had held office in the union for many years.

"I know that Leila," said Bristow, "but we had a television crew here who took some shots of the hundreds marching in through the doors. I bet the company planned the whole thing and arranged things with the TV people."

Leila said the television pictures could backfire and make it appear that those going into work were regimented and not acting as individuals. She said she had asked Julia Cardon to get hold of the various television services to try and get as many as possible to film the rallies they were holding so that would go some way to countering the effect of TV pictures of hundreds of staff crossing picket lines: but it meant that they should have good attendances at each of the rallies. She repeated that the turnout for the strike was good and better than might have been expected, given the circulars put out by the company in the previous two weeks and the pressure that some of the senior management would undoubtedly have put on the staff.

As she was talking to them, and could see that her arguments were having some effect on them and the others in the picket, she saw Leo Patullo from the Press Association approaching. She had met him several times and always found him straightforward. As the PA served a whole range of media organisations they had to have correspondents who were direct and factual in their reporting. It meant too, Leila knew, that it would be impossible to try and pull the wool over Patullo's eyes.

Patullo waited while Leila and Bristow had finished their conversation and then stepped forward. He had a piece of paper in his hand which he kept looking at.

"Good morning again, Mrs Smith," he said. "I've just had this circular faxed through to the hotel I'm staying at. It's from the company and it says that over three thousand of the company's staff have ignored the strike call. Any comment?"

It was a direct question and Leila could not afford—especially in front of those on the picket line—to try and dismiss it.

"I've just come from my hotel and we've received the reports from all of the pickets and organisers at the company's eight branch offices as well. I would estimate realistically—and our people were counting the people going in—that about two thousand eight hundred staff went in. There's about five thousand employed altogether. Our membership at the last count was over two thousand seven hundred. The company's way of looking at it is that between two and three hundred of our members crossed the picket lines but our way of looking at it is to say nearly ninety per cent of our membership has come out. And that's a good figure."

Patullo nodded: "but the strike hasn't shut one office."

"No," said Leila, "and we didn't expect it would. What you must appreciate Leo—" she tried desperately not to sound pompous and she hoped she had succeeded—"is that we had twelve hundred voting for action and almost double that figure has gone on strike. A pretty good figure by anyone's standards. And the company would be daft to ignore this massive show of defiance."

"Just for background can you tell me how many people the company is contracting to companies at any one time and what you think the effect of the strike will be."

Leila outlined how the company worked. It now supplied contract labour for a whole range of manufacturing and service companies, in both the public and private sector, and at any one time there could be up to one hundred thousand people or more on their books. The staff directly employed—the five thousand employees—in the UK head office and the eight branches were basically those who organised the arrangements for the contract staff, liaised with the client companies, paid the staff concerned and recruited new people with the skills that companies wanted. They were continually contacting companies to see if they could contract staff which Industry3M could provide—a form of selling direct.

"The point is, Leo," said Leila "that companies who use the labour that Industry3M supply will not look too kindly if the supply chain of that labour is interrupted, people are not recruited or the staff aren't paid or the supply itself is not there. That's where the effect of the strike will be felt."

"What about the overtime ban—is there much overtime worked?"

"There's a bit here in the head office but not so much in the branches. The effect would be cumulative but we don't expect it to be dramatic. And," added Leila, "don't forget that we have the ballot result in favour of a three day strike if the company don't budge and try and come to a satisfactory meeting with us."

Patullo seemed content. He moved over to talk to Bristow, Davis and the other pickets, asking them what the strength of feeling in the company was and whether they expected the dispute to be settled soon.

Leila then went round to the back of the building and repeated her same message to the pickets there. Next she went to the IT building. She noticed Tony Hammond was still there. She started to repeat the message to him and the other pickets when he interrupted.

"Isn't the truth that we have been out-manouvered by the company?"

Leila started to respond—"but you know, Tony, that we've done everything we could—" and then bit her lip. She was daft to try and argue in front of the others. She smiled and said "I don't think so, Tony."

Hammond said "But what about the lack of publicity and the lack of leadership?" It was provocative and, Leila knew full well, totally unfair and untrue.

Leila looked at the other pickets: "I think you al should ask Tony for details of all the reports and discussions we've had at the national committee and the national executive." She paused and then said "and ask Tony, too, what else he has suggested we should do—at least something that is practical."

She looked at Hammond who started to reply and then turned to the others again and said "but thanks for all you're doing. We have got over ninety per cent of our membership out today and I think that's pretty good. So, see you at the march and rally at lunch time"

A number of the pickets smiled and said they would be there. It seemed to Leila that not all IT people, and perhaps not all of the trots, were as wound up and critical as Hammond. As she left she could hear Hammond haranguing the others. At least, that was what it sounded like. But she also heard what she thought was somebody arguing with Hammond. She smiled to herself: well, that's a bit of progress.

Leila went back to the picket line outside the main entrance to the building. Bristow and Davis had gone but had told the others they would be back at twelve o'clock. Three other union members had joined the picket and were due to stay until twelve. Leila had arranged that all the members had been asked to come to the main picket line at just after twelve and at half past they would then all march to the Royal Liver building by the waterfront. There would still be pickets outside the main entrance, the back entrance and the IT building and—ever hopeful—she and the branch committee had thought that perhaps some of the staff going out at lunch time would decide not to cross the line again to go back to work. Leila knew this was unlikely and now, with the evidence of the organised march into work, she had little doubt that the company had arranged some lunch food to be brought in so that no one would have to leave the building at lunch time. Still, she knew that the picket lines must be maintained until seven o'clock that evening, the time when the office normally closed.

Leila went back to the hotel. Whitchurch told her that he had had further reports from the organisers at all the other pickets outside the company's eight branches. The picket lines were all fully staffed and—as Leila had surmised—some of them had seen provisions being taken into the offices for lunch.

"It doesn't really matter, Alan" she said. They key thing is to have a good attendance at the rally and make sure all the pickets are kept until seven o'clock."

She looked at him: "come on, Alan, it's going well."

Whitchurch nodded—it was unlike him to be so gloomy thought Leila—and then mentioned that Joe Turner of the *Liverpool Daily Post* had phoned and he had agreed that he could come to the hotel and talk to Leila about eleven o'clock. Leila said that would be fine. Whitchurch then said he would go and have a chat with the pickets and stay outside the head office until Leila came back at twelve. While she, and what they hoped would be several hundred members, then marched to the rally he would come back to the hotel and check up again on the other pickets.

Leila telephoned Carmichael at the union headquarters and told him about the organised march into work that had taken place at all the company's offices. He didn't seem surprised and just wished her well at the rally.

Then she telephoned Ian Macallister on his mobile. He was with the Glasgow pickets and sounded very upbeat when Leila spoke to him. About seventy of the staff in the Glasgow office had gone into work but, as far as he and Bruce Cannon, the other member of the national committee from Glasgow, could tell, all of the union members had come out. She congratulated him and asked him to pass on her thanks to the others.

At eleven o'clock Joe Turner knocked on the door of the suite and came in. He Also had a copy of the company's circular that Leo Patullo had shown Leila earlier. Leila explained to him that in her opinion everything was going well for the union and emphasised what she had already said to Patullo: ninety per cent of the union's members had gone on strike and the company would be shown to be totally intransigent if they failed to negotiate with the union now.

Turner accepted the point and told Leila that he had just come from the picket lines and all those he had spoken too were pleased with the numbers on strike and were not in the least upset by the march into work. Leila was pleased to hear this. She and Turner then talked about how the strike was going in the other offices and how it appeared that the driving force behind the company's actions seemed to be John Carr. She mentioned that John Carmichael had tried to speak to Norman Jones, the chief executive, but Jones had refused to speak to him. Instead Carr had come on the phone and merely repeated what the circular had stated.

Turner then left saying he would be at the rally and wished Leila luck. He said also that he hoped he would have a chance to speak to Leila after seven o'clock and Leila stated that she and the branch committee—and probably many others—would be at the Flying Fox pub, about a hundred yards from the company's head office, that evening.

She then phoned her secretary at headquarters. Muriel mentioned the Staff International seminar in Prague and that John Carmichael had spoken to van Mergeren about it. It appeared her diary for the two days concerned was free then. Leila thought for a moment. It would be the Monday and Tuesday of the following week and would probably mean flying out on the Sunday. But if the Swedish and German unions were attending it would a good time to speak to them about how things were going with their job evaluation claims. She told Muriel to make the arrangements.

Muriel then mentioned there was a letter to her marked private and confidential. Leila told her to open and read it to her.

The letter was from Dan Michael. He stated that he was still unwell and his doctor had said it was severe depression and could last for some time. He then stated that in view of all the circumstances he wished to take ill health retirement from the union. At the end of the letter Michael had said he had enjoyed working with the union and had thanked Leila personally for her support.

Leila knew the last comment was sincere: Michael was not the sort of person to make sarcastic comments on such a serious issue. Ill health retirement would fully protect his pension and meant he wouldn't have to wait until the age of fifty-five to draw it. Theoretically the claim for ill health could be challenged but she decided there was no point in going down that road. She asked Muriel to check with the doctor the union retained for staff and get him to liaise with Michael's own doctor and, if they both agreed, then the wheels could be set in motion for Michael to go.

She asked Muriel to check with John Carmichael and, subject to his concurring, to acknowledge Michael's letter and say that she would agree to his ill health retirement request provided they secured the agreement of the two doctors. She would write at greater length when she got back to the office. She knew that Carmichael would agree and that would obviate the need for a messy sexual harassment hearing and all the attendant publicity that could engender, particularly if—as seemed highly likely—Michael was found guilty. At least ill health retirement meant the whole issue could be closed. Also she would follow her usual policy when someone left the union: instead of working out the requisite three months notice she would let the person go at once with three months pay in lieu of notice. So, even if Michael's health quickly improved, which Leila knew would be highly unlikely, he would have a decent lump sum to go with. What the longer term future held for him was something she didn't want to speculate on.

She then asked Muriel, once the agreement of those concerned had been gained, and her letter sent off to Michael, to do a staff notice stating that Dan Michael was retiring on grounds of ill health. She mentioned that she would talk to Sam Askari when she got back.

Just before twelve o'clock Leila left the hotel to go back to the pickets. As she was leaving Alan Whitchurch came back. He seemed more cheerful than before and said the pickets seemed to be in good humour and wished her well at the march and rally. She knew he would have liked to be with her but someone had to be at the hotel to act as the contact point for all the other pickets and the organisers.

As Leila approached the pickets she saw there was quite a large crowd of people by them. It was difficult to be precise on numbers as the crowd was spilling out on the road and the surroundings. She saw Bristow and Davis with a large banner—' *negotiate now*!'—they were holding between them. A number of the others were holding placards—'*talk to us*!'—and some of the others had bundles of leaflets to hand out as they marched to the rallying point by the river.

Leila knew that Whitchurch and the regional organisers had sorted and prepared all the material for the pickets and the marches that were now getting ready at the eight other locations across the country. Leila thought it all looked good. She saw a television camera crew talking to Bristow and hoped that any film they took would be a good counterweight to film of the other staff marching into work earlier that morning.

She greeted Bristow and Davis again and said hello to a number of others. She was pleased to see Larry Brent there and went over to have a word with him. She also noticed that Tony Hammond and June Trevor were holding some placards but she couldn't see what they had written on them. She asked Bristow to come over with her to them.

Hammond looked at her and said nothing. June Trevor said hello. Then Leila saw the placards they had were headed 'Socialism Now' and underneath they said 'Bosses must be beaten'.

Hammond waited for her to say something but Bristow spoke first, pointing to the placard: "That's a bit juvenile isn't it?"

Leila said "You know full well that you can't bring those placards with you on the march."

Both Hammond and Trevor shouted "why not?". Leila sighed and then said firmly: "they are not our placards, they're from a different organisation and we are not having them at our march and rally. Simple as that."

Some others had gathered round them as they were talking. Hammond and Trevor said nothing and then, after a pause, Hammond said "and what do you propose to do about it?"

"If you are going to bring those placards then you must not come on the march. I'll ask Clive and Ted and some others to escort you away." Bristow added that he would be happy to do so.

It was direct and Leila waited while Hammond and Trevor thought about what she had said. She knew that both Bristow and Davis could muster some of their colleagues who would only be too pleased to escort them away and she guessed that Hammond and Trevor knew that.

Hammond laid his placard down and said "you're making a big mistake. We need all the help we can get if we want to win this strike—and already you've made a number of mistakes."

Leila was about to reply when Bristow went up to Hammond and said "why don't you grow up and—more importantly—why don't you support the union instead of trying to sabotage it?"

Hammond pushed him away. Bristow started back to him and for a moment it looked as if a fight would break out. Then Ted Davis came up and placed his large bulky body between them.

He turned to Hammond: "we are all meant to be on the same side, but sometimes with you I'm not so sure—"

Hammond started to speak but Davis said firmly: "we've got the march now and then the rally so let's all cheer for the same side, shall we?"

Quite a few other members had gathered round. Hammond seemed on the point of speaking again but then thought better of it. Bristow moved away.

More and more union members were arriving and Leila thought there must be getting on for five hundred blocking the office and thronging on the surrounding roads. As she was looking at the crowds the same policeman who had spoken to her earlier in the morning came up.

She smiled: "I know what you're going to say, constable. We're only allowed six pickets but this is the beginning of our march and we're off in a few minutes."

The policeman smiled back: "I wasn't actually gong to say that. But if you don't mind I'll come along with you. If there's any trouble I'll call up some assistance."

"Fine," said Leila and hoped he hadn't seen the argument between Bristow, Davis and Hammond.

Bristow had a megaphone with him and through it called on all the members to come along behind himself, Davis and Leila. Then they set off and gradually the crowd of members fell in behind them. Leila couldn't see where the policeman had gone and presumed he would be somewhere near the back.

It took the leading marchers just over twenty minutes to get to the river and as the rest joined them they spread out along the front of the Royal Liver building. Leila looked up at the two statues of what were popularly called the 'liver birds'. She remembered the old Scouse joke that every time a virgin girl passed by then the two statues would flap their wings. The joke was that they hadn't moved in years.

Two of the branch committee members had brought along a box. Leila intended to get on to that and speak through the microphone and speaker that two of the other committee members had brought along. It certainly looked like a good crowd she thought. She asked Davis to get hold of Larry Brent and try to get a rough estimate of the numbers. She noticed that the policeman was standing at the back of the crowd and that a television came crew was just arriving. She couldn't see Joe Turner from the *Liverpool Daily Post* but assumed he must be somewhere among the throng. She didn't see any others from the press that she recognised.

Clive Bristow, as the chairman of the union's branch committee, got on the box first. He had handed the megaphone to Davis and in turn held the microphone. He blew on the microphone and a loud noise came out. The crowd cheered.

"Colleagues," he boomed. "This is a rally of the Clerical and General Union. We're on strike today because the company—the company we all work for—has refused point blank to negotiate with us on pay or the job evaluation claim. It's a disgrace that in the twenty first century a management can behave as they are behaving and we're here to demonstrate that they mustn't get away with it." A few cheers went up. "Now you don't want to listen to me"—an ironic shout of "you're dead right" was heard and a number laughed—but it's my pleasure to welcome our Deputy General Secretary, Mrs Leila Smith, to speak to us. Leila has been heavily involved in the events of the last few weeks along with our General Secretary, John Carmichael. So, Leila over to you."

There were a few claps as he stood down from the box and handed the microphone to Leila. Leila looked round again as she mounted the box. There must be at least five hundred people there. The crowd seemed in a good humour.

So far, so good, she thought. This was the critical moment and she knew she had to make a good speech—a speech that would spell out the basic issues, hold their attention and encourage them all. It could well be that the union might have to implement the ballot vote for a three day strike if the company still stood firm after this day—and if that failed to achieve successful negotiations, what then? She had to reassure them all that the action was worth it and that the union would succeed in the end. When that end would come she had no idea. She guessed that several of the crowd would have been sent to attend the rally by the company to report back to the management and she had to ensure that they took back a report that showed the union members in full support of the action. She had made many important speeches before but this would be one of the most important. She had to be good: and she could not afford to let the members down. The crowd quietened and all eyes were turned to Leila.

I was in my office in headquarters and had just finished dictating to Sheila when about three o'clock Leila phoned in. She had got back from the march and rally and was phoning from the hotel. Apparently there had been about five hundred at the rally and she said it seemed to have gone off all right. The calls from the organisers at the other rallies to her and Alan Whitchurch had all said the rallies had been successful with attendance of thirty—in Bristol—to well over a hundred in Birmingham and in Manchester. Altogether they had both agreed there must have been nearly one thousand members at the rallies.

I was about to congratulate Leila on what sounded a good turnout and reception when Clive Bristow must have seized the phone from Leila because his voice suddenly shouted down the line.

"Leila's being too modest, General Secretary" he said. "Our rally was excellent and Leila herself was bloody marvellous. They were no trouble. She had them all in the palm of her hand: a few jokes, a strong message and an upbeat performance and she got a huge round of applause and cheers when she finished. One of the best union speeches I've heard."

I smiled. I knew Bristow and he was a sound chap. It was good to hear his view. He then apologised for taking the phone off Leila and handed it back to her.

"Sorry about that, John," said Leila. "Yes, it did seem to go quite well. Alan and I are taking it in turns to go back to the pickets until we stand down at seven this evening. I'll give you a ring then."

I told her that would be fine. I would probably be home by seven but, in case not, it would be best to get me on my mobile. I would phone the union's President and Vice-President with the news.

Leila said she would be getting the early train the next morning and hoped to be back in the office by half past ten and would see me then. She asked me if Muriel had told me about Dan Michael and I assured her that she had. I said it seemed the best outcome in view of all the circumstances—but I did feel sorry for him. He shouldn't have done it but it was out of character. However, if he hadn't resigned then the disciplinary procedure for the union's staff would have had to be pursued.

I asked Leila if there had been any problem with the trots. Leila briefly mentioned what had happened at Liverpool and said that the organiser covering the Leeds office had mentioned a slight problem with some of them there but no real problem. I was glad of that. It would have been so nice to have had no problem at all with the trots or anyone else, but then unions—or any group of people—weren't like that.

I said I would see Leila in the morning. In the meantime I reminded her that I was going with the TUC delegation to meet the CBI employment committee, apparently a number of the General Council members couldn't make it but John Miller thought the meeting must go ahead and therefore my attendance was essential ; that was on Thursday afternoon. We were then both due on the Friday afternoon to see Bob Wilson at the DTI. She said she would get in touch with ACAS again when she got back to headquarters but didn't hold out much hope there and I agreed with her. We both knew that we would probably have to think seriously about when—not if—we would call the members out for a three day strike in accordance with the ballot result. I made a mental note to have a word with Christine Buckley, the union's finance officer: we would have to do something about strike pay if the three day strike were to go ahead. I would also mention it to Les Martin and Jane Toff when I spoke to them.

When she had finished her call to John Carmichael Leila said she would go back to the pickets for a while and then, when she returned, she and Whitchurch should do a final ring round the organisers and try and get a complete picture of the day from them. She would phone Carmichael again after seven o'clock and then, she said firmly to Whitchurch, it would be time to go to the pub. Bristow who had said he would be back at the pickets at just before seven, was moving towards the door and told Leila he very much agreed with her last point.

The picket lines at the front and back of the company's head office building were both fully staffed and they all greeted Leila with smiles and a few cheered. The rota system of two hours on and two hours off seemed to have worked well. She knew Bristow and Davis had gone off to get something to eat. She would order something from the hotel when she got back. Two of the pickets told her that about half past four the majority of staff working had come out of the building and walked away. There had been no trouble although they both said the staff looked distinctly sheepish as they went away.

She went round to the IT building and somewhat to her surprise there were only two members on the picket line. She didn't know either of them but they clearly knew her and they looked a bit uncomfortable as she approached. She asked where the other pickets were and they said they didn't know.

Leila thought there would be little point in haranguing them now but made it clear to both of them that the arrangement had been for five to six people to be present on the picket line all day. They looked even more uncomfortable and said nothing. She wondered what Hammond had done and asked them where he was.

"Don't know," said one, a rather chubby little man who looked in his forties. "He said something about a meeting—"

The other man tried to shush him. "We don't know Mrs Smith. We haven't seen him since the end of the rally but we hope he'll be back shortly."

Leila picked up on the point: "what's this about a meeting?"

The chubby man went red and stammered that he didn't know at all. The other man said nothing except that the staff who had gone into work in the morning all seemed to come out together about half past four and presumably gone home. Leila stayed with them for a few moments and thanked them for their picket duty and then left to go back to her hotel.

As she walked back she realised that Hammond must have arranged for a meeting of his left group—perhaps to spell out the line they should take on the day's strike and what they should now press for. There hadn't been any problems with them at the actual rally Leila thought; but they could well be considering something now.

When Leila got back to the hotel she ordered some sandwiches and coffee to be sent up to her suite for Whitchurch and herself. She then telephoned Julia Cardon who was still at union headquarters.

There had been a lot of press calls that day and Julia Cardon had dealt with them on the line that the union turnout had been very good, all the offices had been picketed, a load of leaflets had been handed out to members of the public as they passed the offices where the pickets were and the mood of the union members had been great.

Leila mentioned the television crew who had been at her rally and whom she thought were from the BBC and asked her to try and monitor the BBC's north-west regional news to see if they carried it.

"It all seems to have gone OK Leila," said Cardon. "I think we should get a reasonable press tomorrow and, hopefully, some good photographs will be used. I know that some of the papers sent photographers to cover some of the rallies."

Leila thanked her and wondered why people like Tony Hammond couldn't have the same encouraging attitude as Julia. But, for the umpteenth time she reminded herself that she lived in a democracy and not everyone behaved in the same way.

She got Julia to put her through to Muriel who was also still I the office, and checked her commitments for the rest of the week. Muriel had spoken to vanMergeren about the Prague seminar and she was booked to fly out on the Sunday afternoon, returning on the Wednesday morning. She asked Leila whether she should telephone the SAF union in Sweden and the German white collar union to make sure they had some people at the seminar and Leila said that would be very helpful.

By half past six she and Whitchurch had spoken to the eight regional organisers and were putting together a summary of the day's events. All seemed to have gone well. The apparent trouble outside the Leeds office had been when a group of what the organiser had assumed was the Socialist Workers Party had attempted to join the picket line and hand out their own leaflets to the passers by. The organiser and three other members had had to physically escort them away and, after the organiser had said he would have no hesitation in asking the police to remove them, they had moved on. Jean Asah, the national committee member for the Leeds office, had started to remonstrate with the organiser but the others on the picket line had forcefully told her to shut up. Leila remembered seeing Asah and Hammond talking together at the last national committee meeting and how she had wondered at the time when that meant anything or not. She would have to make enquiries later.

Whitchurch told her that some of the organisers he had talked to were asking when a three day strike was likely—and members had asked them. It appeared that the mood generally was good. Leila thought it would be two to three weeks before they could call out the members again and then a lot would depend on whether the company did anything or not. She told Whitchurch that all they should say to any such question was that a three day strike—if it was considered necessary (and to Leila's mind, realistic)—would probably be held sooner rather than later but the national committee would have to give their view.

They finished the summary which Leila said she would take back to headquarters in the morning and a detailed report on the action would be sent out to all the union's regional and national committees. Whitchurch said he would be going back one more time to the pickets and Leila said she would join him but first she had to make one more call to Ian Macallister the national committee chairman.

Again Macallister sounded upbeat and said the Glasgow rally had gone well and he understood Leila's speech at the Liverpool rally had been what he described as a stormer. Leila said she would phone him the next day to discuss a possible national committee meeting date. Macallister said that he wasn't sure whether they needed another one but would think about it and discuss it with her again.

Whitchurch and Leila then left the hotel and went back to the pickets. There were quite a few more than the six normal people on picket duty outside the company's office. Bristow handed Leila the megaphone and suggested she thank them again and—looking at his watch—said it was now seven o'clock and time to go to the pub. Leila did just that and there were a few cheers and they moved away.

While the others went into the Flying Fox Leila rang John Carmichael on her mobile and brought him up to date and told him she would be bringing back to headquarters the summary that she and Whitchurch had prepared and also mentioned Macallister's point about whether a new national committee meeting was in fact necessary. Finally she referred to the mention of a meeting by one of the pickets outside the IT building and how the full complement of pickets was not there. Carmichael grunted and told her not to worry about it: they would discuss the whole thing in the morning.

Leila was glad they had chosen the Flying Fox as the pub. It was a large building and had a horseshoe type of bar running round the big room on the ground floor. There were apparently two other bars on the first floor. As she entered the place was packed. A number greeted her as she entered. She saw Larry Brent and he asked her what she would like to drink.

"On second thoughts," he said, "perhaps we could try one of the upstairs bars: it might not be too crowded there."

"Good idea," replied Leila and they made their way back to the stairs by the main door. She saw Bristow ordering some drinks at the bar and motioned to him that she was going upstairs. He waved and mouthed that he would join her there as soon as he could.

The first upstairs bar was crowded too but the second was not so bad. She told Brent that she would like a glass of red wine. He went to get it and a pint of bitter for himself. As he went she thought when she had first met him. It was at the open meeting when the egg had been thrown. He had told her he had been in the company for a year. He must be a graduate, she thought, taken on the company's graduate management scheme. Whatever, he seemed a decent chap, fair haired and a bit earnest.

Brent came back with the drinks and they managed to find a couple of seats in the corner.

"Cheers," said Leila, "and thanks—for the drink and for all your efforts."

Brent looked at her: "did you hear about the ultra left meeting?"

She remembered what the chubby man on the IT picket line had said.

"What about it?"

Brent said "it was organised by Hammond of course and they met at five o'clock in that small hall at the back of the IT building. It belongs to one of the local churches and they let it out for small meetings."

Leila was intrigued but didn't like to let on that she knew nothing about it.

"How many do you reckon were there?"

"About thirty, I would say, and they had that organiser from the SPGB speaking. About twenty I would guess were from the union but the others probably not."

"What happened then?" She paused: "and what's the SPGB?"

"The organiser chap made a speech to the effect that it was up to the left—or the ultra left as he called them—to take control of the three day strike if and when it happens. The SPGB is an offshoot of the SWP—the Socialist Party of Great Britain. You know that there's nothing like the far left for splits, divisions and the creation of new parties. People like to lump them all together as trots, but there are differences." He smiled again at Leila as he said it and then went on: "The organiser was apparently originally SWP but moved over to the SPGB when it was formed. I believe they think the SWP is now too meek and mild and not revolutionary enough."

Leila, who knew full well what Brent had just told her, swallowed some of her wine and looked carefully at Brent.

"And let me guess," she said, "they're going to push again for the strike to be run by some sort of representatives committee. And, to be honest, I didn't know too much about the SPGB, but whatever initials you support, there'll always be someone to the left of you."

Brent smiled: "got it in one. And you can come round in a big circle if you want."

Leila had to ask: "how do you know about this?"

Brent smiled: "I was at the meeting." He ignored the other part of Leila's question.

Leila looked surprised but before she could say anything Brent carried on. "Don't worry, I'm not one of them. But they let me in and I think they must believe I'm a potential recruit."

Leila switched tack.

"Where were you before joining the company Larry?"

Brent said he had been in the civil service for a couple of years and then decided to enter the world of industry, and the graduate management scheme of the company looked quite attractive.

Leila smiled "and you have contacts."

Brent smiled back: "yes, a few."

Just then Bristow came into the bar and Leila waved to him.

"Thanks for telling me, Larry" she said, "I'll keep in touch."

Brent said "pleasure" and stood up to let Bristow sit down. He asked if he could get Bristow a drink and Bristow said he certainly could.

"No," said Leila, getting up. "It's my shout and I'll get them."

As she went to the bar she noticed that Joe Turner from the *Liverpool Daily Post* had come in. Turner went up to her.

"Been looking for you. Can I get a quote on the day from you."

Leila smiled and asked him what he would like to drink. When she had ordered and the drinks had arrived she suggested they went and sat with Bristow and Brent. Then she saw Leo Patullo from the Press Association arrive and she asked him he would like to join them. Patullo readily agreed and asked just for an orange juice.

When they had all sat down Leila ran through the events of the day and stressed how, from the union's point of view, things had gone well. She rehearsed the numbers of members on strike, the reports from the organisers round the country and the mood of those on strike. Both Patullo and Turner asked about the likelihood of a three day strike. Leila said it looked as if it would take place but first she would be in touch with ACAS to see if there was any chance of a meeting with the company.

Both Patullo and Turner said they had tried to contact the company but each had only managed to get hold of John Carr. Both Norman Jones, the chief executive, and Tom Chance, his deputy, had been unavailable for comment. John Carr had reiterated to both of them that the company had been working as usual that day and the strike had not made any impact.

Leila said "he would say that, wouldn't he."

Bristow said "someone else once said that" and they all laughed.

They talked about the rallies, the likely effect on the company's business, and, in particular, the union's claimed job evaluation scheme. Turner and Patullo each bought a round of drinks. Bristow was quite talkative but Leila noticed that Larry Brent stayed quiet most of the time. After a while Leila then decided it was time for her to go back to the hotel and to sleep. It had been a good day and a convivial evening but she would have to be up early in the morning. She saw Alan Whitchurch with a group of members in the other corner of the bar; but she knew he was going to Manchester in the morning to talk with the regional organiser there and so wouldn't have to leave so early.

As she got up to go, Turner said that indeed it had seemed to be a good day for the union but the company was showing no sign of being prepared to deal with the union and asked her what the union would do if a three day strike didn't make the company negotiate with the union on its claims.

"Well," replied Leila. "we'll have to think of something else, won't we?"

"Any idea of what that might be?"

Leila noticed the others were all looking at her.

"I've plenty of ideas, Joe. And I'll let you know in due course."

Turner persisted: "and when is that likely to be?"

Leila smiled: "now, that be telling, wouldn't it? But I will tell you that the job evaluation scheme seems decidedly popular with other unions—both here in the UK and apparently on the continent, so a lot of things could happen."

Amid cries of goodnight Leila left them and went back to her hotel.

Chapter Seven

Rumours of Strikes

"Mrs Smith?"

Leila was sitting in the London train when her mobile had rung. She answered "yes."

"It's John Dryden from the CBI. I got your number yesterday from your secretary and I wanted to catch you soonest."

Leila was surprised but didn't say so.

"Did you have a good day yesterday/"

Leila paused and wondered why he had phoned.

"Very good, thanks."

"Look, Leila, if I may call you that," continued Dryden. "It's about the meeting my employment committee has with the TUC on Thursday."

"Yes, I know about that. John Carmichael's going along."

"Well, my colleagues and I thought we could also discuss—apart from the overall subject of employment legislation—your job evaluation scheme. It seems a number of unions are pursuing it and I thought it would help if it could be discussed with my committee." Dryden sounded quite insistent.

"That would be fine," replied Leila, "but it's a TUC delegation and although I'm on the General Council, I'm not one of the senior members and not due to go. You better speak to John Miller at Congress House."

"Leila," said Dryden," I have spoken to him and he's quite happy. I've also spoken to John Carmichael this morning".

Leila looked at her watch. It was only eight o'clock so Dryden must have been busy this morning.

"Your general secretary is also quite happy. Why I'm speaking to you know is to check that you are agreeable and I'll then tell my people to start on a paper for our committee. I'm out of the office until the Thursday morning and we're due to meet that afternoon. If you're OK then everything can be put into motion."

Leila thought there must be some serious concern about the job evaluation scheme for Dryden to ask her to the meeting. She knew that Dick Whetter of the civil service union was keen on the scheme and that Jim Bradwell of the local government union had told Carmichael that he would be pursuing a claim for the scheme. Things must be moving.

She remembered what she had said to Joe Turner in the pub the previous evening. Things must be moving faster than she thought then.

"I'll be delighted to come to the meeting."

Dryden thanked her and rang off.

Leila went to the buffet bar for some breakfast and then returned to her seat. She had bought a copy of that morning's *Liverpool Daily Post* and the *Financial Times* and wanted to see what both of them reported on the strike.

The *Financial Times* report was fairly short. It referred to the numbers the union had said were on strike and included a couple of quotes attributed to Leila. It also reported Carr's comment that it had been business as usual for the company. It was a factual piece but contained no speculation about what would happen next.

Turner's piece in the *Liverpool Daily Post* was quite extensive and had a photograph taken at the rally. He had quoted John Carr as well and then finished with a mention of Leila's throwaway line about other unions pursuing the job evaluation scheme. Leila thought that was just what she wanted Turner to say and was pleased.

Leila came into my office just after half past ten. She had intended to come earlier but had phoned me when the train had stopped for half an hour just outside Euston station. Sod's law, when she had wanted to be early.

Julia Cardon had brought me two bundles of press cuttings earlier and I had had a quick skim through them. Overall the press coverage of the strike had been good and a number of the 'heavies' as well as the tabloids had printed some quite good photographs of the marches and rallies. Strikes were not so common these days and I supposed our strike was newsworthy particularly as it was in an American owned company. When Leila came into the office I passed her one of the bundles.

"Did Dryden get hold of you?" I asked.

Leila told me about his call.

"I spoke to John Miller at TUC this morning and he was a bit mystified about Dryden suggesting you came along on Thursday but was quite relaxed about it. As you know he has to balance the different General Council members and placate their egos."

Leila smiled and said she quite understood.

The TUC General Council had over forty members and seniority of service was one of its main features. The Congress President was always the most senior member in terms of years of service on the General Council—and that was why I was due to be the President in three years time. The TUC General Secretary, though, also had to balance the membership of the various committees and task forces according to the size of the unions the members were from, the sectors in which the unions operated, the seniority of the General Council members and recently what was called the 'gender balance'—and most of the General Council members were very jealous that newer members did not get some of the more senior positions or get involved in Government discussions over their heads.

I told her that six from the General Council were going and she would be the seventh. I asked her to do a brief paper on the job evaluation scheme which we could pass onto the others at the pre-meeting we would hold at Congress House before going to the CBI building for the meeting.

"Will Dick Whetter be going?" she asked me and I told her that he would be one of the key people there. His union was the biggest one in the civil service. Jim Bradwell of the local government union would also be going. The other three apart from John Miller—were from the manufacturing, engineering and transport sectors.

"Do you think there's anything special going on?" Leila asked. "I mean it's not normal for the CBI to ask for specific individuals to be on delegations, is it?"

I looked at her. She was one of the brightest union officials I knew and she would never normally ask me such innocent questions. She must be just thinking aloud.

"Look, Leila, I think we've uncorked the magic bottle with this job evaluation scheme. For whatever reason, there's one hell of a lot of interest in from various unions. I haven't had a chance to tell you yet but Peter Moorhouse was on the phone yesterday and his lot are putting in claims forthwith a number of companies. I know Dick Whetter's pursuing it and apparently Bradwell's executive is keen. The transport union was on the phone yesterday and I put them on to Frank Hallard to talk about it."

I paused: "so either by accident or design the JE scheme is very popular in the unions."

Leila smiled "let's say it was by design. But the key question is what employers think of it. I've been thinking for sometime whether Industry3M decided on its own to reject the scheme—or are they getting advice from someone?"

I smiled: "you're thinking the same as me—that man John Carr couldn't be dreaming all this up by himself."

"Look John, we ought to have another meeting with our officials and see exactly where we are now. I was thinking we ought to meet in a couple of weeks time but I think now we ought to meet sooner."

I agreed that we should meet as soon as practical.

"What about next Monday? There's the CBI meeting this Thursday afternoon and as you know, we've got the meeting with Bob Wilson at DTI on Friday." Then I remembered. I had arranged with van Mergeren that Leila would go to the seminar in Prague then. She reminded me of it too.

"What about Scotland? You're spending some time up there, aren't you?"

I cursed inwardly. I had indeed forgotten. "OK, let's make it Thursday next week, shall we?"

We both agreed and Leila said she would get Muriel to contact the others. She then started to talk about a possible three day strike in Industry3M. She said she had spoken to Ian Macallister yesterday and wanted to speak to him later today.

I asked her "what about a meeting of their GP committee?"

All of our national committees for the different companies we negotiated with had a small sub-committee, usually called a general purposes committee, that could meet between national committee meetings and take decisions on any urgent business that cropped up. She responded that she had been thinking the same. Would it be all right though for something as important as a three day strike call to be discussed by a small sub-committee—and not the national committee?

We discussed it for some time. Leila said the one day strike had gone as well as we could reasonably have expected, the morale of the members yesterday seemed high and Macallister had seemed quite relaxed about another meeting. The reports from the organisers had all been positive. Leila and I both knew, though, that attitudes towards a strike could change quickly, enthusiasm one day could easily become extreme caution the next. And we didn't know what the company would do.

After while Leila said she would speak to Macallister and suggest a general purposes committee meeting be held on Saturday. In the meantime she would have another word with ACAS and would chase up what was happening with the German and Swedish unions

I told her that I was going to have a word with Christine Buckley, the union's finance officer, and Leila said she would like to join me for that. I told her that I didn't think the union's finances could bear any significant amount of strike pay but that's what we would have to discuss.

"John," said Leila, "I've got the summary of yesterday which Alan and I prepared. I must send it out to the national committee—"

I interrupted her.

"I think we might as well send this out to all the national committees, regions and branches. The national executive as well. It's big news at the moment and there's bound to be a lot of interest. Look, I'll do covering letter for your report so leave it with me."

Leila was more than happy to leave it with me. She said she had now to speak to Tino Malik at ACAS and then asked me if it was all right to proceed with advertising Dan Michael's position. She also had to speak to Sam Askari about the resignation.

I told her to go ahead with the advertisement and also said she should get my papers for the Staff International seminar from Sheila. We would have a chat with Christine this afternoon.

⚜

By six o'clock that evening Leila was more than ready to go home. It had been a tiring day.

She had spoken to Malik at ACAS. He had been surprisingly willing to help and had insisted on calling her 'Leila' several times. Leila thought he must now be treating the dispute seriously when at first he had appeared rather indifferent about it. She thought, somewhat unfairly she told herself, that perhaps he was impressed by the press publicity that the dispute with Industry3M had generated and imagined himself being quoted in the press about his own efforts.

The problem was though, as he admitted to Leila, that he didn't think the company would even come to a meeting with ACAS—let alone a joint meeting with the union as well. Apparently he had spoken to John Carr the previous day and had been given short shrift when he suggested another meeting. He had also tried again that morning but only got through to a junior at the company's personnel—human resources they called it—department. The junior staff man had said that if the company's position changed then he thought John Carr would get in touch with ACAS; in the meantime the company did not want to meet either the union or ACAS. Malik told Leila that he would get in touch if there was any change in the company's position but didn't think there was anything more he could do at this stage. Leila agreed and thanked him for his efforts.

She had spoken to Ian Macallister again and suggested they should call a meeting of the general purposes committee instead of the full national committee. Macallister had been phoning round that morning and he said that the general mood was that they would have to go for a three day strike and were waiting for the timing. Afterwards, though, he warned they would have to have a full national committee and think seriously about what they should then do. He also mentioned that some of the members he had been speaking to had raised the question of strike pay. Leila had told him she was of the same view about a long and hard look at the options if the three day strike didn't make the company negotiate. She said she would speak to him further about strike pay and knew that it could become a key issue. They then agreed that Leila would call a meeting of the GP committee for the coming Saturday. It didn't leave much time but she knew that Carmichael would want to have a word with the national executive committee members afterwards and they didn't want to lose the momentum they had achieved by yesterday's strike.

Leila asked Muriel to arrange the GP committee meeting for the Saturday at the same London hotel and for eleven o'clock in the morning. There were five members on the committee including Macallister and—she thought ruefully—Tony Hammond. She also asked Muriel to arrange for the advertisement for Dan Michael's position as head of the union's membership department in the *Guardian* and the *New Statesman*. She knew advertisements there were expensive but the experience of most unions was that they usually got a good response from them and, she also knew, advertisements in other papers or magazines were more expensive. As she often reminded herself, everything was relative.

The meeting she and Carmichael had with Christine Buckley had produced a possible solution. They had gone over various scenarios and figures. If strike pay was to be paid, should it be a flat rate to everyone or a percentage of the pay they would be stopped by the company? Should it be limited to hardship pay only: in other words, just limit pay to those who actually applied for it and made out a convincing case of hardship? But, then, who would be the final arbiter on what was real hardship? In a sense they all three knew that they couldn't win on the issue.

They had drawn up various possibilities. If they paid everyone a flat rate of twenty pounds a day—and there were two thousand people on strike—then that would cost the union one hundred and twenty thousand pounds for the three days. If they made it fifty pounds per person that would mean three hundred thousand pounds. A percentage payment could be more or less depending on the actual percentage but administering it would be more difficult. They all agreed that a flat rate payment could be divisive but the complexities of administering a percentage payment could outweigh that. Either way they would be open to criticism.

In the end Carmichael said he would recommend that the union should pay fifty pounds per day for the three day period. The members would complete a simple form confirming their pay deduction—which was the proof that they had actually been on strike. Leila thought some of the members—and she was certain that Macallister would be one of them—would not actually claim the strike pay but that undoubtedly the majority would.

Leila said she ought to speak to the union's trustees on the recommendation while Carmichael would contact the union's president and vice-president. He would also have a word with both of them about calling another national executive committee meeting. True, he acknowledged, the previous meeting had authorised a three day strike if necessary and therefore they were clear in terms of the employment legislation covering industrial action but they might think it would be best for another meeting to be held. He said he would wait before firmly approaching Les Martin and Jane Toff about a meeting until Leila had told him about the result of the general purposes committee meeting.

After Leila left Carmichael's office she had asked Sam Askari to come ands see her and she had explained that she was now arranging for Dan Michael's job to be advertised. At first Askari had tried to maintain that the sexual harassment charge against Michael should still be dealt with but Leila had talked him down. In the end he had reluctantly accepted what Leila had said.

For the rest of the afternoon she had read over the papers for the Staff International seminar and prepared some notes for what she would say at it. She would make a contribution about the impact of globalisation on union structures in the UK but also on the importance of unions coordinating activities when dealing with common employers. That would make it possible for her then to talk about the Industry3M issue.

She decided she would speak to the union's trustees about strike pay on the next day and also try and speak to the Swedish and German unions about the Prague seminar and, if possible, arrange to meet them on the Sunday evening at their hotel.

At six o'clock she packed her briefcase and left her office. She would have the GP committee on the Saturday and would have to fly to Prague on the Sunday afternoon. She wouldn't be able to see

Deborah or Helen that weekend but would try to fix that she could go and see them the following Sunday.

Leila and I went up to Congress House about one o'clock on the Thursday afternoon. We had a drink and a sandwich in the pub nearby and then went to Miller's office at a quarter to two. The meeting with the CBI employment committee was scheduled for three and Miller had asked us all to be in his office first to decide who should say what. As usual his staff had prepared a briefing paper on the likely subjects for discussion. Apparently John Dryden had suggested they would talk about the employment scene in general, the impact of the latest increase in the national minimum wage, what the TUC was pushing for in terms of changes to existing employment legislation and then he had suggested they could have a brief discussion about our job evaluation scheme. I was still a bit mystified as to why the CBI wanted to discuss the scheme but then perhaps we had indeed opened the magic bottle.

John Miller had a small meeting room next to his office and we all met there. Miller said he would lead on the main issues and suggested which of us should come in on particular points. When it came to the job evaluation scheme he said that he would ask Leila to introduce the subject. Several of my General Council colleagues said they couldn't understand why that was on the agenda although they each hastened to add that they had no objection to Leila being present and speaking on the matter. Mark Thurston from the engineering union, who was also the current president of the TUC, said he would listen carefully to what Leila said as he didn't understand the scheme at all. I didn't think he was completely joking.

As we walked the short distance to the CBI offices at the tower building which used to be called 'Centrepoint' I was talking to John Miller. I noticed that Leila was talking to both Dick Whetter and Jim

Bradwell presumably about how they were getting on with their job evaluation claims.

I reflected, not for the first time, that I was lucky to have

Leila as my number two in the union. I could rely upon her implicitly and knew that she would never be party to any group or faction within the union and that she would always support me fully. I knew that this was not the position in some of the other unions, particularly in those of Whetter and Bradwell where the extreme left seemed much more organised and more of a threat than they did with us, and, in some cases I knew of, the general secretary was hardly on speaking terms with his deputy general secretary.

We got to the CBI building a little early and were ushered into a waiting room. John Dryden came in and bade us welcome. I had always thought him reasonable and was glad he would be at the meeting. I had heard that there were several old dinosaurs on the employment committee. He gave Miller a piece of paper which listed the committee members who would be at the meeting and said he would come and fetch us in about five minutes. John Miller then read out the names to us.

There would be eight members from the CBI present including the CBI President, Sir Malcolm Wise. Miller told us that it was unusual for the CBI President to come to committee meetings. His main job was to preside over the CBI Council, their governing body, to be the leader of representations to Government and to be the second spokesman for the organisation (the principal spokesman being the CBI Director General). Wise was the first banker to be the head of the CBI. For many years, Miller explained, the banks had considered themselves to be so important in their own right—and through their own inter-bank committee structures—that they considered they did not need to belong to a body like the CBI. But attitudes had changed in recent years and most of the clearing banks were now members. It was still a step too far for the merchant banks but that didn't matter so much as it was the clearing banks that were the big employers of people. Wise was the chairman of one of the biggest clearing banks. I had never met him but reports were that he was not too bad a chap.

Leila handed round copies of her briefing paper on the job evaluation scheme. She knew that several of those present were well aware of the scheme but she had also included in her paper details of where the union had submitted the scheme and also had referred to the Swedish and German union interest.

Dryden then came back in and invited us to go with him to the main CBI meeting room. As we entered Malcom Wise came over and shook hands with Miller and Miller introduced Thurston as the TUC President. When we had sat down Wise introduced his colleagues. The CBI Director General was not one of them. Wise explained that he was on a visit to the CBI's Midlands regional council that day. I noted that a tall and thin, and rather ascetic looking individual, was David Adnam the chief executive of Teening & Sykes, the chemical company with whom we had a negotiating agreement and one of the companies where the job evaluation scheme had been claimed. He didn't look very welcoming to me. He must have recognised me for he gave me a curt nod as the introductions were made.

Mark Thurston made a short statement, carefully reading from the script which Miller had given him, I noticed, and then Miller opened up on the general employment scheme. There was quite a consensus on this. We all recognised the growth in employment but Miller drew particular attention to the higher levels of unemployment in the Liverpool and Manchester areas and also highlighted the disappointing figures of youth unemployment and how the current scheme for training youngsters didn't seem to be having much effect. Over half of the young people who had been on one of the Government's youth training schemes had been unable to find a job even six months after they had finished their training.

The discussion then centred on the impact of the national minimum wage with several of the employers present arguing that any further increase in the wage figure could have a bad effect on companies who were anxious to recruit new young people And they particularly were against any lowering of the age for the basic rate. Miller rebutted their arguments which had been made ever since the national minimum wage had first been mooted and for which there was no real evidence except some anecdotal reports from some individual companies and, even then, Miller said there were other factors involved.

We then spent about half an hour on the TUC's proposals for amending the current employment legislation. Clearly the CBI didn't want anymore changes and Adnam from Teening & Sykes said quite bluntly that there was far too much legislation and claimed that the existing burdens on employers, as he described it, were making a mockery of the Government's claim that the UK had an enviable degree of labour flexibility. Miller made some sharp points in response.

It seemed to me that nothing much was being gained from the discussion and nothing concrete would emerge. Miller had stressed to us in our pre-meeting at Congress House that the fact that the meeting was taking place at all was a good thing and that we shouldn't expect too much from it. I appreciated his point but felt that we had to come away with something.

It was about four thirty when we had finished discussions on the main items and Wise then announced that he would ask John Dryden and John Miller to come up with a press statement on the meeting. Both nodded and I could see that they had both discussed a possible press statement beforehand. Nothing wrong in that, I thought, but the statement had to say something positive.

Then Wise stated the meeting should spend a bit of time on our proposed job evaluation scheme. Dryden said he had put this on the agenda for the meeting as there had been some discussion within the CBI on it and also considerable press comment. He made no particular reference to the dispute with Industry3M and we all knew that Industry3M wasn't a CBI member. He then briefly rehearsed the introduction of job evaluation since the late 1960's and how he recognised that there was a need for new schemes to take account of the many changes in the labour market and the ways in which companies now recruited and used their staff. Wise then asked Miller for a comment. He said he shared Dryden's view that new approaches were needed and said that was why he had included Leila on their delegation and invited her to speak.

"Thank you. Sir Malcolm and gentlemen, I've got a summary of the job evaluation scheme of ours here and would like to leave copies with you." Leila paused and then went on: "I assume Mr Dryden will have told you about the scheme as he heard me speak about it at a recent seminar of the Industrial Foundation." She looked at Dryden who smiled and nodded. "I presume also that Mr Adnam knows about the scheme because my union has submitted a claim in his company for its introduction."

Adnam glared at her but didn't acknowledge the point.

Leila then outlined the scheme, the concept of self assessment, how it would operate, the appeals mechanism and how it could apply in both large and small companies. She stressed that the aim of the scheme was to make it transparent and involve the workforce. It would also allow for considerable flexibility in staff mobility. I could see that some of the CBI members seemed quite impressed.

Wise looked round and invited comments. A couple of the employers asked specific questions on how the scheme was administered and then Adnam from Teening & Sykes put this hand up. Wise nodded to him.

"Mr Chairman," Adnam started, "I must say quite bluntly that what Mrs Smith has said fills me with trepidation."

Wise asked gently, "why, David?"

"Because" Adnam responded, "at best the scheme is a recipe for administrative anarchy and at worst it's a blueprint for a sort of workers control."

There was silence for a moment. Miller opened his mouth to speak and I felt like having a go but Wise held up a hand.

"Come on, David, spell it out."

"These meetings are quite congenial, Mr Chairman, but I think it must first be said that the days when unions felt they could run industry—and some felt they could run the country—are long gone.

Different companies have different schemes for their staff—grading, status, payment, promotion and pay. That's as it should be. Of course in some cases we will talk about these matters with the unions but at the end of the day they must recognise that they don't have the power they used to think they had. Management must, after all, manage their own companies."

I could see Miller getting very irritated and he interjected: "is this getting us anywhere?" he demanded.

Before Wise could say anything, Adnam continued.

"What is the reality today? So called collective bargaining covers well under a third of the country's workforce. I believe that in the private sector—the sector that creates the wealth in the first place—union membership is now well under twenty per cent. And what does this job evaluation scheme mean? That people can decide their own worth? Their own grade? Their own pay? Is that what self assessment really means? Are we meant to hand over control of our labour to the unions? No, chairman, it's time to call a halt. We haven't got proper labour flexibility at all at the moment and to have schemes like this one means we're never going to have any flexibility."

Dick Whetter intervened: "why don't you say what you really mean?"

I could see my colleagues smiling at this. Adnam looked at him, his thin face going quite red but didn't respond. He turned to Wise.

"My own company has received a claim for this scheme to be introduced and I have to say quite clearly that we are going to have nothing to do with it."

I thought I must say something and said "this isn't a negotiating meeting, Mr Chairman."

Jim Bradwell said his union was intending to lodge a claim for the scheme to be introduced into local authorities and Whetter added that his executive thought it would be appropriate for the mainstream civil service. I turned to Leila and winked. I think she realised as I did that this discussion was probably just what John Dryden wanted when he had invited Leila to the meeting. She looked back at me and smiled. Yes, she had got the point.

Sir Malcolm Wise then asked for other comments. Both Whetter and Bardwell made short statements as to why the existing grading schemes in the civil service and local authorities were not meeting the needs of the current and future workforce and how they both thought the new job evaluation scheme could benefit both the workforce and the areas where it was introduced.

There was then a pause. One of the employers present was Tom Harding, the chairman of Transport International. A broad shouldered and thoughtful looking man, in his fifties I judged.

He said "my company has received a claim from Mrs Smith's union as has my friend Mr Adnam's company. I don't necessarily go all the way with what David has said but I must say that I can't see how such a scheme can benefit us. It's too open to interpretation and it could easily be abused. One of those schemes, Mr Chairman," he continued, "that looks good in theory but can't possibly work in practice."

Wise then invited Leila to respond. She spoke for about five minutes in a calm and measured tone and, I thought, dealt with all the points most succinctly. She didn't address herself to some of the general points that Adnam had made as she obviously realised it wouldn't do much good.

Wise then turned to Dryden.

"Anything you want to say, John?"

Dryden looked round the table.

"This particular discussion has gone on for sometime and it's obviously something that people feel strongly about. I understand—and it's been confirmed here now—that several unions are going to pursue this job evaluation scheme. I don't think we're going to get much further on it this afternoon but I do think it needs further looking into. I suggest, Mr Chairman, that we ask our trade union friends to join with us in an exercise to look more carefully at the scheme and try and see if it could be applied."

It was a clever move and it confirmed what I had thought as the discussion had started. Dryden had obviously been lobbied by several companies—and possibly by some permanent secretaries in the civil service—if not officials in the Treasury directly—about the scheme and the way to buy time, and, possibly, stifle the scheme from the outset, would be a joint examination of it. On the one hand it would look like a genuine offer to pursue the scheme but in reality it could easily be lost in a mass of meetings and reports and finally never emerge with any agreement. I thought that this was why Leila had been invited to the meeting in the first place. Get if off the negotiating table and into some form of joint review or examination that could bury it.

John Miller said—too quickly to my mind—"we could certainly consider that. What do you think, John?" turning to me.

I decided to play it long.

"I think we ought to discuss it among ourselves first. There are pros and cons."

Wise then stood up.

"Well I think then, lady and gentlemen, we've done all we can this afternoon. John here—" pointing to Dryden—"and Mr Miller will want to discuss the draft statement and presumably Mr Miller will let us know about our suggestion of a joint study of the job evaluation scheme and we can take if from there."

We all got up. Wise didn't come round to shake hands but waved to us cheerily. A very smooth operator, I thought, but then he wouldn't be chairman of a major bank if he wasn't.

***

The TUC General Council members went back to the small waiting room they had first been in, while Dryden and Miller went to Dryden's office. Thurston congratulated Leila on her statement at the meeting—he said with a smile that he thought he could now understand the scheme—and the others murmured approval.

The door opened and both Dryden and Miller came in.

"Just to say," said Dryden to them all, "that I thought the meeting was useful."

Thurston said: "that chap Adnam's a bit Victorian isn't he?"

Dryden smiled: "well, we have our dinosaurs too, you know."

Dryden then left and Miller handed out copies of the press statement he had agreed with Dryden. It talked about their discussion on employment, training, the national minimum wage and then the job evaluation scheme and the proposal for a joint study.

Carmichael and Leila looked at each other. Carmichael then looked at Miller.

"It doesn't say much, does it John? And I don't think we want that reference to the joint study proposal in."

"Well," replied Miller, "I know it's fairly anodyne. The proposal for a joint study on job evaluation was about the only positive thing that came out of the meeting."

They all started to speak at once. Thurston called for order and asked Carmichael to speak. He said the press statement should be merely stating that the meeting, one of a regular series, had taken place and views exchanged on the various topics. He was against any mention of the job evaluation issues. Miller asked him why.

Leila caught Thurston's eye and he invited her to speak.

"I don't believe in the conspiracy theory of history," she said, "but I think that John Dryden wanted the joint study before we even got to the meeting. I don't think it's going to be useful—"

A number of the others looked at her, questioningly.

She went on: "we have claims in with a number of companies for the scheme. Are they to be put to one side while a joint study takes place? How long would the study take? I suspect that either a joint study would come out against our scheme as being impractical or taking too much authority away from management or it won't be able to agree at all. And then, where are we?"

Whetter, sitting beside her, nodded. Bradwell said it might be different if some body like Ruskin College, the adult education

Oxford college with strong links to trade unions—were to do the study. Miller said there wasn't a hope in hell that the CBI would agree to that. Carmichael said why didn't they ask Ruskin to do a study anyway and shelve the idea of a joint study with the CBI. In the meantime unions would continue to press claims for the scheme as they thought fit. Thurston said he agreed with Carmichael and it was clear from their expressions that the others were in agreement with him.

Miller paused, "OK, I'll go back to Dryden and tell him." He looked at Leila. "You're on to something big here, aren't you Leila/"

Leila said nothing and Miller left to have another word with Dryden.

After half an hour Miller came back. Dryden had been very reluctant to omit any reference to the job evaluation scheme but eventually had agreed. In the end the press statement was—again he repeated the word—an 'anodyne' one.

Leila mentioned that Dryden had told her when he rang her about the meeting that he would be doing a brief for his people on the job evaluation scheme. Could they have a copy?

Miller smiled and pulled a paper from his pocket.

"When I was having a chat about the statement with Dryden he went out of his office briefly to give his secretary a draft to type up. I noticed that on his desk were several copies of a paper headed 'job evaluation' and I thought I would take one."

Several of the General Council members cheered.

"I will let you see it in the pub if you like and get my secretary to fax copies to your offices."

"Right," said Thurston, "who's buying the first round?"

The next morning when Leila came into my office we went over the CBI paper which Dryden had prepared and which Miller had lifted from his desk.

The interesting thing, from my point of view, was that it specifically mentioned the Industry3M dispute and—surprisingly as Industry3M was not a CBI member organisation—how the company had contacted Dryden about it. The paper also referred to the other companies where my union had submitted claims and the likely claims for its introduction in the civil service and the local authorities.

Leila said: "the first part is OK but the latter part seems, I'm sorry to say, a rather politer way of saying what Adnam said yesterday. I thought Dryden was going to be more objective. It certainly reinforces our view, John, that we were right to insist that there was no mention of a joint study in the press statement."

I agreed with her point.

"We'll pursue the claim in the companies where we have claimed it and it would be a good idea if you had a word with Hazel Bellini as to why the trots on the Leisure & Sport national committee were not in favour of claiming the scheme now."

Leila said she would and commented that there seemed to be a meeting of minds between the CBI and the trots.

"That wouldn't be too surprising," I said, "but they've each got their own agenda."

Leila said "it almost seems that the CBI—or Dryden in particular—is anxious that unions should not be able to push the job evaluation scheme as a means of making the unions popular again and strengthening our hand."

"Well," I said, "you should take that as a compliment."

<hr />

By mid-morning Leila had spoken to the three union trustees and—after a bit of cajoling—they had agreed to what Carmichael had proposed for strike pay. They had, though, each insisted that it was not to be treated as a precedent and if further strikes were to take place, then they would want to think again. Leila assured them they would be able to think again; but, equally, she knew full well that, like it or not, the flat rate strike payment would inevitably be taken as a precedent.

She had also spoken to Hazel Bellini. Bellini had pronounced herself as mystified as to why the trots on her national committee had not wanted to push the job evaluation scheme as a claim with Leisure & Sport. Perhaps, thought Leila, she realised that she should have pushed the issue harder and was trying to make excuses. It was odd, though, as Hazel Bellini was regarded as one of the most capable of the union's officials.

She had arranged with Carmichael that they would go up to Victoria Street, where the Department of Trade and Industry's offices were, a little early so they could get a bite to eat before the meeting with Bob Wilson, the Minister of State.

They got to the minister's office ten minutes before the due time. His private secretary took them to a small waiting room and asked them to wait. He said he would call them when the minister was ready.

Both Carmichael and Leila had known Wilson when he was a union official. He had worked his way up in one of the small electricity unions and then, when he became general secretary, had been elected to the General Council. His union had been one with under one hundred thousand members and so he took part in the ballot for the smaller union seats. Usually there was a 'right wing' list and a 'left wing list' for the seven seats reserved for the smaller unions.

Leila knew that the terms 'right wing' and 'left wing' were very much relative and they had to be seen in the context of the TUC and Labour Party's political attitudes. 'Right wing' generally meant mainstream Labour; 'left wing' usually meant the extreme left of the Labour Party together with assorted trotskyist and communist groups. Wilson had been firmly of the right wing. She had liked him and while he had only been on the General Council for two years she regarded him as one of the brightest members.

It was therefore no surprise when Wilson was chosen at the last moment for a safe Labour parliamentary seat just before the general election of five years previously. Once elected Wilson had made fairly rapid progress: assistant government whip, parliamentary under secretary in the transport ministry and then minister of state in the Department of Trade and Industry. Even before he had got on to the General Council he had been friendly with John Miller the TUC General Secretary. Both men were from Yorkshire and both had been brought up in Bradford and gone to the same school.

Carmichael and Leila spent some time discussing likely dates for the proposed three day strike. Carmichael thought mid August would be preferable: it was not too late after the July 15 one day stoppage and, in terms of publicity, would be likely to get good coverage as there never seemed much industrial news in that month. Leila said she would put that view to the GP committee at its forthcoming Saturday meeting.

It was twenty five minutes before the private secretary came back to say the minister was now ready to see them. Leila could see that Carmichael was a little irritated at the long wait they had had. She too had felt a little aggrieved that Wilson had kept them waiting but perhaps there was a genuine explanation.

If there was such an explanation they never received it. As the private secretary ushered them into the minister's office Wilson came forward and shook hands. He said he had a busy day and had several further meetings that afternoon. He invited them to sit down and asked Carmichael to speak first.

"I know you're busy, minister—" although he had been 'Bob' to both Carmichael and Leila for some time it was correct for them to call him 'minister'. The private secretary was taking notes and they were speaking to him as a minister of the crown. Carmichael knew that some of his colleagues would try and show off to their colleagues in ministerial meetings by using the first name of the minister as often as they could, but he had never done that.

"We have a serious dispute with the American owned company Industry3M and I understand that John Miller has been talking to you about it."

Wilson nodded. He was a tall and heavily built man, in his mid fifties Leila guessed. He looked a bit stressed and his eyes kept switching from Carmichael to Leila.

Carmichael referred to the company's structure, its global centre in Atlanta, the European head office in London and the UK head officer in Liverpool. He also mentioned the desultory correspondence between himself and the company and the complete lack of any progress in negotiations and the apparent likelihood of the union being derecognised. He stressed to Wilson that he knew he shouldn't bother him as minister with an ordinary industrial dispute, but this was different. The company was American owned and the job evaluation scheme was being pursued in a number of other companies and by some other unions.

Wilson said he knew that but he wasn't sure what the union expected him to do.

Leila suggested he could have a word with the company, particularly the head office in Atlanta and urge sensible negotiations.

"This dispute could be important for foreign companies moving into Britain—"

Wilson interrupted her: "too bloody right, it could be important. We've got one of the best records of foreign investment in Britain and we don't want that upset." He turned to Leila.

"Why can't ACAS sort this out?"

"Well the reason's quite simple, minister," said Leila. "As you well know ACAS can't succeed in any settlement of a dispute unless the parties themselves want to settle it. I've been in touch with ACAS again and they tell me the company will not come to any meeting with them—singly or jointly with us."

Wilson paused and looked again at them in turn.

"You can't expect me to be a sort of ACAS court of appeal, can you? Have you tried to appeal to their head office? Harold Stuckman isn't it?" he said referring to the person he called the company's managing director.

"I've just told you that my letters to Stuckman have not got us anywhere," said Carmichael in a resigned fashion.

Wilson seemed to take umbrage at Carmichael's tone.

"Look, John, you can't expect me to intervene in an industrial dispute." He paused again and then said: "look, if the job evaluation scheme is a problem why don't you try a new tack? Why not have a joint study on it and then take it from there."

Carmichael took a deep breath. The meeting was not going as he had hoped. He told Wilson that he and Leila had been at a meeting with the CBI's employment committee the previous day and that the CBI had suggested a joint study. Leila noted that Wilson gave an almost imperceptible nod at this. He knew, she thought. Someone like John Dryden must have got hold of him, or, at least, one of his officials and told him about the meeting.

"Minister," Carmichael said, "we rejected the CBI idea yesterday as it seems nothing more than an attempt to glance to leg the whole idea and, if a joint study ever came up with a conclusion, it could well go against us."

"Well, that's what might be. But it seems to me that there is such a lot of confusion over this job evaluation scheme that a joint study might help to establish basic parameters."

They argued over the idea of a joint study for the next ten minutes. Wilson kept looking at his watch and then said: "look, John I have to go to another meeting now. I'll think about what you have said but I don't really see what I can do. Yes, we want foreign investment; yes we don't want strikes in foreign owned companies—or any companies, come to that. But I think you both ought to think seriously about a joint study."

His private secretary handed him a note. Wilson looked at it and then added: "and I see that the civil service and local authorities unions are pursuing the scheme. Are you pursuing it elsewhere?"

Leila judged that he already knew the answer to his own question but she decided to tell him about the other companies where the scheme had been claimed. For good measure she also mentioned her talks with the relevant German and Swedish unions. Wilson seemed a bit taken aback at this. He took another look at his watch and then stood up.

"I think we'll have to call this a day," he said. "I will consider the matter further but as you well know in turn, this Government does not favour any intervention into the internal affairs of companies. We've dropped all that. It's up to companies and unions to sort out their own problems. I just hope you and Industry3M can sort this out."

Carmichael and Leila both realised they were not going to get any further in the meeting.

"Well, thanks for seeing us, minister. I just thought a quiet word from you in the right quarter might help. We don't see how a joint study will advance anything. And—" he paused—"we've got a three day strike in the company looming and there'll be more publicity."

Wilson exploded: "are you threatening me John? It's up to you to sort out your problems—the days of beer and sandwiches are long gone."

Leila could hardly contain herself. She broke in: "you know from your own experience how the cards are stacked against us, minister. After all, you have been a general secretary."

Wilson almost shouted at her.

"Yes, and you've never been a minister and you will have to accept that there is a world of difference from putting in claims and taking decisions from a position of responsibility. That's the difference. I have to deal with the world as it is—not as we would like it to be."

Carmichael said "we all used to argue for a better world, Bob." he used the minister's first name deliberately.

Wilson went red again and then swallowed. He looked even more stressed.

"Well, I think we've got as far as we can. Thanks for coming."

The three looked at each other and all knew there was no point in saying anything more. Carmichael and Leila both shook hands with Wilson and his private secretary joined them in leaving the office. Wilson went back to his desk and sighed. He knew he hadn't handled it very well, but they didn't know did they? Power meant responsibility, didn't it? Well, he'd done what he could.

Once outside the minister's office Carmichael whispered to Leila "I must get hold of John Miller before Wilson does. We don't want to lose TUC support."

⁂

I was furious with Bob Wilson's attitude but realised there was not much we could do about it. Leila and I went over to the pub just up Victoria Street from the DTI offices and from there I phoned John Miller on my mobile. He was out but I left a message with Stella to ask if Miller could phone me either at the office or at home so I could tell him about the meeting.

In the pub Leila and I went over the state of play with the other unions and the claims which our union had submitted for the new job evaluation scheme. It was a good thing that we had arranged for a meeting of all the relevant officials for next Thursday and we could take stock of the position. I told Leila that I would ask Frank Hallard to do a brief for the meeting and would myself chase up Dick Whetter, Jim Bradwell and Peter Moorhouse on how their claims were going. With Leila talking to the Swedish and German unions in Prague then we would have a fairly clear picture of where we were.

Leila mentioned that she had spoken to Hazel Bellini and could not understand why her national committee had prevaricated over submitting a claim. She said it seemed that Bellini had not pushed the scheme hard enough, which I found surprising. Still, we would pursue the matter at the Thursday meeting.

We again went over the options for the three day strike in Industry3M and Leila said she would speak to Ian Macallister that evening with our idea of mid-August and try and get the GP committee to endorse that.

As we both went back to Waterloo station and then went our separate ways home, I wondered where all this would lead: a strike and now a three day strike, claims in other companies, other unions making similar claims, CBI interest, the seemingly deliberately hostile attitude of the minister—it seemed we had indeed opened the magic bottle. Or, to put it another and more slightly more sinister way, I wondered whether we had opened Pandora's box.

Leila arrived at Prague airport at four in the afternoon. She got a taxi to the hotel where all the people from the various unions attending the seminar were staying. The hotel was called the 'Pyramida' and apparently before the 'velvet revolution' in the former Czechoslovakia and under the communist regime, the hotel had been built for members of the communist party youth movement. Leila had stayed there before: it was cold, ugly and rather uncomfortable. Still, it was cheap and had good conference facilities.

The plane had been delayed at Heathrow for an hour before take-off and Leila was feeling tired. She would book in, have a shower and change and then as she had arranged would meet Lars Tolmark from the Swedish SAF and Jurgen Bruch of the German DGB at six in the bar. She remembered that the union men usually liked the bar and this was because of the beer which they all said was very good. For herself she found the bar noisy and unappealing, but, she thought, it was better than the ultra smart and highly expensive bars of any of the new western style hotel she had stayed in once in the centre of the city—and where, the union male delegates said, the beer was mostly American and therefore awful. And, she reflected, it was a trade union meeting she was attending.

She was glad the general purposes committee seemed to have gone well the previous day. As usual Ian Macallister had handled it well. After a discussion the committee had agreed that the three day strike should take place on the twentieth, twenty first and twenty second of August. The timing meant it just came within the legitimacy of the ballot vote that had authorised the industrial action. She had spoken on the phone to John Carmichael afterwards and he would circulate the national executive committee about it. The committee had also welcomed the proposal of Carmichael and Leila for strike pay.

Somewhat surprisingly Tony Hammond had not said much at all at the meeting. He had sat, angry looking and occasionally glaring at Leila, but only spoke once and that was once again to advocate a committee of lay representatives to have overall charge of the strike but had not found a seconder for his proposition.

She got down to the bar just after six. Tolmark and Bruch were sitting at a table with two glasses of beer and both jumped to their feet as she approached. They uttered the usual pleasantries of their journeys to the hotel and when they had last met. Leila told herself that much of the conversation of union officials assembled for an international meeting was like that of a bunch of travel agents—however, it seemed to break the ice.

Tolmark said his number two in the Swedish Svenska Arbeiter Forbundet, Per Ulric, would be joining them shortly. In fact, just as he said that, Ulric appeared, shook hands with them all and regaled them with details of his travel experience to the hotel. Bruch of the German Deutsche Gewerkshaft Bund bought some more beer—and a glass of red wine for Leila—and then they listened to Leila.

Leila had faxed over material to both the unions after her initial conversation with them and she now updated them on her union's plans for a three day strike. She also mentioned her conversation with Chuck Pitney of the *Wall Street Journal* and his comments about the financial position of Industry3M.

Tolmark explained how the industrial scene in Sweden was not as healthy as it had been. Many unions were facing increasingly difficult negotiations with employers. The much vaunted talks between the Swedish central employers organisation and the Swedish central union bodies (unlike the UK there were two of them in Sweden, one for manual unions, the LO, and one for white collar unions, the TCO) had failed to agree on measures to halt rising inflation and worrying signs of increasing unemployment.

He mentioned signs of dissatisfaction with the unions from amongst their own membership. Many, particularly the younger members, felt the union structures were too bureaucratic and that the unions were too cosy with the employers and too remote from their own members. Tolmark, large, red faced and in many ways a larger than life character, thought Leila, was no fool and he made an interesting contrast to Ulric, thin and slightly ascetic and very, very serious.

Ulric then told how they had submitted a claim for the new job evaluation scheme to the Swedish company of Industry3M where they had some eighty per cent of the one hundred and fifty staff in membership. The union committee had been enthusiastic about it and groups of members in some of the other companies where they negotiated also were keen on it. Ulric stressed, in his slow and almost pedantic manner, that the scheme was particularly popular with their younger members and thought this was because of the principle of self assessment that lay at the heart of the scheme.

Leila asked about the timetable for pursuing the scheme. Ulric explained that they had settled pay six months previously so the claim was being pursued on its own and so far the company had not made a response.

Tolmark asked Leila: "there's been an American seen in the office of Industry3M. Someone called Tiller. Do you know anything about him?."

Jurgen Bruch, tall and fair haired, looking younger than his fifty years, and whom Leila knew reasonably well—he was one of the few Germans, she often told people, who had a good sense of humour, almost English, she would say—broke in.

"Leila, I was going to ask the same thing." He added with a smile, "you know the Swedes and the Germans often think on the same lines."

Leila smiled back: she wasn't quite sure how to respond as he might have been half serious, so she decided to say nothing. She then remembered what Chuck Pitney had told Carmichael and herself about Tiller. John Carr had been appointed as the HR director for Europe and had beaten an American, Joe Tiller, for the position. She told them what she knew.

"But I've never met him. I can only hope he isn't as bad as Carr," and she explained her view on him with some feeling.

Ulric repeated that they were waiting for a response. Bruch then said they had submitted a claim and it had met with a hostile reaction. His union had made a two year pay deal with Industry3M the previous year and the company was now saying that the claim for the job evaluation scheme was in effect breaking that agreement. Like Ulric he said that other groups within his union had studied the job evaluation scheme and were in favour of it. His executive committee for the white collar section of the DGB had decided to wait and see how things progressed in Industry3M first but it was quite possible that other company union committees would agree to submit claims.

After a few more drinks Leila said she would keep in touch with them on developments. She referred to the civil service and local government unions and their likely pursuance of claims in Britain.

Tolmark commented that it appeared the job evaluation scheme was proving very popular but it would help if one company would agree to its introduction: then others would undoubtedly follow. The others looked at Leila.

Bruch said "it seems that it's up to you first, Leila" and she noticed he wasn't smiling this time.

"Well, we've got a three day strike coming next month and hopefully that will move the company. But I can't emphasise enough that the more both your unions pursue the claim then the better it will be."

She referred to the meeting between the TUC and the CBI employment committee and the suggestion of a joint study. Tolmark, Ulric and Bruch all agreed with her that she and Carmichael had been right to oppose the idea. She said they were still thinking about asking Ruskin College in Oxford to do a study of it but realised many employers would hardly consider them objective or impartial.

Just as she was getting up to go a large figure approached them. It was Hans van Megeren the secretary general of Staff International. He greeted them all and insisted on buying a round of drinks. Leila started to say she just wanted an orange juice but van Megeren cut her off and insisted she had a glass of red wine. He got the drinks and then sat down with them.

"Now let me guess," he said "you're talking about Industry3M."

Leila smiled at him.

"You're very sharp, Hans. And what's been the reaction of the affiliates to the stuff you've been sending out for me—the job evaluation scheme and the rest?"

Van Megeren replied "positive. There's been a lot of favourable reaction. You know, Leila" he said turning towards her, "in your talk tomorrow on globalisation you might mention your dispute with Industry3M and the importance of international action."

"Hans, you have been reading my speech."

"Good, because a number of our affiliates outside Europe have been asking me about it as well"

She started again to get up to go. Tolmark said "why don't you have a word with the Malaysian union Leila: that could be an avenue."

Leila sat down again: "Lars, you're sharp as well. I was going to talk about the scheme tomorrow and how globalisation affect trade union actions and abilities, but I think a private word with them—"she looked at van Megeren—"if they're here "—Van Megeren shook his head—" might also help as well. Well, I'll speak to them on the phone."

She finished her drink and stood up again. They all got up and wished her good night. Leila went up the stairs to the small and uncomfortable room to try and sleep. The conversation had been helpful but it was clear that her union had to make some sort of breakthrough, but how could they given the attitude of Industry3M? She made a mental note to telephone the general secretary of the Malaysian white collar affiliate of Staff International when she got back to her office, or, if she could, sometime during the next two days of the seminar.

Van Megeren introduced the seminar in the morning. Altogether there were some sixty people present, officials and lay members from twenty of the European affiliated unions. In a couple of months time Staff International was hosting a major conference on globalisation for all its affiliates, including unions in north and south America, Australasia and the far east. The European seminar was designed to try and work out a policy for the European unions that could be a central talking point for the world conference.

He then gave way to Jan Pulac, the president of the major Czech white collar union that was affiliated to Staff International. Leila had met Pulac several times during her time with Staff International. Carmichael served as the CGU member of the world executive committee of Staff International with Leila on the European executive. Pulac looked like a professor, she thought, or at least like most people imagined a professor should look like. She had heard that he had been a close friend of Vaclav Havel, the Czech President, and for a while had been imprisoned under the previous communist regime. As she listened to Pulac welcome them all to the seminar she reflected, not for the first time, how little did some of her colleagues in the British trade union movement know of the real struggles that unions in many other countries had gone through—Latin America, eastern Europe before the collapse of communism and several countries in Africa.

Though she didn't want to dignify the trots in her own union as in any way comparable to the forces those unions had dealt with, she couldn't help thinking about them: in particular, why had the trots on the national committee of Leisure & Sport been against the submission of the job evaluation claim?

Her mind was brought back to the seminar when she hear Pulac make a particular point about the job evaluation scheme and her union's dispute with Industry3M. She got out her notes for her address to the seminar and looked at them again. She was the second speaker at the seminar and the title of her talk was 'how can unions deal with international companies in an age of globalisation?' A grand title she thought to herself but there were some relevant points to make; if only, she could talk about a successful outcome of the Industry3M dispute—that really would be the answer to the question in the title.

Her talk went down well at the seminar and a number of the others congratulated her on her talk. Tolmark was particularly enthusiastic and said they ought to have another drink at lunch time. He smiled as Leila seemed reluctant to commit herself to another round of drinks.

"I know there were several drinks last night," he said. "But it's an occupational hazard, isn't it? And I have heard what happened to Per Ulric at your conference that time."

They both smiled and Leila said she would join him at the bar when the morning session finished.

At the end of the session and before she went to the bar Leila got the telephone number of Paul Mugai, the general secretary of the Malaysian union, from van Megeren. She realised that time difference would mean she couldn't get hold of him now but she would try later that evening and catch him as he arrived at the office in the morning.

She remembered what Chuck Pitney had said about Industry3M's expansion plans and how the far east was a likely area. It was definitely worth pursuing.

I got back from my trip to Scotland on the Wednesday afternoon and went straight to the office from Heathrow airport. Fortunately the tube was working all right and I was in the office by four o'clock. There was a pile of papers in my in-tray but first I called through to Leila and asked her to come to my office.

When she came in I asked how the Staff International seminar had gone and she said it had gone well. She mentioned her chats with the Swedish and German unions and then the suggestion of van Megeren about contacting the Malaysian union. She said she had tried to telephone them from Prague but Mugai, their general secretary, had been away from his office. She had just tried him again but to no avail.

I told her that I had got hold of John Miller of the TUC on the Friday evening. In fact he hadn't phoned me but I had phoned him at his home in the evening. I had started to tell him about our meeting with Bob Wilson at the DTI but he had interrupted me and said that Wilson had already spoken to him. Miller had sounded a bit defensive on the phone. I knew that he had Wilson had been friends for a long time and wondered what Wilson had actually told him. Anyway, after a brief discussion we had agreed to have a further chat later in the following week. I told Leila that I would speak to him again after we had had our meeting with our negotiating officials tomorrow.

We discussed the arrangements for the three day strike in Industry3M. Leila thought we should have the same allocation of organisers and pickets as for the one day strike. She suggested that we held a press conference the day before the three day strike and give details of how the job evaluation scheme was being claimed in other companies and refer to the Swedish and German unions claims. She would also keep on to Tino Malik at ACAS. She sounded a bit down as she spoke.

I referred to my talks with Dick Whetter, Jim Bradwell and Peter Moorhouse. Claims for the job evaluation were going in with each of their unions. The bandwagon seemed to be rolling.

"It all seems to be going OK, Leila. Why the long face?" I asked.

"I just feel we've got to have some sort of breakthrough. The other claims are fine but as Tolmark and the others said to me in Prague, they're looking for us to achieve some sort of deal. The scheme is popular and a number of the others at the seminar expressed interest. Van Megeren has circulated all the stuff and several of them want some more detailed papers from me. I've got Frank Hallard sending them more details. It could all go well but I don't like the ominous silence from Industry3M."

I knew she had a point. There had been no communication from the company. I would be writing to them on Friday with the dates of the three day strike as the national executive committee had agreed on a phone round with the decision of Les Martin and Jane Toff after they had got my circular with Leila's report on the one day strike.

"We'll see what reaction we get when I tell the company of the dates for the three day strike." I looked at her. "The troops are still OK aren't they."

Leila confirmed that the GP committee had gone well and Macallister and the others had been solid. She mentioned Hammond's low profile at the meeting. She also said she would be having another word with Hazel Bellini before our meeting tomorrow.

"I do feel a little depressed, John," she admitted. "Yes, the seminar went well and we're doing all we can. I suppose I didn't get much sleep at that bloody awful Pyramida hotel and my plane was a couple of hours late getting back last night. Still, as you say, we are doing all we can."

We talked a little more and her spirits seemed to lift a bit as we went over again all the arrangements for the three day strike. As she left my office she said "it's strange isn't it John, Industry3M membership is about one per cent of our total membership and we're putting in a lot of effort for them. But I do understand the importance of it."

She paused and then added "I'll get a good night's sleep tonight and be fighting fit tomorrow."

I wished her well as she left. I knew her feelings well and many times I had been depressed over the many negotiations and disputes I had been involved in, particularly since I became the general secretary.

Just after she went I had a phone call. Sheila said it was from David Stannard. As she put me through I uttered a cheery 'hello'.

"David, how's it going?"

Stannard sounded very depressed and I immediately thought that all this depression wasn't being very good for me. But what he had to say made me sit up.

He told me that he had had a telephone call from the American, Joe Tiller. They had never met but he knew of him. Tiller had suggested they had an informal meeting and Stannard had agreed to meet him on the Friday at lunch time in the central London hotel where Tiller was apparently staying. I thanked him for telling me that and I then told him privately about the three day strike.

"I get the feeling that Tiller's a hard man, John, and don't know why he wants to meet me."

I asked him if Tiller had mentioned John Carr and Stannard said no.

We talked a little more. I asked him if he had had any joy in getting another job but Stannard said he had been unsuccessful in three attempts but was still trying. After the conversation finished I buzzed Leila on the internal phone and told her about the call. She agreed with me that it might mean some movement but neither of us had any idea of where that movement might lead.

Frank Hallard had produced a briefing paper for the meeting of the negotiating officials on Thursday. He had set out the position in Industry3M, referred to the one day strike on 15 July, the planned three day strike on twentieth, twenty first and twenty second of August and the lack of any progress with ACAS. He had also summarised the membership position in Teening & Sykes, some 6,000 members, Transport International, over 12,000 members (we had taken over the small white collar union that had organised there and built up the membership significantly in the last couple of years), and Hokkaido where we had 3,000 members.

Halard had spoken at length to the three officials responsible for those companies and had put down a likely timetable for the prosecution of the job evaluation scheme. It appeared from what Mathew Singh had told him that the national committee in Teening & Sykes were keen on going for an industrial action ballot in view of the complete rejection of a meeting to discuss the claim. I was not too surprised in view of what the company's chief executive, David Adnam, had said at the CBI meeting the previous week. The other two officials—Adam Turnbull and Brian Hall—had both indicated that an industrial action ballot in their respective companies was a possibility but not quite yet.

Also, Hallard had summarised the position with the civil service union of Dick Whetter and Jim Bradwell's local government union. He had also put down what I had told him of the actions of Peter Moorhouse's Commercial and Tenchnology Union. Moorhouse had lodged claims in three small companies. Progress in the civil service was, inevitably, slow. The grading system was common throughout the service and although Dick Whetter had told me that he had argued that the decentralisation of control meant that individual departments could adopt their own grading structures, the reaction had been hostile. He had suggested that the scheme be tried first in the Department of Trade and Industry—and his committee there had been enthusiastic about the job evaluation scheme—but the permanent secretary and his senior colleagues had rejected the idea almost out of hand.

I thought back to the attitude of Bob Wilson of the DTI at our meeting. It seemed to me that there was quite a network of opposition to our job evaluation proposals—civil service, individual companies, CBI—perhaps Leila and I should indeed take that as a compliment.

I knew that Leila was going to have a word with Hallard to update the report with the news about the Swedish and German unions and that would complete the union picture as far as now. Hallard had written a good piece about the company itself. He had rehearsed information about the company he had got from the *Financial Times* and, as I had suggested to him, Chuck Pitney of the *Wall Street Journal*. Although no American union organised the company in the USA he had been able to get some information from the American Federation of Labour-Congress of Industrial Organisations (AFL-CIO), the US equivalent of our TUC. He had also spoken to Ian Macallister, Ted Davis and Clive Bristow of Industry3M.

Industry3M had eight companies on the continent of Europe of which it appeared that only the Swedish and the Spanish companies were profitable. Surprisingly, the German company was struggling. The company's operation in the US was, of course, the core of its business but it was seeking to branch out into the far east and Thailand, the Philippines and Malaysia were the three most often quoted countries as being on Industry3M's list.

I thought Hallard's brief was good. I hoped our talk with the others tomorrow would be able to move the whole thing along.

Leila thought the meeting with the negotiators had been positive. Alan Whitchurch, responsible for organisation, and Julia Cardon had joined them. Carmichael had also asked Christine Buckley, the finance officer, to join the meeting. Leila knew there would be considerable interest in the decision to pay fifty pounds a day strike pay. The national executive committee had been circulated with that as well as the GP recommendation on the strike days and had agreed to it. Many of the national executive members had though, not surprisingly, said they would want a proper meeting to discuss any further payment of strike pay.

In a way Leila knew they should have had a full debate at a proper meeting of the national executive but there weren't enough hours in the day or days in the week for full discussion on every aspect of any industrial dispute. The trustees of the union had agreed the strike pay proposal and that was important. Of course the decision could be treated as a precedent but the trustees had insisted that they were not bound to a similar decision. And that was the best they could do in the circumstances.

When she had been a lay official of her union in the civil service Leila had often had a difficult time balancing the demands of her job with the time off needed to attend union committee meetings. She knew she was like thousands of others. Although time off was given—and usually it was written into union agreements—and in some cases deputisation arrangements would be made, there was always an inevitable build of work for her to deal with when she got back to work. She knew it was the case even more now with companies in the private sector—and the managements in the public sector—constantly trying to cut down on staff numbers in order to contain staff costs.

The members of the national executive committee of the CGU all had jobs—no pensioners were allowed by the union's constitution to serve on the national executive—and there had to be a limit to the number of meetings and time off requested for them to attend union meetings. She knew that some of the older and more traditional manual unions had small full time executives but she thought that would be dangerous for a union like hers. The members had to be aware of what was going on in their area of work and be in touch with members on a day to day basis.

She had had another word with Hazel Bellini just before the meeting had started. Bellini had obviously thought about their previous discussion. She said she had spoken to a number of the national committee of Leisure & Sport and carefully explained the need for a claim on the job evaluation scheme, particularly as there were about four different types of grading schemes operating within the company at the moment: largely, she explained to Leila, because the company had grown rapidly in recent years mainly through taking over smaller companies with their own staff systems.

Bellini had added that she was fairly confident she could get the claim agreed at the next national committee meeting, but that wouldn't be until September. Leila knew that the same pressures that affected the lay members of the national executive committee also affected the national committee members. There was nothing for it but to wait until September. At least though, Leila was encouraged that Bellini now seemed willing to take on the trots. Although she was one of the brightest of the officials they had, Leila thought she might have been trying to appease the trots when Leila knew there were no medals given nor victories gained for any such appeasement.

Leila had outlined the position with the German and Swedish unions and Carmichael had expanded what Hallard had put in the brief about other unions claiming the job evaluation scheme. She had been pleased when Mathew Singh, the national official for negotiations in Teening & Sykes had outlined a draft timetable for an industrial action ballot. Hallard had referred to the possibility but in the last two days Singh had been speaking to the leading members of his national committee and on that basis had sketched out a likely scenario for a ballot for a one day strike.

As with all calls for an industrial action ballot it would have to go before the union's national executive committee for ratification following a recommendation from the appropriate national committee. But, fortuitously Leila thought, the Teening & Sykes national committee was meeting at the end of August anyway, a meeting that had been scheduled some months ago.

Carmichael had reminded the meeting that the national executive would hold its normal pre-Congress meeting on 2 September and then any demands for industrial action ballots could be considered there and this would fit in with the Teening & Sykes national committee meeting.

Each year the national executive committee would hold a special meeting to go over the agenda for the annual TUC Congress and to mandate the twenty delegates that attended the Congress on behalf of the union. Inevitably there were other items on the agenda and there was precedent for dealing with calls for ballots then.

Brian Hall, the official for Hokkaido, the Japanese motor car manufacturer, stated the national committee there would want to get the company's reaction to the other elements of the major claim they had made on the company. The job evaluation scheme was just one part of the claim. A likely time for any discussion on a ballot over the JE scheme would probably wait until the end of September, or even mid October, assuming that the company refused any discussion of the scheme.

Adam Turnbull, the official responsible for Transport International, said much the same as Brian Hall. There the scheme had been included along with the annual pay claim and he anticipated a clearer picture by the beginning of October.

Again Leila reflected that the decision making process in the union was pretty long winded but she knew it had to be. There had to be proper procedures—not just because of the current employment regulations governing ballots and strikes but because the union decisions had to be taken in a way that small groups of people could not manipulate or short circuit them. As far as they could manage it, decisions had to reflect what actually was the feelings of the majority.

All in all, Leila thought, it had been a good meeting. Carmichael had told them of the press conference they were planning for the nineteenth of August, the day before the three day strike in Industry3M, and how that would generate a lot more interest both within the union but also with the other TUC unions. Julia Cardon mentioned that she had heard from her opposite member in the main civil service union that Dick Whetter was planning a press conference in the same week about the claims he was making for the job evaluation scheme. Some of the journalists would undoubtedly ask Jim Bradwell and Peter Moorhouse for comments on what was happening in their unions so Leila considered they should all get a fair bit of publicity.

It was now the Friday afternoon. Leila had Alan Whitchurch and Julia Cardon with her in her office and they went over the arrangements for the three day strike. They could not afford to be careless about it just because they had held the one day strike. They had to make sure that everything would be ready—posters, leaflets, banners, megaphones, the lists of pickets, telephone numbers to be distributed to the organisers and the leading lay officials, the hotels to be booked, liaison with the local police over the proposed marches and rallies of the striking members. This time Leila decided they would hold a rally at lunchtime on the first day in each of the places where Industry3M had offices and then again a rally after the offices closed on the third day strike.

She knew there was little point in pretending they would close some of the offices this time; they would be fortunate to get the same numbers out on strike as last time. The comments from the union Industry3M branches in the eight offices and the head office had all been encouraging but experience showed they would have to work hard to get the same numbers on strike. There would have to be several leaflets going out in the next three weeks, branch meetings to be held and—as the first time—perhaps open meetings. Leila would speak to Clive Bristow and Ted Davis about another open meeting in Liverpool. She thought it would be a good idea to hold a meeting perhaps in the week before the strike: anyway, she would listen to what they had to say.

Julia Cardon would make all the publicity arrangements and contact the press with the details of the rallies and marches. As before she would stay in the union headquarters with Leila and Whitchurch staying in Liverpool and getting all the reports from the union organisers fed through to them and then to Cardon. She in turn would keep Leila informed of press comment and coverage.

When they had finished Leila called in Muriel and went over her diary for the next few weeks. Carmichael was writing to the company with the dates of the three day strike today and again asking them to agree to a negotiating meeting with the union. She would contact Malik of ACAS on the Monday and suggest he make further contact with the company. Apart from Industry3M she had a number of meetings scheduled which Tim Burke, the national official for Industry3M, would normally have dealt with. She had also agreed to speak at one of the union's weekend schools in the west country that Chris Tuckell, the union's education officer, had arranged and there was another meeting of the finance and general purposes committee to attend.

She suddenly had the thought that when Hazel Bellini's national committee for leisure & Sport next met, then she should perhaps attend. Bellini might object as it could look as if she herself could not handle the committee but, Leila decided, that was too bad. However, it was some time before the national committee was due to meet and a lot could have happened before then. She would mention it to Bellini though.

When she and Muriel had finished going through the diary Muriel asked her when she was going on holiday. Normally John Carmichael went on holiday during the two weeks after the annual TUC Congress whereas Leila would take two weeks during August. But this time Leila had made no arrangements. The continued illness of Tim Burke had given Leila a lot of extra meetings and with all that was happening with Industry3M she thought she would not take her usual holiday but think about later in the year. She had wanted to suggest to her daughter that they go away on holiday with Deborah, her grand daughter, but was glad now she hadn't. It would have been another date she would have had to cancel.

Chapter Eight

More Strikes

"Mrs Smith?"

It was eleven o'clock on the morning of Thursday the twenty third of August. Leila had just got back to her office after the strike of the previous three days. It was her direct line that had rung.

"Yes, Leila Smith here."

"Mrs Smith, I hope you don't mind me phoning you direct and I hope you will treat this conversation as confidential between the two of us."

Leila raised her eyes to the ceiling in exasperation.

"Well, it would help if I knew who you were."

"Oh, sorry. It's Tom Chance here. Industry3M."

Leila sat up. She hadn't spoken to Chance other than at the abortive meeting that evening in Liverpool. And how had he got the number of her direct line? What on earth was he doing phoning her?

"What can I do for you Mr Chance."

There was a pause at the other end of the line.

"After the events of the last three days I wondered if we could have a little chat   but, please, this must be very confidential."

"Yes. I'll treat this as confidential—" she decided to be direct—"but what is it? By the way, how did you get my number."

"David Stannard gave it to me."

Yes, Leila remembered that some time ago when Tim Burke had first been diagnosed with cancer, and she had taken over responsibility for the companies he dealt with, she had asked Muriel to give her direct line number to a number of the key people in the companies with whom Burke dealt. But, Tom Chance? At the meeting in the Liverpool hotel he had been the more antagonist of the two company men.

"Well, can you say what we should talk about?" she asked.

"Look, Mrs Smith," the voice was a bit weary, "I think there are a number of things we might usefully discuss. I'm phoning you because I understand you are completely trustworthy—"

"Thanks very much," Leila interjected.

There was a silence. Chance tried again.

"This must seem a bit odd to you but I've worked for the company since it started here in the UK and I am not happy with the way things are going and—" he paused again—"no one else knows I'm phoning you so that's why I want this treated as entirely confidential."

Leila realised this must be serious and responded in a cautious manner.

"Mr Chance, I'm happy to meet you and will keep this confidential. But, to be blunt, is a chat—informal or not—going to achieve anything?"

"Well, in my view, it must achieve something. We can't go on as we have been doing. That way lies disaster." Chance paused again and then when Leila said nothing he added, "I wonder whether we could meet privately on Saturday? I happen to be coming down to London tomorrow evening and could meet somewhere the following day. I could come to you."

Leila reflected. She certainly didn't want Chance coming to her house but then why not make him come to Wimbledon at any rate? She mentioned a coffee bar in the high street in Wimbledon. Chance said that would be fine. He was staying with his sister in Surbiton and he could easily make it to there. Just before he rang off Leila thought she must tell him.

"One thing, though. Of course I will keep this confidential but I must tell my general secretary."

Chance started to protest but when Leila insisted he reluctantly agreed. The phone call ended.

He was taking an enormous gamble if any one in the company knew he was phoning the union. John Carr, for one—apart from Norman Jones the chief executive—would explode if he learnt of the call. Or so Leila assumed. Was it perhaps a tactic dreamt up by Carr and Jones? No, it didn't sound like it. Several times with other companies she had had private meetings with individuals from company management to try and settle a dispute. It was always difficult. The attempts didn't always succeed and there was the awful problem of who to tell about such meetings and when. If the trots in Industry3M knew of such a meeting then she could guess what they would make of it.

Anyway, she concluded, there was no harm lost in such a meeting now, or at least she hoped there wasn't, and she must tell John Carmichael.

The three day strike had gone off reasonably well. From all the reports from the organisers it appeared that about eighteen hundred of the members had come out for the three days. It was fewer than last time—by several hundred—but it was still a respectable figure and, again, significantly more than had actually voted for the strike in the original ballot. All the company offices had stayed open and the management had done the same as before in bringing in the staff not on strike in one go. The IT department in Liverpool had seen the biggest relative drop in the number out on strike. In the one day strike about thirty per cent of the staff had gone into work; this time, as far as she could get the figures from a clearly embarrassed Tony Hammond on the picket line, about fifty per cent of the staff had gone in to work.

The rallies at lunch time on the first day and at the end of the third day had been reasonably well attended and there had been no trouble at any of them. Hammond and his supporters had planned a rally on the evening of the second day but from all accounts, and Larry Brent had attended this and reported back to Leila, there had only been about twenty there. There had been no attempts to bring in SPGB supporters on the picket line and, all in all, Leila thought it had gone as well as they could expect.

She knew that Bristow and Davis in Liverpool—and she assumed the leading lay members in the other branches of the company—were getting a little dispirited but that was to be expected. There had been a good deal of publicity and the reaction on passers by to the pickets had been supportive on the whole as they were handed leaflets. But there been an ominous silence from the company except for one press statement which Carr had issued: the strike was having no effect on the company, the statement said, and the union support was crumbling. Well, of course, he would say that, wouldn't he, thought Leila. But there was an element of truth in it.

On the train back from Liverpool she had spoken at length on her mobile phone to Ian Macallister. Like at the other company offices, the number of union members who had come out on strike in Glasgow was slightly down and—now that the three day strike was over—there was considerable apprehension among the members. Macallister had said that the mood seemed to be one of waiting for the union to pull a rabbit out of the hat. The strikes had happened; there was no sign of the company moving; there was nothing from ACAS; what could Leila do about it?

Leila could well understand the feelings but was herself feeling considerably apprehensive as it was not apparent what the union could do to break what seemed to be a stalemate. She had told Macallister that she would get back to him as soon as possible. In the meantime she would do a report on the three day action and John Carmichael would send it out to all the national committees, regions and branches of the union.

When she got back to the office Leila phoned through to Carmichael to see if he was free. He said he had just been about to phone her and mentioned a phone call from David Stannard.

Carmichael smiled at her as she entered his office.

"It seems that all went OK then? I've had Alan Whitchurch on the phone. He's gone on to Manchester and saw most of the organisers there. They all seemed pretty upbeat."

She knew that Carmichael would be as worried as she was about what the union should do next and was glad that he was obviously trying to cheer her up. She said she would give him the report on the action in the afternoon. She was about to tell him about the phone call from Tom Chance when Carmichael said: "oh, this call from Stannard. Apparently there was some mix up over dates but it appears he did meet this chap Tiller yesterday and he's just phoned me to tell me about it."

"And?" Leila said.

"And," replied Carmichael, "it appears that if we thought John Carr was a hard man, this man Tiller makes him look like a pussy cat."

Carmichael summarised what Stannard had told him. Joe Tiller had been sent to Europe by Stuckman, the chief of Industry3M in Atlanta. His brief was apparently to visit their companies in Europe but particularly the British one. He had indeed been beaten by Carr for the position of European human resources director—Carr had pulled in a few favours, was how Tiller had explained it to Stannard. But Stuckman was getting increasingly irritated by the publicity that the dispute with the union had been getting, especially in the *Financial Times* and the *Wall Street Journal*. There was a feeling in the head office that the union was getting the upper hand and the whole dispute was giving the company a bad name.

The press coverage after Carmichael's press conference the day before the three day strike had been quite extensive and the press statement by Dick Whetter on his own union's claims for the job evaluation scheme had also got some good publicity.

Stannard had said that Tiller had not given any impression that the strikes had actually hurt the company or lost them any business. His main concern appeared to be the publicity and this had caused several of the company's major share holders to raise the issue with Stuckman himself. Tiller had only been too happy to go to Europe and if he could show that a lot of the adverse publicity was due to ineptitude by John Carr, then so much the better.

It appeared that Tiller wanted to learn from Stannard about why he had been sacked and what the relationship was like between Carr and the two senior men in the British arm of the company—Norman Jones and Tom Chance. Stannard had told him as much as he knew and that seemed all Tiller had wanted.

"The guts of the thing is though," said Carmichael, "that Tiller gave the distinct impression to Stannard that he didn't think the company had been aggressive enough and the company would now start—as he described—to get tough with the union."

"What that means," said Leila "could be a number of things, but none of them pleasant." Then she remembered that both Tolmark of the Swedish union and Bruch of the German DGB had mentioned Tiller to her and she mentioned that to Carmichael.

"It doesn't look too good, does it?"

"No. It doesn't. But I think we ought to treat this as confidential for the moment."

Leila then told him about the phone call she had just had from Tom Chance.

"Well, well, well. The plot thickens."

"It could be good news, John, but in the light of what Stannard has just told you, it doesn't seem likely."

"No," responded Carmichael. "But you must have this chat with Chance—and we'll keep that confidential too. By the way, what's the timetable for Dan Michael's successor?"

Leila had jotted down a likely timetable on the train. The closing date for applications was the second week of September. Because Carmichael would be on holiday immediately after the end of the annual TUC Congress, Leila had suggested an interviewing panel for the position later that month. She said she would contact the union's president and vice-president and see if they could make the date.

Carmichael grunted approval. It was quite a long process but he didn't feel like interrupting his holiday, nor did Leila seek to persuade him.

"I shall be at home on Saturday, Leila. Can you phone me after your chat with Chance?" Leila agreed to phone him as soon as the chat finished and Chance had gone on his way.

Leila got to the café in the high street some ten minutes before they were due to meet. It was a bright morning, the café was a modern one with Swedish style furniture and sold alcohol as well as coffee. Leila knew it was becoming popular with the younger smart set and perhaps two middle aged people like her and Chance would look a bit out of place. But that, she decided, was too bad. It was as good a neutral meeting place as any and she thought she had made a point by suggesting that Chance came to Wimbledon.

She knew little about Chance other than he had appeared distant and dismissive at the Liverpool meeting. A tall man who had been well built, she thought, but her impression now was he was still tall but portly rather than still well built. It had happened to many, she thought.

She was looking at that morning's *Financial Times* with a cup of coffee and then noticed Chance come through the door. Dressed in a suit he did indeed look a bit out of place. More to the point, thought Leila, he looked nervous. A far cry from Liverpool.

Chance saw her and made his way to her table. He said good morning but made no attempt to shake hands. A waitress came over and he ordered a large cappucino. They waited in an uneasy silence until his coffee arrived. Leila looked at him as he stirred in some sugar. He looked at her.

"This meeting is confidential, isn't it?" He sounded almost plaintive.

"As I told you, Mr Chance. I have told John Carmichael but no one else. How about on your side?"

"I've told no one" he replied.

There was more silence. Leila waited for him to say something. He looked increasingly nervous, then took a deep breath and started.

"I wanted to speak to you to see if we could find a way to settle this dispute—"

Leila decided to be brutal: "according to your man Carr, the strikes have not had any effect. So, what's the problem?"

It was a little unkind, thought Leila, but she wanted to see how he would react.

Then the words came out of his mouth like a torrent.

He was worried about the company. It had so far been a success story in Britain and was expanding on the continent. Leila noted that he didn't mention the far east as a potential market. Chance had been annoyed at what he saw as the indecent haste for a strike by the union and thought at the time they would not get anything like a majority in the strike ballot. He had been surprised at the result and even more surprised at the number of members who had actually come out on strike. Then again he had been yet more surprised by the numbers coming out for the three day strike. He had suggested to Norman Jones, the chief executive, and to John Carr that they must try and find a solution. It was not the effect of the strike as such but the damaging publicity.

Chance said that Jones had seemed to waver at his suggestion but Carr had been adamant. The company could not afford to be seen to be weak in the face of the strikes. Chance had almost pleaded for another meeting at ACAS but Carr had said that would be a sign of weakness as well. Jones had then gone along with this.

Leila broke in: "but what do you expect us to do? We are more than happy to meet you direct or with ACAS but if you won't, then you won't."

The waitress came over and Leila asked for two more coffees.

"How serious are you on the job evaluation scheme?"

This was it, thought Leila. No mention of the pay claim or what the company could or could not afford. It was the JE scheme that was worrying the company—and the CBI as well, she reminded herself.

Leila replied that they thought the scheme would be of benefit all round and be a big improvement on the company's existing grading and evaluation scheme. She said she was amazed that the company did not even want to discuss it.

"What about a joint study—to see if it would be practical?"

Leila kept an impassive face. Chance's question could mean a breakthrough.

"Do you mean a study by representatives of the company and the union together?"

"Yes," said Chance, "and we could possibly get some academic to chair the thing. That would be a way out of this, wouldn't it?"

Leila thought this would be significant. Such a study would be miles away from the CBI proposal and also better than just asking Ruskin College to do a study. This would be the company and the union sitting down together to study the scheme and basically that should have been one outcome of negotiations—if they had taken place. She looked at Chance. He seemed genuine enough. She asked him if anyone else had come out with this suggestion and he said emphatically that it was his own idea and repeated that neither Jones nor Carr had any idea that he had thought of it, let alone propose it to the union, albeit informally and in confidence.

She said cautiously, "that might be a way out. The thing is how are we going to get to that stage? If the company won't meet us at ACAS or anywhere at all, what on earth can we do?"

"You could write and suggest it?"

Leila answered that she was going to contact ACAS again but she could ask John Carmichael to suggest such a study in writing to the company.

They discussed a possible letter to the company from the union. Then Leila said why didn't they continue the discussion over a drink. Somewhat again to her surprise Chance agreed. He paid for the coffees and they then left the café and went over to a pub on the opposite side of the road. As it was a Saturday lunch time the main bar was reasonably crowded but they managed to find a small table in the corner. Chance bought Leila a glass of red wine and a whisky—a double whisky, Leila noted—for himself. Chance still seemed nervous but not as much as he had been when he had come into the café. It seemed to Leila that he had relaxed a bit now that he had said what he had obviously planned to say.

Leila realised that he had not made any reference to the financial impact of the strikes on the company's business or clients. He did, though, several times refer to the press publicity and then again he mentioned Tiller coming to the head office and how Carr had seemed very apprehensive at this. Leila got the impression from him that he was worried the company's attitude might well be dictated by the desire of Carr and Tiller to outdo each other in some sort of macho struggle with the union.

Leila asked him outright whether the company had considered actual derecognition of the union and Chance said that of course they had. They had stopped short though because they were in the process of tying up two major contracts for the supply of labour to a primary care trust of the national health service and to a Government executive agency. The company thought they might be unlikely to secure either of those two contracts if they derecognised the trade union. At this moment, Chance added somewhat ominously), particularly because of all the further damaging publicity this would probably engender.

Chance then looked at his watch: "it's time I was going, I'm afraid." He stood up and added "I hope you think this chat has been useful. I repeat again that this must be kept confidential—and we'll await hearing from you."

One last thing." said Leila. "Suppose your company doesn't agree with what will seem to be our suggestion of a joint study? Might they not reject the very idea just because it's come from the union?"

Chance paused. "Look, I can't propose this because they're keeping me out of the loop now. It's Jones and Carr—and probably will be Tiller—who run the show. I haven't really been consulted since we met at the Liverpool meeting."

"And you appeared antagonistic to us then, more so than Norman Jones. Was that your rite of passage?" She was deliberately provocative; and she wanted to see how he would react.

"Look, Mrs Smith, I'm risking my job in coming to talk to you. I don't know if the company will respond positively. If I am asked, I'll support the idea of a joint study. I just think it might be a way out. But this conversation must be kept confidential." He sounded genuine.

Leila said she understood the point and then repeated that she would ask Carmichael to write accordingly to the company. Chance then held out his hand to her. They had, she thought, come a long way since the beginning of their chat. She shook his hand and he left the pub.

Leila wondered whether to get another drink but as she never liked sitting in a pub by herself she decided to go home and phone Carmichael from there.

⚜

Leila had phoned me on the Saturday afternoon. I was as surprised as she was. Could this be the breakthrough we wanted? I had dealt with somewhat similar situations before and was now extremely cautious how they should be handled.

I remembered one occasion when a company's personnel director had had a private chat with me over a dispute we were having with his company. We had both agreed on a way forward: the union would reduce our claim on holidays and the company would offer another one per cent on its pay offer. Then, when it came to the negotiating meeting, I had indicated that we might be prepared to reduce our claim for more holidays but the company side said nothing. The personnel director had merely said that they were not prepared to move on pay.

At the time I had been furious as all that had happened was that the union had reduced an important part of our claim to no effect and I had a row with the personnel director after the meeting. He had said that he had floated the idea of an extra one per cent on pay but his colleagues had rejected this. I had asked him what then was the point of a private meeting and he had merely shrugged his shoulders.

A few months later I had noted that the personnel director had left the company and I had taken a little satisfaction in refusing to attend his farewell party.

But this time we were not being asked to do anything but suggest a joint study of the job evaluation scheme and when I was in the office I had sent a letter to Norman Jones with that suggestion. It was now the Wednesday of that week and I was awaiting a response. In the meantime Leila had mentioned the idea of a joint study to Ian Macallister without telling him about her meeting with Chance and he had agreed that it was worth pursuing.

My door opened and Leila came in.

"Sorry to barge in, John, but I've just had a phone call from Tom Chance."

I looked up: "any joy?"

She smiled thinly. "Absolutely none" she said And then told me what had happened.

Chance had just phoned her in a very agitated state and had started off by saying she had broken their understanding, called her a bitch and said he had just been sacked by Norman Jones. Leila had tried to calm him down and eventually he had. Apparently Jones had got my letter and talked about it to Carr on the phone who was in the European head office in London. Carr had then told him that it was Chance's suggestion and that he knew Chance had had a private meeting with her. Chance had been furious and tried to deny it but Carr knew when the meeting had taken place. Chance thought the only way that could have been known was Leila telling someone. Leila had insisted to him that she had told no one other than Carmichael and said the leak must have come from within the company. Chance had said that was impossible and repeated that as a result of their meeting he was now dismissed from the company. He didn't conclude the conversation but had slammed the phone down.

"It's weird, John. I've told no one—not even Macallister when I put the idea of a joint study to him. It must have been someone in the company but how they knew I just don't know. Anyway this morning apparently Chance was told by Norman Jones to pack his bags and go. It must have been Carr who told him to do that."

Before Leila could say anything more Sheila came into the office and handed me a fax from the company. It was a letter to me from Norman Jones. It was short and to the point. The idea of a joint study was rejected out of hand. He then went on to advise me that the company was making five hundred of their staff redundant. This was because of concern over staff costs and the staff concerned were being told today of the decision. I was furious.

I handed the fax to Leila.

"It never rains, but it pours."

"This must be Carr trying to show Joe Tiller that he knows how to handle the dispute. But what's the effect going to be on their business?"

I said words to the effect that the business effect could be buggered—how could they make five hundred members redundant?

I knew the answer to my own question as soon I had asked it.

"They can't just make union members redundant because of employment legislation," said Leila. "They've probably included a number of non members to make the exercise kosher."

We discussed how to handle the bombshell from the company. It was clear to my mind that the company was upping the stakes considerably and undoubtedly some, if not the most, of the five hundred would be union members. By including some non-members they could say they were not discriminating against the union.

Leila said "I bet it's that smarmy number two in personnel, Collins. He must have learnt of our meeting and gone running to Carr. He must have thought he would get into Carr's good books and get Stannard's job. But how did he know?"

"Perhaps phones were tapped" I said. It was meant to be a piece of flippancy on my part but as I and Leila looked at each other we both realised that that might have been what happened.

When Leila got back to her office she telephoned Tino Malik at ACAS. She was told he was busy in a meeting but would phone back when he could.

She called in Muriel and dictated a draft circular to the members in Industry3M about the redundancy announcement and then a circular to go to the union's national executive committee, regions and branches. Carmichael had said he would write back to Norman Jones and demand an urgent meeting to discuss the announcement and Leila included the text of his letter in the two circulars. Leila had suggested he write to Bob Wilson at the DTI and Carmichael had agreed.

She spoke to Macallister on the phone. He told her the company had issued a circular that morning. It had given no details of where the five hundred redundancies would be made nor how people would be chosen. The only statement on timing was that the company would hope to implement "these unfortunately necessary methods" as soon as possible. Macallister told her that the mood in the Glasgow office was one of outrage. He said that if the company was hoping the announcement would make staff fearful they had miscalculated. He had also received phone calls from many of the leading union members throughout the company and the reaction was similar.

Leila told him she was trying to fix a meeting with ACAS and was also issuing a circular detailing Carmichael's letter to Norman Jones. She didn't mention what had happened to Tom Chance and neither did Macallister. He clearly had not heard, she thought, and she could hardly tell him how she knew about it. They discussed a meeting of the national committee. Leila suggested the Saturday week, the first of September and Macallister agreed. They knew some of the committee members might be on holiday then and some might be reluctant to spend another Saturday on union business but the situation was urgent enough to go ahead with the meeting.

Leila said it would tie in with the meeting of the union's national executive committee the following Thursday, the sixth of September. That was the meeting that would go through the TUC Congress agenda and mandate the union's delegates there on which way to vote on the various reports, motions and amendments that would be the business of the Congress week.

She mentioned to Macallister that the national committee of Teening & Sykes was meeting the following day and Mathew Singh had told her they would be considering a call for a strike ballot in view of that company's complete refusal to discuss at all the claim for the job evaluation scheme. She mentioned that this was not surprising especially in view of the attitude of David Adnam, the company's chief executive at the meeting between the TUC and the CBI. She also mentioned the claim for the JE scheme that the main civil service had submitted to the Department of Trade and Industry.

Macallister asked if there was anything more heard from the Swedish or German unions. Leila told him she hadn't heard but would contact both unions and do a detailed report on what was happening for the national committee meeting.

"The key thing, Ian," she said, "is that we're not alone. Jim Bradwell is also submitting a claim to the local authorities."

"But we're the first over the top" said Macallister in his thick Glaswegian accent. He laughed. "Not for the first time," he added as he rang off.

Leila asked Muriel to come in and they went over her diary. She had two meetings with companies that Tim Burke also dealt with on the following Monday and Tuesday, one in Leicester and the other in London. Fortunately they were not too onerous: in the first company the issue was a new disciplinary procedure and in the second she was representing the chairman of the union's national committee of the company. Normally such representations would be dealt with by one of the leading lay officials in the company or by the appropriate regional organiser. This one was somewhat different in that the national committee chairman was the person who had been given his final warning over his work performance. Tim Burke would have handled it himself so Leila was standing in.

The Saturday of that week—the first of September—was the date she and Macallister had agreed for the Industry3M national committee. The national executive committee was meeting on the following Thursday and afterwards she and Carmichael would be going down to Brighton. The annual Trades Union Congress was being held in Brighton and the General Council would usually meet on the Friday before the Congress week. Some of the members would stay on the Saturday and Sunday; there were a number of union receptions to go to and many of the unions had meetings of their delegations then.

In their case Carmichael had fixed a meeting of his union's Congress delegation for the Sunday afternoon. The Congress started on the Monday morning and went on until Thursday midday. When Leila had first got on to the General Council the annual Congress had lasted from Monday morning till Friday midday but the mergers of a number of unions meant fewer resolutions for debate apart—as the press had pointedly noted many times—fewer delegates in total. Then a few years ago it had been decided that only three and half days were needed so the Congress would finish on the Thursday at midday.

The timetable meant Leila could get home on the Friday evening before the Congress and then go back to Brighton on the Sunday morning. She made a mental note to telephone her daughter Deborah and see if she and Helen would like to come over to her house for a meal on the Saturday.

⁂

I was just about ready to leave my office when the switchboard put through a phone call from John Miller, the TUC General Secretary. He sounded a little apprehensive.

"John, I'm getting a bit of stick from Bob Wilson of the DTI and wondered if you were able to come up and we could have a brief chat."

I replied that Wilson wasn't my favourite minister at the moment in view of what had happened at our meeting with him. Miller said he appreciated that but he still wanted a chat.

I was about to say that I was just leaving for home but decided it wouldn't be the most diplomatic thing to say. I said I'd be up straight away and then asked if he thought it be OK if I took Leila with me. To my surprise he said it would be better just to have a chat with me. I thought it must be serious for him to say that. I put the phone down and walked through to Leila's office.

She was talking to Muriel her secretary when I went in.

"Problem?" she asked as Muriel left the room.

I told her about Miller's call. I said he had sounded a bit odd and clearly didn't want her to come with me.

"You know I could have insisted on you coming and don't want you to think—". Before I could finish Leila had interrupted.

"John, I understand and, in my view, you must go by yourself and see what it's all about."

I heaved an inward sigh. Leila was as sound as a pound. Many other officials in that situation would well have kicked up a fuss and talked about status but I knew she trusted me—and the feeling was mutual.

"Let me know how you get on," she said as she smiled.

"Of course. I'll give you a ring this evening if you're in at home."

"I will be. Good luck."

I got to Congress House just before six o'clock and went straight up to Miller's office. Stella Meadows, his secretary, was still sorting out some papers and looked up at me.

"He's waiting for you."

I thanked her and went in to the office.

Miller offered me a drink from the cabinet in his office and I said I would like a small whisky. He had one for himself and then pointed to the two armchairs in the corner of his large office.

"Cheers."

I had a sip and waited for him to start. Unusually, he seemed hesitant.

"I don't know quite how to put this John," he opened. "But Bob Wilson phoned me this afternoon and he sounded most irate. Apparently he's all steamed up with this job evaluation thing. Dick Whetter has lodged a claim for its introduction into the Department of Trade and Industry. Dick's had one meeting with the department but the claim was just rejected. It appears from what Bob told me that he himself instructed his permanent secretary that the claim should be rejected."

I thought our meeting with Wilson had been bit acrimonious but what on earth was he doing intervening at this stage in a union claim on the department? Miller went on to tell me that the impression Wilson had was that Leila was deliberately stoking up as much trouble as she could by persuading other unions to pursue similar claims for the JE scheme.

"Leila's OK, isn't she, John?" he asked me.

"Of course. She's one of the best union officials I've ever known. I know she and Wilson didn't get on too well at our meeting but then Wilson seemed to me to be deliberately unhelpful." I warmed to the subject, "and the irony is that he kept repeating that he couldn't intervene in an industrial dispute."

Miller nodded: "I know. You told me that. But I gathered that he's under some pressure—wherefrom I'm not quite sure."

"The CBI?" I queried. "You remember what John Dryden tried to do."

"Yes, well it might also be, from what he hinted at, that someone else has been leaning on him."

I suddenly remembered. Each year the ambassador from the USA gave a drinks party for the TUC General Council and the leading officials whose unions did not have a member on the General Council. A number of politicians, including a few ministers, also attended. The party was held in the big garden of the ambassador's residence in

Regent's Park and, though it was usually in July, this time it was held in mid August. Bob Wilson had been there and I remembered I had seen the ambassador take him to one side. They had gone into the large reception room in the residence and didn't reappear for some time.

I told Miller of my recollection.

"How big is Industry3M?" he asked me without commenting on my memory.

I told him that it was not a huge company but it was one of the fastest growing companies in the US and Chuck Pitney had told us about some influential shareholders. It had eight subsidiary companies in Europe and was looking at opportunities in the far east. I could see that what Miller was saying tied in with what Leila had told me about her meeting with Tom Chance. If the company was worried about all the press publicity on our dispute, if Joe Tiller had been sent to Britain to get tough with the union, if some of the major shareholders were worried and if the company (this I didn't know, but it could be) was a contributor of funds to the Republican Party then perhaps someone had spoken to the US ambassador. It was a lot of 'ifs' but it didn't sound too irrational to me. I told Miller my thoughts.

He said, "I know the Government is getting anxious about what they see as declining foreign investment over here and it would be a big blow if Industry3M was to pack up as a result of a dispute with a trade union. You know how that could be seen. The nineteen seventies all over again."

I thought it was time to be specific: "John, what do you want from me?"

Miller replied that he had assured Wilson that he would be seeing me—and he had done that as a means of getting Wilson off his back. He continued "I know that Leila Smith is very good, but I had to ask you because I want to be able to go back to Wilson and tell him that I did. You may be right about American political pressure. In any event you know I'm on your side."

We both stood up. The meeting was clearly over.

"If you want any help from me, John, then let me know" said Miller.

We shook hands and I left. I would phone Leila at home this evening.

On the Saturday morning Leila again got to the hotel early in time for the start of the Industry3M national committee at eleven o'clock. She had spoken to Mailk of ACAS and he had promised to chase up Industry3M for a meeting but he hadn't come back to her, so, presumably, he had been unsuccessful.

She had also spoken to Per Ulric in Stockholm and to Jurgen Bruch in Frankfurt. Ulric told her that the Swedish arm of Industry3M had flatly rejected the job evaluation scheme. His union was now considering a strike ballot and Lars Tolmark was talking to the senior officials of the Swedish white collar TCO—the equivalent to the manual unions confederation LO—and to the Government minister for industry to see if any pressure could be brought on to the company management to make them negotiate. Bruch told her that the German subsidiary company of Industry3M had not only completely rejected the claim for the JE scheme but had also accused the union of breaking the two year pay and conditions agreement they had made the previous November. Again, Bruch was talking to the senior officials of the German trade union centre, the DGB, to see if they could bring any pressure to bear but so far unsuccessfully. He said a strike ballot at the end of September was a distinct possibility.

Bruch had, though, emphasised to Leila that a strike would be difficult. The position of the German Industry3M company was not too good and it was just about breaking even. He stressed to Leila that the basis of the company's operation—supplying contract labour to the public and private sectors of the economy—was not common in Germany. He stressed that there was an ample supply of labour in the former East Germany but accepted that the Industry3M practice could well become much more significant. He was, however, pursuing the possibility of a strike ballot.

Ian Macallister came over to Leila as soon as he arrived at the hotel. He was alone this time. Bruce Cannon the other Glasgow delegate was away on holiday and his deputy was also away. There were in fact several absentees from the national committee. Of the twenty members of the committee Leila expected about sixteen to turn up—and three of those were deputy delegates. But there was no alternative. She had half hoped that Tony Hammond would be on holiday but there was no such luck and she knew he would be bound to attend.

As Julia Cardon went round the table putting copies of all the press reports since the last meeting on the table she told Macallister about her abortive attempts to get an ACAS meeting. Furthermore Norman Jones had not responded to Carmichael's letter seeking an urgent meeting to discuss the five hundred redundancies. She mentioned her phone calls with the Swedish and German unions and also that the main civil service union had submitted a claim for the introduction of the job evaluation scheme in the DTI.

Macallister asked whether Peter Moorhouse's Commercial & Technology Union had pursued claims for the JE scheme and Leila told him that although claims had been submitted in three different companies negotiations were still at an early stage.

"Well, Leila," said Macallister, "what are we going to do?" It was a question she had discussed with him several times in the last two days on the telephone and they had reached no conclusion. Then the previous evening, sitting at home with a glass of red wine and listening to Mozart's Coronation Mass on her CD player she had come to a conclusion and decided that the best course was to be positive and face the national committee with a clear choice—either they took further action or they would have to back down. She was determined not to go down the latter route. It all depended on how the members would react, but they had to be faced with the choice. She had phoned Carmichael at his home that evening and he had agreed with her proposed course of action.

"Well, Ian," replied Leila, "the good news is that the national committee of Teening and Sykes is calling for an industrial action ballot—on overtime and a two day strike. It's going to the NEC next Thursday. So we're not alone. But I think—depending obviously on how people feel—that we have no option but to call for a ballot on an indefinite strike."

She had made it blunt deliberately, partly to see how Macallister would react. He looked at her and raised his eyebrows. Somewhat to her surprise, his question to her was not about whether she thought the members would come out again but "what about strike pay?"

"The NEC's also going to have take a decision on that next week. It could of course be an open ended commitment but I feel we need to do something fairly dramatic."

Macallister looked unconvinced. Leila went on: "Tom Chance has gone. There's this man Tiller over from America here and I've no doubt he will be keen to show his superiors that he can squash the union. But we are not alone and I'm hoping that the threat of an indefinite strike will make the company negotiate with us."

Macallister started to ask her what she would do if the company refused when he looked at his watch. It was nearly eleven o'clock

And the members of the national committee were all sitting down at the table. It was time to start the meeting.

When they started Macallister called on Leila to give an update of the situation. She referred to the three day strike and the numbers who had come out. She spoke about the extensive press coverage, the CBI meeting and the other unions—both British and the German and Swedish ones—pursuing claims on job evaluation. She made a point of mentioning that the national committee of Teening & Sykes was calling on the national executive for authority for a strike ballot and how this would be discussed at their meeting the following Thursday.

She then told the committee bluntly that the company didn't show any sign of coming to the negotiating table at the moment and were refusing to respond to an ACAS call for a meeting. She stressed how in her opinion the union membership in the company now had to face the difficult choice of going forward, which would be risky, or doing nothing which would not be risky but would be an admission of defeat. She referred to the five hundred redundancies and how the company had not even responded to Carmichael's letter.

As she finished she turned to Macallister and said "I don't know, Mr chairman, whether you want me to spell out what I think we should do now or whether you want to take reports from members here on how they think the three day strike went and what they perceive is the mood amongst the membership."

Macallister looked round the table.

"I think you should pause there, Leila, and I'll go round the table and get the reports."

Tony Hammond immediately put up his hand and Macallister called on him to speak.

"This is all a shambles," he almost shouted. "I've said before that the whole dispute has been mishandled and the company has outmanoeuvred us at every point. The publicity has been poor and—"

Macallister broke in: "I want reports on how the action went, Tony, and then we'll discuss what we should do."

Hammond swallowed. "The action could have been a lot better with some positive leadership. That's the view of my members."

Macallister said quietly: "they're not your members, Tony. They are members of our union. And what percentage came out in the IT department?"

Hammond swallowed again and paused.

Leila said "fifty percent of the department was working on the three days, weren't they Tony? That was what you told me."

The members of the committee all looked at Hammond and he realised he had been clearly put on the defensive. He mumbled again about lack of leadership and then shut up except for saying, somewhat lamely, that he reserved the right to come back later.

Macallister decided it was time to be firm.

"You will speak when I call you, Tony. If you don't want to say any more then I'll go round the table with everyone able to say their piece."

Hammond look hot and angry but said nothing. Leila noticed that Jean Asah from Leeds also seemed angry but more at what Hammond had said and how he had said it. She was sitting next to him and pointedly shifted her chair a little way away.

The members of the committee each gave their reports. The consensus was that the three day strike had been as good as they could realistically have hoped. Even Lillian Fairweather echoed that feeling, Leila was pleased to note. The news, the day after about the redundancies had provoked a big feeling of anger and resentment and Leila was pleased at the statements several made that they could not back down now.

When Macallister had finished going round the table he said: "in Glasgow the mood of members is similar to what most of you here have said. They are getting a little battle weary but the redundancy announcement has made them determined that we should do our damnedest to show the company that we are not prepared to lie down with our legs in the air."

He then called on Leila to suggest a course of further action. It was then that Leila referred to the dismissal of Tom Chance and the appearance of Joe Tiller on the scene. She left them in no doubt what this could mean. She said it showed that the company was in a difficult position and it was now, more than ever, that the union had to be shown as taking further action. She was looking round the table as she spoke and noted how they seemed to be hoping she would pull some rabbit out of the hat.

"I haven't got a magic wand, Mr Chairman. My proposal is that we ask the national executive for authority to have a further industrial ballot and that the question of the ballot paper be whether members are prepared to take indefinite strike action."

There was a gasp from several members and, in the silence with which her statement had been greeted, she noted that Hammond seemed quite taken aback. Several members then put their hands up to speak and Macallister called each one in turn. A number asked whether strike pay would still be paid in the event of an indefinite strike, others asked how successful did she think the threat of a strike would be and particularly how realistic was it to have an indefinite strike.

Leila knew that the points were all genuine and she dealt with each in turn. She hoped that the national executive would agree for strike pay to be paid but they would discuss it their forthcoming meeting. She emphasised that she understood the company was getting anxious over the press coverage the union had achieved and there would undoubtedly be more coverage if the dispute escalated. She said Julia Cardon would be issuing a press statement after the meeting and that she had arranged to meet Charles Pitney of the *Wall Street Journal* that evening after the meeting finished. She had spoken to Pitney that morning before she left for the meeting. He had given her his card with his home number on it when they last met. He had readily agreed to see her in the same pub just by Waterloo station. She stressed again to the committee how they were not alone and there would be considerable press coverage of the civil service union and its claim on the Department of Trade And Industry and more if the national executive agreed with the Teening & Sykes strike ballot.

It was all a gamble, she knew. If they did get the authority for another ballot then there was always the chance that they wouldn't win it. If the ballot failed that would be a victory for the company. If they won the ballot and the company still didn't move then the action would have to start and the big challenge was how long they could keep going, how long would the members actually be prepared to come out and lose their pay—even if strike pay was paid by the union. And what would be the effect on the union's finances?

Macallister then suggested that the meeting adjourned and reassemble at two o'clock when they could resume the discussion. As the members left the meeting room Leila noted that Hammond had pulled out his mobile phone. He didn't know how to react, she smiled to herself. In a sense she had spiked his guns, but how would the other members of the committee react?

In the event the committee spent an hour discussing the proposal from Leila when they reassembled. The strike pay was clearly the major issue and Leila repeated how she and the union's general secretary would be recommending to the national executive that it should be paid. There was an evident hope that the threat of a ballot for an indefinite strike would be sufficient to get the company to negotiate but also serious concern at the prospect of getting all the members out on strike if the company didn't move at all. Several members mentioned that the redundancy announcement had made people very angry and repeated the point made to them that if many of them were going to lose their jobs—and perhaps there would be more redundancies to follow—then they had little to lose. Clive Bristow emphasised this on behalf of the members in the Liverpool head office.

In the end the proposal from Leila for the authority for an indefinite strike ballot was carried with twelve votes to nil, the four other members (including Hammond, Leila noted) abstaining rather than voting against. It was as good as Leila could have hoped for and she spoke again to the committee, thanking them for their support. She outlined that she would get the union's organisers to visit the company's offices, a lot of circulars would be issued and she would keep them fully informed of all developments. She was pleased that in spite of all the understandable caution, anxiety and doubt the vote had been decisive. If the national executive on Thursday agreed with the proposed ballot then the die really would be cast.

Leila had spent some time after the meting talking to the various members of the committee. She saw Hammond leave immediately the meeting had finished but many of the others had stayed to talk with each other and with Leila. Both Bristow and Macallister had been particularly supportive of her. Macallister had said he had been taken aback when she had mentioned to him that an indefinite strike ballot would be what she recommended but now thought it was the only practical course for them.

While Leila was chatting to the members of the committee, Julia Cardon was dictating on her mobile phone a short press release on the committee's decision to the Press Association. She and Leila had agreed that this was the best course of action rather than hold a full scale press conference. It was a Saturday and it would be difficult to get the major papers there now. The other factor would be, Cardon had mentioned to Leila, that the Sunday papers would carry the story once the Press Association had circulated their statement and that would allow the nationals to follow up on the Monday morning—so they would get two days of publicity—hopefully. It would mean several of the national correspondents would be on to Leila on Sunday and she thought this could be done without interfering in her arrangements with her daughter and grand daughter for lunch that day. She hoped she was right. She and Cardon had also agreed that a press conference be held after the national executive meeting on the Thursday and, if the proposal was carried there, there should be further press publicity.

Just before they left the meeting room Leila had phoned Oliver Listle of the *Financial Times* at his home. Again she had his home number and knew that he would be interested in reporting the story. She told him of the decision and he thanked her and said he would definitely be there at the press conference on the Thursday afternoon following the national executive committee meeting.

Leila and Julia Cardon got to the pub near Waterloo by half past five o'clock and entered the small bar at the front. Charles Pitney was sitting down holding a half empty pint of bitter. As soon as he saw them he jumped to his feet and ordered their drinks with a further pint for himself.

"Good to see you" he said. He handed round their drinks, red wine for Leila and a gin and tonic for Julia Cardon. "Cheers."

When they had all sat down Pitney got out his notebook.

"Well, ladies, anything for me?"

Leila told him the decision of the national committee and how it would come up at the national executive on the following Thursday. She mentioned the request for a strike ballot from the Teening & Sykes national committee.

"If all goes according to plan, when will the Industry3M strike start?"

"It depends, Chuck"—said Leila.

"On?"

"On the size of the ballot and return and, hopefully, the majority in favour. It depends too whether the company makes any move and if ACAS are able to get any meeting arranged. It partly depends too on how the other unions—both here and on the continent—are getting on with their claims for the job evaluation scheme."

Pitney smiled, "it sounds as if you don't know when it will be."

Both Leila and Julia Cardon knew that Pitney was a likeable man and, if there were sides for a journalist to be on, he was likely to be on their side. But he had a job to do and that was to find out as much as he could. Pitney had told Leila the last time they had met that he wrote the news not the propaganda.

"Chuck," Leila smiled in turn. "I'll let you know soonest. And for Teening & Sykes the ballot will be held—if all goes well—immediately after the meeting and we'll probably allow two to three weeks for it to be held. There's six thousand members there. And the national official for the company is Mathew Singh." She gave him Singh's home telephone number.

"Now, can you tell us anything about movements in the US in Industry3M and over here ?" She mentioned the leaving of Tom Chance and the increasing role that Joe Tiller seemed to be playing.

She didn't mention her meeting with Chance but did say that she had heard from a number of contacts that the company in Atlanta was getting worried about the press publicity.

Piney frowned. "I don't know if they're worried exactly. They don't like the publicity and some of their shareholders have been contacting Stuckman, the chief, about it. But I think they're still fairly bullish and Tiller certainly has the brief to sort things out."

"What about John Carr?" asked Leila.

"That's an unknown for the moment and I'm not sure whether it was him or Tiller who engineered the dismissal of Tom Chance," Pitney replied. He continued, "he wasn't highly regarded in Atlanta anyway. For what it's worth I think you've done the right thing in going for a further strike. That should worry the company but—" he broke off and looked at their glasses. All were empty so he got to his feet and against the protestations of Leila he insisted on buying another round himself—"I think the *Wall Street Journal* has a bit more money than your union," he said as he handed round the drinks.

Leila said "I think that's right. And, if you're going to ask about strike pay, then we'll decide that at the national executive but I'm pushing strongly for strike pay to continue."

"But how long can you last—and with Teening and Sykes as well?"

Leila had known this would be the question a number of journalists were bound to ask. Whichever way she answered could be dangerous and could upset some of her colleagues in the union—the trustees if they thought Leila was trying to pre-empt a decision, the Industry3M members if they thought they might not get strike pay after all, the members in Teening & Sykes who would want to know how they stood before casting their votes in the ballot and the members of the national executive who would not like any idea of a *fait accompli* appearing in the press.

"We've got about twenty million pounds in assets of one type or another, and if two thousand members come out on strike and get fifty pounds a day and six thousand members—the Teening and

Sykes members—strike for two days—well, you can work it out, Chuck."

Pitney put his notebook away, "I think that's the only answer I'm going to get on that." Leila saw him smile as he said it.

They chatted some more about the position of Industry3M in the USA. Leila gave him the telephone numbers of Lars Tolmark in Stockholm and Jurgen Bruch in Frankfurt. Pitney said if he could get hold of them then, with Leila's announcement, that would be a useful report to put in. He would also try and ring Mathew Singh. The Teening and Sykes possible ballot would be another angle to add to the story.

Pitney let Leila buy another round of drinks and then said "I did hear something interesting from a colleague in the *Washington Post* you might be interested in."

"Over here?" asked Cardon.

"Yes, the London guy. Apparently there's quite a lot of interest in your dispute in some quarters in Washington—small, if not miniscule, as your dispute may be."

"Well, go on then" said Leila as she took a sip of her red wine. This would be her last that evening she told herself as she waited for Pitney to continue.

"I understand you and John Carmichael went to see Bob Wilson at the DTI—" he saw the look of surprise on Leila's face as he spoke—"someone in the CBI told me."

Leila said nothing but looked at Julia Cardon. She was equally surprised but also said nothing.

"What about the *Washington Post?*" asked Leila again.

"Well, as I believe the DTI is worried about the effect of a damaging strike on future American investment here, so back home there's a similar concern. Are the old days of strikes going to come back? And, I also understand the DTI itself is facing a claim for the same type of job evaluation scheme that you've lodged with Industry3M. That really mixes it up."

Leila was getting a bit impatient: "what specifically is the *Washington Post* point, Chuck?"

"The specific point, Leila, is that there is Government concern. If there is a strike which lasts a long time that be damaging for the company and cause some US companies to think twice about investment in the UK. If the company conceded your claim, that could also make companies think twice if they're going to see an upsurge in union power."

Leila remembered what John Carmichael had told her about the US ambassador talking to Bob Wilson at the ambassador's drinks party. She told Pitney about it and he again got his notebook out and made a few notes.

"Interesting, isn't it? By the way, isn't that hard man David Adnam the chief executive of Teening & Sykes?" He got up. "I'll call those numbers you gave me and see you at your press conference." He waved to them as he left the pub.

Julia Cardon said "what about strike pay, Leila? We can't pay for ever."

"It's a gamble, Julia. But if we do nothing, then we've lost."

❦

I had spoken several times earlier in the week to Les Martin, the union's president, and to Jane Toff, the vice-president, and I was waiting for them to arrive at the meeting room in the hotel. It was now the morning of the national executive committee and while they were on board with the Industry3M situation—and also the proposed ballot in Teening & Sykes—they were very concerned about strike pay and not just whether it got through the committee. They could see, as easily as I could, the possible disastrous effects on the union's finances if there was a majority for an indefinite strike in Industry3M and a two day strike in Teening & Sykes and if the strikes were then authorised and if neither company moved and particularly if the

Industry3M strike went on for some time. A lot of 'ifs', I told myself, but a genuine critical concern.

I had spoken several times to Leila in the last few days since the meeting of the Industry3M national committee and I could see her strategy. She also told me that she had telephoned Paul Mugai, the general secretary of the Malaysian Commercial Workers Union. I knew Mugai and had met him several times at meetings and conferences of Staff International. She said his union was having discussions about Industry3M's attempt to set up a new company in Malaysia, but it was early days yet. He had promised to keep her informed about those discussions.

Usually the national executive committee meeting held just before the TUC's Annual Congress was to mandate our delegation as to how they should vote on the various motions, amendments and reports that would come for consideration. These days there wasn't too much controversy at the Congress as the practice of compositing motions and amendments had grown to such an extent that, as much as possible, controversy would be submerged in ever lengthening composite motions. On occasions, conflicting views in individual motions were all grouped into one long composite so that the sponsoring unions would be reluctant to vote against a motion that at least contained some of what they had tabled in their original motions.

The other feature of recent congresses was—mainly because of the compositing of motions and amendments, as well as a declining number of unions with more and more union mergers taking place—the shortening of the Congress week. With all the changes in the numbers of unions and the composites there wasn't much left to discuss by the Wednesday afternoon. One feature adopted to deal with this was to invite a fair number of outside speakers, from overseas unions, Government ministers, independent commissions and think tanks and—much to the chagrin of some unions—even from the CBI.

I was not alone in thinking that the Congress increasingly resembled a convention of the American Democrat or Republican parties: more a rally than a meeting place to hammer out policies. I knew that wasn't a completely fair picture but there was some truth in it.

Each TUC affiliated union of the TUC was entitled to submit two motions and two amendments for Congress to debate. This year we had submitted a motion on pensions—which, unsurprisingly, had been composited with five other motions on the same subject, although the wording and emphasis of each differed—and a motion on contracting out of staff by both the private and public sectors. This latter motion had been drawn up to highlight the problems caused by a decreasing central core of labour in companies and an increasing pool of contract labour to service those same companies. This had particular problems for unions in organisation and recruitment, as well as employment protection for the contract staff themselves.

Now I thought this motion—which had not been composited—was an ideal vehicle to refer to our dispute with Industry3M and Leila would be the ideal person to move that motion and I had mentioned this both to Les Martin and Jane Toff and they had been happy with the idea. I myself thought I should speak in the composite motion on pensions. In fact my union was listed as the seconder of the composite motion.

Yesterday the TUC General Council had met to discuss their attitude to the agenda items. They had agreed, naturally, to support the pensions motion and what they called 'leave to Congress' our motion on contracting out of labour. This meant that the General Council was quite happy for the motion to be passed but didn't want to put up a speaker on it. Where the General Council was opposed to particular motions then they would put up a speaker against it and where they were unhappy with some parts of a motion they would put up a speaker to make appropriate reservations. That was a somewhat dubious—but often practised—method of getting doubts put on the record while the original motion was carried. Then when it came to implementation of the motion then reference would be made to the General Council's reservations as well as the actual wording of the motion itself.

Les Martin arrived with Jane Toff. I presumed that they had met outside—or perhaps had arranged to meet for a brief chat before the meeting. They both smiled at me and I took that as a good sign. The idea of having a president and or a vice president trying to undermine me was not one I contemplated with much relish and I was glad I could trust both of them. I knew that this was far from the position in several other unions.

The fifteen members of the national executive had now all arrived as had the others who were members of our TUC delegation who were not on the national executive. Julia Cardon, of course, was present as was Mathew Singh, the national officer responsible for negotiations in Teening & Sykes. I noticed that he and Leila were talking animatedly. I had also asked Christine Buckley, our finance officer to attend and I saw she was speaking to the honorary treasurer.

Les Martin then called everyone to order at eleven o'clock. He was always punctilious, and rightly so, in starting meetings of the national executive dead on time and was a stickler for proper procedure throughout meetings. He had been called pedantic by some but in my view he was quite correct. Any loosening of procedures could easily lead to all sorts of problems, particularly by some of those who wanted to defer any decision.

We spent the morning going through the Congress agenda and I made clear at each motion and amendment what the General Council had decided. We didn't have to do what the General Council recommended but the members had to know. The committee agreed that Leila should move the motion on contracting out of labour and that I should second the pensions composite. They agreed that Les Martin should speak on the debate on employment legislation, where one of our two amendments had been swept up in a very long composite motion, and that Jane Toff should move our amendment to a motion on racial equality where—somewhat surprisingly to my mind—our amendment had not been accepted by the sponsors of the original motion and therefore would be put separately.

I had expected Tony Hammond to kick up about my proposal that we should oppose one of the motions calling for repeal of much of the current employment legislation and in that he didn't disappoint me. He had no support from the other members of the committee. He then tried to get us to support a motion which congratulated Fidel Castro on reaching the age of eighty and called for financial support from the TUC for Cuban unions. I thought the motion was one of the daftest I had ever read in all the years I had been a trade union official and, again, the majority of the committee members agreed with my proposal that we should oppose it. I guessed that Hammond was saving most of his fire for the afternoon debates on Industry3M and Teening & Sykes.

When we broke for lunch I suggested to Martin and Toff that they, with Leila and I, should have a chat with the union's honorary general treasurer and also Christine Buckley. We went to a different pub from the others so we would not be disturbed. I could see the issue of strike pay would be crucial to the discussions and decisions in the afternoon.

We each ordered some sandwiches and I got a round of drinks. We managed to find a table which we could all sit down and, fortunately, there was no piped music spoiling the pub atmosphere and there were not many people in. The fact that there were not many other drinkers was probably due to the fact that the beer was not very good, in fact I doubted whether the landlord had cleaned the pipes to the barrels for several months. It was, though, quiet and gave us an opportunity to talk. You couldn't have everything.

Peter Berenson, our honorary general treasurer, worked for a large firm of accountants and he himself was a qualified chartered accountant. He was in his mid-fifties. Like Les Martin's company, the union didn't negotiate with his company and there was little hope of us doing so, although we had tried some recruitment drives over the years. Berenson himself was very keen on the union and had been the treasurer for several years. His company always allowed him the appropriate time off to attend union meeting during weekdays and he had no complaint of any restriction on his union activities.

I suggested to Les Martin that Leila should summarise what the Industry3M national committee had decided—although they had all had a copy of the minutes of that meeting—and to talk about the strength of feeling on the strike pay issue. She took five minutes and then Martin asked Berenson to speak.

I had never really got to know Berenson. He was always pleasant and had a good working relationship with Christine Buckley the full time finance officer. In fact I had never heard any serious criticism of him from any quarter in the union. But he was regarded as a bit of a loner. No one doubted his commitment to the union. I had long suspected that he had been a member of the Communist Party in the past but had never tackled him about it. I looked with interest at him as he said his piece.

He rehearsed the union's financial position. Of our 260,000 members there were some 30,000 pensioners who paid a nominal one pound a month or else had commuted their future subscriptions with a one off life payment of one hundred pounds. We had 25,000 members under the age of twenty one and they paid three pounds a month. The rest—just over 200,000 paid a flat rate of seven pounds a month. We had in the past tried having different rates according to age or positions held but that was fiendishly difficult to define and therefore collect. We had also considered having subscriptions fixed as a percentage of salary. That would have been ideal if we could get all the employers we dealt with—and we had some eighty procedural agreements and a fair number of members in companies for whom we had no negotiating rights—but that was not the case. So a flat rate was the simplest form of subscription—even though we had two different flat rates.

Our annual subscription income was therefore about eighteen and a half million pounds a year but our annual expenditure was over seventeen million. We could, said Berenson, coast along with that for a long time but the fifty pounds a day strike pay would soon place us in some difficulty. For the Industry3M members it would mean expenditure of about one hundred thousand pounds a day—and the two day proposed strike in Teening & Sykes would cost us £1.2 million.

Against that, Berenson admitted we had to balance the effect of calling a strike with a reasonable amount of strike pay—to try and get as many members out as possible, if the majorities were there, and the impact that would make on the two employers—Industry3M and Teening & Sykes.

"I must say," concluded Berenson, that the publicity we've got over the dispute has been exceptional and, ideally, the threat of strikes—backed with the knowledge that we would pay that level of strike pay—could be a decisive factor." He paused briefly, "but I emphasise the word 'could'."

It was a fair summary of our position and we all knew we couldn't keep the strikes—especially if the Teening & Sykes membership wanted in the future to also consider an indefinite strike ballot,—for very long. And then, suppose our members in some of the other companies also wanted a strike ballot. Les Martin expressed his concern: we had just under twenty million pounds in investments and that could quickly disappear if strike pay was made for any lengthy period. This was the same point that the three union trustees had made forcibly to Leila when she had spoken to them earlier that week.

Jane Toff said she agreed with Berenson's summary but then said forcibly that we had no real alternative but to go ahead.

Leila got another round of drinks and we continued the discussion. Martin asked me what was my specific recommendation—no flannel, as he put it. I could have taken umbrage at this but I saw he was smiling as he said it.

I took a hefty swig of my pint of bitter and looked round at the others.

"Specifically, I think we have no option but to proceed. It's a question of credibility—in the eyes of our members and of the management of the two companies, to say nothing of the TUC and other unions. It could cost us an enormous amount of money and, in the worst scenario, threaten the financial existence of the union but I still think we have to go ahead."

I could see acceptance—at least tacitly—of what I was saying and continued: "we know other unions are pursuing the job evaluation scheme both here and on the continent. There's an interesting line to pursue in Malaysia which Leila will explain this afternoon. We know that Industry3M has been affected by our action so far—particularly by the publicity."

I looked back at Les Martin: "and I suggest we form a small disputes committee to monitor the position on a regular basis."

I had discussed this latter point with Leila. There were pros and cons about it. It could be cumbersome especially when very quick decisions were needed but, on the other hand, it did involve some of the lay members and, if it could be arranged, I would like the three senior lay officials—president, vice-president and treasurer—of the union on that committee. Leila had agreed and I hoped that the idea would go some way towards allaying the understandable apprehension that was clear both with the others in the pub and, more particularly, with the rest of the national executive when we reassembled.

Martin looked at his watch: "OK" he said. "Time to get back. I think we know where we are."

<hr>

Leila was pleased at the outcome of the national executive meeting in the afternoon. John Carmichael had briefly introduced the agenda item on the two strike issues—the indefinite strike ballot call from the Industry3M committee and the two day strike ballot call from the Teening & Sykes national committee. Then Leila had spoken on how the job evaluation proposal was being pursued by unions in the UK and by the Swedish and German Industry3M committees, She referred to her contact with the Malaysian Commercial Workers Union and how that could be important in view of Industry3M's wish to expand in the far east. Then she went into the particular position in Industry3M, the dismissal first of David Stannard and then Tom Chance, the notice about five hundred redundancies and how the Atlanta head office of the company had sent over Tiller allegedly to put some 'backbone' into the company. She emphasised to the committee that the redundancy notice had made the members angry rather than frightened though obviously there was considerable apprehension.

The debate had then started. As she had expected, Tony Hammond made a vicious attack on the union's handling of the dispute and deplored the publicity and alleged lack of direction. She was anxious to respond but Martin called on Peter Berenson to speak. He summarised the union's financial position as he had at the lunch time meeting and then—to the astonishment of most of the committee—made a savage attack on Hammond calling him irresponsible, untrue and totally negative.

Many had not heard him say anything like that before and as he had sat down Carmichael whispered to Leila, sitting next to him, "I always knew the Communist Party hated the trots more than anyone else." Leila grinned. Hammond was clearly discomfited and said no more in the debate.

After an hour's further discussion Martin had called for a vote on the proposal from the Indstry3M committee and it was carried by twelve votes to two. Hammond had voted for the motion because, Leila assumed, he couldn't face the prospect of being against the idea of any indefinite strike as what he called his street credibility would be affected—though he had abstained in the national committee vote. The two who voted against were concerned about the effect of strike pay on the union's finances.

Then the committee had established the disputes committee as recommended by Carmichael. It would supervise the Industry3M dispute and would consist of the three senior lay officials plus Ian Macallister and also Clive Bristow, the chairman of the union's Industry3M head office branch in Liverpool. Carmichael had suggested that the committee could also be called to supervise the Teening & Sykes strike, if it came to that and two members from the Teening & Sykes national committee could be coopted on to it. Again this was agreed.

Mathew Singh had then outlined the position in Teening & Sykes and how the management there had completely dismissed any idea of negotiations on the job evaluation claim. Leila thought he had spoken well and to the point. Negotiations had always been difficult in that company but generally the union had managed to secure agreements on pay and basic conditions. There had, though, been mounting frustration at the way staff were treated and at the relative decline in earnings. Union negotiations had been aimed at doing the best where they could but it was the minimum that could be achieved and gradually staff had fallen behind other companies and that frustration had exploded at the abrupt dismissal of any talks at all on job evaluation. This was especially because the grading system in the company was considered hopelessly out of date and didn't really provide for any right of appeal or objective assessment of the way it worked. Particularly for that reason the union's job evaluation scheme had been very attractive.

After the two issues of authorising strike ballots had been agreed the committee had then agreed the strike pay, again recommended by Carmichael. All in all, Leila thought, a good meeting—and Berenson's demolition of Hammond had been a bonus.

When the meeting finished Les Martin asked everyone to vacate the room as soon as they could as it was needed for the press conference, A number asked to stay behind and listen—Tony Hammond among them, Leila noted—and Martin said that would be all right on the strict understanding that none of them said anything at all, looking at Hammond as he said it.

Julia Cardon left the room to tell the journalists that they could now come in and the press conference would begin. She had asked them to be in the hotel for four o'clock and it was now a quarter past. But journalists, almost more than anyone else, were used to waiting.

Carmichael sat in the middle of one side of the square table with Leila on one side and Mathew Singh on the other. Les Martin, Jane Toff and Peter Berenson sat a little way away. Like the others, they had no intention of saying anything. As Martin had said playfully to Carmichael and Leila as they moved chairs, "there's no point in having a dog and barking oneself, is there?"

Leila saw there were about fifteen journalists coming in and noticed Joe Turner from the *Liverpool Daily Post*, Oliver Listle of the *Financial Times* and Chuck Pitney from the *Wall Street Journal*. Pitney's piece in the *Wall Street Journal* at the beginning of the week had been excellent she thought. He had surmised that the national executive committee would endorse the national committee's proposal for an indefinite strike ballot and also that the union's finances seemed healthy enough for a long strike. It was just what she had hoped he would put.

Carmichael started the press conference by welcoming the journalists and then told them of the decisions taken that day. Leila had then spoken on the position of Industry3M and the feeling amongst the members. She stressed the timing and the size of the redundancy announcement and how this had made the members very determined. She had decided to refer to David Stannard and Tom Chance's dismissal, though was careful not to give any indication of the conversations and meetings that had taken place with them.

"It's clear that the company doesn't really know how to handle this dispute and in a sense seems to be turning inwards on itself—" she knew that this would probably make both Norman Jones, the chief executive and John Carr hopping mad—"and the other thing is that our members know they are not alone. The job evaluation scheme seems to be very popular with a lot of other unions both here and in other countries and we reckon we are on to a winner."

Carmichael thought she was giving a big hostage to fortune in what she said but knew that she was doing it deliberately. They had to get the best possible publicity for the union stance and he thought Leila was just the person to do it.

Mathew Singh then gave a report on the position within Teening & Sykes and how a strike there would be the first time it had happened in that company. He emphasised the feeling of the members on his national committee and the curt refusal of the company to attempt any sort of negotiations.

There were a number of questions on the timing of the two ballots, and Leila said the result of the ballots would probably be in the fourth week of September, and on whether the union would be pursuing similar claims in other companies and Leila referred to Transport International and Hokkaido and that Leisure & Sport would be considering the matter further. Oliver Listle asked specifically about strike pay and how long could the union pay strike pay for in Industry3M, particularly if they were also paying strike pay for six thousand members in Teening & Sykes and Leila gave him the same response as she had previously given to Chuck Pitney.

She added: "we've got the money and that's what it's for—to support members in their struggle for better conditions."

Carmichael thought her comment sounded like a statement from a sixteen year old enthusiast, but again he knew that Leila was choosing her words carefully.

Joe Turner asked for any comment on the presence of Tiller, the man he had heard who had been sent over from Atlanta to sort things out. Leila replied that she hadn't met Tiller but would be happy to do if it would help to resolve the dispute. She added that she even looked forward to further management changes as a result of his activity. There were a few laughs as she said it.

Oliver Listle asked about David Adnam's standing within the CBI. Carmichael said he didn't know what his standing was but mentioned that he had not been the most friendly when the TUC delegation had recently met the CBI employment committee. Singh said he had never met him but would be pleased to do so.

The questions finished at five o'clock. As they journalists left the room Pitney went up to Carmichael and said "that was a bullish performance, John."

Carmichael replied "we've got a lot to be bullish about, Chuck."
Pitney added "Leila's pretty impressive isn't she?"
"Redoubtable is the word you're looking for, Chuck."

Chapter Nine

Congress and other Events

"Mrs Smith?"

It was the Saturday morning and Leila was starting to prepare the lunch for Deborah and Helen, her daughter and grand daughter.

"Yes." Leila waited for the caller to say who he was, though she thought his voice was familiar.

"Chris Rodd here. How are you?"

Leila remembered when she had last seen him in the Euston Station restaurant and she also remembered that she couldn't stand people who asked how she was—especially as they never seemed to wait for an answer. And what on earth did he want?

"Fine," she replied. She thought there was no time to waste on pleasantries. "What do you want?"

Rodd sounded a bit taken aback: "well, I thought I would touch base with you about Industry3M. You remember our previous conversation?"

Leila remembered how she had telephoned him at home that early morning and how she had regretted it afterwards.

"I'm a bit busy at the moment, so please keep it brief."

Rodd sounded a bit more put out.

"I thought you might like to hear what's happening in the company."

Leila swallowed hard: "yes, of course. I'm sorry, things are a bit hectic at the moment but what's the position?"

"I thought it best to phone you at home and—" she could hear him trying to be contrite—"but there seems a lot happening in the company. You know Tom Chance has gone?"

Leila grunted.

Rodd went on: "there's a lot of anxiety over what an American called Joe Tiller is doing. Apparently he's been sent over here to sort things out and he's not going down too well with either Norman Jones or John Carr."

Leila was beginning to get irritated.

"Yes, I know all that. Is there anything specific?"

She could sense Rodd taking umbrage. He said that he was sorry for phoning her at home but it would not be practical to phone from his office. He assured Leila that he was acting from the best of motives and only wished to help. He said that contrary to the circular that John Carr had issued, the company was seriously worried about the impact the dispute was having.

Leila cut in: "what has been the effect?"

"It's the question of future contracts," said Rodd. "The rumour is that a number of contracts the company was hoping to sign up have been deferred because the customer companies have said they are worried about the strikes and basically the continuity of supply. And the press reports yesterday—following your press conference I believe—have aggravated that concern."

Leila thought he was speaking as if he was talking to a seminar but she thanked him for the news, which she thought wasn't really news at all.

"What do you think the company will do, Chris?" She thought using his Christian name would bolster his ego a bit.

"it depends on your new ballot—an indefinite strike, isn't it? By the way, Leila, what's the timetable for that?"

Leila decided that she had heard enough. The news about the indefinite strike ballot was in all the papers but the specifics of the timetable had not been announced and she was quite clear that she was not going to tell Rodd. Was that why he had phoned?

"I can't tell you that, Chris. It will go ahead and—" she thought she would add—"it appears that there's a lot of support for it. We should announce it soon."

Rodd sounded hesitant as if there was a lot he wanted to ask her but was unsure whether to do so. Then he started to talk again about the uncertainty in the company and that the press publicity seemed to be having an effect.

"Look, Chris, I can't say any more and I am busy at the moment. Thanks for calling," and as she started to put the phone down she could hear him almost shout—"hold on, there's one more thing—"

She knew it had been a mistake ever to rely on him for any information and the more he had talked in that rather smooth and intimate manner of his, the more she regretted she had ever taken him seriously. Now, she thought, he was not telling her anything she didn't already know—rather he was trying to get information from her. She heard him saying "hold on" but thought that was just too bad. Enough, she decided, was enough. He shouted again and Leila hesitated.

"I must go, Chris," she said.

"The big news," said Rodd in a hurry, "is that apparently Tiller has given both Jones and Carr three weeks to sort things out, otherwise they will be out."

Leila paused. It could be important news, if it was true and not just company gossip—but why was Rodd telling her anyway? She thanked him, repeated that she must go and then put the phone down. For a moment she felt a pang of conscience that she had been a bit rude but then, why had he phoned? To find out about the ballot timetable? Perhaps someone in the company had put him up to it—if they knew that he knew her. Perhaps he had boasted that he had a direct line to her?

So what, thought Leila and for the umpteenth time she regretted she had ever phoned him at home that morning. She had not told

Carmichael at the time but now she realised she must. If there was any truth in the three weeks deadline that Rodd said Tiller had issued, well that could be important. As for now, she was looking forward to a pleasant lunch and afternoon with Helen and Deborah. She did, though, go over the events of yesterday.

On the previous Thursday evening she had gone down to the Brighton hotel where her union's delegation would be staying and the following day had, with John Carmichael, attended the Friday meeting of the TUC General Council. The meeting had gone fairly smoothly. John Miller had updated the meeting on some new composite motions that had been agreed and given details of the outside speakers that would be addressing the Congress during the Congress week.

Apart from the fraternal delegates from the American TUC equivalent—the American Federation of Labour-Congress of Industrial Organisations—and the Canadian Labour Congress—there would be the chairman of the Health and Safety Commission, the recently appointed new Secretary of State for Work and Pensions and—much to the surprise of Leila and John Carmichael—Bob Wilson the minister of state at the DTI.

The General Council had nodded through agreement with the newly presented composite motions and the list of speakers.

Carmichael had asked Miller after the meeting why Wilson had been invited and he had explained that it was very much a last minute request by Wilson for an opportunity to come and speak. He had sounded out Mark Thurston, the current TUC President, who would be presiding over the Congress, the previous day and he had agreed and he added he was pleased no one—especially Leila or he—had not queried it at the meeting.

"Things are a bit dicey with the Government over a number of issues at the moment, John," he had explained "and we have to tread carefully."

When Carmichael told Leila of this she had remarked that they always had to tread carefully, that she didn't know why Wilson wanted to speak at the Congress and that anything he said might backfire—and that she hoped he himself would tread carefully as well.

Leila had then driven back home. Carmichael would stay on. There were a couple of union receptions he said he would go to that evening and he had been pressurised into playing for the TUC in the annual cricket match with the journalists at the Congress on the Saturday afternoon.

Years before, the annual cricket match had been quite a date in the Congress calendar and it provided for some good photographs and rather obvious captions in the press. Carmichael remembered "general secretary stumped", "president hits out" and "union leaders knocked for six". In recent years the numbers taking part had declined and several Congress House staff of the TUC had actually played for the journalists side in order to make up the numbers. Press coverage was usually now nil.

Carmichael knew that John Miller had been increasingly worried at the decline in press and television coverage of the annual TUC Congress and the poor attendance at the cricket match was but one manifestation of that. It was ironic, he thought, that when there was a Conservative Government in the country then press and television coverage of the unions and the TUC had been generally high; now, with a Labour Government, the coverage was continually declining. Perhaps that was one reason why the Industry3M dispute had attracted so much attention—it involved strikes, a clearly hostile company management—and an American one to boot—and implications for inward investment.

He had arranged with Leila that the union's TUC delegation would meet on the Sunday afternoon and he would then go over the latest information on the state of the Congress agenda, the new composite motions and the outside speakers. He was happy for Leila not to stay over until then and knew that she valued what little time she could spend with her daughter and grand daughter. He wondered again whether she would ever have any time for finding someone else to share her life with. But, it was her life he reminded himself and, really, nothing to do with him.

As Leila carried on with preparing lunch she also couldn't help but go over what could be happening in he company. David Stannard long gone, Tom Chance now sacked—perhaps having had his telephone calls listened to—now Joe Tiller seeming to be in charge. And now Chris Rodd telephoning with news of a three week ultimatum, presumably from the company's head office in Atlanta. Had Rodd been put up to it—or was it his way of pretending to be in the know as to what was happening? And if he had been put up to phone her, then by whom? She realised that she could speculate for a long time. She would phone Carmichael in the evening at his hotel after her daughter and grand daughter had gone home and see if she could catch him before he went to one of the receptions.

In fact she was glad that she had decided not to stay in Brighton for the Friday and Saturday nights. She had been to any number of union receptions at previous Congresses and was getting a bit bored with them. She knew that in a sense she should show her face at them—it was all part of what was called 'the Congress week '—but she had preferred to stay at home.

***

The cricket match had finished and it had just started to rain. We had lost again and I had only scored a miserly two runs and the miserable weather seemed to fit the mood I was in. The coach brought the General Council team—and the wives and husbands who had watched—back to the Metropole Hotel where the General Council were staying. I got the driver to drop me off first at the small hotel where I was staying with my own union delegation. I always liked to stay with them and not with the rest of the General Council at what they called the headquarters hotel. I didn't have to, but I preferred it that way.

As I went to reception to collect my room key the woman behind the desk handed me a letter.

"This came later this morning but you were not here," she said. "I think the post was a bit late today."

I thanked her and opened the letter. It was from Industry3M and signed 'Lionel Collins, acting head of personnel'. That was the two faced blighter who had been Stannard's number two. I had never met him but had heard of him, and it didn't sound too good. Presumably he had got the hotel address from my secretary—but he could easily have faxed the letter to my office the day before.

The letter was brief and I scanned it quickly as I went up to my room. I didn't like to bother Leila when she was at home but thought it best to give her a ring. She answered the phone immediately.

"All OK?" I asked. "And did your lunch go all right?"

Leila replied that her daughter and grand daughter had just left and, yes, the lunch had been a success. I read her the letter.

"We have received your letter to Mr Jones, the chief executive" it started, "concerning the company announcement about some unfortunate redundancy notices. If you wish to discuss this then perhaps you might like to come to my office on Wednesday 12 September at 11:30 am."

"And that's all" I said to Leila. "Bloody cheek. He knows there's a Congress on, his tone is offhand and clearly he's just responding because he has to. And the pensions debate is scheduled for Wednesday morning." I was furious.

Leila told me to calm down—advice that I wouldn't have taken from anyone else but her and then said she could go to Liverpool on the Wednesday—and the union could not afford not to go. The company would undoubtedly trumpet the fact of us refusing to discuss the redundancies; at least, that was how they could portray it.

I agreed with her and said I would ask Sheila to fax through a note t o Collins on Monday morning to say that she would attend the meeting.

I told her briefly some of the comments I had heard from other members of the General Council about our Industry3M dispute. They had sounded genuinely interested. I had never expected so many of them to look at the *Wall Street Journal*: their research and press departments must be on the ball.

Leila then told me about Chris Rodd. I vaguely remembered someone mentioning him to me some time back, something about him and Leila talking rather animatedly at a management seminar once. I hadn't paid any attention to it then as I suspected the person who told me—and I couldn't for the life of me remember who he was—was trying to stir things up for Leila.

"It could be interesting," I told Leila, "if there's anything in the three week thing."

"But I think he was put up to it to find out about our ballot timetable."

"Could it have been that chap Collins?" I asked.

"I don't know John," replied Leila. "I don't know how Collins could have found out that Rodd knows me."

"Perhaps Rodd told him."

Leila paused: "there could be no end to duplicity."

I assured her that no harm had been done and that if the three week deadline given to Jones and Carr was true then it could be helpful. Or, I told myself, it could also be bad news if it meant that Tiller would then take control. As for the ballot timetable, we had agreed at the national executive committee meeting that Leila would mention it when moving the motion on the Tuesday afternoon.

I told Leila that I would see her tomorrow. She said she would get down about midday and we could have a chat before the delegation meeting at two o'clock. After I put the phone down I reflected that Leila was obviously feeling bitter about Chris Rodd but I knew that there were many occasions when I had been almost led up the garden path by people before. People who had told me they had some inside information; people on the management side who assured me they were really on the union's side; people who said they no axe to grind but in fact had personal motives to get their own back on someone else.

I thought it was all part of a union official's experience; or, putting it a bit more objectively, it was all part of life.

I decided to change into a suit in order to go the steel union's reception that was being held that evening in the Metropole Hotel. Just as I had finished changing the phone rang again. It was Alan Whitchurch, our national organiser.

He started to apologise for phoning me at the hotel but I cut him short: "what's up Alan?"

Whitchurch told me that he had just been phoned at home by Jack Treeman, the West Midlands organiser. Treeman had somehow got a copy of a leaflet that the SPGB—the Socialist Party of Great Britain—was apparently going to distribute outside the Congress meeting place, the Brighton Exhibition Centre.

One of the features of Congress was the number of people who would stand outside the conference hall handing out leaflets to the delegates as they went in. They could be other delegates to Congress, members of unions who weren't themselves delegates, or supporters of almost every political, environmental, campaigning group you could think of. I was sure—though I couldn't prove it—that Tony Hammond from my union would be one of those. He was not one of the elected delegates to Congress from the union but would undoubtedly have taken some of his annual holiday entitlement to attend and hand out leaflets for the SPGB.

"I'll fax it through to the hotel, shall I?" asked Whitchurch.

"Good idea. Just a moment. Here's the hotel fax number." I gave him the number. "What's it like?"

I could sense Whitchurch smiling.

"Outrageous. You'll be apopleptic—even at you age, John."

I could take that from him, but not many others. Like Leila Smith, Whitchurch was one of the most solid and reliable union officials you could get. I pressed him as to how he thought Treeman had got a copy of it. Whitchurch said he knew Treeman went drinking with a number of lecturers from the local technical college. He had been a lecturer there himself before becoming a union organiser. As in a number of further and higher education colleges there seemed to be a disproportionate number of trots on the staff and I remembered at the time that Treeman was appointed wondering whether he was a bit of a trot. I had made the usual enquiries and it turned out that he wasn't a member of any extreme left organisation. He had kept in touch though with some of his former colleagues and perhaps one of them had had too much to drink at one of their drinking evenings and boasted to Treeman about how the SPGB was going to lambast his union.

Whitchurch said that, as previously arranged with me, he would be down in Brighton on a visitor's ticket on the Tuesday, so he could hear Leila's speech.

I was not surprised at Whitchurch's news. It had been clear that the trots would do something at Congress and Leila had told me about the shenanigans of Hammond at the national committee of Industry3M and with the pickets during the strikes.

I wondered whether to wait for the fax of the leaflet to come through but then thought I would go straight now to the steel union's reception. The fax could wait a little while. It was time for a drink.

⟨ ✤ ⟩

Leila got to her union's delegation hotel by midday on the Sunday. She met Carmichael together with Les Martin, the president, and Jane Toff, the vice-president, in the bar. She saw Carmichael was waving a leaflet angrily. As soon as she got near he thrust the leaflet at her.

"Look at this cod's wallop" he almost shouted.

Leila looked at the leaflet. It was printed on a small piece of A4 size paper and was headed 'Time to fight'. The others were watching her as she read it.

"Union activists are furious that their union—the Clerical & General Union—is letting them down over the dispute with

Industry3M. The company is behaving viciously and has recently announced it is going to sack five hundred workers.

We say it's time to organise mass pickets and get the TUC to call on other unions to support us. This dispute is crucial for all unions and we must win.

We say the union leadership is too timid and not giving a clear lead. We want all the leading lay representatives to come together in a conference and take the leadership of the dispute away from the union bureaucracy and give it to those most involved—the workers themselves.

It's time to fight: go back to your union branches and get them to pass resolutions urging the above and send copies to SPGB so we can coordinate what's happening."

Leila looked up at Carmichael and handed back the leaflet. He looked at her.

"Well?"

"Well, John, it's wrong in almost everything it says, it's deliberately misleading, it's unfair, it's counter-productive, it doesn't help at all—but what did you expect?"

"You're right, of course, Leila," said Carmichael. "In fact Alan Whitchurch who faxed this through to me said it would make me apopleptic and he was right too."

Les Martin asked if they knew how many SPGB people would be distributing the leaflet and whether they would do it from then until the end of the week. Carmichael said he assumed they would concentrate on distributing it on the Tuesday morning when the motion on contract labour was being moved by Leila later.

"I assume that there'll be another seven or eight causes they'll be pushing this week as well as ours," said Leila. "By the way, I've got our leaflets in my car so I'll bring them in just before the meeting starts. And," she reminded Carmichael, "I've got a suggested list of our delegates who can distribute them and where and when."

Carmichael grunted approval. Jane Toff looked over at him. He looked at her: "what is it Jane?"

"I'm thinking it's a long time since I saw you standing at a bar without a drink in your hand."

Carmichael grinned: "point taken, Jane." He asked them what they would like to drink and ordered from the barman. In fact he knew he had had probably too many drinks at the previous evening's reception and wanted to pace himself for a while.

Les Martin suggested they took their drinks over to a table and go over the afternoon's business. "And don't take the SPGB to heart, John, it's a sign of how worried or angry they must be. The more vicious the attack on us, the better we are obviously dealing with the dispute."

Carmichael told them he appreciated that point but was still annoyed—"just think what the company could make of it," he said, "and some of the right wing press." He got out some papers from his briefcase. "OK, here's the latest I've got from Congress House on the order of business."

He went over the decisions of the General Council on the Friday and what he had heard at the reception the previous evening from John Miller. Bob Wilson of the DTI was definitely speaking and was slotted in for the Monday afternoon. Peter Moorhouse of the Commercial and Technology Union had shown him a copy of his speech to second the motion that Leila was moving. "He's going to give you a copy this evening at the combined civil service unions' reception" he said to Leila. "It seems OK to me. And the good news is that Dick Whetter also wants to speak on the motion."

Martin asked why the General Council were not putting up a speaker on the motion. Carmichael was a bit non-committal. He had wanted to know the same thing but when he had tackled John Miller about it Miller had merely said they were trying to save Congress time—"and it's going to get carried anyway, isn't it?" he had said. Carmichael suspected that perhaps Miller had been leant on by Wilson, or someone else, and that was why he hadn't suggested putting up a speaker.

Leila said she thought there would be quite a bit of support for the motion and that she intended to speak to Jim Bradwell of the local government union that evening to see if he would speak on it as well.

After a few more drinks and some sandwiches Leila went out to her car and brought in a large packet of the leaflets that she had written for our delegates to hand out outside the Congress venue on the Tuesday morning. By two o'clock they were all seated round the table in the meeting room in the hotel and the other members of the delegation had joined them.

I thought the delegation meeting went off all right. Fortunately we didn't have any of the known trots with us this time. Last year we had three of them—but not including Tony Hammond—on the delegation, the price of democracy I thought, and we had had a row over them wanting to join some of the leafleteers and I had formally forbidden it. Luckily they had backed down, but if some had persisted then undoubtedly the issue would have smouldered on and, as ever, we had had enough to do without spending time on that.

We arranged for eight of the delegation to hand out leaflets on the Tuesday morning and for them to be on parade from eight o'clock in the morning until the Congress session started at nine o'clock. I had mentioned the SPGB leaflet and warned them not to try and stop it or get involved in any argument with those distributing it.

Mathew Singh had spoken briefly, and succinctly, on the position in Teening & Sykes. He was not on the delegation but was down for the week on a visitors ticket. He had also got a ticket for the civil service unions' reception and would be talking to a number of other union people there. I had agreed with him that I would speak at three rallies of T&S members that he would be arranging in Sunderland, Manchester and Cardiff and, of course, in terms of the number of union members involved, the Teening & Sykes position was much bigger.

We had discussed for some time whether to get leaflets done on the that position to hand out as well. In the end we had all agreed that we would not. It was no insult to our thousands of Teening & Sykes members but, as Singh put it himself, the immediate issue—and the most advanced in time—was that of Industry3M—and messages to Congress and the wider world had to be clear and, he added, simple. Undoubtedly he would talk about the Teening & Sykes dispute to all the delegates from other unions that he met and I knew that Leila would be referring to it in her speech as well as the possibility of a ballot in Hokkaido (that would set the cat among the pigeons, I thought) but the immediate issue was Industry3M.

After a meal in our hotel Leila and I, together with Les Martin and Jane Toff went off to the reception held by the three civil service unions. It was generally regarded as one of the best of the Congress week but, fortunately, not so crowded that it was like a pub giving away free beer on a packed Saturday night. Dick Whetter met us at the door. He said that he was looking forward to saying a few words on our motion on contract labour. He then whispered to me that there were quite a few trots in the reception, some of them, he ruefully admitted, from his own union.

It was always surprising that there were such a number of extreme left people in the civil service unions—mainly, though, among the clerical grades. Of course there was a serious problem of low pay in the civil service among clerical assistants, cleaners, junior admin staff, porters and the like. And to be fair it was still a problem even after the recent years of a new Labour Government. It was not only that, I knew; there was the problem of the glass ceiling that stopped many from progressing through to higher grades, the monotony and sheer boredom of much of the work and also, though not readily appreciated by many outside the civil service, to say nothing of the dangers staff in some of the job centres and benefit offices were exposed to from what the Government insisted on calling 'clients'.

Put all that together, with some articulate trots and there was a heady mixture in which the easy solutions—though totally impractical—seemed attractive. Dick Whetter and a group of his close colleagues had done a lot to keep them under control and, to be fair again, he had achieved some notable improvements in civil service pay and conditions; but there was a big mountain to climb.

We had been in the reception for about half an hour when I suddenly spied Tony Hammond talking with a small number of others in a corner of the large room. Just as I looked at him so he looked up and saw me. He started to come over, holding a pint of beer which he kept spilling as he walked. Clearly he had already a few and his thin face was flushed.

Leila nudged my elbow. She had also seen him. I thought there was going to be an awkward scene when suddenly two large men appeared through the crowd and grabbed hold of Hammond. He looked at them in surprise and started to protest when they herded him out to the door of the room. He managed to shout but his shouts were more or less drowned in the general hubbub and conversations going on. At the door Whetter leant over and whispered in his ear. Hammond again tried to struggle free but the two who held him were both big and strong and they pushed him out. He tried to get back in but one of the men pushed him hard and he fell backwards into the corridor, his beer spilling over him.

Whetter and the two men blocked Hammond's re-entry and after a bit more shouting Hammond moved off. The others in the group he had been with seemed to be going to protest at what had happened but apparently thought better of it and did nothing. They carried on drinking.

I went over to Dick Whetter.

"That was pretty good, Dick."

Whetter smiled.

"I told my delegation that if anyone got drunk and started to make a scene then we would chuck them out. It's ridiculous, isn't it? The trots on my delegation protested and then demanded a vote on the issue. How daft can you get? But, fortunately the majority of the delegation voted with my point."

"Good thing, democracy, isn't it?"

"As long as you've got the majority," replied Whetter.

I thought the incident had been handled well and hoped there would be nothing similar at our own reception. That was timed for the Tuesday lunchtime and I made a mental note to mention to Les Martin that we ought to raise the matter at our delegation meeting the next morning.

Leila joined us at the door and asked Whetter how things were going with his union's claim in the DTI. He said he couldn't quite understand why the Department was so adamant in not being prepared even to discuss the proposed job evaluation system. I asked him his view on why Bob Wilson, the minister, had apparently been so keen to speak to Congress.

Whetter said he thought Wilson was the problem. The permanent secretary at DTI, he said, was always reasonable, though a tough man to deal with. He confirmed my view that Wilson himself had been lent on and this tied in with my impression from my conversation with John Miller about it.

I mentioned the leaflets we were distributing on the Industry3M dispute on Tuesday morning and he said he would give me one of his union's leaflets which they intended to distribute, also on the Tuesday morning. I asked if any on his delegation were going to protest at Wilson speaking but he said that though they had discussed that, they had decided not to. He thought it would be counter-productive and, if Wilson said anything he considered outrageous, then he could use that in his own speech on the contract labour motion.

Leila said she would have another chat with him after Congress adjourned tomorrow after the morning session.

All in all, the reception was enjoyable and I had realised that, once again, I had probably had more beer than I intended but I was still fairly sober, and it was all part of the Congress week, wasn't it?

As members of the General Council both John Carmichael and Leila usually sat on the platform during the Congress sessions. Sometimes they would—as did the other members of the General Council—go and sit with their delegations but as the Monday afternoon session started they were on the platform when Bob Wilson, the DTI minister, got up to speak. He was introduced by Mark Thurston as the Congress President and he received some applause.

Wilson was quite a good speaker thought Leila as she listened to him. Well, she decided, he ought to be as he had been a former union general secretary. He started by rehearsing some of the achievements of the government since they had first been elected and then spoke about the effect of globalisation on the British economy and how the government was deliberately encouraging foreign investment. Leila thought he lost it when he then went on to condemn those who opposed such investment and how all unions had to be careful in their actions so as not to lend credence to such opposition.

There were a few cries of dissent as Wilson continued but he recovered a bit when he switched to talking about the future intentions of the government in pursuing their goal of full employment and the steps they had already taken and others that they were taking to try and achieve it.

Leila thought his speech was a bit muddled and the bit about not upsetting foreign investment had clearly been intended to refer to the Industry3M dispute. When Wilson finished and sat down there was some polite applause but nothing prolonged. She got our her own speech for the next day's motion she was moving and made a few notes on it.

The rest of the afternoon went without any controversy and by the time the Congress adjourned it was clear that many of the delegates were looking forward to a few drinks and some more of the union receptions that occurred every lunch time and evening while others were going to some of the many fringe meetings that were held during the week. Carmichael and Leila had discussed whether they should hold a fringe meeting on the issue of contract labour but had decided against it.

The next morning Leila went down to outside the Congress hall and joined the members of her union's delegation to hand out leaflets as the Congress delegates entered. There were a crowd of people leafleting, espousing every sort of issue and acting on behalf of a large number of organisations. She saw Tony Hammond with a group of what were clearly SPGB members further down the line ready to hand out their leaflets. She saw Hammond look at her from a distance but neither of them made any move towards each other. That's fine, thought Leila as she helped to hand out her leaflets.

Tuesday was a day for motions and amendments both morning and afternoon with only one outside speaker, the chairman of the Health and Safety Commission. Jane Toff was due to speak in the morning when she moved the union's amendment to the racial equality motion. Leila was due on the Tuesday afternoon.

When she had taken her place on the platform she got out her papers and looked yet again at the wording of the motion she was moving. It read "Congress notes the increasing practice of contracting out of services previously provided in-house by companies and thus the growing numbers of contract labour in the public and private sectors. Further, Congress notes the difficulties in the traditional recruitment of such contract labour and calls on the General Council to set up a special task force to monitor the position and to consider ways in which unions can work together to meet these new challenges. The special task force is to report to next year's Congress with specific recommendations."

She knew the wording of the motion could seem a bit pious but again she knew that was not the point. She had drafted the motion herself and made it such that a number of unions could support it and knew it would provide a vehicle for several speakers to refer to their own position in dealing with contract labour.

Jane Toff's speech on equality had been well received and the amendment she moved was carried, along with the original motion. Leila was still not clear as to why the amendment had not been accepted by the movers of the original motion, and she guessed that her bewilderment was shared by most of the other Congress delegates.

Her union's reception had gone well at lunchtime. John Miller had called in as had the presidents and general secretaries of most of the unions. A number of the press covering the Congress had also showed up. Leila had taken the opportunity to speak to Peter Moorhouse, Dick Whetter and Jim Bradwell. All three were intending to speak on the motion in the afternoon.

The contract labour motion was timed for three o'clock and Leila was sitting with her delegation when Mark Thurston, as Congress President, called on her to move the motion. She went to the rostrum and looked at the nearly one thousand delegates in the hall. She noticed a number of press photographers taking shots of her as she put her notes on the lectern. Under the Congress time limits for speakers she had ten minutes to make her case. She had a lot to say but was determined not to over run her time. It was going to be a tight call, she knew.

"We all think our own motions are the most important," she started, "but in this case I think it's also true." There was a little laughter as she said that. "We recognise that the traditional divide between employers and employees is changing dramatically. Self employment, the reduction of the workforce in so many companies, the huge growth in small businesses, privatisation of so many—I would say too many—"there was some applause at this—"and the growth in contracting out of not only services but also production facilities all mean a large increase in the use of contract labour."

She could see that she had got the attention of the delegates now and continued "I'm not saying that this process needs to be opposed for its own sake or even that we should regret it. It's a fact of life and, like all other facts of life, we have to take account of it and adapt our own methods and activities to meet the challenges that this brings."

There were a few cries of dissent as she said that—most, she noticed, coming from visitors in the gallery. She briefly looked up and thought she saw Tony Hammond in the gallery.

"Yes, of course we can—and in some cases should—press for a halt on some of the unnecessary and ultimately very expensive measures of privatisation. But we also have to deal with the situation as it is now and that's why we put down this motion and ask for specific action to be taken on it." There was some further applause as she spoke.

"The key to organise contract labour is to ensure that we are seen to be relevant to the needs of the working people. It also means we have to organise those who actually organise the use of contract labour." In this she was clearly referring to companies such as Industry3M. She saw now that she had the attention of the hall and she briefly outlined the dispute with Industry3M. She stressed how the job evaluation scheme was designed to provide an objective and fair system within which staff could feel their importance was recognised and how their pay and conditions could be assessed with both traditional employees and also the thousands, if not millions, who were now working as contract labour. A proper grading and evaluation system could be the solution to organising that labour.

She went on to refer to her union's decision to call a ballot for an indefinite strike in Industry3M and then announced that the ballot would start the next Monday and be completed by the middle of the following week.

"We've got ten days to get out the maximum vote and we know that it's crucial to get a big turnout and a big majority." More applause greeted this remark and a number of the press photographers took more photos. "We have got to win this dispute and to show the company that we will not have any company riding roughshod over the wishes of its staff and—" she paused—"tell any foreign investors who come over here that we want them to observe British traditions and customs of industrial relations. We don't want nineteenth century American anti-unionism here in Britain in the twentieth first century."

She had thought for some time as to whether she should say that but in the end decided that it was better to blunt, and she also knew that she would get a lot of support from the left leaning unions for it. She knew she was proved right when large applause greeted her remark.

"And while we recognise the advances towards a fairer society taken by the present government, we also give the same message to ministers as well as employers. And while of course we accept that power brings responsibility let's also remember that power brings the opportunity to change things for the better." The reference to the speech by Bob Wilson of the DTI the previous day was blatant.

"And our Industry3M members are not alone." She referred to the ballot in Teening & Sykes and then the other companies where her union had submitted claims particularly stressing that it looked as if a ballot would be held in Hokkaido. "And it's not just our union—there will be other speakers talking now about how they are submitting claims for the job evaluation proposals and it's just not here but in other countries too."

The yellow light on the lectern came on. That meant she had one minute of speaking time left.

"I emphasise that this is not a dispute with some hidden political agenda. It's a dispute over the fundamental rights of working people for their trade unions to be able to defend and advance the cause of their members. It's a dispute—this and the others that are emerging—that we must win—" she paused again—"and will win."

The red light came on just as she finished. Her timing had worked out all right and there was a storm of applause as she left the rostrum.

Peter Moorhouseof the Commercial & Technology Union rose to second the motion and he was followed by Dick Whetter of the civil servants union and then Jim Bradwell of the local government union. Each talked of the claims submitted and the strong resistance by their respective employers to even consider the new job evaluation system. Whetter put it clearly: "it's clear all the employers just mentioned—public and private—are consistent, the one with the other. They are all opposed to even discussing the system. Well, there's something wrong somewhere isn't there? I've never seen so many different employers so united."

No one spoke against the motion and, when Mark Thurston called on her, Leila waived the right of reply. She thought there was no point in over egging the pudding. The motion was then put to the vote and as far as Leila could see there was a forest of hands in favour but no one against. Mark Thurston declared the motion carried unanimously. Although he should have asked if there were any abstentions neither Leila nor John Carmichael thought it fit to query the procedural point.

The motion had gone as good as could have been expected and Leila hoped the press coverage would be good as well. She had kept the announcement of the ballot dates to give a particular point to possible press coverage, something for the reporters to hang their story on. Also she had agreed with Carmichael that he wrote to both the managements of Industry3M and Teening & Sykes with the ballot dates the previous day so that they could not complain they had heard of the dates first from the press.

⚜

Once again Leila had turned up trumps. All of us on the delegation had given her a rousing reception when she returned to her seat. Les Martin not only shook her hand but leaned over and gave her a kiss on the cheek. After the vote, and when the Congress business had moved on to the next motion, Les Martin suggested that he and I take Leila for a drink in the bar. This was quickly agreed by me and we left the block vote card with Jane Toff, though it was unlikely to be used.

A number of other delegates were in the bar and, by the look of some of them, a fair number had been there for some time. Those who had come out of the hall with us smiled and Leila and one or two congratulated her on her speech.

Les Martin then said that things were all going well so far—"almost too good to be true" he commented. "Also there's been no serious trouble with Hammond or the other trots."

I told him that I had heard there was to be an SPGB meeting that evening in one of the small hotels, in fact the one just next to ours. He asked me how I knew that and I told him that Leila had told me. He turned to Leila and asked her but she said she couldn't remember—it must have been she heard it at the civil service unions' reception on the Sunday evening. In fact as she had already told me, it was Larry Brent from the Liverpool branch who had left a message at the hotel. She didn't want people to know that—even people like Les Martin or Jane Toff.

We discussed when the disputes committee we had set up should now meet and agreed that the following Monday was probably the best bet. Leila said there could well be a problem with leave of absence from the company in the case of Ian Macallister and Clive Bristow—to say nothing of the two members from the Teening & Sykes national committee. She said she would try and have a word with Bristow the next day when she got to Liverpool for her meeting with Collins about the company's redundancy notices and would ask Mathew Singh to chase up the Teening & Sykes members. We knew that if necessary they would all be willing to take a day off work as part of their holiday entitlement in order to attend the meeting but it would of course be better if formal leave of absence could be granted by the two companies Fat chance though, I thought, in the case of Industry3M. Still Leila would have a go.

We each had a second drink and briefly discussed the allocation of our organisers and other full time staff during the ballot period in the two companies. Leila said she would have a word with Julia Cardon about further press releases and Alan Whitchurch about the organisers. She and Mathew Singh would have a chat about newsletters in both companies when she got back from Liverpool tomorrow evening.

Martin said he would also speak to Singh and Whitchurch that evening as both were coming, as far as he knew, to the shop workers union reception that evening. Leila and I would be attending the General Council dinner and undoubtedly would be able to have further words with Moorhouse, Whetter and Bradwell who as members of the General Council would all be there and who had all done well in their contributions to the debate on our motion.

As I said that, Les Martin asked me ; "how are the possibilities going with Peter Moorhouse?" He was referring to the possibilities of his union merging with us. We all knew it would make sense. We operated in similar areas—mainly private sector, white-collar—and a merger could well mean some economies of scale and better combined research and technological services but as always it came down to personalities. Would the full time officials of one union—kings in their own castles—be happy to become just barons in a larger castle? It was, of course, the same in company mergers: who would emerge out on top and—more realistically—who would lose their jobs in the name of 'economies of scale'?

I told him that things were pretty quiet on that front at the moment but once the Industry3M dispute—and the other actual and possible disputes in the other companies—were out of the way we ought to have a long and hard look at merger possibilities with a number of unions including the Commercial and Technology Union.

Leila said it was partly a question of timing. Les Martin said that he thought much would depend on our financial state if the ballots were in favour of strike action and if and when we started paying the pretty hefty amounts of strike pay. If our position became financially very risky then we ourselves could be a likely merger—or worse a take-over—target to some of the other unions.

We left the bar to back into the hall. Leila said she would catch us up and used her mobile to phone our head office.

The General Council dinner in the evening at the Metropole Hotel was enjoyable. Sometimes they were pretty boring and once or twice the speeches had been abysmal. This time the only speech was by Mark Thurston as Congress President and it was surprisingly good. He wasn't normally the best speaker but this time—fortified by a few drinks and obviously a good researcher in his office and the assistance of the TUC office to draft the speech—he was funny and also made a couple of good serious points.

Helmut Karschott, the big burly general secretary of the German trade union centre, the Deutsche Gewerkshaft Bund, was one of the fraternal delegates at the dinner. I had met him several times at meetings of the European TUC where I was one of the British TUC delegates. He had made a point of coming over to me just before the meal started and brought me and Leila greetings from Jurgen Bruch the head of the DGB's white collar section.

"Jurgen says we may well have a strike in Industry3M by early October." He turned to Leila "and that should be helpful to you, I think. By the way, an excellent speech this afternoon." Leila thanked him and we had a very brief chat about how things were going. Karschott said that a number of the leading German employers had been very interested in the Industry3M situation both in Germany and in Britain. The increasing use of contract staff was growing in Germany and they were keen to see if how things would work out. There was the added point in Germany that there was quite a bit of anti-American feeling among a number of employers as well as unions, much more than in Britain.

After the dinner was over Leila and I decided to walk back to our hotel. I said that it was a good thing that Bob Wilson had not been at the dinner as it might have put a dampener on the dinner—particularly if he had spoken at it. In fact he had gone back to London shortly after his speech on the Monday. Leila said she wondered whether there would be any further approach from him now the die was cast in the ballot timetables in the two companies.

I had been up for a few more drinks after the dinner but Leila said she wanted to get back to our hotel. She would have to catch an early train to London the next morning and then cross to Euston for the Liverpool train so she could get to see Collins of Industry3M at half past eleven and I thought it would be the decent thing to make sure she got back to the hotel safely.

As it turned out it was just as well as I went with her. It must have been about half past ten as we strolled back along the sea front. There were quite a few people about; some going to parties and pubs, others coming out of receptions, some going to restaurants, all seeming fairly merry if, at times, a little loud. It was when we were about half way from the Metropole Hotel to our hotel, also on the front, that it happened.

Leila saw them first: "there's several over excited men" as she pointed out at a group who were walking towards us on the pavement. They were shouting but not at anyone in particular. They also seemed to be swaying a bit and clearly they had had a lot to drink. I looked at the one in the front of the group and then it hit me. It was Tony Hammond and just then he seemed to recognise the two of us.

I remembered that Leila had told me the SPGB were having what they called an open meeting that evening. Presumably the meeting was over and several of them had been in the pub afterwards. Nothing wrong with that I thought to myself, I had done it many times myself. But this was a bit different.

We saw a couple in front of us being pushed almost off the pavement and onto the road by Hammond and what I now saw as four others. The man who had been pushed shouted at the group but that was the signal for them to shout back, and the man and woman quickly moved away. Leila whispered to me that we might have a problem and she was right.

As Hammond and his companions came up to us we stopped walking. They did the same. Hammond was looking flushed and was sweating. "Been living it up with the rest of the General Council?" was his opening statement.

I asked him if he and his mates had been living it up in the pub.

One of the others asked Hammond in a loud voice "are these the two wankers you told us about, Tony?" Another called out "you should have been at our meeting."

Leila then called out that if they had been there they would have probably doubled the number in the audience. I was surprised at her—and so were they. Hammond was clearly very angry and put his face towards mine.

"Your girl friend thinks she's funny, does she?"

Things rapidly got worse. One of the Hammond group, a tall man wearing a dirty T-shirt over what was very much an expanding waistline, went right up to Leila: "give us a kiss, love?" Two of his companions tried to pull him away but this seemed to make him more belligerent and he pushed them away and reached out to grab Leila. I tried to push Hammond away and go over to rescue Leila. There was a bit of pushing and shoving and then I saw the tall man fall backwards onto the pavement and he was groaning. He was shouting what sounded like "you bitch, you tart" but it wasn't particularly clear.

By this time a number of other people were walking towards us and we were creating quite a scene. I pulled Hammond towards me and hissed at him; "why don't you bugger off?" I said. A number of the newly arrived people started to call for calm and one went over to the tall man who was writhing on the pavement. "You all right, mate?" I recognised him as one of the engineering union delegates.

"She kicked me, the bitch," he blurted out. Leila was standing still and looking at him on the ground. His companions then managed to get him to his feet. Hammond swallowed hard and turning round said to them that they ought to move on. They half lifted, half carried the injured man away and the crowd which had been gathering now dispersed. The engineering union delegate asked Leila if she was all right and she smiled and said she was fine.

I went over to Leila and also asked her if she was all right. She gave the same answer, she smiled and repeated she was fine.

"What did you do to that man who tried to grab you."

She looked at me, her face a little flushed: "I kicked him in the balls and he went down."

I looked at her again: "you are redoubtable indeed," I smiled. "Let's get back to the hotel."

When we got there she collected her room key and went up the stairs to her room. I went to the bar and joined several of our delegation who were there. They asked me how the dinner had gone and I told them it had been OK and then recounted the incident with the trots and Hammond. I told them what Leila had said and done and they all laughed.

"She's a good girl," said one of them and this seemed to be the general reaction.

I stayed with them for a few more drinks.

The next morning Leila had got up at six o'clock and showered and dressed. She collected each of the leading newspapers that the hotel had laid out on the reception desk and entered the taxi outside. She had booked it the night before as well as making some telephone calls from her room. She reckoned she would get to Liverpool about eleven fifteen and had arranged to meet Ted Davis and Clive Brisow in the Flying Fox pub about one o'clock. She imagined that her meeting with Collins would be over by then.

Fortunately for her the train to Victoria was punctual and she got to Euston in good time for the Liverpool train. She got a bacon sandwich and a cup of coffee from the buffet at the same time as inwardly regretting that the full breakfast that used to be available on the early morning trains was no longer on offer.

Leila looked through the various newspapers. Oliver Listle of the *Financial Times* had written a large piece about her speech and the Industry3M dispute and had particularly emphasised the ballot timetable and the union's decision on strike pay. He had written that the union was taking a big gamble if the ballot produced a majority in favour of indefinite strike action and had mentioned the likely drain on the union's finances—especially if the Teening & Sykes ballot also produced a majority for the two day strike there. He had concluded his piece with the statement that "if the union succeeds in getting effective negotiations with the two companies on its new and somewhat revolutionary job evaluation scheme then it will be a major boost to the influence of all trade unions and one which will be of concern to the CBI as well as the Government. It could, though, be a major breakthrough in the treatment of contract staff across the economy."

She read the reports in the other papers. All had referred to her speech and the ballot timetables, even the *Sun* had a paragraph saying "union bosses are balloting members in Industry3M for an indefinite strike. The American company has so far firmly resisted union calls for negotiations over a new grading system. The ballot result will be known in two weeks time." The *Daily Mirror's* piece was a bit longer and had a photo of Leila at the top of the article which was headed "Leila gets tough with Americans".

The *Daily Telegraph* had been downbeat and dealt on the union's likely financial state if the ballots were in favour and the strike actions took place. In contrast to the *Financial Times* it had said that the result could be a severe blow to not only the Clerical & General Union but all unions if a settlement with the companies was not resolved and added that there seemed little indication that any settlement could be achieved. The paper had also carried a photograph of David Adnam the chief executive and had him quoted as saying 'this company will not hand over its staffing policy to a trade union'.

The *Times* had carried a photograph of Leila speaking at the rostrum and had given the background to the dispute as well as mentioning the ballot in Teening & Sykes and the possibility of ballots elsewhere. The *Times* had also made the point that Japanese companies might well be worried if there was industrial trouble in Hokkaido, one of the largest Japanese owned companies in Britain and that this worry would undoubtedly be shared by the Government. It had also specifically drawn attention to the remarks of the DTI minister, Bob Wilson, in his speech on the Monday.

Leila thought the most interesting report was by Chuck Pitney in the *Wall Street Journal*. He, she thought, had obviously done his homework again. He had referred to the Swedish and German unions' claims in their Industry3M companies and also the position of Teening & Sykes and the strong competition in the chemical markets it was now facing and how a two day strike could affect that. He had also mentioned the concern by several of the major US stockholders in Industry3M and had hinted at the internal difficulties Industry3M was facing with the sacking of Tom Chance the former UK deputy general manager and the impact that Joe Tiller was having. He had concluded with "Industry3M is a small company in the UK and Europe but has been a growing one with considerable importance in the rapidly expanding area of contract labour and its organisation. Its anti-union position was welcomed by many in the USA but now there are doubts as to whether a successful indefinite strike by the union could have a disproportionate effect on its future. Equally an indefinite strike could well have a disproportionate effect on the union and its finances. The stakes are high for both the company and the union."

Considering how little coverage there usually was in the press for the TUC Congress and individual unions, Leila thought the coverage of the debate on contract labour and the ongoing disputes was very good. Having finished scanning the papers she decided to telephone head office and speak to Muriel.

"I saw you on the BBC news last night" was the first thing Muriel said. Leila said she hadn't seen it.

"There was about three minutes on the Congress and they showed you speaking."

"Well, that's something, I suppose," responded Leila. "Anyway, I phoned to see if there's anything dramatic happening. As you know, I'm on my way at this moment to Liverpool and am going back to Brighton this afternoon."

"I'm glad you phoned. There's two things really. One is a letter from John Dryden at the CBI asking if you would like to meet him for dinner one evening and the other is a letter from Sam Askari with a large staff pay claim."

Leila thought for a moment. The Dryden invitation had to be because of the disputes—perhaps David Adnam of Teening & Sykes had been on to him? She told Muriel to contact Dryden's office and fix a date for the dinner.

"The staff pay claim: what's the amount?"

Muriel paused, "well, it's for eight per cent with an extra three days holiday a year for everyone."

Leila of course knew that the staff pay review date was the first of October and had wondered why the claim had not been submitted earlier. Askari was still relatively new in the position of chairing the staff side in negotiations with the union and perhaps that was it. But, eight per cent? Leila thought that was pretty steep.

"Is there any rationale in the letter?" she asked Muriel but Muriel replied that there wasn't any.

"I want you to circulate the letter to the national executive committee and the trustees and then contact Peter Berenson to see what dates he can manage for a meeting with the bargaining unit. I'll have a word with John, Les Martin and Jane Toff this evening when I get to Brighton and will phone tomorrow". She rang off.

Leila had almost added that she could have done without this at the moment with all else that was going on and with the tremendous financial implications of the possible strikes. But she knew it wouldn't have been fair and there was no point in saying it to Muriel anyway. The union was, in one sense, an organisation like any other. They employed one hundred and fifty staff in the head office and eight regional offices. Just as the union pressed employers to have proper grievance and disciplinary procedures and annual pay reviews so it was fair for the union to have those things within its own administrative procedures. As any observer of the trade union scene would have told her, they had to practise what they preached.

Even now she knew that some, if not many, outside the union scene had somewhat simplistic views that administering a union was an easy task because everyone worked for the same end. In a sense Leila knew they did, but life was not that simple. In many ways running an organisation like a trade union was almost impossible. All the officials knew full well how to argue and pressurise to get their point of view accepted and to use the procedures to try and get what they wanted. It was one of the reasons why the position of chairing the staff side bargaining unit was one of the most unpopular jobs and equally one of the reasons why nobody had opposed Sam Askari when the position had come up for election the previous year. Whether anyone thought he would do a good job was—for some—another matter.

Although Leila accepted that the union had to be whiter than white in its own internal organisation she did think that some—but not all—of the officials, and perhaps more of the staff, thought of the union as an organisation that was permanent and prosperous and paid little regard to the fact that in many ways the union's continued existence was always precarious. True, they had built up financial reserves and owned the freehold of their head office and four of the eight regional offices but all that might well be in jeopardy if the disputes with Industry3M and Teening & Sykes continued and even more so if strikes were to happen in Hokkaido and possibly Transport International and Leisure & Sport.

The train reached Lime Street station just five minutes late. Unfortunately for Leila there was quite a queue for taxis and by the time she got to the concrete and glass structure that was the Industry3M head office it was nearly twenty to twelve. She walked through to the reception desk and said she was due to meet Lionel Collins. The middle aged and rather sad looking receptionist telephoned through to Collins' office and then told Leila that he was tied up but would see her as soon as possible.

"He is expecting me" said Leila brusquely but then bit her tongue. It wasn't the receptionist's fault. The receptionist asked her to take a seat in the reception area and said she would call her as soon as Mr. Collins was available.

Ten minutes later she called over to Leila and said "Mr Collins will see you now. Please go the third floor and his secretary will meet you at the lift."

This is a bloody good start, thought Leila to herself but knew she would have not to let herself be provoked. She entered the lift and got out on the third floor. She was met by a smart looking blonde woman in what appeared to be an expensive suit who announced that she was Collins' secretary and asked Leila to follow her. Leila had never met Collins before and knew little about him except that he had a reputation as being smooth and—as far as the union in the company was concerned—totally unsympathetic.

The secretary stopped at a large glass door—there's a lot of glass in this building, thought Leila—knocked and entered. "Mrs Smith," she said.

It was a large office with a table and some chairs on one side and a settee and a couple of armchairs on the other side. Collins got up from behind a rather large desk and came over to meet her. He was younger than Leila had imagined. Tall, well built, fair haired and, she had to admit to herself, rather good looking. He made no attempt to shake her hand. He gave a small and somewhat supercilious smile,

"Sorry to have kept you but I understand you were late."

Leila smiled sweetly: "eight minutes actually. Train and taxi problems."

Collins motioned for her to sit on the settee. He sat in an armchair. The secretary left them.

"Thank you, Lana" called Collins as she left.

This office is like a TV soap opera set, thought Leila. She waited for Collins to begin. Collins looked at his watch and said nothing. Leila still said nothing. Collins looked at her: "well?"

"Well what?" asked Leila.

"Well, what can I do for you, Mrs Smith? I've got another meeting coming up."

"I'm sure you have," said Leila sweetly.

Collins started to go red. He looked at his watch again.

Leila looked at her watch: "it's five to twelve," she said.

Collins asked: "do you want to talk about the company?"

Leila had had enough by now.: "the company wrote to my general secretary about five hundred possible redundancies. He responded and you then wrote to him and fixed this meeting. Here I an."

Collins heaved an exasperated sigh: "yes, I know that. Do you want to run with the ball first?"

Leila pretended she didn't understand what he said and waited for him to say some more. Eventually he did.

"Yes, as the law requires, we advised you of the redundancies we might have to make—"

Leila broke in—"is it' might' or 'will be making'?"

Collins realised that he was not going to provoke Leila into losing her temper and switched tack.

"We do not want to make anyone redundant but in company management you have to take tough decisions, you know—or I assume you know." He looked again at Leila. She looked at her watch again and said "it's five past twelve."

Collins went red again. Leila guessed that he was trying to behave as he imagined company executives ought to behave and appear worldly wise and also wrestling with the cares of office. In fact It was neither one thing nor the other. Leila had met his sort before and thought he was—unfortunately—one of the newer breed of personnel people, or human resource executives as they preferred these days to be called. Probably he had been to a minor public school and had the arrogance to show for it. But, she realised, he had none of the charm of a major public school as well. He would fit in well with Industry3M she reasoned but there was no time for any further fencing around.

"I'm here to talk about your announcement," she said. "Yes, you are required to notify the recognised trade union about redundancies and I've come here from Brighton this morning to discuss with you the company's proposals on where the redundancies might fall, when and how will those concerned be chosen. You also will be well aware that my union is dead against any compulsory redundancies and if it's going to be voluntary redundancies then I'm here to talk about the level of compensation and the timetable involved."

Collins leant forward: "I can't say when or where exactly the axe will fall. We don't think it's practical to call for volunteers. We know there is slack in the departments and we shall of course pay the statutory redundancy pay."

Leila well realised that the discussion had started badly and it was now going downhill from there. She would have enjoyed goading Collins some more but knew that the jobs of many members were involved and it was an extremely serious matter. She asked how the company had arrived at the figure of five hundred and how they knew there was what he called 'slack' if they didn't know where. She repeated that she sought some idea of timescale and how the redundancies were to be chosen. She looked at him.

"I'm afraid I can't tell you," responded Collins. "We're still kicking the ball around and we're not ready to bell the cat."

Leila had had enough.

"That's a mixed metaphor," she said.

Collins got to his feet, his face getting more red but still tried to give another slightly supercilious smile.

"I don't think this is getting anywhere, Mrs Smith. I was prepared to listen to what you had to say. The handling of redundancies is a matter for the company. We're the ones who have to manage the company. We are required to notify the union and the law lays out the amounts of redundancy pay. If you weren't recognised then of course you wouldn't be here at all." The threat was obvious. He finished "If you've got nothing positive to say then I think we should call it a day."

"Are you worried about the company's financial and trading position?—is that the reason for the redundancies?" asked Leila. She looked at her watch again. "And, by the way, it's thirteen minutes past twelve." She paused but made no effort to get to her feet.

Collins opened his mouth to respond to what Leila had just said but before he could say anything Leila continued: "You heard what I said about compulsory as opposed to voluntary redundancies and our union's position and you've heard what information I have sought—who? when? And how? And if you can't tell me or behave in a courteous manner then I shall notify my members accordingly and also write to ACAS."

Collins, she thought, had put himself in a difficult position. He was still standing and he must have imagined if he sat down again then he would have lost face. He continued to stand and contented himself by saying "I've got an important meeting to go to now, so my secretary will show you to the lift."

Leila got up, picked up her briefcase and went to the door. She saw that Collins had pressed a button on his desk and his secretary then came in. Just as Leila left she turned back to Collins and said: "you've certainly helped us win the forthcoming strike ballot, Mr Collins."

Before Collins could say anything she quickly left the room and went to the lift, leaving the secretary to try and catch up with her. Leila turned round to her, "I'll find my own way out, thank you."

Six minutes later she was in the bar of the Flying Fox. Bristow and Davis were already at the bar.

As Leila walked over to them Davis said: "Leila, from the way you're looking—to say nothing, as they say, of your body language—I think you need a drink."

Leila smiled and said she would like a large gin and tonic: "I did honestly keep my temper, but it was very difficult." She then recounted what had happened. Collins, she explained, had not mentioned the strikes or the forthcoming ballot. He had not mentioned the TUC Congress. He had made the obvious point about union recognition but made no effort at all to give Leila any information about the proposed redundancies. Also, she concluded, he had made no effort to be pleasant.

"You had a useful chat then" smiled Bristow. "We didn't expect anything else." Davis added that he had never met Collins but he had heard that those who had had all been unimpressed.

Bristow said that there couldn't be a greater contrast than the reputations of David Stannard and Lionel Collins.

"Bring back the past" said Leila.

Davis and Bristow then explained how many rumours had been circulating in the office in the last few days. Far from frightening the staff it seemed the redundancy announcement had now caused great anger and made a lot of people more determined to support the union. Much to Leila's relief they were both upbeat and keen to pursue the ballot and discuss the arrangements with Leila.

Davis and Bristow had one more pint of beer each and declined any more as they had to go back to the office. Leila ordered another gin and tonic. Gradually she had calmed down and went over the arrangements for the next few weeks which she had sorted out on the train and had discussed with Carmichael on their way back to the hotel the evening before—and before the incident with Hammond and the others from the SPGB.

As Leila had announced in her Congress speech, the secret ballot for indefinite strike action would commence on Monday 17 September and the closing date was Wednesday 26th. The ballot in Teening & Sykes had the same timetable and in both cases the result of the two ballots would be declared in the afternoon of the Friday of that week, September 28th. Leila explained that John Carmichael would announce the results in a press conference that afternoon. The following day, the Saturday, the union's national committees in Industry3M and Teening & Sykes would meet and decide their recommendations to the union's national executive committee. The national executive committee would then meet the following Saturday the sixth of October and if all went well—a big 'if' emphasised Leila—then the strike action could start on the Monday two weeks after that—the twentieth of October.

In the meantime the disputes committee set up by the union would meet on the next Monday, the seventeenth of September and then again on the Wednesday of the week after the press announcement of the ballot results. That committee would oversee arrangements for the disposition of organisers, the issuing of news letters, approaches to both companies and responses to any moves the companies might make. Leila would undertake to keep the committee posted on developments in other unions and on the actions of the Swedish and German unions. Teening & Sykes did not have any subsidiary companies outside Britain but Leila would ask Mathew Singh to liaise with Van Mergeren of Staff International about contacts with those unions on the continent that dealt with some Teening & Sykes key suppliers.

As well as the three senior honorary officials of the union the disputes committee would also have Ian Macallister and Clive Bristow from Industry 3M and the two senior members of the Teening & Sykes national committee on it. John Carmichael and Leila would be members of it and Mathew Singh, Julia Cardon and Alan Whitchurch would also attend. Leila expected the disputes committee to meet weekly. Although the Teening & Sykes strike would only be for two days, the possibility of the Industry3M strike going on and on meant that it would have to be carefully monitored: the stakes were high and they all knew that the future of the union could well be dependent on how things went.

As Leila rehearsed the timetable and meeting arrangements Davis commented that it all sounded like a military operation. Bristow commented that he would be using up a lot of his holiday entitlement to attend the various weekday meetings as Industry3M would be hardly likely to grant leave of absence for the meetings. Leila said she would apply formally for the leave but all three knew it would just be going through the motions. Most union procedural agreements had clauses relating to leave of absence for members but there was always another clause which referred to the needs of the company in an emergency. Industry3M would certainly accept that this was an emergency for the company and not grant leave.

The three of them provisionally fixed an open meeting in Liverpool for the Monday evening after the ballot results had been announced and the national committee had met and decided their recommendations on the Saturday. She mentioned that the major open meetings for the Teening & Sykes would be done by John Carmichael.

It was nearly two o'clock by now. Leila asked whether there was any more news about Joe Tiller and mentioned the alleged three weeks period for the company to sort out the dispute. Neither had heard specifically of the three weeks notice but said there were all sorts of rumours about what the company might do. The key thing though, Leila stressed, was to get the maximum possible turn out for the ballot and both Davis and Bristow would telephone the leading lay representatives around the company in the next couple of days.

"It's going to be a busy time," said Bristow. "A good job we're all fully relaxed and ready." He looked at Leila. She smiled, "you have got a sense of humour, Clive." She was pleased that both of them seemed so upbeat and determined.

They then left the pub and Leila hailed a taxi to go back to the station.

My pension speech had gone down well and all of the delegation were pleased at the press reports of Leila's speech. Julia Cardon had been in the gallery for the speech and this morning had circulated a sheaf of the press cuttings to each of our delegation. So far then the Congress week had been fine but I wondered how Leila was getting on with Collins at Industry3M.

It was one thing to get caught up in all the meetings, speeches and excitement of the Congress but quite another to deal with some of the myriad of mundane issues that cropped up every working day in the outside world, let alone such a crucial meeting as the one which Leila would undoubtedly have had with Collins. I remembered the first Congress I had attended and how I had got home on the Friday evening after it had finished. I had been married for six months and was bursting to tell Elsie all about it—the people I had talked to, the BBC and press people I had seen—and I had even spoken to one or two—and she had just smiled and said that she was glad that I had enjoyed it. And that had been that.

I knew that several of my colleagues on the General Council always brought their wives to the Congress for the week but Elsie had never pushed me into taking her with me and, to be honest, I was glad. Apart from the conference sessions, some of which I had to admit were pretty boring, it was a long round of receptions and drinks and she didn't drink much and I had to keep reminding myself that what was fascinating to me—the personalities, the manoeuvre ring, the lobbying—was not particularly fascinating to Elsie. Nor, I admitted to myself, for the wives who did attend. I had seen too many of them at receptions trying to look interested but in reality just standing there by their husbands and all too often just holding glasses of warm white wine. And the one or two who did keep an interest in what was going on were, frankly, a bit of a nuisance. After all, what had it got to do with them?

Our delegation had all behaved themselves though one or two had spent a little too much time at the bar of the conference hall rather than actually being present during the debates. I couldn't do too much about that as I had been guilty of the same offence in the past. Les Martin did mention it at one of our morning meetings with the delegation and most did take heed of his point. Fortunately we had seen no more of Tony Hammond. He may have gone back home after the fracas yesterday evening. He could have gone anywhere for all I cared.

After our delegation meeting in the morning, which we held at eight o'clock, I had gone to the regular pre-session General Council meeting. These meetings were held from Monday to Thursday mornings half an hour before the start of the Congress sessions. John Miller would give an update on Congress business, what motions and amendments had been withdrawn, composited or remitted to the General Council without debate. This morning Miller had come over to me at the end of the meeting and just as we were going into the hall. He suggested he and I had a chat after the afternoon session finished. I agreed to meet him in the pub just down from the conference hall.

When I got there I saw several groups of union delegates in different parts of the main bar but the pub was fairly big and there was a quiet corner where I saw Miller already ensconced, nursing a pint of bitter. He got up to buy me a pint and we both then sat down.

"Problems, John?" I asked.

"None but the usual," was the reply. "Actually it's all going reasonably well—except that the Bob Wilson speech didn't go down too well, did it?"

I wondered whether he was a bit worried about our disputes. If he was anxious about the effect of our strike in Industry3M then he would be perhaps even more worried about the repercussions of a strike in Hokkaido, the Japanese owned motor car company. I thought he would certainly have picked up the single reference in Leila's speech.

I was right. Miller told me that he was coming under pressure from various ministers in Government—and not just Bob Wilson he stressed—about the effect of any industrial action on inward investment. He asked me about the timing and likely extent of our action and I told him about the dates we had fixed and how there could well be a strike ballot in Hokkaido.

"So this could all escalate?"

"It could indeed," I replied. I emphasised the momentum gathered not only in Industry3M but also Teening & Sykes and probably in Hokkaido.

"And it's not just a few thousand members," I reminded him. "In Teening & Sykes we're talking about six thousand members and if there is a ballot in Hokkaido then we'll be balloting twelve thousand members."

Miller paused and then finished his pint of bitter. I got up and got two more pints. I could see that he was indeed worried.

Miller asked, "suppose I fixed up for you to see the DPM?"—he meant the Deputy Prime Minister.

"With respect, John, what good would that do? He'd huff and puff but what practically could he do?"

"You know very well that he could lean on the companies—if he wanted to."

I thought it was time for some plain speaking.

"Look, John, of course I'll see the DPM. I'd be daft not to and if he can lean on Industry3M or the others, then that would be fine.

But be under no illusion. We have no option but to pursue the claim in Industry3M—equally in Teening & Sykes. If we back down now then all our credibility is gone and what does that mean? Why should anyone join our union—or any union, come to that—if they are powerless to do anything?"

I warmed to my theme: "yes, I know this dispute could cost us an enormous amount of money and if it goes on and on then it could bankrupt us anyway. And if that happens then the union is finished and what remains of us would be ripe for being swallowed up by one of the big four unions."

I was referring to the four largest TUC affiliated unions who had some three million members between them. Miller nodded.

"I appreciate all that and I wish you luck. But ministers are getting very jumpy. All the talk about flexible labour markets which they're pushing is now being counter-balanced by the strikes and threats of more strikes."

We looked at each other. Then Miller said he would try and fix a meeting between me and the Deputy Prime Minister. He paused again. There was clearly something else on his mind.

"Between you and me," he said, "I've decided to go next summer."

I looked at him in surprise. He could stay on as TUC general secretary until he was sixty five and I didn't think he was much over sixty years old.

"I'm sixty two next month, John, and I've decided to go in the next twelve months and next summer seems the best time. Next Congress can elect my successor."

"And is that likely to be Arkwright?" I asked.

"Possibly not, and that's what I wanted to ask you." He leant forward in his chair and lowered his voice. "I understand that Mark Thurston might stand and I wanted to know how you and your group would feel about that."

'My group' as he called it was a number of mainly moderate sized unions whose general secretaries would meet from time to time and discuss who to support for various TUC nominations to outside bodies, who to vote for on the TUC executive committee and who to support—as far as we could—in elections for some of the special seats on the General Council. We were called by the left wing unions 'the right wing group' and it was true that we were generally, and specifically on certain occasions, opposed to some of the left and extreme left attitudes and personalities of other unions.

Of course all of us were supporters of the Labour Party and most of us were individual members of it even though a number of our unions were not affiliated directly to the Party. The terms 'left wing' and 'right wing' were all relative and had to be seen in that context though in the left wing case there were some who were members of various of the extreme left and trotskyist parties and, I believed, one general secretary who was still a member of the Communist Party. Some dinosaur he must be.

"I didn't think Mark would want the job."

Miller chuckled: "there's no limit to some people's ambitions."

He was referring to the fact that Mark Thurston, as one of the senior General Council members and now the current TUC President, served on a number of bodies such as ACAS, the conciliation service, the European TUC executive committee and the committee of inquiry into pension provision that the Government had recently set up, as well as doing his job as general secretary of the engineering union which was one of the big four.

"Do you think he would beat Arkwright?" Arkwright was deputy general secretary, the number two in the TUC hierarchy and usually—although it was never guaranteed—the positions of general, deputy and assistant general secretaries were filled internally from among the TUC staff, although the actual decisions were taken by the General Council or the smaller executive committee However Len Arkwright was regarded as too friendly with some of the left wing unions and that might count against him.

I told Miller that I would sound out my colleagues in 'the group' and get back to him. "As far as I'm concerned," I continued, "Thurston wouldn't be too bad. I have my doubts on Arkwright."

Miller then asked me: "what about your position? How much longer have you got to do? I know you'll be TUC President in two years time but—after then?"

The office of TUC President was dealt with in the most traditional manner, though again there was always an election at the General Council. It always went to the person with the longest service as a member of the General Council, even to the extent that if there were two members with equal years of service then the choice was made alphabetically. The President was then formally elected at the meeting of the General Council held immediately after the end of the Thursday session of the annual Congress. The system meant that there was never any rivalry for the President position and in many ways a contested election for the position could mean the big unions having too great a say in who it should be. I had long worked out that it would be my turn in two years time from now.

"I shall be fifty nine when my year as TUC President finishes and I retire from my union at sixty so I've got three years to do."

"And Leila Smith will take over—subject to the democratic process of course,?' he added with a smile.

"I haven't actually discussed it with Leila" I said—which was true and neither had she ever spoken to me about it—"but I imagine that she would be the strongest, if not the only, candidate."

I wondered, why was John Miller raising this with me. I could understand the point about his successor and him asking me to sound out people about Mark Thurston, but my successor in my own union? Was it politeness or was there something else to it?

We both decided we didn't want any more drink for the moment. There were several more receptions to go to in the evening and I had arranged to meet the others on my union's delegation at the bar of our hotel at half past six. It was now ten to six. I thought to myself, it's all go, isn't it?

Chapter Ten

Going Global

"Mrs Smith?"

The telephone had woken her up. She looked at the alarm clock: it was just seven o'clock. She was normally awake by now and she then remembered that she had forgotten to set the alarm the previous evening when she went to bed. It wasn't the first time that had happened but she knew she couldn't afford to let that happen too often. However, thank goodness for whoever it was that was phoning her now.

"Yes, Leila Smith."

"Ah, Leila, sorry to ring so early. Hope I didn't wake you."

"Is that Chuck Pitney?" She thought she recognised the voice.

"Got it in one. I didn't wake you, did I?"

"I'm not telling you." Leila smiled. The few times she had met him she had grown increasingly to like him.

"I'll take that as a yes," said Pitney. "Anyway I'm in Dublin at the moment and I wanted to check what time your press conference is this afternoon."

"Three o'clock. And what are you doing in Dublin?"

"We have lots of Irish—American readers you know. Seriously though, I'm doing a bit on the latest saga in the power sharing story. And the attitude of the Irish politicians. I do have to get around for my editor, you know."

"Three o'clock at the same hotel as before—"

"Yes, Leila, I can remember that. You feeling hopeful?"

"Always, Chuck. See you then." She rang off.

It was Friday the twenty-eighth of September: a key date for the union and its future, Leila thought. It had been a hectic two weeks since the end of the annual TUC Congress and the ballot results would be crucial. The disputes committee had held a successful first meeting on the Monday after Congress and allocated resources and people to the different parts of the campaign in the two companies. The union organisers had been round as many of the Industry3M and Teening & Sykes union branches as they could. Leila had been to three of the Industry3M ones—Leeds, Bristol and Glasgow.

Bristol had the lowest proportion of union members but the reaction of the branch committee had been encouraging and they said they had managed to recruit some twenty new members in the last couple of weeks. Leeds, one of the strongest branches had also been encouraging. Leila was particularly pleased that Jean Asah, whom she had thought was becoming a bit too close to Tony Hammond on the national committee, had had a private chat with her and said she had lost all faith in what Hammond was trying to do—"whose side is he actually on?" had been her question to her. Glasgow had been a bit disappointing but Ian Macallister had assured her that the members there were determined and would be voting heavily for the indefinite strike. She had put down the rather dour reception she had had there to traditional Scottish caution rather than any lack of enthusiasm.

She had contacted Tino Malik of ACAS about the abortive meeting with Collins on the redundancies. He came back to her with the news that he had contacted Collins at the company but he had refused to attend any meeting, either with the union separately or jointly with ACAS and the union. Malik reported that Collins had said he had held the meeting with Leila but it was clear to him that she had no real interest in discussing the issue but merely tried to score cheap points off him. "She blew it" was how he put it, said Malik.

Leila knew that was a travesty of what had happened. She had issued a newsletter to members the day after the abortive meeting, and it had been sent throughout the company, stating that the company had refused to tell her about where or why the redundancies would fall and had blatantly said they would pay only the minimum statutory redundancy pay to those involved. The company had not issued any circular. Leila had pressed Malik to try again for a meeting but he had said that while there was no timetable for the company's redundancy proposals there was little he could do.

Carmichael had written again to Norman Jones the chief executive asking for details of the redundancies but had as yet received no reply. He himself had been visiting several of the Teening & Sykes union branches and had spoken at a well attended open meeting in Sunderland where one of the largest plants of the company was.

Her dinner with John Dryden of the CBI had, she reflected as she showered and dressed, been a bit of an anti-climax. It had been pleasant but nothing of significance had emerged. Dryden had chatted about the job evaluation proposals and the situation in other unions that were pursuing them. He had emphasised that naturally the CBI could not get involved directly in any industrial dispute and that was why he had wanted to see Leila before the ballot results were known. Then towards the end of the meal he had casually asked Leila if the meeting with the Deputy Prime Minister had been fixed.

Leila had been surprised. Carmichael had told her about his chat with John Miller on the Wednesday afternoon of the Congress week and the idea of seeing the DPM. Who had told Dryden of this?—she thought it couldn't be Miller himself. And what was the proposed meeting going to achieve unless the Government leant on the companies to negotiate with the unions? And, she knew, they were hardly likely to do that given their oft repeated stance of—like the CBI—not getting involved in individual disputes.

She had also told Dryden that she had heard that Joe Tiller had apparently given an ultimatum to Norman Jones and John Carr that they should "sort out the union" in three weeks but he said he had no knowledge of that; nor did he know of Tiller. Leila had told him the three weeks was soon up and what did he think would happen; but Dryden declined to make any forecast. He had merely repeated that the situation about inward investment was very important and what he called 'old fashioned strikes' would certainly frighten off many potential investors.

She had one cup of coffee for her breakfast and then left to go to the office. She wanted to get there early as there were a number of things she had to do that day before they got the ballot results and then held the press conference.

She got to the office by a quarter to nine and spent the first two hours clearing up the paperwork on her desk and sorting out her diary with Muriel.

Muriel had given her the applications for the position of head of the union's membership department now that Dan Michael had gone. Leila reflected that his departure had been a sad occasion. He had not wanted any sort of party and had even declined a drink with Leila and Carmichael. A quick handshake and he had gone. He had been an efficient official and worked hard for the union but, she thought, he would be remembered by many for the manner of his going rather than all the work he had done for the union. Why was it, she asked herself, that one mistake—and she assumed it was only one mistake in Michael's case—could make all the difference when for the rest of his time his behaviour had been exemplary?

There were sixteen completed application forms, one she noted from Sarah Mackenzie. That must be a joke she thought. She had neither the experience nor the aptitude for the job but, because of the standing requirement that all internal applicants—those from the existing union's full time staff—had to be given an interview then she would have to add her to the short list.

There were some good applicants she decided and put down four for short listing. She asked Muriel to check with Jane Toff who, as the union's vice-president, would chair the interviewing panel, what her short list was and hopefully marry the two lists together. The interviews would take place on the Monday week.

She had prepared some notes for her speech at the open meeting that was arranged for the coming Monday and went over them again. It would be a key meeting. The ballot results would be announced today and the national committee would recommend what to do at its meeting on the Saturday. If all went well, and the open meeting was a success, then the national executive committee would undoubtedly authorise the indefinite strike and the battle would then be well and truly joined.

At eleven o'clock Carmichael looked in her office. She raised her eyebrows to see if he had the ballot results. He shook his head and said: "not yet, Leila. But I've just got a fax from Jones at Industry3M. It's the list of redundancies—four hundred and eighty two, to be precise. Here's a copy." He handed Leila a photocopy of the fax.

"Have a look now, and we'll have a chat at the meeting."

He had arranged for the senior officials of the union to meet in the meeting room at half past eleven.

Leila thanked him and looked at the list. It listed the redundancies by head office/ branch, department and then alphabetically. Carmichael had asked Eliza Astobe in the membership department to do a check on who on the list was a union member and she had put an asterisk by the relevant names.

She looked first at the head office list and saw Ted Davis' name but not that of Clive Bristow. She looked at the Glasgow list. No Ian Macallister but Bruce Cannon, the other Glasgow delegate on the national committee, was listed. She quickly scanned the names. Lilian Fairweather from Brighton—her name was listed as was that of Jean Asah at the Leeds office. She could not see any rhyme or reason for the names and reflected wryly that was probably why Lionel Collins had not answered her questions. Nowhere could she saw Tony Hammond's name so it would appear that the company had not just picked on all the active union members, or, she wondered, was that just being naïve on her part?

She looked at the summary totals on the last page. There were four hundred and eighty two people selected for redundancy and of those some three hundred and ninety were marked as union members.

"Grim, isn't it?" said Carmichael. "See if you can make sense of it and then come along to my office by half past."

"Just a minute, John—what did the covering letter say?"

Carmichael snorted. "It was from Collins, not from Jones. It merely said 'here's the list' and then stated that they would pay those concerned the statutory amounts of redundancy pay. It's about the worst treatment of any redundancy issue that I can remember."

He left Leila's office and went away still clearly fuming.

Leila had a longer look but still couldn't see any pattern to the names. She knew they could go to ACAS and point out that the mere presentation of a list did not really satisfy the legal requirements for proper detail to be given to the recognised trade union, but, realistically there wasn't much they could do about it. They could see if any of the individuals would be prepared to take out an unfair dismissal claim to an employment tribunal and, in some circumstances, that might prove to be a useful weapon to beat the company with—but that could take several weeks.

Carmichael was right. It was grim, but Leila thought, brutally, that the way this was being handled by the company could stir up a big show of protest and support for the union. But then, she wondered, suppose the union could not get the company to start negotiations proper: support for the union could go down almost as quickly as it might go up.

❦

The disputes committee had been a success so far and I was once again grateful that in Les Martin and Jane Toff we had two able and helpful people as the two most senior lay officials in the union. I knew we would soon expand the composition of the committee as the situation in Hokkaido developed—and if Transport International and

Leisure & Sport were to be involved then Adam Turnbull and Hazel Bellini would have to be coopted as well as two lay officials from each of the companies. It could make the committee a little unwieldy but there was no way round that. The lay members had to be represented and the full time officials had to be present. They would just have to make it all work.

As well as the regular disputes committee meetings I also intended to have regular meetings with the officials so we were all aware of what was going on.

The officials and I were all sitting down in the meeting room by half past eleven. Leila was the last to join us and I could see she was almost as angry as I was after she had studied the list of Industry3M redundancies. I opened the meeting by saying that I expected the ballot results to come through by fax by twelve o'clock and reminded the others that we had the press conference fixed for three o'clock. I told them of the Industry3M redundancies and asked Leila to update on the situation.

She said she would be writing to ACAS about the redundancies but realistically she did not expect to get any result from that. She referred to her meetings with the union branches in the company, the open meeting planned for the Monday evening in Liverpool and the pointers for a majority vote for indefinite strike action. Mathew Singh reported on the Teening & Sykes position and how he anticipated a reasonable majority in the ballot for the proposed two day strike.

I asked the others to report on their own companies. Brian Hall said it was now likely that the union's national committee would ask for a strike ballot in Hokkaido as the management there had—surprisingly—sent him a letter saying simply that they were not prepared to discuss the job evaluation scheme now or in the future. I thought they must have had a rush of blood to the head to say anything like that but apparently they had. He—and Turnbull for Transport International and Bellini for Leisure & Sport—asked for the chances of an NEC meeting later in October where they could be asked to authorise industrial action ballots. The next scheduled national executive meeting was in early November—but we had the special meeting tomorrow to consider the ballot results in Industry3M and Teening & Sykes. I said that undoubtedly we would have to have another national executive meeting later in October.

I knew anyone unfamiliar with the workings of a trade union would be amazed at the number of different meetings at different levels that were held and that was partly why a union's procedures could be held up by some as excessively bureaucratic. It was, though, essential that the twin imperatives of taking proper decisions and involving all the members concerned were both met. And I knew—as did my colleagues in other unions—that it would be relatively easy for an unhappy or recalcitrant member to complain to the agency set up by the previous Government which could look into the internal affairs of a union if there was a complaint that it had not behaved constitutionally or legally. And that would set in motion all sorts of bureaucratic problems.

By now it was twelve o'clock and almost on the dot Sheila came into the room with a fax from the Electoral Reform Society, the body which had actually conducted the two secret industrial action ballots. I quickly glanced at the figures and inwardly uttered a big sigh of relief. I looked round and the others were all looking expectantly at me. I asked Sheila to get enough copies of the fax to hand round to the others and then reported the figures.

"Good news, colleagues," I said rather formally. "The figures are positive." One or two of the officials gave a small cheer.

I went on: "the Industry3M figures are that we have two thousand three hundred members, a little down from three months ago, out of five thousand staff in the company—and that includes the nearly five hundred redundancies. One thousand seven hundred members voted—that's nearly three quarters of the membership—and of those, twelve hundred voted for indefinite strike action. That's the same figure as voted for the original one day strike in July and is over fifty per cent of our membership. Pretty good I think we would all agree."

I could see Leila smiling.

"In Teening & Sykes we have six thousand members which I believe is about two thirds of the eligible staff—" I looked at Mathew Singh as I said this and he nodded—"and some five thousand voted in the ballot for a two day strike. Of those who voted there were three thousand two hundred and fifty in favour of the action, again over fifty per cent of our membership and, again, pretty good I think you would agree."

They all nodded and it was clear that there was relief all round.

I asked Leila to expand on the Industry3M position. She outlined the position in Sweden and in Germany. The SAF in Sweden had declared a formal dispute with the Swedish company of Industry3M and talks were taking place with the TCO, the white collar central trade union organisation, which would then raise the issue with Government ministers. Lars Tolmark, the general secretary, had told her that if there was no progress by the end of October then the union would call a ballot of its members in the company and recommend an all out and indefinite strike. The white collar section of the German DGB had made no progress with the German arm of Industry3M but, interestingly another German company had responded positively to the union's claim for the introduction of the job evaluation system. Jurgen Bruch had telephoned the previous day and had been quite excited over the news when he relayed it to Leila.

The company concerned was a small life assurance company and Bruch had emphasised that if they made progress with it then there was a large number of financial institutions where similar claims would be lodged.

"It's the first breakthrough" said Leila and she then briefly outlined the situation in other British unions. Dick Whetter of the main civil service union had told her that the ballot papers for a one day strike in the Department of Trade and Industry were going out the following week and he had stressed that good ballot results in Industry3M and Teening & Sykes would, he reckoned, have a very positive effect on the DTI union members. Peter Moorhouse's Commercial &

Technology Union had claims for the job evaluation system lodged with three different companies but nothing definite had yet emerged from discussions with them.

The position in local government could be very helpful, she said. Jim Bradwell had told her that the claim had been lodged for the system and had been discussed at two meetings with the local authority employers body. It was too early to say whether they would make progress or whether there would be a breakdown and then possibly an industrial action ballot. However from what Bradwell had discovered, it appeared that a number of Labour controlled local authorities were in support of the job evaluation scheme and were pressing their representatives on the employers negotiating body to support positive negotiations on it.

I could see that the officials were being encouraged by the news. Of course they all realised the tremendous financial implications for the union if the strikes in Industry3M and Teening & Sykes actually went ahead and strike pay was then paid. But I sensed that they thought that progress was being made—and I didn't think it was just wishful thinking.

I asked Mathew Singh to update the others on Teening & Sykes. He said that the company did not have any subsidiary companies or branches in other countries but they were reliant on imports from a number of countries of different raw materials for their chemicals production over here. He had been in touch with Hans van Mergeren of Staff International. Van Mergeren had circulated all the affiliated unions with a statement that Singh had prepared for him and asked those unions which negotiated with companies that did supply Teening & Sykes with their raw materials to write to the head offices of those companies supporting our claim and stance.

Singh stressed that he was not expecting any of the foreign unions—and he didn't know how many of the supplying companies were unionised—to take any sympathetic industrial action. While secondary sympathetic strike action was banned by law in Britain it would be daft to expect some unions abroad to take it on our behalf.

But letters to the companies stressing their support for us could raise queries with some of the managements and there could be worries about the continuity of their exports to the UK. In response to a query from me he stated that, as far as he knew, the countries in which the companies were situated included Tanzania, Venezuala, Guyana and Spain.

Singh concluded with "from what Leila and I have just reported it's clear that we're going global." I thought this was a neat way of putting it and resolved to use the phrase this afternoon at the press conference.

A number of queries were raised. Alan Whitchurch said he would be speaking individually to the various officials about the deployment of the organisers in the next few weeks. Julia Cardon emphasised that while officials could deal with any press questions in the future, the officials must keep her informed.

It was now half past one o'clock. I said that Leila would be doing a report on all that had been said at the meeting and distributing it to all officials and organisers and also the national executive committee. Officials could send it to their own appropriate national committee if they wished. Leila looked at me as I said that and I remembered that I had forgotten to mention this to her beforehand. I could see, though, that she was smiling and once again I was grateful she was the deputy general secretary of my union.

We got to the hotel for the press conference at half past two and just had a quick chance to get a drink and a sandwich at the bar. Julia Cardon had brought copies of the formal letter from the Electoral Reform Society giving the ballot figures. Before I had left the office I had asked Sheila to telephone the two chairmen of our Industry3M and Teening & Sykes national committees with the news so at least they would know before they read the result in the newspapers. Detailed newsletters to all the offices of both companies would follow on the Monday.

I was pleased at the turnout for the press conference: some twenty journalists had turned up together with a BBC News television crew. I read out the results, said the national committees for the two companies would meet tomorrow and make their recommendations to the national executive committee the following Saturday. If action was authorised then the executive would fix the dates and Julia Cardon would issue a press statement with the details. I emphasised that we were prepared to risk the future of the union in the disputes and were determined to get both companies to negotiate in good faith.

Several of the press asked why we were taking such a big risk. Leila looked at me and I indicated that she should answer.

"The fundamental point about trades unionism is to be able to work effectively to protect and improve the working lives of our members. It's basic and if we can't do this then there's no real reason for our existence. We're not just for legal advice, important though that is. We're not just for discounts and cheap goods and services—we're not a glorified sort of bucket shop."

The man from the *Daily Telegraph* interrupted her: "but suppose the two companies won't negotiate? Then you're risking the future of the union."

"Of course it's a huge risk," replied Leila. "But it's worth it. We are dealing with a big British chemicals company that's at the cutting edge of modern technology and an American owned company that's dealing with the new phenomenon of contract labour. If we don't win then the implications for all unions in the twentieth first century are grim."

I could see Chuck Pitney from the *Wall Street Journal* smiling. Then the *Daily Mail* pressman asked again about our finances and how long could we continue to pay strike pay. I reiterated what Leila had said before—that we would pay strike pay until we achieved what we wanted.

Mathew Singh then outlined how a two day strike could affect the position in Teening & Sykes. After that we were winding down and the questions had stopped when Oliver Listle from the *Financial Times* raised his hand. I nodded to him.

"In this dispute what would you hope to achieve by meeting the Deputy Prime Minister?"

I was a bit taken aback but tried not to show it. Leila looked at me. I could guess what she was thinking. She had told me about her dinner with John Dryden of the CBI and his similar question. It couldn't be that John Miller had been spreading the idea. It couldn't be staff from the DPM's office because—as far as I knew—no date had been arranged for such a meeting. Who on earth told Listle about the proposed meeting?

I was slightly irritated at Listle's question and wished he had raised it with me privately. Now all the press would know about the possibility—not that it would in fact achieve anything if it took place. But I well knew that although Oliver Listle was a nice chap and relatively straightforward in his dealings with us, he was basically a journalist whose first responsibility was to provide his newspaper with stories. He had obviously thought that by raising the point now at the press conference he might get an interesting reaction from me.

I thought the best thing to do would be to play it with a straight bat.

"There has been a suggestion that the Deputy Prime Minister might intervene. You will know from other unions how claims for the same basic job evaluation scheme have been lodged in both the public and private sectors—including in the Department of Trade and Industry. You will have heard Bob Wilson of the DTI refer—somewhat obliquely in his Congress speech—to our dispute. But we will of course go to any meeting with the DPM if asked; but we haven't been asked yet. And even if we did go I am not sure what such a meeting might achieve."

Then I remembered the quote I had meant to use: "as Leila has said, there are a number of other unions pursuing claims like ours. And it's not confined to this country. Unions organising Industry3M on the continent are also going ahead with similar claims and possible action and, as Mathew Singh can tell you, our international—Staff

International, our international trade secretariat—is helping us contact a number of unions in South America and Africa about supplies of raw materials to Teening & Sykes. You could say that the whole issue is going global. So it might be that the DPM wants to be updated on the situation from our point of view."

This started a couple of the other journalists asking about a meeting with the DPM but I merely repeated the essence of what I had already said.

As the press conference ended the BBC man came over and asked if he could do a short interview with me. I suggested he do the interview with Leila and he thought that a good idea. After all, Leila was a lot more photogenic than I was and it would be a change for a smart and articulate woman to be the voice of the union rather than yet another white, middle aged and slightly overweight man like me.

Mathew Singh, Julia Cardon and I watched while the other journalists left and the BBC television crew set up the chairs and lights for the interview. Just before he left Chuck Pitney came over to me and said he couldn't help smiling earlier—"I haven't heard so many soundbites in one paragraph before as Leila uttered. And you're 'going global' caps it all." I smiled at him and said that if he waited in the hotel bar we would join him for a drink after Leila's interview was over.

As I expected Leila came over well in the interview. It lasted about five minutes and though the BBC would probably only use one or two minutes of it that would be fine. She, as well, managed to get the 'going global' quote in what she said.

We all then went to the bar and joined Chuck Pitney there. He hadn't met Mathew Singh before and I let the two of them have a chat while I talked to Leila and Julia Cardon. We all thought the conference had gone well. Leila said to me that the one thing she hadn't said—and she had been debating whether she ought to say it earlier—was about the so-called three weeks ultimatum that had apparently been given to the Industry3M UK management.

Julia Cardon pointed to Pitney and Singh and suggested that I should mention it to Chuck. If it was only him that knew then he might give it a fair wind in his own piece for the *Wall Street Journal*. Leila said she thought that an excellent idea and when he had finished asking Mathew Singh about the Teening & Sykes position I pulled him to one side and told him. I couldn't tell from his expression whether he knew about it already but he scribbled a few words in his notebook and remarked that several of his paper's readers might find it very interesting.

Mathew Singh, being a strict Muslim, didn't drink any alcohol himself but insisted on buying another round of drinks for us with an orange juice for himself. We chatted a bit more and then I thought it was time to go. We all finished our drinks. Pitney said he would be in touch and I said I was sure he would be. I then wished Leila and Singh the best of luck at their national committee meetings the following day and left.

✦━━━⟨⟡⟩━━━✦

"Mrs Smith?"

It was the morning of the eighth of October. Leila was in her office and sorting out a mass of correspondence, reports and newsletters. Julia Cardon had, as usual, supplied her—and all the other officials—with a weekly bundle of press cuttings.

"Yes."

"It's Tino Malik here. A bit of good news perhaps."

"Good news is always welcome, though in short supply."

Leila had written to Malik of ACAS about the redundancy notices and again requested a meeting with the company at the ACAS offices. Carmichael had also written again to Norman Jones of Industry3M but had again received no direct response.

"I've just had a phone call from someone called Joe Tiller on behalf of Industry3M. I'm not quite sure what position he has in the company. From his accent he's American."

"Yes, he is. Allegedly sent over from head office in Atlanta to sort out the company here and a hard man, I am led to believe. What did he say?"

"Well," said Malik, "this good be the good news. He says he is prepared to meet your union here at ACAS and talk about the redundancies. He's emphasised though that he's not prepared to discuss anything else—your claims on pay or the job evaluation proposals. I contacted the chief executive last week—Norman Jones, isn't it?—and was put through to someone called Collins. He sounded particularly unhelpful but he must have passed on my message and now I've had Tiller saying they will meet you."

Leila asked when Malik could fix up a meeting. He said that Tiller had suggested the Thursday of that week. Leila immediately said they would make that date. She wasn't sure offhand whether she had any other commitment on that day but the chance of a joint meeting was too good to miss.

Malik then said he had read the press reports following the union's national executive meeting on the previous Saturday and the announcement that the strikes would start on the twenty second of October. The Teening & Sykes strike would be on the Monday and Tuesday of that week and the Industry3M indefinite strike would also start that Monday.

"Oh, one more thing," said Malik. "You know how status conscious the Americans are. He insisted that your general secretary attend the meeting."

"I don't think that's a problem, but I'll check his availability and get back to you. I will attend as well and bring with me the chairman of our national committee and the chairman of our Liverpool branch, which is the head office branch. That's assuming that they can get leave of absence to attend but I would hope that the company would give them leave of absence to attend."

Malik said "I'll have to leave that to you but I'll assume now the meeting on Thursday is on. I'll get back to this man Tiller and confirm. Eleven o'clock all right?"

Leila signified assent and put the phone down. It was good news, at least she hoped so. Did Tiller's involvement mean that the three week ultimatum—though it was more than three weeks now since she had been told of it—was in operation? And what had happened to John Carr? She decided to phone Ian Macallister and Clive Bristow to check with them about the meeting and see if they had heard anything else.

It had been another busy week. On the previous Monday evening she had spoken at the Liverpool open meeting and was pleased that the attendance seemed even bigger than at the one held in July when the dispute had been starting. This time there had been no problem with Hammond and the other trots and, she reflected wryly, no repeat of the egg throwing incident.

She had told the meeting that the national committee had recommended that the national executive should authorise the indefinite strike and the mood seemed determined. Several of the questions and statements from the floor of the meeting had been about the redundancies and this had clearly strengthened members' resolve. The meeting had then passed its own resolution asking the national executive to authorise the action.

Afterwards Leila had gone for a drink with a large number of the members in the Flying Fox and had had a private chat with Larry Brent. He had told Leila that as far as he knew the trots were keeping a low profile. Leila had said that there wasn't much they could protest about as it was likely that the union would call the indefinite strike. Brent had said that he had heard that they were biding their time so they could have an attack on the union if—or 'when' he had heard them say—the strike collapsed. Then they would have a good go at the conduct of the dispute. Leila had told him that she didn't expect them to do anything else—and for the umpteenth time had asked herself whose side the trots were on. Brent had said that he would not be surprised if some of the SPGB actually wanted the strike to fail—that would show the union in a bad light and they would try and use that to boost the trots and their organisation.

She had then had a chat with Joe Turner of the *Liverpool Daily Post* and briefed him on the position with the Swedish and German unions and how things were progressing with the other British unions. He had been making his own contacts with the unions and said that he would do a report for the next day's paper with a fair amount of background. Although the paper had never been noted for its sympathy towards trade unions he had assured Leila that the paper was anxious to cover the dispute as widely as possible. With all the history of labour relations in Liverpool over the years this dispute, he had emphasised, was of importance to the city.

The next day when back in London Leila had gone to see Tim Burke in hospital. She had meant to go and see him earlier but, as always, time had been at a premium. She knew he must be depressed that as the national official for Industry3M he had been away during the whole dispute. He had gone into hospital in May and had had several weeks of chemotherapy for his cancer. Then in July he had undergone six weeks of radiotherapy.

When she saw him in hospital now she thought he looked dreadful. He been a well built man in his mid-forties but now had lost all his hair as a result of the chemotherapy and also seemed to have lost a lot of weight. Leila felt a stab of conscience that while she had been heavily involved in the dispute she had not gone to see him earlier. She told him about events since July and the news seemed to brighten him up a bit but overall he seemed but a shadow of his former self.

He had been reading the reports and press cuttings that Leila had made sure her secretary had sent him but was clearly pleased to hear from Leila in person. The one thing he told Leila that he hadn't told her before was that, when he first had been given responsibility for negotiations in Industry3M, he had met Norman Jones the chief executive. His view was that Jones had been favourably disposed to the union but he reckoned he was a weak man and since then had been clearly influenced by the Americans from head office. He was not surprised at what Leila told him had happened subsequently to Tom Chance nor David Stannard.

After Leila had been with him for half an hour he was clearly getting very tired and Leila leant over to kiss him on the cheek.

"Good luck" he had whispered. It was all very sad, thought Leila. She said she would come and see him again as soon as she could and suggested that success in the dispute would be a big boost to him—"we're going to win both the battles, yours and ours." He had smiled weakly as she then left.

The rest of the week had been taken up with a number of meetings with companies that Tim Burke had also dealt with before his illness, with discussions with Askari and the other representatives of the officials and staff bargaining unit on their pay claim and the appointment of Dan Michael's successor as head of the membership department.

As she had expected, Sarah Mackenzie had been hopeless at interview and if she hadn't been on the staff already there was no way in which she would have been even short listed. After the interviews they had appointed a woman from the Commercial & Technology Union to the position. She had been the number two in that union's membership department. And Leila thought that that wouldn't hurt if there were ever realistic merger talks between her union and the CTU.

It was now the start of another week and the news from Tino Malik had been encouraging. Just before she left her office to go and tell John Carmichael about it her phone rang again. It was Paul Mugai, the general secretary of the Malaysian Commercial Workers Union.

"Good day Mrs Smith." Leila knew he was always pedantically polite.

"Good day to you, Paul. How are you?"

Mugai replied that he was fine and that he wished to speak to her on a matter of great importance.

"I think I told you a few weeks ago that my union was involved in some approaches by the American company called Industry3M."

"Yes, you certainly did."

Mugai then went on to tell her that as his union was one of the largest in Malaysia, and the biggest one that organised white collar staff, the Malaysian ministry of labour had suggested to Industry3M that the company should have talks with the union. Mugai explained that, as the Malaysian economy was one of the success stories in south-east Asia, the Malaysian government had tried to keep some order in its labour practices and unions by taking an active part in assisting both companies and unions to reach an understanding of proper industrial relations procedures.

It was not out of any particular feeling of goodwill towards either the managements or the unions but to ensure industrial peace at a time the government was encouraging foreign investment and also was itself engaged in major technological infrastructure investment. Mugai, as one of the most important union figures in the country, was often consulted by various of the government ministries. He was a large—fat some would have called him—chain smoking Christian Malay. As a practising Christian Mugai was an exception in his country but he was shrewd enough to make sure he got on well with his fellow Malays who were Muslims, the few Hindu practising Indians and especially the Chinese. He had met Leila at several of the international conferences hosted by Staff International and he seemed to get on well with her.

Leila's mind raced as he was talking. This could be a major advantage in her union's dispute with Industry3M and all sorts of possibilities occurred to her.

As Mugai paused for breath Leila said "this is very interesting and I would like a longer chat with you. Can I phone you back in about an hour's time. Oh, by the way, what is the time over there?"

Mugai said it was nearly four o'clock in the afternoon and if Leila were to phone him by five o'clock their time, then that would be fine.

She went to Carmichael's office. He was putting the phone down as she entered.

He looked at her. "That was the DPM's office. They suggested this Thursday afternoon for us to go along to his office."

"As it happens," explained Leila, "that could fit in nicely." She told him about the conversation with Malik of ACAS and the date of the Thursday morning for the joint meeting with the company. Carmichael confirmed that he could make the meeting.

"There's one thing that bothers me, Leila, apart from a host of other things."

"Well?" said Leila as she sat down in the chair by the side of his desk. "Let me guess. What are the trots up to?"

Carmichael's eyes widened: "that's exactly it. You must be psychic."

"No," said Leila. "I have wondered about that. We really haven't heard much—if anything—from them since the TUC Congress and, as you know, Hammond was almost well behaved at both the national committee and the national executive meetings. Well, he didn't say much at either meeting—that's what I mean."

Carmichael nodded: "they must be planning something."

Leila told him about her conversation with Larry Brent after the Liverpool open meeting and Carmichael said that was probably the explanation.

"It would be fanciful, I suppose, to think they might actually come out in support of what we are doing. By the way, how does this Larry Brent know so much?"

Leila smiled: "let's just say he has some civil service connections. He did come from there before he joined the company."

"I suppose I better not ask anymore," commented Carmichael. "But I'll be waiting for them to do something. Anyway, it's good news about the ACAS meeting and I'll be interested to meet this Tiller chap."

Leila then told him about Mugai's phone call. Carmichael had also met him several times and, like Leila, had a high opinion of his capabilities. He listened as Leila explained what Mugai had said and then broke in: "why don't you go out there for a couple of days and talk to him and his colleagues?"

Leila said, "I was hoping you would say that. If I could talk to their executive committee and explain our job evaluation scheme and—" she was getting excited as her mind raced ahead—"if they were to get it established in the new company that Industry3M want to set up in Malaysia then—."

"We could be on a very good wicket" cut in Carmichael. "Yes I think you should go out there—next week if possible—before the strike starts on the twenty second, then it could be very helpful."

Leila looked at her diary. "Perhaps I could go out on next Tuesday and come back on Friday. I think everything's in order for the start of the strikes on the Monday and though I don't really want to be away that week, this could be important."

Carmichael agreed with her and she left to phone Mugai back and to sort out the flight arrangements with Muriel.

On the Thursday morning Julia Cardon, Leila and myself met Ian Macallister at the ACAS offices. The meeting had been postponed from eleven to half past. Macallister had flown down from Glasgow that morning and Bristow had got the early train from Liverpool. We waited for Tino Malik to come and fetch us from the waiting room. We didn't see anything of anyone from Industry3M.

At half past eleven Malik came from his office and took us to the meeting room. There were two men sitting there, neither of whom I recognised but assumed that they were Joe Tiller, the American and Lionel Collins whom Leila had previously met. When we entered the room they both got up and, somewhat to my surprise, moved towards us to shake hands. I saw Collins smile as he shook Leila's hand and thought I heard him say "nice to see you again". I did see Leila return a very frosty smile.

Malik took the chair at the head of the table and we and the two
Industry3M people sat facing each other.

"Perhaps we all better introduce ourselves," opened Malik. "I'm
Tino Malik and am the chief regional conciliation officer of ACAS."
The thickset and fit looking man with a crew cut said "I'm Joe Tiller
from Atlanta" and Lionel Collins said his name and that he was the
acting head of personnel.

As we introduced ourselves Leila leant over and whispered to
me that the Industry3M men were remarkably pleasant and said I
had better watch out. I didn't really need her to say that to me but I
appreciated her point.

Looking back I suppose we spent an hour with them and indeed
Tiller seemed seemed to know what he was talking about. He took
the lead for the company and produced a lot of figures of staffing in
the different branches and departments, average lengths of service
and the annual turnovers. We asked a number of questions and Leila
asked why it was that while we had just over fifty percent membership
nevertheless the number of union members who were being made
redundant was over eighty per cent of the total. I watched Tiller
closely as she asked that. I could see Collins was keeping his face
expressionless.

"There's no connection between union membership and those
earmarked for redundancy and I think we—" I noted he kept saying
'we' when talking about the company—"had no idea who was or was
not a union member."

I opened my mouth to say something about the list of cash payers
which had been provided to the company and all the other names
listed because of the check-off system of collecting subscriptions but
thought better of it.

Tiller smiled in a friendly way as he answered Leila's point. Then
he went on: "and, for the record, we have as you know said that we do
not want to operate the procedural agreement with you as we don't in
fact believe that you have a majority of our staff in membership—at
least that's what the check off figures indicate. So we are not really

obliged to tell you all this detail but for the sake of good relations we thought we ought to. And I emphasise that while we obviously have the union check off figures for subscriptions, because we actually operate the check off system, we did not marry up those figures with the redundancies list."

He was certainly doing his best to appear reasonable. But as I said to the others afterwards, appearances were very deceptive. He did say that they would pay the statutory redundancy pay and that was all, that it was not practical to have a voluntary redundancy scheme and he had made the point about the procedural agreement though he did not actually say that the company was withdrawing recognition from us. From his point of view it was a good performance.

Malik had sat back during the meeting. As Tiller was quite prepared to discuss the redundancies in detail and tempers seemed calm, there was nothing really he could say. Collins said nothing at all though I saw that he did take fairly copious notes.

As we were making our last statements Leila suddenly looked at Tiller and said that we had been expecting John Carr to be present—where was he?

"He's the European Group HR director and at the moment he's in his office." Tiller was brief and gave nothing away as he spoke. I saw Leila looking at Collins as Tiller spoke. He seemed to go a little red in the face but still said nothing.

Malik asked us whether anyone wanted to say anything else. I nudged Leila to make a closing statement.

"Just to reiterate what the general secretary has said, Mr Malik" she said. "We do not accept the principle of enforced redundancy but we are prepared to discuss voluntary redundancy terms. We regret the company is not prepared to discuss this nor is it prepared to offer any more than the statutory terms."

I could see Tiller and Collins trying not to look bored as Leila said this. Then they both became alert as Leila went on.

"For the record Mr Malik," again she addressed her remarks through the ACAS official, "we are a little confused at the changes in the company in dealing with us. Last July it was Mr Jones, the chief executive, Mr Chance the number two and Mr Stannard the personnel director. Oh, and John Carr was there from Group. Now Mr Chance has apparently gone. Mr Stannard has gone and it would also appear that Mr Carr has, at least for the moment, gone as well. Has the company got problems?"

Leila smiled as she said the last bit and, for the first time, I could see that Tiller was annoyed but he said nothing. Malik looked at him and Collins but they both just sat there, mute but not, I thought, deaf.

"Well," said Malik, "I don't think there's any more we can do, is there?"

We gathered up our papers and stood up to leave. Surprisingly, Tiller came round and shook hands with each of us, smiling as he did so. I admitted to myself that he was a bit of a class act. He had conceded absolutely nothing but had been polite throughout. I remembered what Leila had told me about her meeting with Collins and assumed Tiller was trying to teach Collins how to conduct himself. It seemed to be working because Collins looked uncomfortable and tried a weak smile; but he made no attempt to shake hands again.

When we got outside the ACAS offices I suggested we went for a drink and Leila said that was a surprise. When we were in the pub I asked Macallister and Bristow for their impressions of the meeting.

"He's a smooth bastard, isn't he?" said Macallister and Bistow echoed the point. I told them that was my impression too.

"But," Macallister continued, "what happens now?"

I told him and Bristow about Leila's phone call from the Malaysian union and they both brightened considerably.

"That could be very helpful" said Bristow. I told him he was right and how Leila would go and see Mugai. Leila assured both of them that she did not want to leave the members in the cold while she went off to the sunshine in Malaysia—"at least, that's how some might view it"—she said.

"Hammond for at least one" responded Macallister. "But you would be daft not to go." Bristow again agreed.

I was relieved. Even some of our best members had a blind spot when it came to meetings with our international trade secretariat, Staff International, with the old fashioned British attitude that as soon as someone went abroad they were somehow 'living it up'. But both Macallister and Bristow were shrewd enough to see the overall picture. Macallister asked when Leila was likely to go and when she said the following Tuesday he saw the point. If Leila could bring back some positive news that could be the breakthrough we were seeking. Bristow mentioned the open meeting planned for the Monday evening in Liverpool on the first day of the strike and Leila could tell them about it—if it was good news.

Macallister assured Leila that he would speak to the leading members of the national committee and ensure that there would be no criticism of her going off in the critical few days before the strike though, he added, he couldn't be responsible what the trots might say. Bristow said he was sure the majority of the branch committee would welcome Leila going to Malaysia.

Julia Cardon commented that it was still a mystery to her why the trots were quick to condemn any trips overseas by union officials when they themselves—in her words—were always banging on about international solidarity. Workers of the world unite, she said and then "did you know it wasn't Karl Marx who coined that phrase, but Karl Schapper some time before?" I was surprised—I had not believed that that was something Julia would know.

After a couple of drinks and a sandwich we got a taxi outside the pub and went to the office of the Deputy Prime Minister at the far end of Whitehall. Bristow wished us all the best and Leila said she would phone him that evening at home.

I was pleased at how Macallister and Bristow had reacted to the suggestion of Leila going to Malaysia and also at how the meeting at ACAS had gone. I don't think anyone of us had expected anything positive to emerge from the meeting but the fact that it had taken place at all, and that Tiller himself had been there, was, to my mind, encouraging. And it could mean that the three week ultimatum was true. It might of course mean that things could get worse—but, equally, they might possibly get better. At least things wouldn't stay the same and in any industrial dispute the worst thing that could happen was no movement at all. It was up to us to make sure it was an improvement for the better.

"What the hell is this bloody job evaluation thing all about?"

The Deputy Prime Minister, a thick set man with a florid face and a broad Lancashire accent, was clearly annoyed and he had said that as soon as Carmichael, Leila, Cardon and Macallister had entered his office. A tall grey haired man then came over and introduced himself.

"Hello. I'm Lawrence Lascelles, the head of the DPM's office." He spoke to Carmichael. "I know this is Leila Smith", smiling at her., "Perhaps you could introduce me to your two colleagues."

Carmichael explained who Ian Macallister and Julia Cardon were and they shook hands. The DPM then said "excuse my language, but I've just had a most frustrating meeting with a group from the Scottish Parliament. I'm not sure what they wanted, but they certainly didn't get any joy from me." He sounded a bit triumphant but then shook hands with them and motioned to the chairs round the oval table at the side of his office.

Leila thought, this is a good start. She and the others sat down. Apart from Lascelles and the DPM there was a young civil servant woman who was obviously the note taker.

"I've got a deputation from the local authorities coming next. It's going to be one of those days."

Leila could see Lascelles smile thinly.

"Now then," said the DPM, "what have we got here?"

There was a pause, then Carmichael spoke.

"I understand, Deputy Prime Minister—" Before he could carry on the DPM said abruptly "call me Jack. We're all union members here, aren't we?" He turned to Lascelles: "you're a member of the top civil servants union, aren't you Lawrence?"

Lascelles nodded and his smile became thinner.

Carmichael continued: "I understand that you called us here to discuss our dispute with Industry3M and the wider actions that are also being pursued by unions in connection with the job evaluation proposals of ours. We're happy to discuss this with you, Deputy Pri—" he stopped and then continued—"Jack. It's a serious position."

The DPM heaved a sigh: "I know it's a bloody serious position. I've got the Trade and Industry Secretary telling me his staff is likely to go on strike. I've had the CBI onto me asking me what I'm going to do about it. I've even had the American Ambassador asking me the same thing and I understand the Japanese Ambassador is seeking a meeting." He seemed to calm down, "so what's it all about?"

Lascelles said "it might be helpful if you gave us a brief background to the proposals and what you hope to achieve by them."

"That's just what I've said, Lawrence," the DPM said, but this time with a smile.

Carmichael said that it would perhaps be best if Leila outlined the background as she was the principal architect of the proposals. The DPM nodded.

"OK, Leila isn't it? We've never met but I've heard a lot about you. So, fire ahead."

Leila outlined the basis of the job evaluation scheme, the principle of self assessment and how that assessment could be carried over into different forms of employment. The growth in contract labour had prompted her union to come up with the scheme. It meant that each time contract labour was allocated to a company the grading—and thereby their potential and valuation—could easily be understood by the company that hired the labour. It also meant that the staff concerned could know that they were properly assessed and could feel they were being fairly treated in whatever company they were currently being employed.

Leila could see that Lascelles was taking it in although she wasn't sure about the Deputy Prime Minister. She said how it seemed that the traditional world of employer and employee was changing irrevocably—mobility was the future, she stressed, and the use of contract labour—particularly because of the impact of technology—was here for good. She then outlined the history of Industry3M and how, with its recruitment and allocation of contract labour for a whole range of companies and agencies in the public and private sectors, it was central to the position of contract labour and therefore very important and how the union thought an application of the job evaluation scheme there could be beneficial for all concerned.

Before the DPM could speak Lascelles quickly said "yes, I can see the theoretical importance of the scheme and how its adoption by Industry3M could be useful. But the reality is that the company will apparently not have it."

The DPM said "and we don't think that's it's going to be much use in the DTI. And, I believe, the CBI don't like it."

Carmichael said "but the central point Dep—er, Jack—is that no one seems prepared to negotiate with us about it. Why not? Why not talk about it. What have they got to lose?"

The DPM responded, "well, Malcom Wise, the CBI President tells me that his members see the scheme has handing over responsibility for their staff to the unions."

Leila explained again how the essence of the scheme was that, while the principle of self assessment was fundamental, there was objectivity in the scheme which could assist the employers and make it easier to get the staff with the appropriate skills and training that they needed.

She went on, "Deputy Prime Minister, you must be familiar with the CBI reactions from your own time as an active trade unionist. They would say that, wouldn't they?"

Lascelles quickly said, "I can see the basis of your scheme and its appeal, Mrs Smith, but you must appreciate that the strikes and threatened strikes are doing great damage to our efforts to encourage foreign investment here. The figures of that investment literally run into billions of pounds. If the Americans or the Japanese are going to be frightened away, then they will go away and probably won't come back."

The DPM said, "and you know where they might go—bloody France—and we don't want that, do we?"

Carmichael thought it was time to focus the discussion. He looked at the DPM.

"What do you want us to do? We have legitimate claims and if an employer won't negotiate with us, and if ACAS is powerless to do anything, then what precisely is your advice?"

The DPM was getting angry again.

"Look, don't lecture me. Look at all we've done for the labour movement since we came to power. Minimum wage, the social chapter, the New Deal—we don't want to jeopardise all that. It's the strikes that are causing the publicity and the apprehension among British and foreign employers. And look at the DTI—they may be having a one day strike at the end of this month."

Leila thought the discussion was getting nowhere and wondered why they had been called to the meeting.

"Deputy Prime Minister, why won't the DTI negotiate with the civil service unions and discuss the job evaluation scheme in detail. I think it could work and, indeed, would be of advantage both to the civil servants and to the department."

She could see Lascelles look at the DPM and raise his eyebrows. The DPM gave a slight nod.

"Well, if we suggest that the DTI examines the scheme, what are you going to do in return?—suspend the strikes?"

"You know we can't do that, Jack" responded Carmichael, "but sensible negotiations in the DTI might take away a lot of the apprehension among employers and encourage them to sit down us and the other unions.".

There was a further pause.

The Deputy Prime Minister then looked at Leila. He said "I said that I've heard a lot about you and I can see that you have thought up a scheme that could be popular among your members. But, to be blunt—and you know I have a reputation for being blunt—I have heard that that it's the trots who are driving this scheme. To some it's like a new version of workers control, and we're not having that."

Carmichael was getting irritated: "nothing could be further from the truth, Jack. None of us here have any truck with the trots or any other extreme left group—or right wing group, come to that. If any of the relevant employers think that, then they must be using that as an excuse and not a reason."

The Deputy Prime Minister looked again at Lascelles: "perhaps we ought to have another word with the DTI and suggest they talk again to Dick Whetter of their union."

Leila thought that was as good as they were going to get. If there could be genuine negotiations within the DTI then that could be a useful move. It could also be abortive if the DTI didn't move at all, but at least it was worth pursuing.

There was then a further discussion about the application of the scheme and Leila referred to the claims put in by the Commercial & Technology Union and the Swedish and German unions. Carmichael mentioned the position in Teening & Sykes and the likely developments in Hokkaido.

"We know about that," said Lascelles. "A number of people have been on to us about it. But I emphasise the effect of strikes and threatened strikes on foreign investment."

The Deputy Prime Minister had had enough: "OK, we'll have a word with the DTI, but I do urge you to try and settle this peacefully. For what it's worth, I'll see about having a word too with the American and Japanese ambassadors and explain your position. That might be some assurance for them, but they are very jumpy. It's taken years for them to accept that the unions here are not all hell bent on some left wing agenda and stirring up trouble. You can see their point of view."

Carmichael decided it was time to end the meeting. "You can rest assured that we have the trots under control—at least in our union, Jack. But I think your suggestions could be helpful and I'll certainly take back to our members your points about strikes. We certainly don't seek strikes for their own sake and you'll be aware of the financial impact of them on our union—" he could see the Deputy Prime Minster nod at this—"and if we can settle all this peacefully, then it would be a major step forward."

The Deputy Prime Minster then stood up. It was the signal that the meeting had finished. They all shook hands and Lascelles escorted them to the door. As they went, Lascelles murmured to Leila "I can see where you're coming from and we will do our best, but it is difficult you know."

Leila smiled at him: "I appreciate that. And, perhaps we could keep in touch." Lascelles said he would like that and they then shook hands and left.

As the four of them left the office Carmichael said "well, I think that was slightly better then I anticipated. Let's have a chat about it in the pub."

<hr />

We got to the Red Lion pub just opposite from the Parliament buildings, at the start of Whitehall. As Leila insisted on buying the first round I thought I would try and ring Dick Whetter of the civil servants union. Fortunately he was in his office and I briefly told him about our meeting with the DPM. He sounded quite excited. I told him we were in the Red Lion and he said he would come down from his office and join us, if we were likely to be there for a while.

I told him this was highly likely and then rang off. After I had swallowed a mouthful of bitter I told the others. I noticed that Macallister seemed particularly pleased.

"It looks as if things might be happening" was his comment and I could understand why he was pleased. As the chairman of the national committee in Industry3M he must have been under a lot of pressure in the last four months since the dispute with his company first started. That, together with the forthcoming indefinite strike being called—and no prospect until now of any breakthrough—must have given him a hard time.

We went to the corner of the pub. It was half past four and already the pub seemed to be filling up. Julia Cardon could see me looking around.

"You wonder why all these people aren't at work" she said, deadpan.

"I don't wonder anymore," I replied. "I've given up wondering."

I asked Leila to summarise the position as she now saw it.

"Well, we have the strike scheduled to start on the twenty second. That's next Monday week. I think everything is hand for that," looking at Macallister as she spoke. He nodded. "We know," she went on, "that the union in the DTI was planning to send out ballot papers for a one day strike next week. Whether the DPM's comments will mean that negotiations could after all take place, we shall have to see. Perhaps Dick will give us his view when he comes here. Then we have the German life assurance company actually sitting down with the union and discussing the job evaluation scheme.

"As for Industry3M I've mentioned the so-called three week ultimatum that ran out some time ago. But it might now have come into force. I thought the absence of John Carr this morning was significant—"

"And probably helpful" I butted in.

"Yes, said Leila," but we don't know if in fact Tiller will be more against us than Carr and I guess that Tiller's got more clout with the company's head office than Carr had—whatever he may have thought. But I agree with you, John. At least we talked to him this morning—and you may have noticed how Collins seemed almost too frightened to say anything."

Macallister said, "and the biggest opportunity might well be what happens in Malaysia. I know that the company is anxious to expand into south-east Asia. It has put a lot of effort into expanding in Europe but it is a fairly crowded market. If Industry3M can get established as the main supplier of contract labour in Malaysia then that would be a major boost for them."

A voice behind me said "I think that's absolutely right."

I turned round. It was Chuck Pitney, holding a pint of bitter and smiling broadly.

I asked him how he knew we would be in the pub. At first he declined to say and then Leila asked him again. He seemed anxious to please her—and he told us.

He had been talking to someone in the American embassy this morning and had apparently been told that we were meeting the DPM this afternoon. He had also been told that the American ambassador had been told this by someone in the DPM's office.

"Your Deputy Prime Minister must be anxious to keep in with us," he joked. "But, whatever, it's clear that the ambassador must have thought the news of the meeting was important because it was all over the embassy."

"And you put two and two together, Chuck," said Leila "and assumed we would be in the pub after the meeting."

"Right," replied Pitney. "I did phone the DPM's office and they—surprisingly—told me what time your meeting was so, yes, I did put two and two together. Now, what's everyone drinking?"

Like Leila, I had not met Pitney before the Industry3M dispute had started and I was warming to him every time we met. I thought that was also true of Leila if her expression was anything to go by and also wondered, briefly, how warm she would get. But that was not for me to guess.

Just as Pitney had brought a round I saw Dick Whetter enter the front door of the pub and waved him to come over. I introduced him to Julia Cardon, Ian Macallister and Chuck Pitney. I told him that Chuck Pitney would be very discreet over what he wrote for his paper and Chuck himself assured him that he would check beforehand with him if he were to say anything about his union and the DTI. He also said that before coming to the pub he had checked with the press office of the Deputy Prime Minister and had been told that the meeting with the union had been positive. "Positive and encouraging was what their press man actually said." Julia Cardon suggested that was what she should say to the press as well and I agreed that would be the line to take.

Leila then amplified what I had told Whetter over the mobile phone and asked him "how does this affect your ballot timetable, Dick?"

Whetter paused. He was one of the brightest of the current crop of union leaders that I knew. He had been a civil servant himself, working in the Work and Pensions Department and an active lay official of the union. When the previous general secretary had retired he had stood for election and to the surprise of many—and the fury of the trots who had fielded their own candidate for the position—had won with a handsome majority.

Whetter told us what we really already knew—that ballot papers were due out next week. "It's Thursday today and the papers are due to be despatched on Tuesday next so if anything's going to happen it will have to be very soon. It's always possible, of course, to have negotiations while the ballot papers are being distributed but I should imagine that if the DPM is going to do anything then our permanent secretary might contact me tomorrow or Monday."

Macallister asked him about the position in the other departments of state and Whetter told him that there was some enthusiasm for the job evaluation scheme across the civil service but his executive had thought they would wait and see how things went in the DTI before pushing it harder in other departments. He explained to

Macallister how the changes in the civil service now meant a great deal of autonomy in the different departments—"a long way away from the good old days of national negotiations and the civil service pay research unit" was how he put it. He added "autonomy, that is, under the watchful eye of the Treasury. And the key seems to be the increasing use of contract labour throughout the service—and the same job evaluation scheme for them and the permanent staff has a lot of attractions."

I then briefly told Pitney and Whetter of our meeting in the morning with Industry3M at ACAS and how Tiller had represented the company and there was no sign of John Carr.

Pitney told us that he had checked with one of his colleagues in New York who knew one of the senior management in the Atlanta head office of Industry3M. The three week ultimatum had indeed been made and as a result Tiller had been sent over here with executive authority. He had never liked Carr since they had both been contenders for the position of the European personnel director and was apparently keen to show his superiors that he could sort things out. He added that the head office was worried about the possible strike in their Swedish company as well as the position in the UK and finding someone to blame was becoming increasingly popular among the management.

"If Tiller doesn't sort things out to their satisfaction, then of course, his own position will become dodgy," Pitney smiled. "And I should imagine that Carr has some contacts in Atlanta who would not be unhappy if Tiller falls on his face." He looked at Whetter: "the private sector's nice, isn't it?"

Whetter grinned, "it's all human nature really" and Pitney said he had to agree. He added that in the public and private sectors they were all human beings and human nature was common to them all.

"I suppose it's what the structures let people get away with that's the key thing" said Whetter. "Anyway," he continued, draining the last of his pint of bitter, "I must get back. I've told my senior colleagues that I would give them a report after I had spoken to you."

He turned to me: "and thanks John for pushing our case with the DPM. It'll be splendid if something does come of it."

I demurred: "it was Leila who did most of the pushing, Dick" I said.

❦

The following Tuesday Leila booked in at Heathrow's terminal four for the British Airways flight to Kuala Lumpur. It would be a long flight and she would arrive there in the early morning. She had spoken to Mugai again and he had arranged to pick her up at the airport and for her to speak to his executive committee in the afternoon of her arrival. He had been most solicitous about her meeting them having travelled overnight but she assured him she would be all right.

It would have been nice for her to travel club class on BA but she had always made a practice—both on planes and trains—to travel economy. It wasn't just to avoid criticism within the union for apparent extravagance but she herself thought the fares for club or first class were outrageously high and would be an unnecessary expense for the union. She hoped she would be able to get some sleep on the economy flight but, anyway, she thought, adrenalin would keep her going.

Fortunately the queues at the check-in desks were small and it didn't take long to book her luggage in and collect her seat ticket. She looked at her watch: she had nearly two hours before boarding. Time, she thought, for a cup of coffee in one of the cafes in the terminal and have another look at her notes for the meeting with Mugai's executive committee.

As she collected her coffee she had a quick look round at the others in the café. She always tried to avoid anyone she knew when catching a flight—and was very unhappy at having to sit next to someone she knew. She preferred the silence when she could read or sleep without having to make polite conversation to someone. It would be just my luck, she said to herself, if someone like Chris Rodd came up to her or, even worse, was travelling to Kuala Lumpur.

She remembered how when she had first met Rodd at one of those management seminars he had appeared confident, easy going and also very pleasant. How wrong she was, she thought, and it showed what she called her naivete in assessing some men. She knew she had been very naïve when she had got married over twenty years ago. For a while they had lived happily and then when Leila became more active in trades unionism—first as a civil union lay official and particularly when she joined the Clerical & General Union as a full time official—things became difficult. Her husband, an architect with a large property company, became very jealous and angry at the nights she spent away and constantly complained that she was taking him for granted. Arguments had then became regular and Leila could see that their daughter Helen became very miserable as she inevitably heard some of them. In the end when she had returned from her union's annual conference in the afternoon, and Helen had not yet come back from school, she found a note from him saying that he was leaving. He was sorry but living with her was now impossible for him. He had packed some of his clothes and left.

As it happened she knew that she would have left him sooner or later, taking Helen with her, but was glad that it was he who had taken the decision. She had only seen him a couple of times shortly afterwards when he had collected the rest of his clothes and his books. He had never tried to get custody of Helen. She reflected that he had been fond of Helen but had told her that it was better for all of them if he disappeared from their lives. She had not seen him since.

She got out her papers from her briefcase and as she did she wondered about Chuck Pitney. She knew many journalists, the labour and industrial correspondents of the newspapers, the BBC and ITV, and had generally got on well with them. She particularly liked Oliver Listle of the *Financial Times* but Pitney was, somehow, different. He seemed confident but not arrogant and, although she thought him a bit over-weight, he did seem quite handsome in a dishevelled sort of way. She thought he was amusing and he had certainly been helpful during the dispute.

She knew nothing about his personal life. Was he married? Divorced? Any children? Living with a woman? She hadn't asked him and thought it would be stupid to ask him. Anyway, she had to look at her notes and also prepare some notes for her speech to the Liverpool open meeting on the first evening of the strike. She had more than enough to do without thinking about Pitney's personal details.

Leila had packed copies of the union's job evaluation booklet in her suitcase and Frank Hallard, the head of the union's research, had given her copies of his report on the major job evaluation schemes already used in some of the major companies in the private sector. She read through it and then her own booklet on the job evaluation scheme. She had also brought with her the notes she had made for her speech to the Industrial Foundation on job evaluation and read that again. By the time her flight was called—and she had finished her third cup of coffee—she reckoned she could use job evaluation as a specialist subject on the BBC television show 'Mastermind'. She looked forward to having a gin and tonic on the plane and then, hopefully, going to sleep.

The plane was only fifteen minutes late taking off and while it was reaching its cruising height and the safety demonstration was taking place Leila wondered again about the meeting with the Deputy Prime Minister. Yes, it had gone better than either she or Carmichael had thought. If the DPM did have a word with the Secretary of State at the DTI as he had indicated he would—then that could be a significant move. But as of yesterday, Monday, at five o'clock, Dick Whetter had told her on the phone that he had received no call from either the minister or the permanent secretary and that the ballot papers would have to go out on the Tuesday—this day—as scheduled. She couldn't understand why nothing had happened; Lascelles had seemed quite genuine and had given every impression that something might develop.

Perhaps those people—whoever they were—that were opposed to the job evaluation scheme had persuaded the DPM to do nothing. If so, were they the same people who had suggested to the DPM in the first place that he should talk to the union? And, this was the point that had been bugging her for weeks now: why was their such opposition to the scheme at all? She could see that the David Adnams of the world would see it opening the door to a new lease of life for what they would see as irresponsible union power; but not everyone was like Adnam of Teening & Sykes, were they?

She thought she ought then to get out her draft notes for the speech she would make the following Monday evening at the Liverpool meeting but thought she would leave that for the moment. The atmosphere in the plane was stuffy` and the man sitting in the seat next to hers was already asleep and snoring: hardly conducive, she thought, to more work. She closed her eyes.

She was woken by the stewardess asking her if she wanted the lamb or the fish for her meal. She had slept through the initial serving of drinks. She opted for the fish and asked if she could now have a gin and tonic. The man besides her must have woken some time before; there were two empty gin miniatures on his table and he was now asking for a bottle of wine. She fervently hoped that he wouldn't spend the entire journey either drinking or snoring. Still, she thought, she probably wouldn't have to talk to him then.

The plane landed at Kuala Lumpur airport about half an hour late. Leila had managed to get a bit of sleep in spite of the snoring by her side. At one point the man had woken and had tried to start a conversation with her but she had pretended to be asleep when he spoke and, fortunately, he hadn't persisted. It was a difficult choice but, on balance, she preferred the snoring.

She knew Mugai would be meeting the plane and thought she would ask him to drop her at the hotel where she was booked so she could shower and change her clothes. She had to be ready for the meeting with Mugai's executive. But she thought she would also try and speak to Carmichael at his home from the hotel—it would be late evening in Britain when the plane landed at Kuala Lumpur in the early morning but she knew he wouldn't mind. He had, the previous Friday, written to Norman Jones, the Industry3M chief executive in

Britain on the threatened strike from the twenty second of October and again asking for negotiations: she wanted to know if there had been any reaction.

Although she and Carmichael had been genuine when they had told the Deputy Prime Minister that they would inform members of his appeal to suspend the strikes—and Leila had circulated the members of the two national committees on this on the Friday following their meeting—it was clear by the Monday from the phone calls received that there was no willingness by either the Industry3M or Teening & Sykes committees to agree. Macallister's reaction in the pub, after the meeting, to the idea of suspending any action had been dismissive; the members, he had said, were geared up for the strike. It would be foolish to suspend the strikes now as, he put it, once suspended they might not get sufficient motivation among the members to re-introduce them. Mathew Singh had told Carmichael the same on the Monday morning.

Leila collected her luggage from the carousel at the airport and walked through the 'nothing to declare' exit. There was quite a crowd of people waiting to meet the passengers from the plane and for a moment she couldn't see Mugai. Then she saw his large figure waving to her.

Mugai gave Leila a large wet kiss on the cheek and insisted on taking her luggage. They went out of the airport and Mugai led her to his car parked just across the road from the entrance. It was hot but it must be the rainy season, thought Leila, as there were pools of water on the road outside.

"We'll go straight to your hotel, Leila and then I'll leave you to book in. Is it all right if I then pick you up at half past one this afternoon for our executive? They meet at two and are all looking forward to hearing you. Are you tired from your journey? Did you manage to get any sleep?"

She knew that Mugai always talked in a rush as if he was running short of time. Most times he never seemed to pause for an answer to the questions he asked but this time he did ask again whether she was refreshed enough for the meeting. Leila assured him that she was fine and was looking forward to meeting his colleagues.

As they drove to the hotel Mugai gestured to the railway station on their left: "there's a piece of old England as well as a bit of new Malaysia" he said. Leila agreed; she had been to the station before and with its old fashioned architecture and pillars she thought it was indeed a piece of old England.

"There's also been a lot of new building here hasn't there, Paul? The new twin towers and the financial district".

Mugai nodded assent.

"There's a lot going on" he said. "Malaysia is booming. People talk about the tiger economies of Singapore, Taiwan, Hong Kong and more recently Dubai and Bahrein but in many ways we are the most successful. It's not just manufactured goods but finance as well."

He went on and described how the Malaysian government had done a lot to encourage the growth of what he called Islamic banking, "and the expansion of financial services is not just traditional retail banking. We're moving into more sophisticated markets for bonds, equities and options. It's all happening here, Leila. And just imagine how much Islamic money there is."

Leila wished he would not keep turning to her as he spoke but concentrate on the many busy and fast vehicles on the road. She also wished he wouldn't keep smoking another cigarette as soon as he had finished the last one but kept her feelings to herself. Mugai did see her blink her eyes a lot because of the cigarette smoke and asked if she minded him smoking. She said she didn't mind in the least. It was his car, and it was his country.

She asked him about Industry3M and Mugai explained how the use of contract labour was just starting in the Malaysian economy and how it seemed that Industry3M had seen the potential in that market and they had already had had talks with the government ministers of labour and finance about setting up a company to supply that labour.

"But they'll have to start from scratch, won't they? Where will the contract staff come from?"

"It's the permanent staff of many companies—and banks—who are leaving full time employment and going into the contract market. They like the freedom it gives them. But the key is that there is no main supplier of contract staff here so individuals have to approach companies themselves; it's all uncoordinated. That's why we all think the Industry3M approach is so important. If they can establish themselves as the hirer and supplier of contract staff then they'll be in pole position."

They arrived at the KL Hilton Hotel and Mugai stopped the car outside the main entrance. Just before Leila got out he put his hand on her shoulder.

"I know you know this, Leila, but just to remind you. We are a mixed country here. Malays, Indians and a lot of Chinese, Muslims, Hindus and some Christians. There is a bit of scepticism among the Chinese members of the executive about your job evaluation proposals and—how they describe it, forgive me—your union's unsuccessful try at getting Industry3M to adopt them. You will have to convince them."

Leila smiled at him.

"I quite understand, Paul. There was a lot of scepticism back home at first. It's inevitable but I'll be happy to talk to all your committee and explain the scheme and what's going on in the UK."

She noticed one of the hotel doormen hovering outside the car, obviously waiting to open the door and collect her luggage.

""There's a lot going on and it involves not only us in the UK but other countries as well. The scheme seems to be catching on internationally."

It was a slightly presumptuous boast but, she thought, basically true.

Mugai smiled as the doorman opened the passenger's door.

"You mean you're going global, Leila?" He chuckled and the said he would pick her up at half past one.

Chapter Eleven

Malaysian meetings

"Mrs Smith?"

It was the hotel receptionist.

"Yes."

"There was a message an hour ago from a Mr Carmichael in England reminding you to phone him when you had booked in."

She had arranged to phone him. He must have some news and thought he would remind her. She thanked the receptionist and then dialled Carmichael's home number. When he answered she said she was sorry it was late and asked him what the time was in England. Jokingly he told her that he assumed she was not phoning him to ask what the time was. She smiled. She liked working with him and, in contrast to many trade union officials she knew, he almost always retained his rather dry sense of humour.

"I'm just going to bed, Leila. It's half past eleven in the evening and I've just finished watching Newsnight on BBC Two. Elsie's already gone to bed, telling me that she's had enough of Newsnight filling her with stories of gloom and doom. I assume that Paul Mugai's met you."

She said he had and he then told her that late that afternoon—when Leila was at Heathrow—he had received a call from Dick Whetter. The DTI permanent secretary had called him that morning and had arranged for a meeting to discuss the job evaluation claim with the civil servants union on the Wednesday. Whetter had thought it good news and although the ballot papers in the DTI had gone out on the Tuesday as scheduled he said they would be daft not to go.

Leila said that the Deputy Prime Minster must have done what he said he would do and Carmichael concurred. "There is some good in everyone" he said. Leila thanked him for the message and said she would call him when she could and then rang off.

She unpacked her suitcase and thought she would try and sleep for an hour. She reckoned she had had about four hours somewhat fitful sleep on the plane. She set her alarm clock for one hour's time and lay down on the bed but she couldn't get to sleep; her mind was going over the events of the last few weeks and what was going to happen now. Everything that could be done over the strikes had been done and the industrial action should start on the following Monday but she knew how crucial the next few weeks would be and how the future—if not the very existence—of the union could well be determined by what happened then.

After half an hour she got up, turned off her alarm, undressed and took a shower. She then dressed and decided she would go down to the hotel bar and get something to eat and also drink some orange juice. Any alcohol now would probably make her feel sleepy when she was with Mugai's executive committee and she knew she had to be on the ball for them.

In the bar she looked again at her notes and then drafted out some key points for her speech at the Liverpool meeting. At half past one Mugai came into the bar, saw her and said it was time to go.

The headquarters of Mugai's union was not too far away. It was in a small modern building and, as she saw when they arrived, hopelessly over crowded. The building, which Mugai proudly told her, was owned by the union had four small offices and a large open plan office where she could see about fifteen people at desks almost touching each other. There were filing cabinets along the walls and piles of papers on each desk. She could see all the desks had computer terminals on them and she wondered why there was so much paper about. There was also a meeting room where Mugai led her.

The Malaysian Commercial Workers Union was an amalgamation of the Malaysian Clerical Workers Union and the Malaysian Banking Union. They had merged some four years ago to form the new union and it was—in terms of total membership—the third largest union in Malaysia. The same factors that prompted union mergers in the UK were also prevalent there. Mugai was one of the leaders of the Malaysian trade union centre—the Malaysian TUC—and he said he would be the president of the body in the following year.

Mugai told her that the chairman of the executive committee—not called 'president' Leila was pleased to note—was Sammy Nam. She had met him once at a meeting of Staff International. A small Malay who always seemed nervous but, Leila remembered, very bright.

As Leila and Mugai entered the meeting room she saw twenty people—including Nam—sitting round a large circular table. Again there were filing cabinets around the walls and there seemed an enormous amount of papers on the table. Looking at the people round the table she did a quick count and reckoned that, apart from only two women members there but—judging by their appearance—there were about seven Chinese on the executive. All were looking at her expectantly.

She remembered that her father, who had been with the British Army there during what was called the Malayan emergency in the late 1940s and 1950s, had told her that when Malaya got independence from the British there had been an unofficial rule that senior positions in the public and private sectors of the economy would be restricted for the Chinese inhabitants. There had been a feeling that with the indigenous Malays being regarded as rather slow and easy going, the more dynamic and efficient Chinese would capture most of the positions unless there was some quota or restriction. Now, Mugai hold told her, there was no such rule—official or unofficial—and he assured her that in his union the only criteria for serving in a senior position was the ability of each person. Leila was surprised therefore that there were only seven Chinese malays on the executive but she said to herself that this was probably an out of date attitude.

Mugai and Leila went to the two seats reserved for them at the table. Sammy Nam greeted them both and indicated that Mugai should take the lead. Mugai stood, referred to Leila's position within her union in the UK and said he would not introduce her individually to each executive member but asked them all to state their name and from where they came when asking Leila questions.

"Mrs Smith" he said, "has come over here specially to talk to us about the job evaluation scheme invented by her union and how it might be of benefit to us. You have the details of the scheme. She will also talk about her union's dispute with Industry3M which, as we all know, is keen to establish a company here." Somewhat embarrassingly for Leila he then continued "Mrs Smith is one of Britain's leading trade unionists and we are very grateful she has found the time to be with us."

Leila got to her feet and looked again round the table. She saw most of the members of the executive were smoking and the air was getting both warm and smoky. She didn't mind that as she herself had been a smoker until some ten years previously: and when she given up she had resolved never to behave like she knew many reformed smokers did and make complaints about others still smoking. Any way, she reminded herself again, it was their country and they could do what they liked.

She opened by distributing copies of the job evaluation booklet, although she saw that most members had copies already, and then briefly described the main points of the scheme. She emphasised that in the UK economy more and more people were becoming contract workers and the old concept in some of the traditional companies of people joining at an early age and staying until retirement was now gone for ever. Mobility was now the key and she said that was the basis of the job evaluation scheme. Individuals could be assessed for their personal qualities—training, work experience and aptitude—and their own self assessment was underlying the evaluation. There were a series of objective criteria in the evaluation but the essence of the scheme was that when a company was taking on contract labour it knew what it was getting—and the individual concerned would know he or she would be fairly treated in terms of their grading and, of course, pay.

Industry3M was, she told them, one of the expanding hirers of contract labour and if they adopted the job evaluation scheme for staff it would be of considerable benefit when supplying companies with the numbers of staff which they wanted as contract labour. If the individual companies themselves also adopted the job evaluation system, then that made it easier all round.

She looked at her watch. She had spoken for some forty minutes and, as far as she could judge, all the executive members had seemed interested and were following her address closely but she saw several of the Chinese members looking puzzled.

Nam looked at Mugai and indicated he should conduct the questions and answers. Mugai asked for questions and one of the Chinese put up his hand. Mugai nodded to him.

"John Ho" said the man, "from the Malayan Banking Corporation. I don't understand why the job evaluation scheme described has been opposed so much in the UK. Is there something you haven't told us?"

It was a fair question, thought Leila. She got to her feet again and explained how she and the union's research head, Frank Hallard, had devised the scheme and why they had.

"All the previous job evaluation schemes in companies seemed to be implemented from above, that is the individual members of staff seemed to be told what their grade was and although they could appeal there was little input they could make to it. That's why the system of self assessment at the initial phase is so important."

Ho broke in, "yes, I understand that, but why are so many employers opposed to it?"

Leila described how many of the schemes that companies operated had seemed beneficial in the first instance, particularly when they replaced the traditional age related pay scales and management dictated job descriptions. "But now," she went on, "the scene has changed. As I said, mobility of staff is now the key. In recent years it was increasingly common that staff would change their jobs every four or five years. Now that's old fashioned. Constant mobility is the name of the game and that's why contract labour is becoming so popular. Our endeavour is to make sure such staff are fairly graded and treated and that's what our job evaluation scheme is designed to do. In short, staff carry their grading with them."

Ho put his hand up again. "Yes, again," he said, "but why won't companies negotiate over it?"

"Because," answered Leila, "there's considerable apprehension that with the element of self assessment, many employers feel they will have no control over the allocation and grading of staff. Taking that further, several UK employers have wrongly stated that the scheme hands over control of their staff to the unions. Others—" she thought of David Adnam of Teening & Sykes—"have said the whole scheme would see a return to what they call 'irresponsible union power'."

She looked at Ho and smiled: "and all the old cliches about unions taking control have been trotted out."

Another Chinese member put his hand up: "Christopher Xandhu. Malayan Chemicals. Some of us think, Mrs Smith, that you are here to get our support to solve your problems with Industry3M. Why should we?"

"That" replied Leila, "is another fair question. We had hoped that we could get proper negotiations with the company but they decided to tell us to go away. Remember—" she looked round the table as she spoke—"that Industry3M is an American company and, traditionally, they are not pro-union, to put it mildly. In my own view, once they had taken the decision then they did not want to change, because they thought they might lose face."

She saw several of the Chinese members smile at this.

One of the two women members put her hand up and Mugai motioned for her to speak.

"Mohini Traval, the railway corporation", she said. "How does the scheme affect the role of women and the guarantee of fair and equal treatment?"

And so the questions flowed. Leila answered each in turn and could sense she was winning over the majority of the committee. She assured Traval of the explicit undertaking in the job evaluation scheme of guaranteed equal treatment and to another questioner said that, in contrast to the scheme she was proposing, many of the existing schemes could be manipulated so although equal treatment of men and women was declared, the schemes could be implemented without it really happening. She recounted what was happening in the Industry3M dispute in the UK and then talked about the situation in Germany and Sweden.

Leila thought she should be quite open with them and recounted how there had been considerable debate within her own union over the job evaluation scheme and there had been opposition from those who had worked for years in companies which had some of the old fashioned schemes of grading. "But, to be fair," she added, "it was understandable there should be opposition especially when some of them—and I'm being quite blunt with you here—had benefited under old schemes and perhaps wouldn't be treated quite so well under our new scheme. In a way, I'm talking about what could be described as the over-graded."

Altogether the questions and answers lasted for nearly one and a half hours and Leila felt quite exhausted by the end of it. Mugai called a halt and asked her if she herself any questions.

The one question that Leila wanted to raise was on the status of discussions between the union and Industry3M about setting up a company in Malaysia. She said there were a number of points but this was the main one. Mugai responded by saying that after the government minister of labour had contacted both the company and his union there had been some discussion but no real negotiations. The company, he added, seemed to have been taken aback by the ministerial insistence that peaceful agreement should be reached before the company could get the go ahead to set up operations.

Sammy Nam then thanked Leila for her presentation and, particularly, the way in which she had answered the questions. The members of the committee—especially the Chinese members Leila noticed—gave her a warm round of applause. Mugai then escorted Leila out of the meeting room. He explained that there were some other items of business for the executive committee to deal with and said he would arrange for one of his staff to take Leila back to her hotel.

"I hope you can join us for dinner this evening" he said. Leila smiled and said she would be pleased to, hoping that she would manage to stay awake then. Mugai said he would pick her up at seven o'clock.

Once back in her hotel she e-mailed Carmichael and said that she thought the meeting seemed to have gone well. She would be meeting Mugai and some of his senior colleagues that evening. So far, so good, she thought.

❦

On Thursday I got back to the office about eleven o'clock. I had got the early morning train from Plymouth and I wanted to get back as soon as possible. Although everything was in hand for the strikes starting on Monday I wanted to be in the office in the event of any last minute alarms. And I wanted to have a chat with Leila in Kuala Lumpur.

Mathew Singh had arranged for an open meeting of our Teening & Sykes in Plymouth. The company had a large processing plant just outside the city and about three hundred of our members had turned up, a pretty good turnout these days, I had thought. All had gone well although there had been a couple of trots who tried to get support for an indefinite strike and—as they always seemed to do—get a national committee of lay representatives to be responsible for the action. It was the old trick of trying to by-pass the official union structure. And establish one they thought they could control. Fortunately several of the members there had spoken against their idea and it was clear that there was little support for them.

One of the highlights of the meeting came in the middle of my speech. I had referred to the circular that Adnam had issued to all staff of the company saying that the company believed our job evaluation scheme was a recipe for industrial anarchy and how he was determined that the company would not be going back to what he described as 'the bad old days'. Then someone had shouted out that Adnam was looking forward to the bad *new* days and that brought a lot of laughter and applause.

Mathew Singh had done a good job, together with our west country organiser, in arranging the meeting. I had not really got to know Singh in the five years he had worked for the union. We travelled down to Plymouth together and I found he was an amusing, if slightly cynical, chap. His family were originally from Sri Lanka. He himself had been born in Leicester and had gone to school and then college there.

He told me that he had written to the appropriate unions in Guyana, Tanzania, Venezuala and Spain about the dispute and they in turn had written to their local managements and also to the head office in Britain. They had sent copies of their letters to him and he was pleased that they had all followed his suggested brief.

Teening & Sykes imported most of its raw material from the four countries and without a guaranteed supply then their chemicals production in Britain would be severely affected. Singh had suggested to the unions that they outline their concern at the forthcoming two day strike in the company and whether that would mean a cut in production and therefore a reduction in the amount of raw materials needed. They had then said to the management of the home companies that mined the raw materials that they were concerned at the possible loss of employment if the amount of raw material exports to Teening & Sykes was cut back. They had made the same point in the letters they sent to David Adnam in Britain.

It was all good stuff and I hoped it would at least make the company apprehensive. It was a big company, though, with a considerable market capitalisation and Adnam would no doubt think they could shrug off the effect of any two day strike—or a longer one.

Singh was confident that there would be a good turn out for the strike next Monday and Tuesday and several of his national committee members had told him that some of the senior management were getting a bit concerned at the hard line that Adnam had adopted. However Singh conceded that in many ways the key issue was the effect of the indefinite strike in Industry3M. If that went on for a long time and nothing tangible was achieved then the financial consequences for us would be considerable and the management of Teening & Sykes would be highly unlikely to move from their current position.

He was right, of course, and much now depended on how Leila was getting on in Kuala Lumpur. It was a common belief in the trade unions that the threat of a strike was often much more powerful than the strike itself and the next few days would be crucial. In Teening & Sykes we would assess the situation again after the two day strike. But, if nothing happened to cause Industry3M to negotiate properly with us and that strike drifted on, then it could be disastrous. After a while, inevitably, a number of members would have second thoughts about staying out on strike and domestic pressures would add to this concern. Once a drift back to work started then it could easily gather momentum and the ultimate nightmare would be a collapse of the strike and the bankruptcy of the union.

Then those opposed to the strike in the first place would say 'I told you so'; many loyal members would be disheartened; many members would undoubtedly leave if they thought the union was ineffective and the trots would have a field day and blame the leadership and our tactics.

Singh stayed on in Plymouth to talk to the local branch committee at lunchtime while I came back to London. On the train I drafted out a note to send to the national executive committee on the happenings of the last few days and what I had learned from some of my colleagues at the TUC General Council meeting yesterday morning.

Dick Whetter had told me he and his colleagues were moderately hopeful that the meeting with the permanent secretary and other senior officials of the DTI on Thursday would be helpful. They had not attempted to call back the ballot papers which had been issued on the Tuesday; that would have been administratively confusing so the decision had been taken to let the ballot run its course. Their executive committee would then consider the figures once the ballot had finished at the same time as assessing whether any progress had been made in discussions and, hopefully, negotiations.

Jim Bradwell of the local government union had told me that he had another negotiating meeting with the local authorities employers body next week and was now hopeful that the pressure from some of the Labour local authorities would have some effect. Peter Moorhouse of the Commercial & Technology Union had, unfortunately, been absent from the General Council and I made a mental note to phone him when I got to the office.

I looked at my watch. It was just after nine o'clock and the train was due in Paddington station at ten. I would be in the office before eleven and could phone Leila at her hotel then.

<hr>

On the Tuesday evening Paul Mugai had picked up Leila by car and taken her to what he described as the best Chinese restaurant in town. Leila thought it looked pretty run down as they approached it and it wasn't in a smart part of town. Mugai could see her expression as he parked the car and they walked to the door of the restaurant.

"It's not the smartest," he said, "but it's the best."

Leila smiled and said she was sure it would be fine.

As they entered Mugai led her to a large circular table in the middle of the room. There were Sammy Nam and eight others present, including she noted, John Ho and Christopher Xandhu. As they got to the table she heard a voice behind her.

"You are going global, Mrs Smith."

She turned and saw a large, quite handsome American with a crew cut. It was Joe Tiller from Industry3M sitting at a table with two Chinese men.

Tiller was smiling as he spoke. Leila smiled in return. "international solidarity, Mr Tiller. That's what it's all about."

There was a pause and then Leila walked on. Mugai had noted the interchange and whispered to her "you obviously know Joe Tiller then."

Leila was surprised—both at Tiller being in the restaurant and then that Mugai knew him. Then she thought that really neither point was all that surprising. She should have realised that Industry3M would have someone out in Malaysia to take charge of the company's efforts to establish a Malaysian subsidiary. She should also have realised that the ministry of labour would have probably put the company in touch with the union.

The dinner was very pleasant and though Leila felt tired she tried not to show it. Mugai was good in involving the others in the conversation and Leila was pleased that all of them seemed to think the afternoon's meeting had gone well. Mugai was solicitous at ensuring that Leila had enough time to eat as well as responding to the comments and questions from the other and—though he seemed to keep smoking his cigarettes at every opportunity and the atmosphere was getting warm as well as smoky—Leila didn't feel as tired as she had thought she might. Sammy Nam didn't say much and again left Mugai to act as the host. It was different in the UK she thought: there it was invariably the leading lay official—whether called president or chairman—who would take the lead. Here it seemed more logical, the man who effectively ran the union also conducted the occasion.

She glanced at Tiller at the next table. He was in deep conversation with the two Chinese and didn't look at Leila at all. During a lull in the conversation she whispered to Mugai: "when did you meet Tiller?"

Mugai explained that he and his senior colleagues had met Tiller at the ministry of labour offices two days before. The ministry had arranged the meeting. Tiller at first had apparently been dismissive of anything the union said, but the official from the ministry, who chaired the meeting, had told him sharply that the ministry expected progress to be made and then—not too subtly—had described the process by which any foreign company had to get a licence to operate in Malaysia.

Leila asked "and what effect did that have?"

Mugai smiled: "a complete transformation. Once the ministry man had spoken, and Mr Tiller could see the way the land lay, he was a different man."

Mguai stopped and lightly tapped the table with his spoon. The others all looked at him.

"Friends," he said "Mrs Smith is asking me about Mr Tiller who, as some of you will have noticed, is seating at the table over there with Niem van Hui and Chi Jintao." He turned to Leila. "Those two are two of the sharpest business people in the country and it is with them that Industry3M is hoping to establish itself here."

He looked round the table: "now I will tell Mrs Smith about our meeting at the ministry and if anyone thinks I have not been accurate, then please say so."

He told her that four of his colleagues had attended the meeting with him, including Sammy Nam the chairman of the union. Mugai himself had done all the talking: apparently that was the normal way in the union. Anyway, reflected Leila, it would be difficult for anyone else to get a word in once Mugai had started.

Tiller had outlined the sort of working conditions they envisaged for the company, the numbers of people they would want, the numbers of contract labour they envisaged supplying to the public and private sectors and—after some pushing by Mugai—the sort of pay levels they would implement. Mugai had then raised the job evaluation scheme and had said his union was discussing it. Apparently Tiller had at first objected loudly to any discussion of the scheme but, after another intervention by the ministry man, had merely said that Industry3M was not enamoured of the scheme and saw it as totally bureaucratic and impractical.

Mugai had then said that Leila was coming to meet his executive committee and suggested that they have another meeting later in the week after they had talked with Leila. Tiller had seen that there was nothing much he could do about that except mutter that he was not going to negotiate with a British trade union official over terms and conditions of a company in Malaysia. The man from the ministry had said he would like a separate meeting with the union and that was fixed for Thursday. Mugai suggested to Leila that she might like to come along to that and observe what was happening.

Leila said she thought that was a good idea and she would be pleased to attend. She told him that she had an appointment with the British High Commission in the morning. It was something that Leila had arranged the day before she left England. She would normally arrange to contact the appropriate British high commission or embassy in whatever country she was visiting. Sometimes it was just a courtesy call but, on occasions, she had found it useful as had the officials she had met. This time she wanted to discuss the high commission's view of foreign companies getting established in Malaysia. She thought it could be very helpful—more so now that Mugai had suggested she accompany his team to meet the ministry of labour man.

Mugai looked round the table. Sammy Nam said he had covered all the points and echoed Mugai's view that it would be a good thing for Leila to go with them tomorrow to the ministry. The others nodded. Leila said she would be at Mugai's office at half past one o'clock. She had fixed the high commission meeting for ten thirty and that would give her ample time.

By now they had all finished eating. Leila saw Tiller and the two Chinese get up and leave their table. Tiller made no attempt to look back at Leila as they left. As they went Mugai said to Leila "those two Chinese are two of the most devious people. If he is not on the ball they will have Tiller for breakfast."

"I don't believe he's a slouch," said Leila "and they in turn will have to be careful."

"Well," said Mugai, "the wily occidental and the devious orientals." John Ho heard him say this and added, with a grin, "it could be the title of a new musical show, couldn't it?"

Leila looked at him: "I'm glad it was you who said it" ; and Ho smiled at her.

By the time I was able to speak to Leila on the phone it was eleven o'clock on the Wednesday evening—six o'clock on the Thursday morning in Kuala Lumpur. What with the time differences, the long meeting I had had with the disputes committee and the difficulty of catching Leila in the hotel, I was lucky, I supposed, to have got hold of her at all.

I apologised for catching Leila so early but explained there was little alternative. She said she was awake anyway. She mentioned the meal she had had in the Chinese restaurant. It had been fine but something had kept her awake most of the night. She said she hadn't been sick but had not felt too good. Still getting over jet lag, she said that she felt very tired but was looking forward to the two meetings she had today: the meeting with the high commission people and then the meeting at the ministry with Paul Mugai and his colleagues.

When she told me she had seen Tiller in the restaurant I was surprised, particularly when she mentioned what Mugai had told her about the two Chinese men he had been with. It appeared that the intentions of Industry3M to establish a Malaysian subsidiary company were progressing faster than I had previously thought and the news of the reaction of Mugai's executive committee to Leila's talk on the job evaluation scheme was encouraging.

"There's a bit of bad news," I told her. "A number of the disputes committee—the three senior lay officials" I said, meaning Les Martin the president, Jane Toff the vice-president and Peter Berenson, the honorary general treasurer, "are apparently all getting a bit of stick over the financial effects of paying strike pay. They're holding the line so far but a hell of a lot depends on how the strike will go with Industry3M next week. Everyone seems OK on the two day strike in Teening & Sykes, but it's the implications of the indefinite strike that are sinking in with a lot of people."

"That bit of bad news is understandable," said Leila. "Anything else?"

I then told her about the SPGB leaflet which had been passed to me by Jack Treeman, our west midlands organiser. "Hold on to your sick bag while I read it to you."

It was the most scurrilous piece of paper I said and then read it out to her. One bit in particular was outrageous.

"At this critical time it is beyond belief that the union's deputy general secretary, Mrs Leila Smith, should decide to go swanning off to Malaysia leaving our members to fend for themselves—"

Leila broke in, "What on earth does that mean—fend for themselves?"

I told her to hear the rest.

"We understand Mrs Smith has taken her swimming costume with her—" I could hear Leila shout 'balls' as I said it—"and will be hoping to top up her tan." I then told her the essence of the leaflet was not the personal abuse of Leila but the last bit: "we must press again for a committee of lay representatives to be set to run this dispute properly. It is clear that the national executive committee is failing to organise the dispute properly."

"That's what they're after" I said to Leila. "As you know, they think that they could control such a lay representative committee far easier than try and influence the national committees or the national executive. I reckon too that they are almost hoping for the strikes to be a failure and then they'll really start crowing."

"It's all right, John," said Leila, "your call has now got me very wide awake and I'll try not to let the trots get to me." She went on to express the hope that if the ministry of labour in Malaysia could be persuaded to lean a bit on the Industry3M people then there could be a significant breakthrough. She mentioned the Chinese members on Mugai's executive committee and how she hoped Mugai would be able to somehow get talking to the two Chinese whom Tiller was with. She told me then about John Ho's crack about a possible new musical show. I laughed and was pleased to hear Leila chuckle as well.

She must be knackered I thought but I knew she wouldn't appreciate me making a comment on those lines. I wished her all the best for the two meetings and she said she would either phone me at the end of the day or send an e-mail if she couldn't get hold of me.

I had arranged with Dick Whetter that he would phone me at home on the Thursday evening after he had his meeting with the DTI officials: progress there might be useful for Leila to pass on to the Malaysian union.

Leila arrived at the British High Commission at half past ten. It was a bright morning and she felt refreshed after a long shower and some breakfast. She knew the tiredness would hit her later but the two meetings that day could be crucial, particularly the meeting with the ministry in the afternoon.

Tom Holliday, the deputy head at the Commission, came down to reception to meet her. He was a tall, thin and slightly ascetic looking person. Leila had been told nothing about him by the Foreign & Commonwealth Office in London except that he had been the deputy for two years and his next move was likely to be as an ambassador in one of the smaller countries in south east Asia.

"Mrs Smith" Holliday said as they shook hands. "Good of you to come. I'm sorry the High Commissioner is not here today but he sends you his regards."

Leila smiled: so far, so diplomatic.

Holliday escorted her to his office on the first floor of the commission building and motioned her to sit in one of the comfortable chairs next to the window. He asked if she would like some coffee but Leila declined.

"Now, how can I help you?" asked Holliday.

Leila briefly summarised the reason for her coming to Malaysia and her union's dispute with Industry3M. She mentioned her forthcoming meeting with the union and the ministry and asked him to give her an overview of foreign investment in Malaysia and how he saw contract labour developing in the economy.

Holliday smiled: "well, how much time do you have?" implying that he could talk at length. "But, seriously," he went on, "you know that the Malaysian economy is in pretty good shape and there are a number of countries talking about setting up subsidiaries here, hoping to cash in on the diversification of the economy. It's not just western countries but China as well, we believe. And it's not just rubber and tin anymore. Finance is one of the big opportunities—"

Leila cut in: "Islamic banking I understand."

Holliday replied: "you've got it. That's one big area. Another is IT manufacture. They're a bit behind Singapore, Japan and Hong Kong but there's a huge market here now. And you mention Industry3M. They are hoping to be in on the ground floor in terms of supplying contract labour—and that is a very much growing market."

Holliday talked for some time on how the idea of new companies employing large numbers of contract labour with only a small number of core staff was increasingly attractive. He had heard that Industry3M itself was proposing to employ about five hundred staff directly but then build up an availability of thousands of contract staff which they could supply to both public and private sector companies.

"If Industry3M can get in now, then they could have a great future. And I've no doubt they are hoping to be the first of several subsidiary companies in other south east Asian countries. So it's important for them to get the necessary licences and agreements to operate here."

Leila told him about Industry3M's operations in the UK and on the European continent and then about the dispute with the union. She mentioned the disputes in the Swedish and German companies and then the indefinite strike due to start on the following Monday. She thought Holiday had clearly been well briefed on the company's position and while he was at pains to explain that the high commission could not be seen in any way to be directly intervening in the dispute he did stress that he understood the Malaysian government was anxious to have stable and peaceful industrial relations throughout the economy. He added that he understood Paul Mugai was well regarded by the ministry of labour.

He asked her again if she would like some coffee and this time Leila said yes. As they waited for Holliday's secretary, a locally recruited Malay, to bring in the coffee, she told him how her father had served in the British army during the Malayan emergency and how she had nearly been born in Malaya but had actually been born in England shortly after her parents had returned to England once her father's posting had come to an end. And, she said, this was the first time she had been to Malaysia although she knew Paul Mugai and other leading trade union officials from her union's involvement in Staff International.

She then told him the outline of the job evaluation scheme the union was pursuing and how she reckoned it could be useful, not only to the employees, but also the company itself. By half past twelve o'clock Leila thought it was time to go. She was meeting Mugai at his office in one hours time and she could not afford to be late.

Holliday asked why the company was so against the scheme. Leila said she thought the initial response from the company was due to the traditional suspicion of American companies to dealing with British trade unions and how she thought that once having determined an attitude they were digging in so as not to be seen to be weak in the face of union action. "They've never discussed the scheme with us at all" she said, "and that's what is so galling."

Leila looked at her watch and saw it was now getting on for one o'clock. She stood up and explained that she had to go. She thanked Holliday for his time and the background information he had given her. He smiled and repeated again that he could not afford to take sides but, as he led her out of the office and downstairs to the reception, he whispered "I think you're on a good wicket here: and it's just the right time"

Holliday asked the receptionist to order a taxi for Leila and then wished her well. Leila thought the meeting had been very useful: now it was time for the ministry.

She got to the union's offices just before half past one o'clock. She didn't have time for any lunch; anyway, she thought, she still wasn't feeling all right after the big Chinese dinner the evening before and then not sleeping too well. She realised that Mugai might have another dinner arranged for the evening but she would be quite happy to have something to eat in the hotel and then have an early night. She was scheduled to get the early flight back in the morning which, with the time difference, meant she would get back to England in the early afternoon.

Mugai came down to the entrance when the receptionist told him Leila had arrived. He seemed more ebullient than ever and greeted her with a warm hug.

"I hope you had a good meeting this morning; we certainly did here."

He explained, as he took Leila to the meeting room that he, and his four colleagues who would be coming to the ministry meeting, had been discussing the meeting on the previous afternoon and what had been said at the dinner afterwards. Everyone, he told her, had been most impressed by the talk she had given on the job evaluation scheme and there had been agreement amongst them all that the union should insist on the adoption of the job evaluation scheme as a prerequisite for the granting of a licence to Industry3M by the ministry.

Leila told him that if they did that, then she thought it would force Industry3M to come to terms. She tried not to sound too excited but inwardly realised that such a breakthrough here would be tremendous.

In the meeting room Mugai again introduced her to the others who would be going to the meeting. Sammy Nam shook hands again and she smiled at the other three, all of whom had been at the dinner last evening: the two Chinese—John Ho, Christopher Xandhu and Michael Keennu one of the local malays. He had said nothing at either the executive committee or the dinner and had wondered whether he had agreed with what she had said; but she assumed he had in view of what Mugai had just told her.

As they sat down Mugai asked Leila if she had eaten any lunch but she told him she didn't want any—and the prospect of eating any of the sort of rolls she had seen at the receptionist's desk in the entrance hallway had diminished any hunger she might have felt.

Sammy Nam then said how pleased they all were that she was joining them at the meeting and how much they appreciated her coming over to Malaysia in what was a very important time for her union. Leila acknowledged his statement and stressed how pleased she was to have met them all and how she hoped they would have a successful meeting that afternoon.

Mugai explained that the main man from the ministry, a local malay called Ashu Colomba, was in fact the number two in that department. He was not particularly helpful to the unions in Malaysia but he was realistic and Mugai hoped that if he realised that the only way to get the acceptance by the union of a new company established by Industry3M was to support the job evaluation scheme then he might well be helpful to them. However, he warned, if he thought the company could get established and recruit enough staff without union involvement then he would not be sympathetic to the union at all.

Leila asked about the possible recruitment of contract labour. Mugai said that the main areas would be in companies—and the Malaysian civil service—where there were indications that the relevant managements had indicated they would be moving into the employment of contract labour, and the laying off of full time staff. In those areas Mugai said that several unions had established agreements, including his own.

Leila wanted to pursue the point but Mugai then said it was time to go. Two taxis were ordered and the six of them went out to go to the meeting.

It was Friday morning and I had another meeting with my officials to make sure that all was in hand for the actions starting the next Monday. I had been expecting Leila to look in at the office in the afternoon if her airplane was on time but I received a long e-mail from her when I arrived earlier.

Apparently the meeting which she had attended between the ministry of labour and the union on the Thursday afternoon had, after several difficult moments, gone well. She had gone on at some length about the ministry man, Ashu Columba, and how at first he had been somewhat dismissive of the job evaluation scheme which Paul Mugai had said they wanted introduced by the new company that Industry3M sought to establish. At one point, Leila had written, Mugai had said they would end the meeting as it was obvious that the ministry were merely repeating what the American, Joe Tiller, had said at the previous meeting. He and his colleagues had actually stood up and moved towards the door of the meeting room when Columba had called them back. Leila said she wasn't too sure whether Mugai would actually have gone out through the door but, in any event, it was Columba who blinked first.

Columba had then stated he could see the points the union was making and then, somewhat to her surprise, had asked Leila several questions about the job evaluation scheme. A number of them were quite technical on the scoring and assessment processes. Leila said it was obvious that Columba was very bright and he had indicated some approval of the scheme. He had, though, emphasised that it was up to the company whether they wanted to implement the scheme: he had stated that he could not see how the introduction of the scheme could be a necessary condition for Industry3M to set up shop.

I reflected that it was a good thing Leila had put it all down on an e-mail. I had asked Sheila to copy it for distribution to the officials. I still wanted to speak to Leila, though and wondered when the best time would be.

The e-mail went on: at the end of the discussion Mugai had stated that he could understand Columba stating that the introduction of the scheme could not be a condition but he reckoned it would be legitimate for the ministry to state that at least the company should discuss the issue with the union. Columba, however, had again said that was up to the company to decide. The most he was prepared to do was to say that in his personal opinion the scheme had much to commend it.

Leila said she had had whispered to Mugai that he should press for a joint meeting under Columba's chairmanship and that, if at all possible, she would love to attend it.

Then, apparently, Columba had agreed to call Tiller, and the two Chinese he was working with, to a meeting the next day—here in England, now, that meant today, Friday—with himself and the union. He had also stressed that while in no way could he insist on the embryo company accepting the job evaluation scheme he would insist on them attending the meeting. Again, much to Leila's surprise, he had said he thought it would be a good idea for Leila to attend such a meeting.

The e-mail concluded with details of Leila's rearranged flight home. She would now come back to London on the Saturday—fortunately it had been quite easy to switch her flight.

I e-mailed Leila back to say I had read her e-mail with great interest and congratulated her on the progress so far. I also telephoned her hotel in Kuala Lumpur and left a message as to when I would be in the office or at home so we could, if possible, speak on the phone.

At the officials meeting everyone was pretty upbeat. Mathew Singh reported that there had been some attempts by local managements of

Teening & Sykes plants to put pressure on staff by issuing circulars emphasising that the strike would not achieve anything except perhaps jeopardise some of their main customers. Some members had complained to him about these circulars but Singh had told them that it was perfectly legitimate for the company to do such things. It was the union's job to counter such statements and to maximise support for the action: it was a dispute, after all.

I then told them about my call from Dick Whetter the previous evening at home. Whetter and his senior colleagues had met the permanent secretary and two others from the DTI for an informal discussion on the union's claim for the job evaluation scheme on the Thursday afternoon. After a bit of fencing around both the permanent secretary and Whetter had agreed they would have a formal negotiating meeting on the following Wednesday. In the meantime, as Whetter had previously advised, the ballot was continuing. The fact, though, that the DTI was prepared to get involved in negotiations was somewhat promising.

Hazel Bellini reported that after some pressure from herself, the leading lay officials of the national committee for Leisure & Sport were now sympathetic to the idea of formally pushing a claim with the management. At its last meeting she had worn down the arguments of the two SPGB members on her committee that it would be premature to lodge such a claim and the committee had then agreed she would raise the issue informally with the company and see what the reaction would be to a formal claim.

Adam Turnbull reported that the claim had been presented in Transport International but a series of events—deliberate procrastination he said it was—had not resulted in any negotiating meeting yet to consider the claim. First the personnel chief had been away at meetings at the time the normal negotiating meetings would be held; then the independent chairman they used for the negotiating meetings had been ill for a couple of weeks and finally when a date had been agreed the company had called up the day before to say they were not quite prepared and requested a further delay. However a formal start for negotiations had now been fixed for the end of the following week.

Alan Whitchurch reported on where the organisers would be for the two strikes; he himself would be in Liverpool at the same hotel as he had used before. Julia Cardon said she was putting out a press release on the Sunday to catch the Monday morning papers. She told them that quite often there was relatively less news to fill the Monday papers so a weekend press release was likely to get more coverage then. From Monday onwards she would be in union headquarters and reports on the strikes from the organisers and officials, together with any difficult press queries, should be relayed to her. I said I would also be in headquarters and that Leila would be going up to Liverpool to join Alan Whitchurch. Assuming that Leila did get back on Saturday she would travel up to Liverpool on the Sunday.

After the meeting with Columba at the ministry of labour had finished Mugai had suggested that he pick up Leila at her hotel at seven o'clock to go for dinner with the others at the meeting. Leila would much have preferred to decline but realised that she couldn't. Now that he had asked her, she found it impossible to refuse. It was not every day that any senior official from Britain visited Malaysia and, especially in view of the close ties between the Malaysian union and her own, if she refused then it would be seen as a bit of a rebuff—and that was the last thing she wanted.

John Ho said to Leila that he thought she had won Columba over—a very difficult thing to do: "it's a good thing you're not Chinese," he said, "that would have been even more difficult."

Leila responded "that's good of you, but he was very careful not to give any hostages to fortune. Basically he only said he would arrange a meeting."

Ho replied, "yes, but that's what you haven't yet got in Britain, is it?"

She knew that John Ho was sharp and what he said was true. If she had got any negotiations started with Industry3M in Britain then the whole situation might have developed very differently. She remembered Christopher Xandhu's point at the executive committee meeting: was she in essence getting the Malaysian union to win her battle with Industry3M in Britain?

"If you can get the job evaluation scheme here then that would be good for your union—in my opinion. Yes, of course I admit it would also be good for us. It would be a precedent."

Ho smiled: "I know that, Mrs Smith. I'm really winding you up. It's a traditional Chinese tactic."

Mugai hailed two taxis and they all went back to Leila's hotel. Leila got out and the others went back to their union office. Leila said she was looking forward to their meal that evening. It was now five o'clock. She would e-mail Carmichael with the result of the meeting and then hopefully have a rest until seven when Mugai would pick her up again.

In fact by the time Leila had called the British Airways office and confirmed her rearrangement of the flight and then sent the long e-mail to Carmichael it was nearly six o'clock. She decided to have another shower and change her clothes. She was too keyed up to attempt to have a short sleep and decided then to go and have a glass of red wine at the hotel bar.

Just as she was going out of her room the telephone rang. She thought it must be Paul Mugai calling her and was surprised to hear the tones of Chuck Pitney from the *Wall Street Journal*.

"I hope I haven't called at an inconvenient moment, Leila".

Leila assured him he hadn't and then asked how he had tracked her down.

"It was your secretary, Muriel. I sweet talked her into giving me your hotel number. How's it going?"

Leila paused. She liked him but knew she had to be careful: she couldn't afford to say anything that might jeopardise the next day's meeting, and he was a journalist.

"It's all very nice here. The first time I've been to Kuala Lumpur. The weather is good; the hotel is fine and I'm going out for another Chinese meal this evening."

"Thanks for the itinerary. Anything you can say about Industry3M?"

"No, Chuck. I can't. I'm sorry."

She could almost see Pitney smile as she spoke.

"No, I didn't think you could," he replied. "Actually I have some news for you which you might find useful."

Pitney then told her he had been in contact again with some of his sources in New York and in Atlanta. There had been concern for some time among the major stock holders in Industry3M at the continuing dispute in the UK and now it appeared that one of them—a major US bank, he told Leila—was rumoured to be going to make a takeover bid for the company. Harold Stuckman junior, the CEO, had held a press conference to talk about the company's plans for expansion in both Europe and more particularly in south east Asia. That bit had gone down well but then when questions were asked about the likely success of the company in its efforts Stuckman had stumbled. He had not been fully briefed—or didn't seem to be—on the local conditions in Malaysia or Thailand, which he had also mentioned, and the company's share price had fallen when the papers reported what he had said.

Leila asked him what was likely to happen next. Pitney told her that apparently Stuckman had thought Tiller had already got provisional agreement for their projected Malaysian company to be licensed but when he himself had contacted the Malaysian ministry of finance it appeared he had not. It was they who had told them about discussions with the ministry of labour. Pitney had known Leila had gone to Malaysia and then put two and two together.

"That's helpful, Chuck," said Leila, "but I still can't say anything. I can say, though, that I will phone you as soon as I can report anything, but you must appreciate I can't say or do anything that might upset my colleagues in the Malaysian union."

She thought she could say one thing—provided that he didn't use it until she said he could.

"There's a natural concern here that I'm trying to use the union to solve our own problems: but please don't print that until I give the all clear."

"I'll respect that, Leila. But I would appreciate a call at any time from you. Things are going global, aren't they?"

There was a pause. Pitney said "well, I hope you enjoy your meal, and please let me know when you can." Leila assured him she would and then rang off. She thought about e-mailing John Carmichael again but decided against it. There wasn't much in what Pitney had told her that was hard fact and she decided to leave it until she could speak to him. It was now time for that glass of red wine.

⌖

The next morning she had booked an alarm call at six thirty. She had slept well and felt much more relaxed that she had for the previous two days. The Chinese meal had been at a different restaurant than the previous one and it had been equally good, though, she noticed, a lot more expensive. And there had been no sign of Joe Tiller at the restaurant. Mugai had seemed confident that they would have a good meeting at the ministry and they had all seemed confident. Leila hoped they weren't being too optimistic.

She checked her e-mails on the laptop she carried with her. Carmichael had sent her a brief note about his conversation with Whetter. She realised that it wasn't negotiations but at least it was movement and the actual negotiations later the next week could be very helpful.

She e-mailed Muriel with her new flight details and also sent an e-mail to her daughter Deborah. She had talked with her before she left for Malaysia that they might get together on the Saturday but that was now impossible. She knew Deborah would understand, though also feel frustrated. It wouldn't be the first time.

After breakfast in the hotel dining room she got a taxi to the union offices. They were due at the ministry at ten o'clock and had agreed to meet first a half past nine.

Mugai and his four colleagues went over the tactics to employ at the meeting. Originally, Mugai had previously explained to Leila, his union had been content to find out what sort of conditions the embryo Industry3M company would introduce and he had determined to get the highest possible terms. Now they had all agreed that the introduction of the job evaluation scheme would be of considerable benefit and that they should push for this as a necessary condition for the union's agreement, Leila had stressed to them that if the scheme were introduced then it would be worth a lot for the future employers of contract labour who would know what degree of training and skills the contract labour would be. It would also make it all the easier for the new company to recruit contract staff on to their books if they themselves operated the same scheme.

Mugai asked Leila if she would wish to speak at the meeting. Leila said firmly that it was not her intention to say anything—the negotiations were theirs—but if asked by Columba or the company men then she would be happy to speak. She asked them all if they were happy with that and they all agreed.

As they approached the ministry building Leila reflected again on the curious mixture of oriental, native and old English styles that a lot of the buildings had. The result for some was that they looked a mess: for others they looked attractive, if a bit mysterious. She recalled that on the previous day the ministry building seemed an ill fitting collection of different types of walls, roof, entrance area and surrounding pieces of garden. Inside it resembled, in a way, the offices of Mugai's Malaysian Commercial Workers Union: lots of desks, lots of paper, lots of people apparently very busy but with no sense of orderliness or structured activity. Still, thought Leila again, it was their country and they could behave as they wanted to. And the Malaysian economy was one of the strongest in south east Asia.

They went to the same meeting room. Joe Tiller and his two
Chinese associates were already sitting down. Astu Columba got up
as they entered and shook hands with all of them. Leila saw Tiller
looking at them but he made no attempt to get up and greet them.
His two Chinese companions merely looked at them with disinterest,
although Leila thought she detected a look of recognition between
one of them and John Ho of the union.

When they had all sat down facing Tiller and the other two
Columba spoke.

"Lady and gentlemen, I am glad we are all here." He looked at
Tiller. "I asked you and your colleagues to come to this meeting
because I want to try and get some agreement on the conditions under
which your company can establish its Malaysian subsidiary here
and—" looking at Mugai—"I asked you here again to see if we can
all avoid any sort of industrial trouble to such establishment."

Columba's voice was quiet and once or twice Leila had to
listen very carefully to hear what he said. As yesterday he appeared
emotionless and somewhat pedantic, even old fashioned in his use of
English.

Columba waited but no one seemed to want to speak first. He then
gestured to Tiller to speak.

"Mr Columba," said Tiller, "we have come here because you
asked us to and we want to have good relations with the ministry
of labour here and with all of the Malaysian government. I have
already outlined how we see the establishment of our company as
being beneficial to your country and to its leaders in both the public
and private sectors. We have told you how many staff we envisage
employing directly and how many contract staff we aim to have on
our books to supply those sectors."

Columba was nodding as he spoke. Tiller went on: "We aim to
be among the market leaders in terms and conditions of service. We
envisage that Mr van Hui—" gesturing to his right—"will be the
chairman of the company and Mr Jintao—" looking to his left—"will
be the chief executive. The company will be a subsidiary of Industry3M

which, as you know, is headquartered in Atlanta, Georgia, in the US. We also envisage that around forty per cent of the share capital will be offered on the exchange here for local stock participation."

Leila thought Tiller's statement had been concise and succinct. Columba nodded again and then looked at Mugai. Leila hoped he wouldn't be too verbose.

"Mr chairman," Mugai began. "We are grateful to you for arranging this meeting. We hope that Industry3M can establish a subsidiary company here and are pleased to note the forty per cent stock participation mentioned by Mr Tiller. We would like the company to go further than this in terms of Malaysian involvement but forty per cent is a start."

A good point to make first, Leila thought to herself.

"I know that Mr Tiller's two colleagues will know all about our union but for Mr Tiller's benefit can I just say that we are the third largest trade union in this country, we are the second largest in the private sector and our record in honouring agreements is second to none. We accept the trend towards contract labour and realise that whoever gets in on the ground floor in supplying to other companies will be providing a useful and expanding service."

Leila reckoned it was a somewhat convoluted way of saying it but, again, the point was an important and she could see that the two Chinese with Tiller were paying attention to what he said.

Tiller waited until Mugai had finished his sentence and then, looking directly at Columba, asked "why, Mr Chairman, should we be concerned at what the union says? We haven't even recruited any staff yet so what's the relevance of what the union may say?"

Columba didn't smile but looked at Mugai: "perhaps, Mr Mugai, you might like to answer that before I do."

Mugai was smoking furiously. Leila thought he must have anticipated the question, but how would he deal with it?

"My understanding, Mr chairman," he said, "is that the government rightly is concerned at stable industrial relations and that means good relations between employers and unions. My union has over one hundred procedural agreements in the private sector in Malaysia, some big and some small. We anticipate that many staff who are thinking now of switching from full time employment to contract status will be members of our union. We will obviously try and recruit all those who are not. If Industry3M wants to starts its operation in Malaysia on an amicable basis then I would have thought they would want good relations with us."

Leila was watching Tiller as Mugai spoke. His face was impassive.

Mugai went on: "you will know, Mr chairman, of our record as a trade union and our commitment to the prosperity of the Malaysian economy. I would have hoped that Mr Tiller and his colleagues would welcome our positive approach. And we will recruit the members, make no mistake about that."

Leila could see Tiller look at his two Chinese colleagues.

Mugai continued: "and have no doubt about it, we want the company to introduce the job evaluation scheme we have proposed so that things can get off to a flying start. It will be of great benefit to the company."

There, thought Leila, he has nailed his colours to the mast. There was no point in beating about the bush: he had explicitly set out the union's stall. She saw Jintao, one of the two Chinese with Tiller, lean over and whisper something to him. Tiller looked at Columba and asked "exactly how will this untried and theoretical job evaluation scheme help us here in Malaysia?"

It was his big mistake, thought Leila. He had opened the door for a discussion about the scheme. She looked at Columba. He nodded to her and said: "perhaps I could ask Mrs Smith from the UK to answer that important question."

Tiller opened his mouth to protest but Leila didn't give him the chance. She started speaking immediately. She outlined the basis of the scheme, how it would operate, the principle of self assessment and the safeguards on objectivity that it contained. She was looking at Tiller and the two Chinese as she spoke. She thought she detected a note of interest from the expressions of both Jintao and van Hui. Tiller sat there impassively.

"I can see the attraction to Industry3M of setting up a company here and in effect being the first major recruitment company here in Malaysia. We see the job evaluation scheme as being of considerable help to them—and, more importantly—to all the staff they will employ and the numbers of contract staff they will recruit for placing in the companies that will want them. They will be the first in the field here, and the scheme will be of benefit all round." Leila then paused.

Jintao spoke rapidly in Chinese to van Hui. Van Hui nodded and then whispered to Tiller, Tiller listened but gave nothing away as he listened. He's a clever negotiator, thought Leila.

Tiller then looked at Columba.

"Mr chairman," he said, "perhaps we could have a recess."

Columba looked at his watch. It was nearly half past eleven o'clock.

"I suggest we adjourn for fifteen minutes" he said. "Mr Tiller, you and your colleagues can stay here and I will take the union side to another room. Please let my secretary know when you're ready to resume, but I trust that fifteen minutes will be enough for you."

Tiller nodded. Columba then motioned for Mugai, Leila and the rest of their team to follow him.

When the union side were sitting down at a table in another, and much smaller, meeting room, Columba asked them: "how do you think it's going? You see, I have to report to the finance ministry on the progress here. They, I know, are of the view that Industry3M should be allowed to establish a company here but they do want reassurance that it will not be a signal for a prolonged union dispute."

Mugai said "if the company will agree to our view then it will be of considerable advantage both to the company and ourselves. But" he smiled "I know that you know that, Mr Columba."

Columba said he would contact them when the company was willing to resume the meeting and that he would chase them if they didn't contact him in fifteen minutes time.

After he left Mugai asked John Ho what Jintao had said to van Hui. Some malays could speak Chinese, and Mugai was one of those, but he wanted Ho to spell it out to the others.

Ho said he hadn't caught all that Jintao had said but from what he had heard it appeared that he was impressed by the statement of Leila and could see the potential benefit for the company in being the first in the field. He looked at Leila: "I think we might be making progress. But that man Tiller is a hard man."

Leila responded "yes, he is. But I think he's also realistic and he seems to have a direct line to the head office in Atlanta." She decided then to tell them about her conversation with Chuck Pitney and the pressures on Industry3M from some of their stock holders.

Mugai said he was not surprised and told her that they had heard rumours to a similar effect. He explained that Jintao had been the head of the investment division of Malaysia's largest bank and that van Hui had been the deputy chief executive of the major rubber company. They had both left their jobs to start up a number of joint ventures, the proposed Industry3M company being the biggest.

"In fact, Leila, I understand it was the two of them that approached Industry3M first. They saw the potential there is here in Malaysia and—apparently—the company had been making some enquiries about suitable people they could get to run such company here."

Sammy Nam said he thought Columba had been helpful and added that this was a change from his own previous dealings with him when he was the head of his local union branch and they had had a dispute with one of the banks over pay. Then Columba had steadfastly refused to get involved and said it was up to the union and the bank to sort things out. In the event the union had failed to secure a settlement over pay. Mugai said that presumably Columba could see now how his own stock would rise if agreement could be reached on Industry3M. Undoubtedly, he said, the Malaysian government would be pleased if the company and the union could agree. It meant that Malaysia would be among the foremost of south east Asian companies in the new employment world of contract labour.

Columba then knocked and put his head round the door: "the company is willing to resume the meeting" he said.

When they re-entered the meeting room Leila could see Tiller talking animatedly to Jintao and van Hui. She thought he looked tired and a bit exasperated. He stopped when he realised the union team was in the room. Columba took the chair at the head of the long table. Mugai, Leila and the others resumed their seats.

Columba cleared his throat. Mugai lit yet another cigarette. Jintao smiled at Leila. As usual, Sammy Nam kept nervously looking from side to side.

"Well, Mr Tiller," opened Columba, "you asked for the recess so perhaps I could ask you to speak first."

Tiller ran his hand through his thick crew cut and took a deep breath: "yes, Mr chairman. We have had a brief discussion but are not ready to change our attitude—"

Leila tried not to look disappointed.

"And we need some more time to consult with the parent company in the US. I'm sorry about this but the original remit we had has not changed."

Mugai asked whether they had been prepared to come to an agreement at all or whether the meeting had just been one big waste of time. Then, to the surprise of everyone on the union side Jintao spoke.

"Mr chairman," he said in a soft lilting voice, "Mr Tiller has said what the current position is. For myself and Mr van Hui—" he gestured towards his Chinese colleague—"we have listened with interest to what the union—and, particularly Mrs Smith from England—has said and we can see some advantage in the job evaluation scheme that has been outlined. But unless Industry3M are prepared to agree to it then we are indeed wasting all our times."

Mugai was puffing furiously on another cigarette. Leila wondered what Jintao would say next.

"So you are all aware of the position I wish to emphasise that it was Mr van Hui and myself who had the idea of setting up a recruitment company. It was we two who approached Industry3M as they are recognised as one of the leaders in this field today. They have the experience, the contacts and the money. To be clear, though, they may not be the only ones."

Leila saw Tiller go pale as Jintao said that. The threat was clear and she could sense that Mugai and his colleagues had realised that too.

Tiller spoke again: "it is the middle of the night back in the south of the US and perhaps not so easy to contact them but I will try. We are keen to get a new company established here in Malaysia. We recognise the stability of the country and its economic structure and we think Industry3M would be an important mainstay of that stability if we got off the ground."

Leila could see that Tiller's remarks were aimed at Jintao and van Hui as much as the union.

Tiller went on: "I suggest we adjourn until later this afternoon."

There was silence. Leila could see that what Tiller was actually suggesting was time for him to seek to persuade the chiefs back in Atlanta that they change his mandate.

"I repeat," said Tiller, "that communication with Atlanta will be difficult at this time but I will do my best."

Columba looked round: "I think we ought to adjourn and meet again—would four o'clock be acceptable? How about you Mrs Smith, when do you intend to return back to England?"

"I'm all right, Mr chairman," responded Leila. "The important thing is whether this proposed further adjournment is acceptable to Mr Mugai and his colleagues."

Mugai grunted and quickly looked round at the others. He could see where this was leading but he didn't want to let Tiller off the hook.

"We would be prepared to meet again this afternoon at four; but I sincerely trust that we will not continue to be wasting our time." Mugai then sat back and took out another cigarette.

Columba said that he too hoped a further meeting at four o'clock would not be a waste of time for anyone. No one else spoke so Columba then said "well, four o'clock it is then."

I had just showered and was starting to get dressed when the telephone rang. It was Leila calling from her hotel in Kuala Lumpur.

"Sorry to call so early," said Leila. "It's early afternoon here and we've just adjourned the meeting and will resume at four o'clock this afternoon. I trust things are all going well with you."

I assured her that everything was going all right. David Adnam of Teening & Sykes had written to me complaining at the scheduled two day strike and emphasising that he and his company would not give in to what he called 'union blackmail'. From the reports of the organisers it seemed that the spirits of our members in the company were holding up and we anticipated a successful response to the call for action on the Monday and Tuesday.

She asked about any developments in Industry3M. I told her that Ian Macallister had spoken to me yesterday and told me of the many rumours now circulating in the company. I hadn't had any response from Norman Jones to the last letter I had sent him and there hadn't been any sightings of John Carr at all. Macallister told me that he had heard Collins had drafted a circular condemning the union's call for an indefinite strike but—surprisingly —it had not been issued. Then Macallister said there were rumours of ructions in the head office in Atlanta and talk of some sort of takeover moves. He didn't know any more than that. I had tried to get hold of Chuck Pitney of the *Wall Street Journal* but so far had been unable to reach him.

Leila then told me of the meeting at the ministry of labour and the attitude of the two Chinese who were scheduled to be the chairman and chief executive of the new company. She sounded optimistic and spoke highly of the part played by Paul Mugai in the meeting.

We discussed the possible outcomes—from the worst scenario of no progress at all and the ministry giving agreement to the establishment of a new company, without any participation by the union, and the best scenario whereby the union would be recognised and the job evaluation scheme accepted.

"I think the key is the attitude of the two Chinese and how much of a mandate Joe Tiller has from head office. He's under pressure but he's no fool and won't be a push over if he's convinced he's got the necessary authority from Atlanta to hold out" said Leila.

Not for the first time I regretted that no American union had been able to organise the staff in Atlanta, but that was unfortunately the norm in most of white collar employment in the US. I asked Leila how much the ministry of labour man was just going through the motions and how much did they really want a settlement that would involve the Malaysian union. She replied that on balance it appeared that the ministry man seemed genuine in wanting a settlement that did involve the union but was not sure how far he would go to achieve it.

I told her that I had been in touch with van Megeren at Staff International who had told me that the German white collar arm of the DGB were making progress with the small insurance company that had reacted favourably to their claim for the job evaluation scheme but the German subsidiary of Industry3M was proving obdurate. The Swedish union was well on its way to a strike ballot in the Industry3M company there.

Leila then asked me to put her through to Muriel, her secretary, and I did so.

From what Leila had said it seemed that there could be a breakthrough and that would be excellent news. But I had been in that position before over the years and I didn't want to count the chickens yet: it could all go wrong.

As I dressed and then had a bite of breakfast I knew I must see Julia Cardon as soon as I got to the office and do an e-mail to the disputes committee members on what Leila had told me. I must, too, speak to Macallister and—if possible—get hold of Pitney to check with him about these rumours about the company in the US.

Leila had gone back to her hotel during the adjournment where she had telephoned Carmichael. Mugai and his colleagues had gone back to the union office. They had agreed to pick Leila up again from her hotel at half past three and then go back to the ministry.

When they arrived back at the ministry of labour building and the meeting room they sat down with Columba once again in the chair at the head of the table. Columba explained that Tiller had said they were not quite ready to resume the meeting but hoped they wouldn't be long. Mugai whispered to Leila that he hoped so too, but he reckoned the delay would be, on balance, to their advantage.: "I am an optimist," he said to her.

They waited for fifteen minutes and then there was a knock on the door. Tiller and the two Chinese entered and took their places opposite the union side. Leila thought Tiller looked very subdued and a bit dejected but could discern no emotion on the faces of the two Chinese.

Columba looked at Tiller: "well, Mr Tiller?"

"Mr chairman," began Tiller, "I—we have had a discussion on our side and I have been in touch with my head office in Atlanta. It is the middle of the night over there and there have been some developments." He paused, breathed in deeply and continued ; "it appears that the ownership of the company may be changing. Apparently yesterday—Thursday in the US—there was a lot of movement in the share price of Industry3M with the price climbing quite a bit. Some of our stock holders, particularly one of the major US banks, has been buying up stock in a big way."

Leila, Mugai and the others tried to look impassive as Tiller was speaking. Leila knew this could be very significant. Sammy Nam kept looking around nervously. Mugai lit another cigarette.

"It appears that there was a late night meeting of the executive board of the company and as a result they are now recommending acceptance of an offer by the bank for the remaining shares they didn't manage to buy yesterday. In fact the bank only needs a few more to get the majority."

There was silence. Leila thought she saw one of the Chinese winking at her. Columba looked again at Tiller.

"Where, then, does this place your company's desire to get established here in Malaysia?"

Tiller responded: "this is the key point, Mr chairman. The takeover bank has made it clear that it wants to pursue the plans for the establishment of the company as quickly as possible." He looked at some notes he had obviously just scribbled down and went on: "if we get agreement to operate the company here in this country then we will agree—if the union gets fifty per cent plus one of the staff of the new company within six weeks of establishment—then we will recognise the union for collective bargaining purposes."

Leila saw Mugai looking at Tiller through clouds of his cigarette smoke but he said nothing.

Columba asked Tiller "anything else?"

Tiller looked down at his notes again: "yes, Mr chairman, we are prepared to discuss the introduction of the job evaluation scheme with the union. In fact, to be precise, we are prepared to introduce the scheme whether the union gets the required membership for recognition or not."

Leila had not anticipated that Tiller would say that. Her mind raced at the import of his words. The company was saying that they would introduce the job evaluation scheme whether there was a union recognised or not. In a sense the company would be claiming ownership of the scheme—and where would that leave the union?

Mugai put out his cigarette and said "we are glad to hear what Mr Tiller has just said but we must be clear on exactly what it is that he has said."

Tiller replied a little angrily that he thought what he had said was quite clear. Mugai smiled at him which seemed to make him more angry.

"We've got six weeks to recruit half the staff you are going to employ?" he asked. Tiller nodded. Mugai went on: "then I assume we will have full access to the staff in order to recruit, to distribute material and to address the staff?"

Tiller said "within the confines of the business of the company not being disrupted."

Leila thought that statement could be used to justify no facilities at all for the union to recruit and whispered to Mugai to make it clear that the company should recognise the union in principle and get the company to formally sign a recognition agreement after the six weeks—or before, if the union had recruited the necessary number before then. Mugai grunted agreement to her and put the point to Tiller.

Before Tiller could reply Jintao interrupted and said "we don't want to waste any more time. We will recognise the union and sign the agreement when there is a majority of staff in membership and, naturally, the union will have the facilities to recruit."

Tiller looked astonished at Jintao but the Chinese ignored him and continued, "and, of course, we accept that the introduction of the job evaluation scheme clearly implies that there will be a union to be part of it. In fact I cannot see how the scheme could operate effectively without the participation of a body to represent the staff." He looked across Tiller to van Hui. Van Hui nodded and spoke to Jintao in Chinese.

Columba broke in and said that what Jintao had said would mean that the union would presumably agree to the establishment of Industry3M's subsidiary in Malaysia. Mugai confirmed that that was the case and suggested that Columba should write down the points that had been agreed and that the company and the union should sign it.

Leila inwardly heaved a sigh of relief. The danger of what Tiller had said was passed. And she realised that Tiller's attempt to stonewall over union recognition and involvement in the job evaluation scheme was a last ditch attempt to salvage something but equally she saw that the two Chinese were not prepared to mess about anymore. They wanted the new company established and—she surmised—the two Chinese could also see the commercial advantages of the job evaluation scheme being implemented.

Columba asked if both sides would recess for a moment while he went away and drafted a 'heads of agreement' which would summarise the points agreed. Mugai said his side would indeed be prepared to adjourn while Columba did that. Tiller looked for a moment as if he was going to make a long statement but then shrugged his shoulders: "OK, Mr chairman, we'll agree to that."

Leila whispered again to Mugai: "you've done it."

Mugai looked at her and replied "yes, but only with your help."

I had just got back to the office after a few lunch time beers with some of the officials in the pub when Leila phoned me from Kuala Lumpur again. It was late in the evening and she sounded a bit tired, but also happy.

"John, I think we've got somewhere at long last."

She told me about the ministry meeting and that Columba had produced a statement of heads of agreement. The union was recognised in principle and now had six weeks to recruit half of the staff. Mugai had told her that this would be—as he put it—a 'piece of cake'. Importantly the company had agreed to implement the job evaluation scheme though they wished to discuss several aspects of it: but, Leila stressed, the company had agreed that the union would be totally involved in the implementation and, even more importantly, its operation.

I asked her what had caused the change of mind. Leila referred to the impending change of ownership and how she believed that the likely new owners—the leading American bank—must have given Tiller an instruction to get the position sorted and agreed. They didn't want to waste any more time. Apparently one of Mugai's side, John Ho, had heard what the two Chinese had said to each other and that was the basis of Leila's belief.

"Are you quite happy with the heads of agreement statement" I asked her and Leila replied that she and Mugai both were; and so were the other members of Mugai's team. The union would now recommend that the company get the necessary licences to operate from the Malaysian government.

"It's a big change." said Leila. "The company will give lists of those staff whom they recruit to the union and Paul said they would contact them as soon as possible and was confident they could get them to join the union. Many of them would undoubtedly be from companies where the union already operates and thus they would be members anyway."

I asked about the likely timescale now and Leila told me that the company had said they would aim to recruit some five hundred staff in the next four weeks and Mugai had reckoned that they would easily get the necessary membership within the six weeks.

She added "Paul and the others are delighted. They are going to have a meeting of their executive committee next Monday but anticipate no problems at all at that—and the heads of agreement does specifically say that the company recognises the union in principle now."

I asked Leila to fax a copy of the heads of agreement to me. She said she would do that as soon as she got back to the hotel. At the moment she was speaking from the union offices. They had all been out for another meal—a malay curry restaurant this time, she added, and then she had gone back to the offices with Mugai.

"What about the press, Leila? What can we say here?"

"Well, the union has put out a statement just now and Paul tells me that if we want to put out the heads of agreement then he's quite happy. I suggest that Julia puts out a copy of that as soon as possible."

I said that I would then fax a letter to Norman Jones, the chief executive of Industry3M here, asking for an urgent meeting to discuss our claim. Leila told me not to forget the pay claim which we had submitted at the time we had originally claimed the new job evaluation scheme and I assured her that I had not forgotten that.

"What about the strike on Monday—what do you think, Leila?"

Leila said that that would have to go ahead. She told me how Tiller had reacted after the long adjournment and how he looked as the Chinese had spoken at the meeting: "he may well try and say that the Malaysian agreement has got no relevance in the UK or anywhere else. By the way, can you send a copy of the heads of agreement statement to van Megeren and directly to the Swedish and German unions? In the meantime I don't think we've got any alternative but to let the strike proceed."

I said I would send out the copies of the fax as soon as I got it and would also telephone my fellow union general secretaries, Dick Whetter, Jim Bradwell and Peter Moorhouse. I would also speak to John Miller at the TUC.

"It's great news Leila and I congratulate you. If I could, I'd buy you a large drink now, but no doubt you have that in hand."

Leila told me that she was now going back to the hotel with Paul Mugai and they would have a few drinks to celebrate. She would fax the stuff over first.

Finally I asked if she would phone me when she arrived back at her house tomorrow and she said she would.

"One last thing," said Leila, "I think it would be a good idea to phone Chuck Pitney and tell him the good news. I've got his mobile number and I did say I would let him know as soon as we had anything positive to say."

I smiled. I took it for granted that she would contact Pitney, or the other way about, but I supposed she was letting me know the formal reason for her speaking to him: I guessed that she would want to speak to him anyway. They did seem to get on well together.

Chapter Twelve

Life goes on

"Mrs Smith?"

It was the reception in the hotel. Leila had asked for a call at half past five o'clock in the morning as she was not too confident that her alarm clock would wake her up and she had to leave the hotel by half past six to get to the airport in time to check in for the flight home.

She had slept well. With the curry and the drinks there at the restaurant and then, after she had phoned Carmichael, several more drinks at the hotel when Mugai had brought her back, she had slept like a log; in fact it seemed only a few minutes since she had gone to bed. She couldn't immediately remember what time she had got to bed but it must have been just before midnight. Perhaps, she thought, she could sleep on the plane. Anyway, it had been a nice meal and all Mugai's team had been in good spirits and most appreciative of Leila's efforts.

She had sent the fax to Carmichael and then had managed to speak to Pitney. She hadn't been able to contact him at first but had left a message on his mobile. He had phoned her back. He had been aware of the news about the bank looking to take over Industry3M but had not heard of the heads of agreement between the Malaysian union and the company. He had been full of congratulations when she had told him and they had agreed to speak further when she got back to the UK.

She showered, dressed and decided to try and phone Tom Holliday at the British High Commission from the airport. Holliday had told her he usually was in his office by eight in the morning and had specifically asked her to let him know how things were going before she returned to the UK.

She arrived at KL airport in good time and checked in. The flight was apparently on time and was not crowded. She went to the bar and ordered a cup of coffee and a croissant. When there she tried Holliday at the high commission and—true to his statement—he was in his office. She briefly told him of the meeting the previous day and the heads of agreement signed with the company. He had sounded pleased. Leila suggested he contacted Paul Mugai that day to get the whole story in more detail and he promised he would.

As Leila was finishing her coffee she noticed Joe Tiller advancing towards her in the bar area. He did look quite fit and handsome, she had to admit, and this time was also looking quite pleased with himself.

"Good morning Mrs Smith," said Tiller as he came up to her. "I assume we are travelling on the same plane."

"You're going back to England then," responded Leila. Tiller said he was. He did sound quite upbeat and Leila wondered whether he was in fact pleased with how things had gone at the meeting. She asked him if he would like to join her at the coffee table and Tiller readily accepted.

"You look perky," she said, "in contrast to how you looked yesterday."

"It's another day, Mrs Smith—or may I call you Leila?" Leila smiled and nodded assent.

"My name is Joe and I'm glad I've seen you here and even more glad we'll be on the same plane. Club class I hope?"

Leila shook her head. Tiller raised his eyebrows: "you're obviously a woman of principle—but I'm not sure what that principle is."

Leila knew he was joking and also thought he was trying to be a bit flirtatious and again wondered at the change in his whole approach and demeanour. Tiller noticed her look and said he would welcome a chance to chat to her.

Leila said they still had some time before their flight boarded and that now was as good a time as any. Tiller went over to the bar and ordered a cup of coffee. He looked at Leila and asked if she would like another coffee but she shook her head. He got his coffee and sat down beside her.

"Yesterday was yesterday," he said as he sipped his cup. "We have to deal with the reality of the position."

Leila thought it was time to stop fencing around and asked if he was really pleased at the heads of agreement they had agreed at the meeting.

Tiller said "of course. We've got a result and that's progress. Look, Leila," he leaned forward as he spoke, "we Americans are realistic above all else. It's a new ball game now. By the end of the day the bank will have brought up enough of Industry3M's shares to give them control of the company and they are the ones calling the shots."

"What about Harold Stockman junior?" Leila asked with a hint of a smile.

"He'll be there for a few weeks and then the bank will announce a whole new change of the top management structure." Tiller went on to explain that because of Indutsry3M's growth, and the enormous growth in the contract labour market in the US, Industry3M had been regarded as a company that a number of institutions wanted to take over. "It clearly has a bright future," he explained, "and, quite frankly, Leila, the bank doesn't think the existing management is astute enough to take advantage of all the opportunities that are now opening up."

"That's why the bank wanted the situation here sorted out as soon as possible," commented Leila.

"You've got it in one" said Tiller. "I must admit I did try and get something for our previous position but, as you must have noticed, the two Chinese were getting fed up with all the messing about. So, we got a deal."

Tiller explained how his mandate from the company had at first been to resist any deal with the union—that showed how out of touch the company was in relation to Malaysia, he said—and was going on about the naivety of some of the management when Leila looked at the departure board and said the plane was now being boarded. Tiller said he would try and catch up with her on the plane: Leila said he could always downgrade his seat. She then left him finishing his coffee while she went to the departure gate.

It was about an hour and a half later, after boarding, finding her seat, stowing her hand luggage away, watching the safety demonstration and waiting until the plane was given the all clear to start engines and it then took off, climbed to its cruising height and the seat belt sign was switched off, that Leila relaxed. She thought about what Tiller had said. He was almost too good to be true: was he being genuine in being so forthcoming about the company and its new owners or was there some hidden agenda?

After a rather unappetising late breakfast had been served to the passengers she saw Tiller coming down the aisle towards her seat. Fortunately she was in a window seat and the seat next to her was empty. Tiller smiled at her and gestured to the empty seat. Leila nodded and he sat down.

"Now, where were we?" Tiller asked.

"Tell me what's going to happen now in your European subsidiaries. As you know we've got the strike starting next Monday," said Leila.

"Yes, I do know that and so does the bank back home. And I know about what the Swedish and German unions are up to." He looked at her: "can I talk quite frankly?"

Leila said she would prefer if he did.

"The new owners want to start with a clean sheet. I guess they had no idea that the trade unions in Europe could be so—er, what's the word ?—"

"Positive? Strong? Awkward?" Leila was smiling as she answered him.

"Let's just call them a big factor. That's pretty neutral, isn't it?" Tiller then went on to talk about the traditional reluctance of most American companies to get involved with trade unions. Outside of the traditional industries of coal mining, steel, road transport—'trucking' he called it—and motor car manufacture, unionism was weak and in many industries practically non existent. Many of the managements had only a vague idea of collective bargaining and union/employer relations throughout western Europe and Tiller said that, while most American managements remembered the battles that Mrs Thatcher had had with the unions in Britain over twenty years before, they knew nothing about the everyday course of industrial relations now.

"When your union put in the claim for a new grading and evaluation system then the management in Atlanta thought it was the start of some sort of latter day communist takeover."

"But what sort of reports did the UK management send back to head office?" asked Leila.

"I guess they told the head office basically what they thought they wanted to hear," said Tiller "and—to be quite honest with you—that man John Carr was not anxious to correct their apprehensions. The bastard," he added.

Leila remembered what she had heard about Tiller, that he had lost out the European post to Carr and asked "to be quite honest, too, how much is your view coloured by not getting the European job?"

Tiller grimaced a little: "yes, I should have known you would have found that out. But it's not just that. Whatever Carr said to the interviewers when that job came up, well, he's now being seen as a big bag of wind and he's being blamed for a lot of the trouble with your union."

"Well then, what's going to happen?"

Tiller paused before replying, then said: "I've got to contact Atlanta as soon as we get to London."

"There's no point in my asking you how you're going to respond to the strike, then". Leila knew he would not commit himself on that; and nor would she have done if she was in his position.

Tiller replied "and I suppose there's no point in me asking you how long you can keep your members out on strike. But, seriously, we'll have to wait and see. I've got to speak to Atlanta before anything else."

"I understand that, Joe. My general secretary has written for the umpteenth time to Norman Jones in Liverpool and if we get no positive response then so be it. The strike will go ahead until we do."

Tiller looked at his watch. It was now nearly twelve o'clock midday in Malaysian time. He asked Leila: "time for a drink?"

Leila looked at her watch, "why not?"

Tiller saw a stewardess walking down the aisle and asked Leila what she would like. Leila said she thought a gin and tonic would be nice. Tiller said he also thought that was a good idea and asked the stewardess for the two drinks.

Leila realised that Tiller was no push over. Yes, he had been very forthcoming about the company—and John Carr in particular—but in fact he had given nothing away. He hadn't tried to be too clever in trying to stitch up some sort of deal now and she respected him for that.

They chatted for a while when they had got their drinks. Tiller asked whether she had been to Malaysia before and Leila told him about her father's military service during the Malayan emergency. He told her about his background—graduated in law, practised law for a while in San Francisco and then gone into what he described as 'human resource management'. Leila told him that, in England, was still called 'personnel' by many people: Tiller replied that it sounded more impressive the way he had put it.

"It depends on what you're impressed with" commented Leila and Tiller smiled.

"There's nothing more I can say about the future" he explained "except to say that Atlanta will be very pleased at what we've now got in Malaysia. We'll be the first big player in the contract labour market in that part of the world and the opportunities are tremendous."

Leila said "that's what I told you and your colleagues at the ministry" and Tiller laughed.

They talked about the publicity the dispute had generated. Leila asked him whether he knew Chuck Pitney of the *Wall Street Journal*. Tiller said he had never met him but had heard a bit about him. He had quite a reputation as an investigative reporter and was generally well respected. Leila asked if he was married. Tiller, for a very brief moment looking puzzled, said that he had been but apparently his wife had been killed in a car crash some years ago. He had one daughter who, he thought, was at university. Leila noted the information and suggested they had one more drink.

It was Saturday afternoon and I had just finished watching one of the autumn rugby international matches. England had just failed to beat the Australians, though not by much. Elsie had been out shopping. Try as I might, I had failed to get Elsie interested in rugby and after several attempts had now given up. She didn't mind me watching the matches though, and I thought that was progress. I made a cup of tea and then thought I ought to make some phone calls.

Just then the phone rang. It was Leila and she had just arrived at her home. Her flight had landed on time, she had caught the tube to Wimbledon and thought she ought to phone me first before doing anything else. I reckoned she must be very tired after the events of the previous four days and the jet lag from her journey. I said as much to her but she told me she was going to try and stay awake until the evening—she always said she tried to operate on the local time whenever she went abroad.

"A pretty successful trip," she said and then told me about her conversation with Tiller at the airport and then on the plane. It all sounded pretty good but, as she said to me, there was no guarantee that anything would happen here. Apparently Tiller was going to speak to his head office in Atlanta and had indicated to Leila that, depending on what they said to him, he might go to Liverpool on the Monday.

I told Leila about the progress that Dick Whetter seemed to be making at the DTI and how he was hoping his meeting with the permanent secretary next Wednesday would be a big step forward. He would get his ballot result on Monday and anticipated the result would be a reasonable majority in favour of a one day strike but he didn't think his executive would want to activate it until after the Wednesday meeting.

We went over the arrangements for the following week. Leila said she would phone Ian Macallister as the Industry3M national committee chairman and suggest that, if at all possible, he come down to Liverpool on the Sunday and be with her for the start of the strike the next day. I told her that I had received no news from Norman Jones but she seemed to hope that there might be a response on the Monday. She wasn't exactly pining her hopes on Tiller and his talk with Atlanta but thought it would be prudent. She said she would also phone Clive Bristow and Ted Davis and suggest that they, and Macallister should all meet in her hotel on the Sunday evening. Alan Whitchurch would also be there so, if anything did happen, they would all be together.

"I'm going to phone the members of the disputes committee at home now, but I'll leave the Industry3M members to you then. By the way, thanks for the fax you sent—and you've got a copy of the heads of agreement with you?"

Leila assured me she had a copy of the agreement and said she would speak to me again when she got to her Liverpool hotel tomorrow.

She's certainly had a busy time, I thought to myself. Then I remembered what a general secretary of another told me once: he had been speaking to a large meeting of members and explaining how busy he was with negotiations and meetings and rushing around the country. Then one of the members present had shouted out "well, you wanted the bloody job didn't you". It was funny, but also true.

Leila got to the Liverpool hotel by six o'clock on the Sunday evening. She had spoken to Macallister, Bristow and Davis the previous evening and they had agreed to meet in the bar of the hotel at seven. She knew Alan Whitchurch had been aiming to arrive at the hotel in the evening and she had left a message at reception for him to join them in the bar as well.

The hotel receptionist handed her a message. It was from Joe Turner of the *Liverpool Daily Post*: could he have a chat with her later in the evening? He would be in the bar at about eight o'clock. Leila thought she would phone him back and agree. He had been helpful in his coverage of the dispute so far and Leila thought she ought to give him the latest developments. Julia Cardon had telephoned the Press Association with a statement about her fax to Carmichael but undoubtedly Turner would want to get some more detail about how she thought the Malaysian agreement could affect the dispute in Britain.

She handed the receptionist the heads of agreement statement and asked her to make ten copies. She then collected her key and went to her room, unpacked her bag and before phoning Turner she rang her daughter Deborah. She had tried that morning before she got the train from Euston station but had only got her answer phone. Fortunately Deborah was now at home and Leila agreed that she would go over to her house the following Sunday for lunch. It would be good to see them again and, not for the first time, Leila said she was sorry she hadn't contacted her in the last few weeks but, she explained, things had been rather hectic. Deborah had said she appreciated this and told Leila not to worry about it. Next Sunday would be fine. Leila knew she was much more understanding than her ex-husband had ever been.

After phoning Joe Turner at his home she left her room, collected the copies of the heads of agreement statement and went to the bar. Three of them were already there and greeted her with a cheer.

Macallister, Bristow and Davis all insisted on shaking her hand as she joined them and were full of congratulations over the agreement in Malaysia. She then saw Alan Whitchurch come into the bar and he too congratulated her.

Leila brought a round of drinks and they sat down at a table. She told them about the days in Malaysia, the meetings, Paul Mugai and his colleagues, the involvement of Joe Tiller, the part played by Ashu Columba the ministry man and then handed out copies of the heads of agreement statement.

She asked Macallister, Bristow and Davis how members were feeling about the strike on the next day. They all said that as far as they could judge the mood was a mixture of obstinacy and defiance. The statements by the company over the previous five weeks had made most members more determined to take the necessary action to force the company to move from its entrenched position. The rumours about what was happening to the ownership of the company had also strengthened the union position. Whitchurch said that he understood about three hundred new members had been recruited since the ballot result had been declared and he echoed the views of the others of how members were currently feeling.

Macallister got up and went to the bar to get another round of drinks. As he did so Leila's mobile phone rang. It was a number she didn't recognise.

"Hello, Leila Smith here."

"Mrs Smith, it's Lionel Collins from Industry3M." Leila looked at the others and mouthed the name of Collins to them.

"Yes?"

"Mrs Smith, I'm sorry to bother you but you may recall you did give me your card with your mobile number on it."

"Yes," said Leila, slightly irritated, "but you didn't phone me up to tell me that." She thought she heard a slight nervous laugh at the other end.

"As you may have guessed, Mr Collins, I'm here in Liverpool. What do you want?"

There was a pause. She could almost hear Collins taking a deep breath.

"I'm calling on behalf of Norman Jones. He wonders whether you would be available for a meeting with him tomorrow afternoon."

Lela thought his manner had changed dramatically from when she had first met him but knew that nothing would be gained by rubbing it in.

"Yes, I think so but for what purpose?"

It was not a daft question. Leila had been fobbed off in the past by different companies who had asked her for meetings and then had tried to pretend that it was Leila herself had asked for the meeting. That way the companies could claim that they had not refused to meet the union but in fact had made no move at all.

"It's about the strike and your claims—pay and the job evaluation system. Mr Jones thinks a meeting might be helpful—and—" he paused again—"he wonders whether you could call off the strike while we have the meeting."

Leila almost exploded: "you must be crazy, how on earth can we call off the strike at this hour? How can we contact anything up to two and a half thousand members on a Sunday evening?"

She calmed down and waited for his response.

"OK, Mrs Smith, I do understand that but Mr Jones asked me to put the point to you. Can we still meet tomorrow afternoon at, say, two thirty?"

"Can I phone you back," asked Leila, "I'll have to have a word with my colleagues. I won't be long. What's your number?"

Collins gave her his number. Apparently he was phoning Leila from his home.

Leila rang off and spoke to the others: "you probably gathered what that was about."

Bristow said "he's asked you to call off the strike? Just like that?"

Leila realised that they wouldn't have heard all of what Collins had said about a meeting. She explained and asked if they could all come to the meeting with her.

"Alan," she said, "you better remain here as the point of contact, but I think if the three of you—" looking at Macallister, Bristow and Davis—"came along, we might be hearing some positive news."

They all thought that a meeting could be good news, though, at first, Davis wondered whether the company would just be going through the motions for publicity purposes. "Remember," he added, "I'm one of those selected for redundancy and I don't trust them at all. However, I certainly think we should go."

Leila phoned Collins and told him she and the others would be at the head office by half past two in the afternoon and stressed that he explain to Norman Jones that there was no practical way the strike action could be suspended now on a Sunday evening. Collins repeated that he did appreciate that. She said that she assumed there was no harm in telling any newspapers that asked, that there would be a meeting. Collins said he couldn't see any problem with that. He seemed anxious to get off the phone as if phoning her about the meeting had been a most dangerous task. Hard luck, thought Leila.

"Now, just suppose," said Leila to the others: "if we get some good news at the meeting then we must consider how to get the news out and what to do about the strike."

They discussed possible scenarios at the meeting. Davis asked whether they should raise the question of the five hundred announced redundancies and Leila said they must raise it. Macallister wanted to know what pay offer they thought would be acceptable to the membership. Bristow queried how they could consult the national committee. Whitchurch got another round of drinks.

Leila then summarised what they had provisionally agreed: they should press the company on the redundancies—on making them voluntary and not compulsory and also pressing for significant increases over and above the minimum statutory pay requirements; as their pay offer was for an eight per cent increase across the board they should not settle for anything below five per cent; the company must accept the principle of the job evaluation scheme and agree to working out a plan for its implementation with the union.

Macallister grinned: "well, we've sorted that out, but it may all be pie in the sky. Suppose they suggested the meeting so they could read us the riot act—or worse, announce the closure of the company?"

The others were silent. Although Leila had thought of that as a possibility—though very remote—she had not mentioned it to anyone else. Anyway, given the plans of the bank that was taking over Industry3M, and given what Tiller had said to her on the plane, she thought that possibility was highly unlikely.

Just then Joe Turner of the *Liverpool Daily Post* approached them. Leila looked at her watch; it was a quarter past eight.

"Sorry to be late," said Turner. "I did get here earlier but saw you were all engaged in deep conversation so I thought I would wait." He smiled at Bristow and Davis and then said to Leila "I don't know your other two colleagues." Leila introduced him to Macallister and Whitchurch and asked him to sit down with them. Whitchurch asked what he would like to drink and then went to the bar to order another pint of bitter.

Turner explained that he had written his piece for the Monday morning edition but wondered whether there was any more background for the piece he would write for the Tuesday morning. He said that he had heard some rumours about a takeover of the company and asked Leila if there was anything she could tell him.

Leila thought she might as well that Turner the whole story. She gave him a copy of the Malaysian heads of agreement statement, told him about the takeover by the bank and then mentioned the call from Collins and the meeting with the company scheduled for the Monday afternoon.

"And the strike goes on?" asked Turner.

"Of course. The issue we were just discussing is how we deal with it if the company decides to negotiate properly with us and make us some offers." Leila didn't tell him what they had just decided for dealing with that. "The strike starts tomorrow and all indications are that it will be widely supported."

Turner had been scribbling furiously in his note book as Leila had been speaking. He looked round at the others and asked them if they had comments. Macallister replied that they were all optimistic that there would be a good turnout for the strike and also had a cautious welcome for the meeting with the company the next day. The others murmured agreement.

Turner then shut his note book and got to his feet. "I had better phone the office—I'll try and get in a piece about the meeting with the company and your comments about the likely turn out for the strike. Before I go, can I get you all a round of drinks?"

"Why not," said Whitchurch, "and, by the way if Leila is not here in the hotel tomorrow then I shall be."

"Thanks. I'll probably come round to the pickets in the morning and then catch up with you after your meeting—or, perhaps, you could phone me" he said, looking at Leila. She nodded.

Turner then got a round of drinks at the bar and waved them goodbye.

"This," said Bristow, "is almost too good to be true—"

"What? A journalist buying us a drink?" asked Davis.

Bristow smiled: "no. Two days ago we faced the prospect of an indefinite strike with no movement whatsoever from the company, a load of redundancies announced and I know a lot of members, determined as they are, were very apprehensive of what could happen."

"I know what you mean, Clive," said Macallister, "and that prospect could still face us tomorrow."

"Quite right, Ian," said Leila, "we shall have to see."

I got to the office by eight o'clock on the Monday morning. I knew the organisers would be phoning in soon afterwards with details as to how the strike at the Teening & Sykes plants and offices were going. I also wanted to speak to John Miller at the TUC and tell him about the heads of agreement between Industry3M and the Malaysian Commercial Workers Union.

Julia Cardon came into my office soon after I got there. She had the cuttings from the Sunday newspapers and this morning's. Overall the press coverage, though not great, was generally factual and—if anything—in our favour. Oliver Listle of the *Financial Times* had done quite a good piece. He had referred to the possibility of the bank taking over the company and also specifically mentioned the result of the Malaysian negotiations. Apparently he had got hold of Julia on the Sunday and she told him about the agreement. There was a note of caution in his piece—"it remains to be seen if agreement in Malaysia means agreement in the UK" but, I supposed, that was fair enough.

As the calls came in from the organisers I thought the two strikes were being well supported and there had been no problems with the picket lines. Surprisingly there had been no sign of the trots causing any trouble. Jack Treeman, the west midlands organiser, told me that he had been told the trots would be keeping a low profile to begin with but—if the Teening & Sykes management made no peace moves towards us, and particularly if the Industry3M strike dragged on for a while, then they would launch a big attack on the union's handling of the disputes.

I thanked Jack for the information and for his parting comment that I shouldn't let the bastards get me down. I then phoned Miller at the TUC and had a long chat with him over what was happening. He was upbeat in his view of how things would go. Apparently he had spoken to Dick Whetter the previous day and this morning had got a call from Bob Wilson, the minister of state at the DTI. Wilson had learnt of the agreement in Malaysia and also the impending takeover of Industry3M and the discussions Whetter was having with the DTI and the negotiating meeting planned for the Wednesday. Miller thought Wilson now appreciated that the job evaluation scheme of ours could be useful to a number of companies and was even criticising those who objected even to talking about it. I asked him whether Wilson had been on the road to Damascus and John had laughed.

I told John that I would keep him posted and he in turn said he would try and speak to Sir Malcolm Wise, the president of the CBI. Apparently he knew him reasonably well and thought quite highly of him.

Alan Whitchurch phoned me at ten o'clock and confirmed the organisers' view of how the two strikes were going. He told me that Leila was currently at the picket lines but would phone me later that morning.

I had sorted out most of the letters and reports that were in my in-tray by eleven o'clock when Leila phoned me. She had returned from the picket lines and said that all was well. She estimated that the same number of members were out on strike who been out before. The only difficulty had been at the company's IT department where there had only been two members on the picket line. They had told her that over half the IT staff had gone into work and there had been no sign of Tony Hammond or June Trevor. I suggested that that was both bad and good news and she agreed.

I told her about the reports from all the organisers and she mentioned that Alan Whitchurch had confirmed these and had been optimistic that things were going as well as reasonably could be expected. I also told her about my call to John Miller and she seemed pleased at that. She said she was meeting Macallister, Bristow and Davis at two o'clock at the hotel for a last minute chat before they went to the meting with the company. Then she outlined the steps they had proposed for contacting the national committee and the members throughout the company if there was definite progress at the meeting with the company. I wished her well.

***

Just before half past two o'clock Leila, accompanied by her three colleagues, went into the company's head office. The pickets outside gave them a rousing cheer and Leila promised to update them as soon as they had finished the meeting.

Inside the building Lionel Collins was waiting for them in the reception area and in a somewhat embarrassed way he greeted them and took them to the meeting room on the first floor. He didn't say any more than "hello, please come with me" and Leila didn't want to say anything to him either. As they entered the room Leila saw Norman Jones, the chief executive, and Joe Tiller both sitting down at the table. Jones didn't look up as they entered. Tiller did and smiled at them.

After they had sat down there was a silence. Then Leila said "I think you know my three colleagues, Mr Jones, but for the record I will introduce them with their union positions." She did so and then asked "you suggested this meeting, Mr Jones, so what have you got to say?"

Jones cleared his throat: "thank you for coming. I want to ask Mr Tiller to speak first." He nodded to Tiller.

Tiller said "we see that you managed to cross the picket lines". It was a weak joke, thought Leila, but then perhaps Tiller would not be familiar with industrial disputes and their practices. She responded "and then I see that you also crossed the lines."

Tiller smiled again: "let's cut the crap" he said abruptly. "We have asked you to this meeting in order to sort out the dispute."

"And? How do you suggest we do sort it out? You know our claims and what we have been urging for some time. And you've got over half your staff on strike and they want to know—as we do—what you propose." Leila was short and brutal in her remarks.

Tiller said that the company had been having a lot of discussion recently and wanted to see if there was anyway they could resolve the dispute and get on with their business of recruiting contract staff and supplying them to companies. "That's what our business is," he said, "and we want to get on with it."

There was another silence. Then Leila said "there's three issues—apart from the overall position of the union in the company to which you—"looking directly at Norman Jones—"have referred in the past. The issues are the redundancy notices, our pay claim and our claim for the introduction of the job evaluation scheme."

Tiller looked at Jones and then responded: "we've got something to say about all points but first I must ask you to call off the strike so we do not talk to you with this action going on."

Leila replied that there was no way they could call off the strike at the moment. If they did make some progress on the three issues then they might consider suspending the action—but it was up to the company to respond to the three issues they had raised. There was another silence.

To Leila's surprise Norman Jones then spoke.

"As Mr Tiller said, we want to get down the basics—although he did put it more colloquially—" Leila smiled—she had not heard any glimmer of humour from him before—"and I think I ought to explain where we now are."

"Good idea, Mr Jones," said Leila. "We would appreciate that."

"I think you will have heard that the First American Bank have made an offer for the shares of Industry 3M and the executive board of our company is recommending acceptance of it. We expect the bank to have bought the majority of the shares by the time the New York stock exchange closes today, Monday."

Jones' tone was precise and unemotional. He continued: "the bank, as the new owners, will be announcing tomorrow—assuming all goes well—the names of the new chairman of the company and its chief executive. Mr Harold Stuckman—" he paused.

Leila broke in: "Mr Stuckman junior".

"Quite so, Mrs Smith." Jones couldn't help smiling a little as he said that. He went on: "Mr Stuckman junior will become the president of the company, president emeritus I believe they are calling his position, and the new international executive director will be Mr Tiller here. I myself will be taking early retirement in a couple of months and they are considering who my successor will be. You may recall Mr John Carr from our European head office—" Leila nodded—"and he will be leaving us at the end of this year and again the new owners are considering whom to appoint as his successor. As for Industry3M in the UK, we shall be appointing a new personnel director. In the meantime Mr Collins here will continue to act as acting head."

Leila and the others digested the information Jones had given them. Macallister spoke first: "it's all change then, Mr Jones."

Jones replied that it was indeed all change and therefore he proposed that Tiller should conduct the rest of the meeting for the company. He lent back in his chair and breathed heavily. Leila thought he looked relieved now that he had spelt out what was going to happen. She noted that Collins was looking distinctly unhappy: presumably, she thought, because he might have been given an indication that the new head of personnel for the UK company would not be him.

"Let us be clear, Mrs Smith and colleagues," said Tiller. "First American want to start with a clean sheet and, as I have already said, we want to get on with our business. I hear what you say about not calling off the strike and I regret it. However I am authorised to respond to the three issues you have mentioned and then perhaps we'll see where we go from there."

Leila's pulse was racing. So far, so very good. If only the company had said that when they met in the summer, which seemed so long ago, and perhaps all the anxiety, meetings, speeches, strikes and emotions of the last months would have been avoided. But she knew that this was now and there seemed—from Tiller's words—an opportunity to make real progress.

"Right," said Tiller, "your three issues. First, we are prepared to suspend the redundancy notices and introduce a short period during which we will call for volunteers for redundancy. We shall also discuss with you specific redundancy payments over and above the statutory minimum requirements. But, so there's no misunderstanding, if we don't get enough volunteers, then we shall have to consider compulsory redundancies—" Leila opened her mouth to speak but Tiller held up a hand—"but we'll have to discuss that with you at a later date. But, be clear, we are currently over staffed and the numbers have to be reduced. If, as we hope, our business expands then we might well start recruiting staff again, but for the moment we have to reduce numbers."

Bristow whispered to Leila "not too bad, so far" and she nodded.

"On the issue of pay, well you haven't made any rationale for the substantial increase you have claimed nor do we know what your arguments are—" again Leila opened her mouth to speak and again Tiller held up a hand—"but we have looked at settlements elsewhere and taken advice and so as to make progress I am authorised to propose an across the board increase of five per cent backdated to the first of July this year."

Tiller could see that Leila and her three colleagues were all anxious to say something but he quickly carried on: "as for the job evaluation scheme you have put forward, we have now had a chance to examine it in some detail and again have taken advice. We think the scheme has potential and are prepared to accept it in principle and discuss with you how best to implement it."

Tiller sat back and watched their faces.

Macallister was the first to say something: "I never thought I would actually meet Father Christmas in person, or that he came from America."

Leila said that she thought that what Macallister meant to say was that they would like a recess so they could consider the import of what Tiller had said. Macallister grinned and said that that was indeed what he had meant to say. Tiller asked Leila if she was pleased: Leila replied that she would answer that question after the recess.

"One point before we recess, however," she said. "In view of the statements made to us before by the company—both verbally and in writing—can we be assured that the company will continue to observe the terms of our procedural agreement with you: in other words, Mr Tiller, that the union will be fully recognised for collective bargaining purposes.?"

Tiller confirmed that that would be the case. Leila and her colleagues then got up and went out of the room. Collins, still saying nothing, went with them and took them to another room.

"Well," said Ted Davis as they all sat down and after Collins had left them, "Leila, what do you think of it so far?"

"First," replied Leila, "we must get what Tiller has said about union recognition in writing and that must go out throughout the company. That's the bottom line. And the three offers—what do you all think? I would prefer to hear your comments and then tell you what I think."

They all thought there had been a fundamental change in the company's attitude.—as Clive Bristow said "there can't be anything else to say, can there?" Macallister said that he thought the national committee would be very pleased; Bristow then said he would be prepared to suspend the strike while they carried on discussions; Davis said he didn't like the point Tiller had made about over staffing but he recognised the statement about calling for redundancy volunteers and the prospect of more pay for those who went.

Leila pursued Bristow's point: should they suspend the strike action and could they get the message out in time? They discussed this for about ten minutes. The time was getting on for a quarter to four and if they were going to contact the national committee then it had to be soon. Leila thought, why am I always fighting time? There never seemed enough time to do everything that needed to be done. But then, she reminded herself, she wanted the job, didn't she?

Leila summarised what she thought they ought to do: fix a negotiating meeting with the company for a few days time; phone round the national committee and get their agreement to suspend the strike in the light of the company's proposals and a further negotiating meeting; all going well, they could announce the decision at each of the open meetings being held that evening: Alan Whitchurch and the regional organisers had arranged for open meetings to be held in the eight towns and cities where the company had offices, as well as in Liverpool, the site of the head office. They would have to rely on the branch officers in the eight offices phoning round the members.

Leila added that she would ask Whitchurch to get out a message detailing the company's proposals by fax to all the offices in the morning and Leila said she would follow up with a newsletter when she got back to her office the next day. Macallister said that the company would undoubtedly want to send out a circular to all its staff. Leila agreed but stressed that the union must send out the information itself—the members deserved to hear the news from the union irrespective of when the company sent it out.

Macallister looked at his watch and said they ought to be getting back if they were going to do all the things they had agreed.

The first issue Leila raised when they got back inside the meeting room was a further negotiating meeting to carry forward the company's proposals. Tiller agreed and they fixed the meeting for the following Monday morning. He then asked about calling off the strike now. Leila replied that—assuming the company would put its proposals, as outlined by Joe Tiller, in writing then they would move quickly and try for agreement to suspend the strike. She outlined what they had agreed during the recess.

Tiller pushed a piece of paper across the table: "you can have the proposals in writing now." Leila glanced at them. It was all written down. She said that in the light of that they would suspend the strike so they had better adjourn now and would start making telephone calls. Tiller offered the use of the head office but Leila said they would prefer to do it from her hotel.

Just as the four of them were leaving Tiller motioned Leila to one side: "a quiet word, if I may." The others had left the room and didn't see Tiller pull Leila to one side. He whispered to her "I hope this could be the start of a new era with the union," Leila said she hoped so too. He then lowered his voice even more ; "what would you think about taking the job of head of personnel here?"

Leila opened her mouth in astonishment: "what? No, certainly not. Never."

Tiller made a quietening gesture with his hand: "OK, I'm only asking. Don't be too affronted. The terms and conditions would be pretty good."

Leila calmed down: "I am sure they would be, but no, no thanks. I'm happy where I am."

Tiller reassured her "It's just my suggestion and shall we keep this conversation to ourselves?"

Leila agreed and said she would tell no one about it. Then, relenting a little from her stance of outrage, she said "I appreciate the offer, Joe, but I couldn't possibly even consider it."

"OK, enough said. See you next Monday then and here's my card. If you want to get hold of me in the meantime, just give me a ring." He handed Leila his business card and she noted his mobile number on it. She hurried down the stairs to the ground floor reception and caught up with the others there. She explained that Tiller had just wanted to confirm the arrangements for the following Monday's meeting and had agreed that the union could release the proposals to the press if they wanted.

"I'm dying for a drink or two," Bristow said, "but I suppose we must get on with the telephoning." Leila assured him there would be time for several drinks after they had made all the arrangements and after the open meeting that evening—"then we really shall have earned it".

The two day strike in Teening & Sykes seemed to have got off to a good start. The reports all indicated a reasonable turnout and there had been no sign of any major problems.

Then about midday I had a telephone call from John Miller at the TUC. He had spoken to Sir Malcolm Wise the president of the CBI. He in turn had spoken to David Adnam the chief of Teening & Sykes. Apparently Wise had been impressed by the decision of the DTI, particularly its permanent secretary, to start proper discussions with the civil service union about the job evaluation scheme. Then Miller had told him about the heads of agreement in Malaysia and the deal between the Malaysian union and Industry3M. Wise had told Miller that he would speak to David Adnam and urge him to, at least, ask his people to talk to the union.

I thanked John for his call and his efforts. I said that I was expecting a call from Leila in the late afternoon and would keep him posted.

Mathew Singh, our national officer for Teening & Sykes was in Sunderland during the strike. It was either Sunderland or Plymouth and in the end he had thought Sunderland would be best. It was the largest plant of the company and not too far from some of the company's other plants in the north-east. We had considered picketing the company's head office but it was only a small office in central London and I didn't think we actually had any members there, so we had decided to leave it alone.

By half past four o'clock I had dealt with all the phone calls and papers and was chatting to Julia Cardon in my office. We went through various scenarios for a press conference, depending on what Leila would tell me about her meeting with Industry3M.

She telephoned me just after five. She had got back to the hotel and her three colleagues were phoning round the national committee on their mobiles with the result of the meeting. Leila told me the result of the meeting and then read out the text of the proposals which Tiller had handed her. She said she would get the hotel to fax it through.

It appeared from the phone calls they were making that all the members of the national committee they had spoken to were in favour of suspending the strike and then awaiting the result of the negotiating meeting scheduled for the following Monday. The only exception apparently was Tony Hammond.

Macallister had offered to be the one to phone him. Hammond had said it was far too premature to suspend the action and had, to be fair, made a valid point that once industrial action was suspended it would be very difficult to reinstate it. Macallister had said to him that the other committee members, of course, had all been aware of that but in view of the company's written offers they were all in favour of suspending the strike—even including, Leila had been pleased to note, Jean Asah from Leeds who was thought to be a follower of Tony Hammond.

I asked Leila about notifying the members and she outlined what they had agreed. She would be speaking now to Alan Whitchurch about contacting the regional organisers. It was a bit messy but it would be absurd to continue with the strike the next day in the light of all that happened. I agreed with her and said I would do a quick e-mail message to the national executive committee members and follow up with phone calls to the three senior honorary officials.

I could see Julia Cardon mouthing something at me while I was speaking.

"Just a minute, Leila, I'll put Julia on to you."

Julia Cardon asked Leila about any press embargoes and whether she had been contacted by any journalist. Leila told her about speaking to Joe Turner the previous evening and how he had said he would be at the open meeting. They discussed the best way of getting a decent press coverage. In the end Julia suggested that we hold a press conference tomorrow afternoon. In the meantime she would send out a press statement to the effect that Industry3M had made offers and it was likely the union would suspend the industrial action. She would also phone Oliver Listle of the *Financial Times* and brief him.

I said to Julia that she should ask Leila to phone Chuck Pitney of the *Wall Street Journal* and I could see her smile as I said that.

"John suggests," said Julia to Leila, "that you phone Chuck Pitney with the news, but I imagine you have that in mind anyway." She chuckled at Leila's response.

Leila got to the Friends Meeting House, where the meeting was, at six o'clock. It had been a hectic time in the hotel where they had made all their phone calls. Leila had thought it best to start the meeting at six thirty: this would allow for members to come straight from the pickets which stood down at six. She reasoned that if they started later then many members might go home and not turn out again. The meeting room could take about a hundred people sitting down but with space for quite a few more standing round the sides of the room. She remembered the first meeting in the summer when the place had been packed. She remembered too the incident of the egg and how that had turned out to be a big success for her. She hoped, though, that the incident would not be repeated: her aim might not be so good this time.

As before, Clive Bristow, as the chairman of the head office branch of the union, would take chair at the open meeting and again they had arranged for Ted Davis to move a resolution at the appropriate time—appropriate, Leila thought, when questions had been asked and the mood was judged to be right.

She was pleased at the reaction of the Industry3M national committee to the news of the company's proposals but knew that the key to the meeting would be to be realistic: the company had made a u-turn in its attitude to the union. The pay offer was reasonable and the decision to accept the job evaluation scheme in principle was a major breakthrough. There would always be those, though, who—having embarked on the indefinite strike—would want to go on. She had to convince them that it was time now to conclude an agreement with the company and carry on the negotiations in a week's time.

She knew that the redundancy issue would be difficult. There would be those who would argue that now the company had moved, then the union should press for the company to abandon its redundancy proposals altogether. The chances of that, however, were slight if non-existent but to put that across to the meeting might be difficult. It was the only sensible course, though, and she hoped that people like Davis speaking from the floor would reinforce the wisdom of agreeing to the company's proposals as the basis of a settlement.

Leila saw Joe Turner of the *Liverpool Daily Post* enter the room and waved to him. He came over to her.

"You've scored a victory" he told her. "Congratulations."

Leila smiled at him: "thank you, Joe, but we've got to see how the meeting goes."

Turner looked surprised "but you've got what you wanted."

Leila replied "I think so, yes. But some may well have the bit between their teeth now. And they are all only human beings. But, we shall see."

The room was filling up and a number of members came over to Leila and said they had heard the good news. They all looked pleased and she could sense excitement among them. She wished she could have had more time to prepare what she was going to say as in many ways the decision whether to suspend or call off any industrial action was always the real test of a trade union leader. But time, as ever, was short and there had been no opportunity to work out her speech in detail.

Just before half past six o'clock Bristow called them all to order. All the chairs were now full and there were, Leila guessed, about another eighty or so people standing round the room. She wished she had time to get the written proposals from the company circulated beforehand but that had not been possible.

Bristow announced that he was asking Leila to speak to the meeting, would then take questions and comments and said he had been advised of a resolution that had been agreed with the national committee.

Leila spoke for about thirty five minutes. She briefly rehearsed the origins of the dispute and the union's claims. She mentioned the takeover bid by the First American Bank and the likely changes in the management structure that might result but was careful not go into too much detail as they had not been formally announced by the company yet. She told them about the result of discussions between the company and the Malaysian Commercial Workers Union and then went over the result of the meeting she and her colleagues had held that afternoon. She read out the written statement the company had given her. There were a few cheers as she did so and the atmosphere seemed good. She mentioned the national committee's decision as a result of the phone round that the strike be suspended and how that decision was being communicated to the members. Then, after a few factual questions on the proposals had been asked and answered, it happened.

Bristow saw that Tony Hammond had been holding his hand up as soon as Leila had finished speaking and he now called upon him to speak.

"Brother chair," said Hammond in his thin and rather nasal voice, "I don't think the company's proposals go anywhere near far enough. The threatened redundancies are still there. The pay offer isn't good enough—" there were a few groans as he said that—"and what does accepting the job evaluation scheme in principle actually mean?"

Leila got up to answer his points but Hammond continued: "and I listened with interest to Mrs Smith saying there would be some management changes at the top. Perhaps Mrs Smith could say something about the company offering to make her the new head of personnel."

There was a stunned silence in the room, quickly followed by a buzz of excitement as people digested Hammond's words. Leila was amazed: how on earth had Hammond learned of that? It was a confidential discussion between her and Joe Tiller. No one else could have known about it. Had Tiller deliberately told others about it—and for what purpose? If he couldn't be trusted over that, then what price all the talk about starting with a clean sheet and a new relationship with the union?

Leila hadn't told Macallister or the others about the offer Tiller had made her and she could see Bristow looking at her with concern. She stood up.

"First, Mr chairman, the factual points. The company want to reduce the number of people they employ—but they are going to ask for volunteers and they have agreed to negotiate with us over levels of redundancy pay. We'll be doing that at next Monday's negotiating meeting and in the meantime the company will withdraw the earlier redundancy notices they issued."

As she spoke she could see the meeting calming down and she went on: "five per cent is their pay offer and we have to consider that against pay increases in other companies, the prices index and a host of other factors and, again, we'll discuss that at next Monday's meeting. And the acceptance of the job evaluation scheme in principle means that they will introduce the scheme—and we have to make sure, after negotiations, that the implementation will be fair and effective"

She could see a number of heads nodding as she spoke but could sense an uneasiness still amongst many. She knew she then had to tackle Hammond's point about the job offer directly. She looked straight at him.

"I don't know who you have been talking to about the so called job offer made to me, Tony. In fact I have often wondered about the source of some of your comments in the past—"

She paused and could see that her point had gone home. Hammond was not popular with many in the company and his previous actions and statements—although many did not know about his behaviour at the annual TUC congress—had not endeared him to the majority of the members who came across him in the national committee or at other meetings.

"Yes, it's true that an official of the company did make that offer verbally to me earlier today." There was a further pause and she could see that they were all waiting for what she would say next. "And it's equally true that as soon as the offer was made, I completely rejected it. I can't prevent the company from saying what they did, but I can say that there are no circumstances whereby I could accept any job within the company. I was surprised they made the offer, I didn't want it and I do not wish to be anything other than an official of this union—a union I am proud to serve. I can only wonder at why the company made the suggestion—and, more importantly, why someone chose to tell you, Mr Hammond, about it."

There was a big round of applause as Leila said that. She breathed a sigh of relief. Her words had gone down well and she could see Bristow smile at her. Hammond made no attempt to speak again.

But she was still seething at what she regarded as a disgraceful trick played by Joe Tiller. She hadn't asked for a job with the company, nor would she have entertained the notion of one: had Tiller made the suggestion so as to deliberately undermine her? And could it really have been Tiller who had spoken to Hammond? As far as she knew, there was no reason why Tiller should have any knowledge of who Hammond was.

Before she could pursue her thoughts she heard Bristow call on Ted Davis to move his resolution.

"Mr chairman," he started, "before I read out the words of the resolution can I express the thanks of myself—and, I am sure of all union members in Industry3M—to Mrs Leila Smith for her leadership and skill in conducting our dispute with the company." There was a large burst of applause as he said that and several cries of 'hear, hear'.

He went on: "the resolution reads 'this meeting of union members notes the written proposals by Industry3M in response to our claims of June 2007 and that a further negotiating meeting is to be held on Monday 29 October 2007. Further, this meeting congratulates Mrs Smith, the deputy general secretary of the union and the officers of the national committee on the progress made in pursuing the union's claims. This meeting therefore endorses the decision of the Industry3M national committee of the union in suspending the current strike action while negotiations continue."

There was some more applause after Davis had finished reading the resolution. Bristow then asked him if he wanted to say anything more.

Davis said he would like to add some further points: "It may well be that we can't stop redundancies. It's happening everywhere throughout the economy and it's a fact of life. And before anyone shouts, may I remind the meeting that I was on the original list. But we've got the company to agree to asking for volunteers and to negotiate with us over redundancy payments—before, it was compulsory and no payment over and above the statutory minimum. I think we've made progress."

Bristow called for a seconder for the resolution and a number of hands shot up. He asked for any more speakers. Macallister got to his feet and Bristow gestured for him to speak.

"For those here who don't know me, I'm Ian Macallister, the chairman of the national committee. I'm from Glasgow and we speak frankly there. So I don't apologise for doing so now." He looked round the room and saw he had their attention. "And I want to say that in essence we have won the dispute. Don't lets talk this down. Yes, we've got negotiations next Monday and possibly after that—but look at the company's written proposals. Who would have thought we could have got anything like them even a few days ago? This is one of the few occasions in today's world where a trade union—our union—has forced a company—an American owned company, I must add—to move from a position of outright hostility and no offers at all to one where we have realistic offers on all points. And the introduction of our job evaluation scheme will, in my view, be of major benefit to all our members both now and in the future."

This time the applause was thunderous. Bristow said he would put the resolution to the vote. A forest of hands went up in favour and, when he called for those who wished to vote against, there were no hands showing. He declared the resolution carried and that the meeting was now closed.

As the nearly two hundred members who had been at the meeting all went out of the building, most of them heading to the nearest pub, Leila said to Bristow that she would catch up with him in a few moments: first, she wanted to make a phone call.

She stood outside the main entrance to the Friends Meeting House and once the crowd had gone away she phoned Joe Tiller on her mobile. He answered almost immediately and from the background noise Leila assumed he was at a restaurant.

"Is that you, Mr Tiller—Joe?"

The American voice answered that it was indeed him. He recognised Leila's voice: "how did your meeting go, Leila? All well, I hope?"

"Yes—except for one thing." She told him about Hammond's reference to the job offer by the company. She was keeping her temper in check but Tiller could sense that she was very annoyed.

"How could you do that, Joe? I thought we were building a position of trust between the company and the union and between you and me. Now you've blown it—"

"Hey, hang on, Leila. It wasn't me." His voice was tinged with a bit of desperation. As far as Leila could tell, he must have realised the import of what she had told him.

"Come off it, Joe. We agreed we would keep the matter confidential between us: so why did you tell Hammond?"

"I didn't, Leila. I promise you that I didn't—" he broke off, paused and then said "oh my God, I know what happened." He told her that during the recess at their meeting in the afternoon Norman Jones had asked Tiller when he would make the job offer to Leila. He said to Leila that he and Jones had discussed the matter before and he—Jones—had gone along with Tiller's suggestion of the job. Tiller had said he would put the idea to Leila after that meeting.

"Of course, that little shit Collins was in the room. He didn't say anything but must have realised the significance of the exchange between Jones and myself. It must have been him who told Hammond. The bastard."

Leila thought quickly. It could be true. She remembered how it was Collins who put up the young man Curtis to throw the egg at her at the original meeting in the summer. She recalled her brief meeting with him and its abortive result. Clearly he had nailed his colours to the mast of defeating the union. He must have been in touch with Hammond on a number of occasions. Yes, it all made sense.

"Are you still there Leila?" She could hear that Tiller was a bit upset. She said she was listening.

"You may have noticed Collins' expression when Norman Jones told your team about the senior management changes. I guess that Collins blames the union for not getting the personnel job. You must believe me, Leila. We do want to get off to a fresh start with your union so please don't think I deliberately told anyone about it. I wish now I had never made the offer. And don't worry, I'll sort the little bugger out."

Leila said she believed him and wouldn't mention it again and she wasn't worrying: whatever he did to Collins, she didn't want to know.

He asked about the mood of the meeting and she told him the result of the vote on the resolution that Ted Davis had moved. Tiller sounded pleased and said the company would be pleased to try and conclude the outstanding issues at their meeting the following Monday. Leila replied that she hoped they could reach agreement on all the issues then and then rang off.

It was time to join the others in the pub.

❦

Leila had told me that she hoped to be in the office by eleven o'clock, assuming there was no hold up on the Liverpool train. I had called the other officials for a meeting in my office at noon. I was looking through the press cuttings that Julia Cardon had handed to me when I had arrived, when the phone rang. The telephone receptionist told me that the caller was a Mr Adnam and I told her to put him through.

"Hello. John Carmichael here."

"Mr Carmichael, it's David Adnam from Teening & Sykes. I wanted a private word."

The only time I had really met Adnam was when we went to the meeting at the CBI and, to put it mildly, he had not exactly been helpful then. I waited for him to continue.

"I've been speaking to Sir Malcolm Wise and he suggested I speak to you."

I waited again. I was damned if I was going to make the running in the conversation, but I was pleased that Malcolm Wise had spoken to him. I assumed that that might have been prompted by John Miller from the TUC.

"You may think I'm a bit of reactionary, Mr Carmichael"—that to my mind was a considerable under statement—"but I am also a realist. I have seen the press reports which indicate that your union and Industry3M are close to an agreement on your claims and that the strike there has been suspended."

I still said nothing.

"I also understand that the DTI is negotiating with the union there over the job evaluation scheme that you lodged with us as well."

I thought I had to say something so I said "yes, I believe that there are going to be some negotiations involving the DTI permanent secretary tomorrow and, as far as Industry3M is concerned, there is a further negotiating meeting next Monday where I think there is a good chance of making an agreement on the outstanding issues."

Leila had telephoned me last night and in spite of the loud noise I could hear from the pub where she was, I gathered that everything had gone well. She had then phoned me again from the train this morning.

"Well," said Adnam, "you've got your second strike day today with my staff"—it was a funny way of putting, I thought—"and I thought I might suggest that you and your colleagues come to my offices on Thursday to see if we can settle our differences."

It was tremendous news. David Adnam, known as a hard man throughout union circles and, indeed, in the CBI, was suggesting a meeting with my union to, as he said, to 'settle our differences'.

"I think that would be a good idea," I told him. I'll have a word with my national officer who deals with your company—"

Adnam broke in: "I want you at the meeting, Mr Carmichael."

I paused. Mathew Singh was the national officer concerned and the person who would ordinarily lead any negotiations in Teening & Sykes. He would still be up at Sunderland coordinating things there on the second day of the strike. I knew that some union officials would complain bitterly if they thought they were being superseded by their general secretary. Union officials were as status conscious—if not more so—than any managements in companies. I could see though that Adnam would want me there as he was reputedly very status conscious too.

"I was going to say, Mr Adnam, that I will have a word with Mr Singh and I am sure he will be able to come with me to the meeting you propose."

"Ah well," said Adnam, "that's fine. Perhaps you will confirm with me later today."

I assured him I would phone him later and thanked him for his call.

It seemed to me that things were now happening fast. For months we had met resistance from companies—to say nothing of problems with the DTI minister and others—and now we were within sight of getting agreement with Industry3M and Teening & Sykes, at least that's what I hoped would be the case as that must be the point of the meeting that Adnam had proposed. And if Dick Whetter's union did get an agreement with the DTI on the job evaluation scheme that would be seen as a significant breakthrough in the public sector. Then there were the claims we had in with Hokkaido, the Japanese owned motor car manufacturer, Transport International and now—after their initial delay—Leisure & Sport. I would discuss this with the officials at our midday meeting: but there seemed no reason why our claims shouldn't now proceed smoothly. The dam had been breached.

I finished reading the press cuttings. They had all been positive and Joe Turner in the *Liverpool Daily Post* had done quite a big piece including a report of the previous night's meeting and the stuff about Leila's alleged job offer. Julia Cardon and I discussed whether to still hold a full scale press conference this afternoon but now came down in favour of a conference the next Monday. If Leila finished her meeting with Industry3M in the morning and then got the train back to London we should be able to hold the press conference about five or six o'clock that early evening. We didn't want to hold it any later because we might miss some of the first editions of the newspapers and the early television news programmes. Like a lot of things these days in industrial relations, it was partly a question of timing.

When Leila came into the office just after eleven o'clock she looked tired but happy. I congratulated her again on the progress made in Industry3M and told her about David Adnam's call from Teening & Sykes. I handed her the press cuttings and said that, on balance, Julia and I had agreed to hold the press conference next Monday rather than one before then. That way we should have some news on not only Industry3M and the meeting with Teening & Sykes but also the other companies where we had submitted claims and hopefully also by then Dick Whetter would have made some progress with the DTI. And I proposed to have another word with Peter Moorhouse of the Commercial & Technology Union: perhaps there would be a better chance now for merger talks in the future but I would have to play that quietly for the moment.

Leila agreed and said she would update the other officials on what had happened since their last meeting. Yes, she said, it did all look promising.

❦

Leila breathed a huge sigh of relief as she and her union team came out of the Industry3M UK head office building in Liverpool on the following Monday. Their negotiating meeting with the company had just ended and they had concluded an agreement. This time there had been only two representatives present for the company: Norman Jones, the chief executive and Joe Tiller. She had noted that Lionel Collins was not there and imagined that Tiller must have done something about him since the meeting the previous week.

It was now nearly half past twelve and she had to catch the two o'clock train from Liverpool Lime Street. She suggested that they went for a drink in the railway station bar so she would be sure of not missing her train.

On the previous Wednesday Leila had called a meeting of the national committee and, given the relationship now between the company and the union, there had been no problem about getting leave of absence for the meeting to be held in working time. As before the meeting had been held in London; the tone of the meeting this time had been very upbeat and the committee had congratulated Leila and the negotiators on their success so far. They had also agreed that—at a pinch—the pay offer of five percent could be accepted, that the negotiators should get what they could in terms of extra redundancy pay and firm up the position on the new job evaluation scheme. Tony Hammond, she had noted, had not attended the national committee meeting and no one had seemed to know why.

Now, after the negotiating meeting with the company was over, Leila reckoned that there would be agreement all round the national committee on the basis of what had just been concluded. Leila had promised to telephone Tiller later that day after the members of the national committee had confirmed acceptance. In the event, the pay offer had been increased to five and a half per cent, backdated to the first of July and redundancy pay—over and above the statutory amounts—was to be one and a half week's pay for each completed year of service. The company had said they hoped there would be enough volunteers now to avoid any compulsory redundancies. On the job evaluation scheme, the company and the union had agreed to issue a joint statement accepting that the scheme should be introduced in principle and that a joint company-union committee would be established to determine how best to implement the scheme. The timescale for the scheme's introduction was aimed at three month's hence.

Leila had taken Macalister, Bristow, Davis and also Jean Asah from Leeds, to the meeting with the company and all were very pleased with the result. Leila had also asked Jean Asah if she knew why Hammond had not been at the national committee the previous Wednesday but she said she had no idea. "And I don't really care," she had added.

Leila insisted on buying the first drinks in the station bar and, when they had sat down, she thanked them for all their efforts both in the meeting that morning and throughout the dispute. They discussed the mechanics of getting the news out and Macallister said they must use the agreement for a big recruitment drive in the company. Leila said she would ask Alan Whitchurch as national organiser to have a word with him about that. She also said she would get out a newsletter to all the members in the company and would try and dictate one to her secretary when she phoned her from the train.

She had told them the previous evening when they had met again in the hotel bar that the negotiating meeting at Teening & Sykes, that Carmichael and the leaders of their national committee in the company had held with David Adnam and his personnel director on the previous Thursday, had also been positive: and Carmichael had told her it was obvious that the news about Industry3M had been the central factor that had changed Adnam's whole attitude. They too had agreed a that a joint company and union committee would look at how to implement the job evaluation scheme. She had said then that they should press for that with Industry3M and this they had agreed.

Leila asked Macallister to oversee the phoning of the national committee that afternoon and he said he would phone Leila as soon as the phone round was complete and she would then phone Tiller. Ted Davis said he was sure there would be no dissent from the national committee to ratifying the deal of that morning providing, he added, that they were unable to contact Tony Hammond. Leila insisted that they did try and contact him—they couldn't afford to go outside union procedure. However difficult, Hammond was an elected member of the national committee and had the right to be consulted. Whether he would observe the same procedures if the boot was on the other foot was, Leila said, immaterial.

Then. looking at her watch, she realised that she would have to be quick to catch the two o'clock train. She downed her drink, thanked them again all for their efforts and rushed out of the bar. As she went they all called goodbye and wished her well.

It was always a question of time, she thought, as she got on to the train and sat down in her carriage. She had had a busy day yesterday, Sunday. She had arranged to go to her daughter's for lunch and she knew should couldn't let her down again—particularly as Helen, her grand daughter, would be most upset if she did. So she had gone to Deborah's house, but had left them shortly after lunch to get the Liverpool train and had arrived at the hotel just after seven o'clock in the evening. She had arranged to meet the others in the hotel bar and they were already waiting for her when she arrived.

Yes, she thought, time was always at a premium—but there were lots of things to do. She had hoped to spend the previous Thursday and Friday in the office catching up on all the work that had been piling up during her absences. As it happened she had been unable to do so. At the TUC General Council meeting on the Wednesday Len Arkwright, the TUC deputy general secretary, had button holed her and said there had been a last minute cancellation by one of the three union officials earmarked to sit on a TUC disputes committee on the Friday of that week. The disputes procedure was central to the TUC's authority and relationship with its affiliated unions and she could hardly turn down Arkwright's request.

The dispute was over a recruitment battle between two unions in the construction industry and one of the three man TUC nominated panel had fallen ill. It was a high profile case and Leila could understand why they wanted a reasonably senior General Council member—as she was—to stand in for him. She was an obvious candidate and had agreed. The disputes committee had sat all day on the Friday and she had spent most of the Thursday evening at home in reading the papers for the disputes committee.

On the Thursday she had attended a meeting of the union's administration committee and that too had taken all day: John

Carmichael had attended for a couple of hours and then had gone to the Teening & Sykes meeting. She had hoped to get to the office early that day and spend an hour looking over all the papers in her in-tray but there had been a breakdown on the railway line from Wimbledon and she had spent that hour frustratingly on the train until it was fixed.

It was basically now two weeks since she last been able to spend some time sorting our her correspondence, read the many papers on her desk, make a number of phone calls and check her diary.

She saw the steward pushing the refreshment trolley along the carriage and bought a cup of coffee from him. Then she thought she ought to start telephoning. There were immediate things to do.

She phoned Carmichael on her mobile and told him about the agreement they had now made with Industry3M and how the national committee was being phoned to secure their acceptance. He told her he was very pleased and then told her that he had got a phone call from Jim Bradwell of the local government union that morning. Apparently the Labour members on the local authorities' negotiating body had managed to get the majority on it to agree to open negotiations with the union over the introduction of the job evaluation scheme. What with that, and Dick Whetter's successful meeting with the DTI the previous week, it seemed good news all round.

"It was the Industry3M breakthrough that did all this," Carmichael said.

Leila responded "it was the Malaysian union that was the key to that."

"With your help, Leila."

She thanked him and then asked him to put her through to her secretary. She dictated a short newsletter on the Industry3M agreement to Muriel and asked her to make arrangements to send it out—but only after she had checked with Ian Macallister that the national committee was in agreement.

"Apart from Industry3M there's a number of things, Leila, that are pending because I haven't had a chance to go over them with you" Muriel said. Leila took a deep breath and told her to start.

"Well, there's a couple of companies that Tim Burke would normally have dealt with if he was not still off on sick leave. Their national committees are asking you to go to their meetings and both companies are pressing for negotiating meeting dates. I've told the two national committee chairmen that you do hope to go to their meetings and I've told the two companies' personnel people that you will deal with negotiating dates when you get back here. There's a couple of the union regional councils who would like you to speak at their next council meetings and I said I would get back to them after speaking to you. Then, there's Sam Askari—he has been pressing me several times now as to when he and the other staff representatives here can talk to you about their pay claim. As you know the implementation date is now long gone."

Leila groaned inwardly. That had not yet been dealt with amid all the activity of the last few weeks. Still, she must deal with it soonest.

"Then there's the arrangements for the week end school that Jack Treeman has at the end of this week in Coventry. You will remember that some weeks ago you had agreed to speak at it."

Muriel ploughed on. "I've had a call from the Industrial Foundation asking you to speak at a seminar next week and I've also told Per Ulric from the Swedish union and Jurgen Bruch from Germany that you will speak to them as soon as you can. They both phoned this morning. I know that John Carmichael has spoken to van Megeren at Staff International but both Ulric and Bruch insisted that they wanted to speak you."

Leila's head was whirling.

"Nothing else, Muriel?" she said wearily.

Muriel laughed: "Well, yes, there is. The trustees want to fix a meeting with you and Peter Berenson, the treasurer, about the union's financial position." She could sense how all these matters must be piling up in Leila's mind. "I know, Leila, but there's many other things on hold too. As you well know, whenever one industrial dispute is solved—and congratulations by the way—the rest of the world still spins: life goes on."

Leila knew she was quite right. She had been so involved in the Industry3M dispute that she knew there were many other matters that she hadn't got round to. She told Muriel she would go over it all with her in the morning.

She thought she would now phone Ulric in Sweden and Bruch in Germany and bring them up to date on the Industry3M position. She hoped they would both now be able to conclude agreements with the Industry3M subsidiaries in their countries. Just as she lifted up her mobile phone again, it rang. It was Clive Bristow.

"Leila? It's all going well here and there's no problem with the national committee. They all seem very pleased. Ian will confirm that with you after the last couple of calls he's just making."

"Good, thanks Clive."

"But there's one particular piece of news we've just heard." He paused.

"Go on, Clive, I'm listening."

"Well, I heard from one our chaps in the head office that Tony Hammond has apparently handed in his resignation from the company. And I did try and contact him as you said, but there was no answer from his phone."

Leila was surprised: "thanks for that information, Clive—but why he's done that? Anyone know why? What's his agenda—or, more precisely, whose agenda is he following?"

"No one seems to know the answer to those questions," replied Bristow. "No one either seems to know where he's going; but I'm assured it's true that he is going. It is all good news isn't it?"

Leila thanked him for his call. She was indeed pleased about Hammond but knew from bitter experience that someone else would no doubt come along in the future to fill his shoes. Human nature almost demanded that things would never always go smoothly and also almost demanded difficult, questioning and negative people—let alone groups of such people—in any walk of life, but especially in an organisation like a trade union. Indeed union structures seemed to encourage the emergence of them. And, apart from its basic collective ethos, a union was above all a collection of individuals with all their foibles, characteristics and, sometimes, different agendas.

She felt a wave of tiredness come over as she then started to dial Per Ulric's number in Stockholm. She then abandoned the call and thought it would be prudent to close her eyes for a short while.

In fact she slept on the train until it was pulling in to Euston station. She woke with a start as the train slowed down, realised where she was and got her bag down from the overhead luggage rack. She looked at her watch. The train was on time. She had now to get a taxi and go straight to the hotel where the union press conference was being held. She knew she must freshen up when she got to the hotel.

The queue for taxis had been long and it was just after five thirty, after a hasty call to the cloakroom, when she met John Carmichael in the hotel room where they were holding the press conference. Julia Cardon was putting out copies of the agreement they had made that morning with Industry3M. Ian Macallister had faxed it through to the hotel while she had been travelling on the train. Mathew Singh came up and congratulated her on the agreement and she in turn congratulated him on the success achieved with Teening & Sykes. Carmichael seemed in a particularly jolly mood and was greeting the journalists who were now entering the room.

Leila suddenly remembered she had yet to phone Ian Macallister to get formal confirmation that the national committee had agreed and then phone Joe Tiller and tell him the national committee had formally agreed the settlement they had negotiated that morning. She could have kicked herself: it would be the height of idiocy not to confirm to the company that after all those months—and just before going into a press conference to announce the details—that the dispute was over and a good settlement achieved.

She quickly phoned Macallister who was still at the Liverpool hotel. He explained that he had tried to phone her while she was on the train and she realised that she must have been asleep when he did. He then gave her the confirmation that all the members of the national committee had formally agreed the settlement and she then phoned Tiller: he sounded pleased and said that no doubt they would meet again. She said she would write formally to him with the union's agreement the following morning.

In spite of sleeping on the train she still felt tired and wished she could now take a few days holiday: but knew she couldn't, at least not yet. There were so many things to do and time, as ever, was short. She thought it wouldn't be so bad if she had someone whom she could talk to when she got home in the evenings, someone to confide in, who would listen to her and understand all the pressures she was under. Her former husband had never filled that role although he had expected her to fill that role for him. He had regularly told her about the pressures of his job but had never shown any real interest in hers.

Although she had, now, long grown accustomed to living alone, she did think it would be nice if there was someone waiting for her at the end of the day. She enjoyed her job and thought it worthwhile but she wished sometimes she could talk to someone about it all, someone who was not part of the union but who would understand and sympathise and appreciate all the problems, the long hours, the meetings, the travelling, the arguments, the constant pressures of time, the setbacks as well as the victories.

She noticed that Carmichael was now sitting down at the table and beckoning her over to start the press conference and then realised that someone was saying something to her. She shook her head and looked round to see Chuck Pitney by her side. About twenty journalists and two television film crews had now come into the room and they were now all sitting down ready for the conference to start. She hadn't noticed Pitney nor heard what he had been saying to her and said: "sorry?"

"You seemed miles away, Leila," he smiled. "By the way, everyone reckons you've scored a big victory—and I do too. The whole job evaluation bandwagon is now rolling fast. I should think all unions are proud of what you and your union have achieved: and it's not often these days that I write about a union success. You're the lady of the moment, Leila—and you are indeed redoubtable, aren't you?"

Leila looked at him. Yes, slightly over weight, his suit a bit crumpled and he didn't seem to have combed his hair that day at all. But he was a nice sight and he looked pleased to see her and she liked his smile.

"I won't keep you now, Leila, because I think everyone's ready to start but I wonder whether you might be free after this press conference for a bite to eat,: I won't badger you about union matters, but it might be nice just to chat." He looked at her expectantly and added "I know you must have a thousand things to do; one problem solved but another six coming along—but that's life and life goes on."

She smiled back at him: "yes, Chuck, a bite to eat would be very nice—and a chat with you as well."

Lightning Source UK Ltd.
Milton Keynes UK
10 April 2010

152593UK00001B/26/P